Sailing Against the Tide

Sailing Against the Tide

Carol Busby

This book would not exist but for the assistance of my two 18th century experts.

Thanks to Ann Colby who kept my heroine properly clothed (and no longer putting her underwear on the outside) and for all manner of information about mores, manners and customs. And thanks to Ann's husband Bill MacLeod for his knowledge of sailing ships in general and 18th century ships in particular.

Huge thanks to my writing partner Paula Mahon whose wisdom and insight made the book a lot better. Paula, you're in my head whenever I write.

This book is dedicated to my husband Rick Davidson who was patient and loving throughout the writing process. He turned out to be an excellent editor as well.

PREFACE

"[Anne Bonny] was of a fierce and courageous Temper ... [O]nce when a young Fellow would have lain with her, against her Will, she beat him so that he lay ill of it a considerable time.

...she marries a young Fellow, who belonged to the Sea, and was not worth a Groat; which provoked her Father to such a Degree, that he turned her out of Doors ...

... when any Business was to be done in [Jack Rackham's pirate ship], no Body was more forward or courageous than she, and particularly when they were taken; she and Mary Read[e], with one more, were all the Persons that durst keep the Deck ...

The Day that Rackham was executed, by special Favour, he was admitted to see her; but all the Comfort she gave him was, that she was sorry to see him there, but if he had fought like a Man, he need not have been hang'd like a Dog."

From *A General History of the Pyrates* by Captain Charles Johnson (possibly Daniel Defoe), 1724

CHAPTER ONE

15 June 1721 - Spanish Town, Jamaica

Anne Bonny lifted her head off the slouch hat that covered a rock which acted as her pillow. It was raining and her side of the prison was dripping water on her. Slowly and awkwardly, she managed to get her heavily pregnant body standing, grabbing the hat as she went. She hobbled, her leg chains clanking, to the other side which was, for the moment, dry. The dirt and sand floor would get wet eventually and seep over if it rained enough. For now, however, it was the better spot. She began to sob, knowing that this babe, like the one born in Cuba, would be taken away from her, a knowledge made worse by the fact that it had saved her life. The British didn't hang pregnant women. They waited until after the birth. Anne couldn't imagine what after the birth would look like. She just wanted to survive this hellhole and the act of giving birth itself.

Then her waters broke, soaking that side of the cell. She had been measuring time by the growth in her belly. She wasn't surprised then when the process started.

Maneuvering herself onto the floor, she put the hat back down onto a familiar rock on this side.

She was tired of being hungry, thirsty, covered in mud, and bitten by rats and fleas. And of being pregnant, even though it was the only thing between her and the hangman's noose after being convicted of piracy.

She had lain down for about ten minutes, waiting for the pains to start, when she heard a voice at the entrance to her cell. She rolled a little and looked at the bars. There stood a guard and a man dressed in fancy clothes. She never did get used to being a side-show, but she also never let anyone know how it hurt.

"Yes, Sir Jonathan," the guard she recognized as Williams was saying. "That is indeed the infamous female pirate Anne Bonny."

She saw the other man snort. "How the mighty have fallen. Deservedly. I am Sir Jonathan Woolrich and you pirates brought a fever that killed my wife and son."

Williams murmured something vaguely sympathetic.

"Killed my friend Mary Reade too, bastard," Anne called out.

"She deserved it," Woolrich said. "My wife and son didn't. And the last ship you and your disemboweled partner took was mine. I lost over £1000 on that cargo."

"Well then, glad to meet you," Anne sneered.

"I'll see you hanged if it's the last thing I do."

"Ye're a coward, and I trust ye'll rot in hell."

Williams bowed slightly to Woolrich, who seemed reluctant to leave. "We must go, sir."

Woolrich spat at Anne. "I hope you die in pain," he said. "And lose the babe."

She heard them walking away. She was staggered by the cruelty in his last remark.

The first labor pain hit and Anne groaned. She knew it would be a while, because of her previous birth. They hadn't let her see the boy – just hustled him away. The pain never left her.

Anne managed to doze through the early contractions. Around midnight, her eyes popped open. The pains were worse and closer together. They took her breath away. Once she had it back, she screamed, which brought two guards running. One opened the cage door and ran to Anne's side.

She panted. "Baby. Need midwife," she said as she collapsed back onto the ground.

"How do you know?" one asked.

"This ain't my first time, you idiot. Get me a midwife!" She never saw the guards leave.

A while later, she didn't know how long, a woman came into the prison cell. "Oh my lord," she exclaimed. "She can't give birth in this filth. And look at her."

"Master's orders are she's not to be moved so you'll have to make do," said Guard Williams, who had brought her to the cell. He re-locked the door and left.

Anne started to scream. Next thing she knew, there were kind hands on her telling her to roll onto her knees and pant. The midwife put out a clean sheet and Anne moved onto it.

Five hours later, Anne bore a healthy, bawling son. She collapsed, panting and relieved. "Can I see him?" she asked.

"I'm sorry, love, but my orders is no. You might get attached and there's no point." The midwife had cut the cord and was wrapping the baby in a clean towel.

"Please," whispered Anne. "I had another who was taken before e'er I saw him. Can I just look?"

The midwife looked up and saw that the guards were gone. "All right. I hear you're to be hanged so this will be your only chance."

She handed Anne the baby boy. With tears running down her cheeks, Anne kissed the baby and whispered, "Ye've got my red hair." She gently stroked the fuzz on the baby's head with a finger. "Yer name is Jack. Not John but Jack. Whatever they call ye, it's Jack. Like yer father, Captain Jack Rackham."

Light was dawning when they heard the guards marching towards the cell a few minutes later. With tears streaming down her face, Anne gave the baby back to the midwife.

The guards came in. "Midwife, your work is done. Take the baby and leave."

"I have to deliver the afterbirth, gentlemen, and only then will I leave. Mrs. Bonny is quite exhausted and will need rest." The midwife stood defiantly before the guards.

"All right. We can give you a little time but not much."

"Thank you."

The midwife took as long as she dared to finish her duties. The guards remained outside the cell.

"Good luck to you, Madame," she said as she took Jack away from his mother.

* * *

Anne laid on the sheet the midwife had brought with her head on her hat and her back to the cell door. She knew that any day they would come to hang her so she was as quiet and inconspicuous as possible, hoping to prolong the time while knowing full well they wouldn't wait long. She was too famous.

It was dark three days later, about midnight, when she heard a key scrape the lock and the cell door open. She almost vomited with fear but held it in. A lantern shined around the cell.

"What do ye want?" she asked.

"I've come to take you home," answered a voice she hadn't heard for a long time.

"Father?" she asked as she rolled over. Her eyes widened. When she had been thrown out for marrying John Bonny, she had never thought to hear that voice again. *I wonder if I've died and his voice has come to haunt me.*

"Yes, Anne. It is your father. We've brought a pallet. If anyone sees us, they'll think ye've died."

Anne stared at him incredulously. "Where are you taking me?" she asked weakly.

"To my ship, Anne. Home to Carolina."

Two men came over and, although she cringed at first, their hands were soft and they helped her up and lifted her onto a canvas pallet and covered her with the dirty sheet she'd given birth on. As they started towards the cell doors, Anne cried out, "Wait. My hat."

The three men could barely see in the cell but when Anne pointed back to where she had been, they moved the lantern and saw a battered leather slouch hat. "That rag? Why on earth do you want that nasty thing?"

"It's all I have left," Anne said, continuing to point. "Get it." Then she added, "Please." Tears welled up in her eyes.

One of the men held onto her while the other got the hat which she tucked under the sheet. They carried her out of the prison and down a long walkway. It was dark with a new moon. Suddenly, someone called out: "Who goes there?" She recognized the guard William's voice. As quickly as she could, she put the sheet over her face, letting her red hair spill out on one side.

Her father saw her actions and answered the guard. "Anne Bonny as was. Dead now so no one will be needing to set the noose."

"Let me see 'er," William said as he approached the pallet. He pulled the sheet from her face and, recognizing it, gasped. "I weren't told. Sorry. Where you taking her body?"

"Somewhere no one will find it and dig it up. Think she deserves that for all she's been through."

"Yeah okay. My shift's done anyway and I have a large thirst." They all laughed. "Go on," Williams said as he turned and headed back towards the guard house.

The men rushed as fast as they could to the dinghy waiting to take Anne out to her father's ship, *Killarney*.

The trip to South Carolina took four days. They hit a squall but nothing else to slow their progress. No ships followed.

Anne spent the time on a cot – a real luxury for a pirate – being attended to by the ship's doctor. He cleaned and bandaged her open sores and checked on her recovery from childbirth. Anne told him about conditions in the prison. "Dear God, woman, it's a miracle you're alive. And that the babe survived."

Anne started to cry and the doctor immediately apologized. "We men don't really understand how having a baby affects a woman. I am sorry to have upset you."

Anne blew her nose. "I had another, doctor. Also alive. Also given away. The first was easier. I was young and my life at sea wouldn't allow for having a family. This baby was much more important. He saved my life. And he was Jack's baby. All that's left of Jack. Yet I'll never see him again."

"Can I get you anything?" the doctor asked.

"Yeah. A bottle of brandy – or rum. I'm not particular," Anne niffed again. The doctor started to laugh, then realized she was serious.

He decided to bypass the captain and Mr. Cormac, Anne's father. The cook was happy to provide the brandy and a glass.

Anne was still weak when they landed in Charles Town, but at least she had her emotions in check.

"It's nice to see a harbor again," Anne mused.

Her father shot her a worried glance. "You aren't even remotely considering going back to that life are you, my dear?"

"No, Father. That life has already ended for me and most of the others. I got out alive but most didn't. With the British actively looking for them, they'll soon be hanging on scaffolds."

As they got closer, Anne's keen eye looked over the ships in the harbor. "Lovely harbor, 'tis. No wonder so many trade here." She breathed deeply of the sea air then went below decks to fetch her slouch hat for the trip to her father's plantation.

CHAPTER TWO

21 June 1721 - Thousand Oaks Plantation
Near Charles Town, South Carolina

They spent the night in Charles Town and reached the plantation the next day. The house slaves were delighted to see Anne and worried about her health.

Sarah, the slave who had taken care of Anne from the time they arrived from Ireland until she ran away, hovered especially and ordered the others around. Anne stayed in bed for a week, regaining her strength.

As time passed, Anne got stronger: walking, riding, swearing and regaining her defiance, although she didn't understand why this place brought out the worst in her. One day, her father called her into his study.

"Anne, I see ye're back in good health." Anne nodded.

"It's time for you to move on. I have found a husband suitable to me and, I think, to you as well. His name is Joseph Burleigh and he has agreed to marry you even though I told him you can be a foul beast at times."

"Well, we'll be starting off on the right foot at least. Thank ye, Father," Anne growled.

"We're heading to Charles Town tomorrow. You'll be married and board a ship to Virginia. I've bought you a plantation. Not a big one but one of a moderate size that two people utterly unfamiliar with farming should be able to learn on. And some coin and tobacco notes for things you'll need."

Anne stared at him. "We went through this before, Father."

"I know, Anne, and it didn't turn out well because you took it into your head to run off with that horrible James Bonny. I'm asking you to try it my way this time."

"I ran off with the man I loved. He turned out to be a rotter but I couldn't see that then." Anne kept her father's eye even as she knew that Bonny had been a terrible mistake – turning into an informant after the pirate amnesty.

"Yes, my dear, but ye have to admit at this point that he was a bit of a disaster. Meanwhile, ye let Mr. Buckles, my choice, get away." She detected a bitter edge in her father's voice.

Anne kept his gaze. "Ye've a point. Besides I don't see I have much choice in the matter."

"No, I'm afraid ye don't. But wouldn't ye agree it's a much better result than hanging from a gibbet off Jamaica?"

"I can't argue that."

"Good, it's done. Pack and we'll be off tomorrow." Her father looked down to the papers on his desk and dismissed her with a wave of his hand.

I still get angry even though I know he wants the best for me. Why is that? Why does this place drive me crazy? Anne left the room.

As she watched Sarah pack the three outfits her father had bought for her with the help of a lady friend who, Anne suspected, would be his wife as soon as she was gone, she realized that the plantation, and her father, represented restrictions and rules. Anne had never been fond of either. Piracy, with its egalitarian society and lack of anything remotely resembling slavery, was more to her liking. *He's not a heart-*

less bastard as I've so often thought. He's a father who revels in the rules and I'm his bastard daughter who won't follow them. He's probably as frustrated as I am.

At the end of the next day, they found themselves again staring at the ships in the harbor of Charles Town. Her father dropped Anne off at a boarding house. She watched him drive away and immediately went walking through the town. As it was Sunday, there was little foot traffic.

She stopped to look in the window of a jewelry store. A pinchback brooch with an openwork floral spray set with pearls and garnets caught her eye. She looked around but the street was empty but for a couple of drunk sailors staggering on the other side of the street. She backed up to the door and tried the doorknob, but it was locked. As casually as possible, she ducked around the side the building. A window stood slightly open only five feet back from the front. Looking around and seeing no one, Anne tested the window and found it unlatched. She peeked inside and saw the room empty except for a table and displays of jewelry, handbags and other items attractive to ladies. And a chair, right below the window.

She lifted the framed glass and hoisted herself, bottom first, through the opening. Without hesitation, she scooped up the brooch, stowed it in the pocket under her skirt, and moved back to the window, using the chair to get up to the sill. She dropped onto the alley below, shut the window and sauntered back into the street.

When she figured her father would be returning, she went back to the boarding house. In less than five minutes, there was a knock on her door.

"Yes?" she called out.

"Anne, it's Father. With Joseph."

Anne had dreaded this moment. Joseph Burleigh, her husband to be, a person she had never laid eyes on, waited on the other side of the door.

Standing beside her father was one of the most handsome men she'd ever seen. Tall with deep blue eyes and curly dark hair, his smile lit up his whole face.

"By God, you are more beautiful than your miniature," he said, leaning over to kiss her on the cheek.

Anne involuntarily shrank back. "Miniature?" she asked.

Joseph reached into his coat pocket and pulled out a small painting of Anne. She remembered when it was done. She was about fifteen and left home shortly thereafter.

"He gave it to me the day we met and made our bargain."

"Bargain?" Anne asked.

"Well, neither of your nor I are in the position for a long courtship, but we can talk about that later. For now let me say, I am most pleased to meet you and most impressed with your beauty." Joseph bowed.

"Fine. What now?" Anne turned to her father.

"We'll spend the night. I've arranged with a vicar to marry you first thing in the morning and then you sail on the early tide. For now, we go to get some supper at a publick house up the street. Put on your cloak and come with us."

"That an order?" Anne asked.

"No, my dear, it's a request. It will give you a chance to get to know Joseph a bit."

Anne shrugged and put on her cloak.

She came down and found Joseph and her father already at the publick house. "We were just talking about farming. Tobacco. The land you and Joseph are going to is already planted for the season. Joseph is not an experienced planter so I have been giving him some counsel," her father said.

Anne nodded. She had no intention of learning to farm, so she looked around the dining room. Most of the guests were dressed well but not extravagantly. She saw little jewelry or fancy embroidery work on the women's attire. Her own clothing, she realized, was probably the nicest in the room.

The men finished discussing the fine points of fertilizer and leaned back, each taking a deep drink from his tankard of beer. "Where's mine?" Anne asked with some annoyance.

Joseph laughed. "I must apologize, Mistress Cormac. I didn't think to request a glass for you." He looked around and waved at the waiter. "Another beer, good sir," he called out. The waiter nodded and disappeared.

Anne ignored them as she drank her beer. Finally Joseph turned to her, "Mistress ..." he began.

Before he could say the name, Anne interrupted him. "If we're to be married, ye must call me 'Anne.'" She said and then looked away, surprised to find herself blushing.

"Anne. It's a lovely name. I was just saying that I would hope that with a year's good crop, we can make improvements to the property. The house is rather small and needs expanding. We will need some more furnishings as well. For now, there is enough in the house to live in." Joseph reached out as though he would take her hand but Anne pulled it off the table and into her lap before he could reach it.

The waiter brought a third glass. "Thank you. Bring us supper, please. Whatever the cook is making this evening," her father told the waiter.

Anne continued to watch the diners as the men discussed tobacco farming. *That one's got a full pocket*, she thought, looking at a sea captain who furtively patted the bulging pocket of his waistcoat as he ate. *But he won't for long. If I can see it, so can others.* On the far side of the room, a couple sat waiting for their food. The woman fingered a knife, weighing it between her fingers. *And they may be the ones to relieve him of it.*

"Anne?" asked her father. She came out of her reverie and saw that both men were watching her.

Those are the darkest blue eyes I have ever seen, she thought looking back at Joseph. *And full o' mischief they are.*

They finished supper and returned to the boarding house. In the lobby, her father said, "Be up at six o'clock, Anne. The marriage will be at seven." She nodded and her father left for his room.

She and Joseph stared awkwardly at each other. He pointed to a pair of chairs. "Let's chat a little."

"Starting tomorrow, it's just you and me. I wanted to tell you that I am very glad to have you come with me. I haven't farmed before but I am excited about the chance to start over," he said as they climbed the stairs.

"Start over?" she echoed. "Start over from what, Joseph Burleigh?"

He laughed. "From living here. And for you, from Jamaica."

Anne made a mental note to ask more questions when they were on their way north. "Yes," she said, "we will surely be starting something over." She turned to face him as they reached her door. "I don't know what my father has told you about me ..." she began, but before she could finish, Joseph held up his hand.

"Enough," was all he said. Then he smiled. "I know enough," he said. "And I promise I won't force myself on you. It would be better if we got to know each other a little before ..." he broke off and turned bright red.

They sat in an embarrassed silence for a bit. Finally Joseph asked, "May I walk you to your room?"

She nodded. They walked up the three flights of stairs and she unlocked her door

"Good night, Anne," Joseph said. "Truly, I am delighted to be marrying you, temper and all." Although she detected a twinkle in his blue eyes, Anne could feel his sincerity.

Wish I could say the same, she thought.

"Indeed. I will see you early. Good night..." she hesitated, then added, "Joseph."

He grinned and bowed. "Anne."

Anne threw herself onto her bed and cried until she couldn't cry any more. Then she took one of her kerchiefs, blew her nose, wiped her eyes and stood up. "I will make the best of this," she said loudly to the room.

She undressed, climbed into bed, and fell into a deep sleep.

CHAPTER THREE

22-25 June 1721 - Hampton, Virginia

Anne and Joseph were married by the vicar promptly at seven o'clock in the morning. The ceremony was witnessed only by the vicar's wife and Anne's father. Anne wore a simple white bodice over her shift and a skirt embroidered lovingly by Sarah with blue lines representing waves at sea. Joseph wore the same coat and breeches he had on the night before. After they said the vows, Joseph put a small gold band on her left hand. She felt like it was choking her whole hand bloodless. Then she realized, *at least he's given me a ring.* James Bonny had married her without benefit of jewelry, something Anne had never quite forgiven him for.

After the ceremony, they walked to the ship that would take them to Virginia. "She sails on the mid-day tide," said Joseph.

"So you said. About one then?" Anne looked out at the ship at anchor and recognized the captain as the man Joseph had been laughing with when they arrived.

He nodded. "We have to be on board by noon. I assume you've packed the things in your room? We should get them onto the ship soon."

"Can we inspect her before we board?" Anne asked.

"No," said her father.

She put the glass down and glared at him. "Why not?" she asked, turning to face him.

"Because Captain Stoutley says we'd be in the way. He comes highly recommended by friends of Joseph, in case you were wondering," he added, waving a hand at his new son-in-law.

"Yes, through a former ... uh ... business partner. Stoutley seems quite competent." Joseph told Anne, who continued to glare. "Although you would be a better judge of that than I."

"Thank you," she mumbled.

The dock bustled with activity and although she refused to acknowledge it, Anne realized that Stoutley had been right. She would have said the same thing.

They strolled back to the boarding house where Anne packed her good clothes into a valise her father provided. The rest of her trousseau, such as it was, had been put in a trunk with some linens and dishes. It was already on board the ship. She changed into a loose gown over her shift, tied on her pockets and skirt, carefully hiding the brooch, wrapped in a piece of linen, inside a shoe. *Men's clothes are so much more comfortable,* she thought, shaking her head.

When she was done, she lay down on the bed and fell fast asleep.

A knock on the door woke her. "Yeah?" she called out, shaking the fuzziness out of her head.

"We need to go to the dock, my dear," replied her father's voice. "Give me the valise and come down so we can send the boy with it."

Anne pulled herself up to a sitting position with her legs dangling over the side of the bed. "Be right there."

After she inspected the room, she picked up the leather bag and went downstairs.

Joseph met her at the bottom and immediately took the valise. "The boy's right outside."

At the dock, a sailor stood by the pier looking impatient. Joseph went up to him. "For the *Waverly*," he said.

The sailor nodded and, muttering "about time," led them down to where a rowboat bounced in the water. He climbed in and looked up at the passengers.

Anne turned towards her father, keeping here visage neutral. "Well, Father, once again, farewell." She stood, uncertain what to do next. Her feelings about her father had changed since he had rescued her. She recognized now why he had opposed her marriage to Bonny, although she would never agree that she shouldn't have left. She also realized how stupid she had been at sixteen.

Her father stepped forward, put his arms around her, and squeezed her breathless. Anne curled her hands around his back and hugged him back. "I wish ye good fortune, Anne. Better than you have had to now. Write if ye will. Ye are my daughter and I love ye dearly. We will likely never see each other again, but I would like to know now and then that ye are well."

Anne nodded, silently. She knew she should say more but she didn't know what. Finally she managed, "Thank you, Father. For rescuing me. And for taking care of me."

He kissed her on the cheek and stepped aside, offering a hand to Joseph. The men shook warmly and then, to the surprise of both, William Cormac hugged his son-in-law. He let go, turned, and strode back up to the wharf without a backwards glance.

Anne watched him go, a single tear rolling down her cheek. *I'll never see him again. Just when we were beginning to trust each other.* She reached up and brushed it away. Taking a deep breath, she stepped, with Joseph's unnecessary assistance, into the boat.

Once they had climbed aboard, Joseph went off to talk to Captain Stoutley, but Anne remained on the deck as the ship drifted out of the harbor and hoisted her sails. She watched Charles Town recede in the hazy summer sun. She glanced up to the Quarterdeck and spotted Joseph standing with the Captain, laughing and watching the activity on board with interest. *I wonder if this'll be my last voyage,* Anne thought, overwhelmed by conflicting emotions: sad, trapped, angry, curious and excited. After they had cleared the harbor, Joseph appeared at her side.

"Captain Stoutley has invited us for brandy in his cabin," he said.

Anne nodded. "I will go change," she said without looking at the man she was now bound to.

In the small cabin, a narrow cot, built into the side of the ship, had been made up with sheets and a blanket. Anne's trunk sat against one wall with a chair next to it. A small table jutted out from a third wall. She opened a second, smaller trunk to find Joseph's second set of clothes and some personal items. It suddenly dawned on her that he had a smaller wardrobe than she did. *Who is this man?* she wondered, not for the first time.

Stoutley and Joseph chatted and laughed for over an hour while Anne listened. She was a good mimic and she would need that skill to blend in. She occasionally threw in a comment, but she mostly held back. *The quicker I can learn to talk like regular folk, their speech and small talk, the safer we will be.*

Finally, the Captain rose, which prompted Joseph and Anne to stand as well. "I have kept you too long from your honeymoon bed," he joked with a wink at the couple which caused both to blush deep red.

"Quite all right, Captain Stoutley. Anne and I will manage." Joseph said. The captain bowed, as did Joseph. Anne remained standing until the captain opened the door to let them out.

They walked in silence to the tiny cabin which was back under the Quarterdeck, close to the captain's quarters. Joseph held the door open. They each gave silent thanks that none of the crew were nearby to snigger.

The newlyweds stood in the small cabin, only a foot apart, and stared at each other.

Finally, Joseph broke the silence. "I will not take you against your will, Anne. I know you are experienced, but not with me. I do not condone force. When we join, we must join by mutual desire."

Anne nodded. "Thank ye," she said. "If ye'll turn, I'll undress."

Joseph replied, "If you will also turn, I will undress as well."

Joseph slid onto the cot first, and rolled onto his side facing the wall. Anne joined him in the bed, lying on her side and facing the room. They both lay listening to the other's breathing until finally Joseph heard Anne's soften and become regular. He smiled to himself. *Matter of time*, he thought as he fell fast asleep.

Late afternoon on the third day, the *Waverly* landed at Hampton, Virginia. Anne and Joseph stood at the rail watching Stoutley skillfully manoeuver the ship into the harbor, drop anchor, and call for the jolly boats. By six o'clock that evening, they had found lodgings at Mistress Johnson's Boarding House. Joseph went off to see about the horses and wagon.

Anne stood on the porch looking at the harbor in the increasing gloom. Lights had begun to flicker along the waterfront and on the ships bobbing in the harbor. Her mind raced forward and backward and then settled. "Goodbye old life," she whispered. Turning her back on the water, Anne Cormac Bonny Burleigh walked slowly back to the Mistress Johnson's and closed herself in her room.

Joseph found her there an hour later. She was sitting in a rocking chair with her feet up on her trunk. She looked up at him, expressionless as her mind roiled with uncertainty and fear. *Can I do this? Can I be who I am and be his wife? A farmer's wife? Although I don't think he's ever been a farmer.*

Joseph sat on the bed. "The horses are secured and the wagon. We can leave in the morning as planned." He waited but she did not speak. "It's time for supper. There's a place up the road that the captain recommends."

She realized that she was hungry. So she put on a simple bodice of linen over her shift and a plain skirt. Her hair was pulled back from her face but fell loose down her back. The fancy clothes remained in the trunk.

"I think you look bewitching, my dear," Joseph told her, rising to offer a hand to help her up. She swung her legs off the trunk and took it. For the first time, she felt a slight jolt of electricity at his touch. She gasped a little, but covered it with a cough.

The dining room of the King's Raven was almost full when they reached it. Joseph led the way to a small table beneath tall windows that looked out onto the passing traffic. They sat uneasily on chairs that faced each other, each deliberately avoiding eye contact by staring at the people and wagons going by.

Anne noticed a woman on the far side of the street carrying a bundle of packages, some ribbon tailing out the back. *Lovely color, that orange*, she thought. Another woman went by on their side wearing an engraved gold locket. *Oh, that's nice. At least ten doubloons.* She caught herself and looked across at Joseph, who was now watching her.

"Appraising the locals?" he asked.

"What if I am?" she retorted.

"Fine with me," he raised his hands defensively. At that moment, they were rescued by the waiter. They ordered food and Madeira, Anne's favorite wine.

"Well, that's done then," Joseph said. "Back to the window?" he asked. Anne blushed briefly then laughed.

"Looks like a pretty prosperous port," she noted. "Nice clothes. People well kempt. Streets clean." She paused, then glancing back at Joseph asked, "How big is it?"

The waiter brought the food and drink.

"About two thousand and growing. Tobacco going out; goods coming in. The port is indeed prosperous, as you have discerned," he nodded to her.

"Have you been here before, then?" Anne asked him.

"Only once, to see the property. It will take some work to make it a comfortable home but we can live in it as is."

"And how, Joseph, do ye define 'comfortable'?" Anne asked.

"Comfortable chairs, a good bed, a well-stocked larder, nice silver and china and tobacco growing happily outside the door." He looked at her, his head cocked. "And you?"

"Not sure about the tobacco, but I agree with the rest." She looked at him. "Is this getting to know each other talk?" she asked.

Joseph laughed. "Yes, I suppose it is."

"And are ye a religious man, Joseph Burleigh?" Anne looked at him from above a spoonful of soup.

"Nay. And I can't believe that you are either," he said with a big smile. "I think that's enough for tonight. We can get more information out of each other on the road."

Joseph poured the last of the wine into the two glasses, handed one to Anne and lifted the other. "To us," he said, "and our new life together." He clinked his glass on hers.

Anne stared at him and gulped. "'Tis a new life, isn't it?" She looked down at the table for a moment before taking a long drink and then moving the glass over to clink against Joseph's. "To all that," she said.

After they finished, they decided to delay the evening further by taking a walk around the town, Anne leading Joseph away from the bluff and its view of the harbor. He asked her questions about what foods she liked, what colors for her clothing, and did she ride horseback.

"Most assuredly," she answered. "Do we have horses?"

"Indeed. Two for now, but I'm hoping to build a stable."

She looked at him in surprise. "To breed?"

"Yes, diversify our income. Not all in one crop with nothing else." They stood watching the sun go down in a blaze of red against distant clouds scudding across the sky. The evening was hot and muggy.

"Ye're full of surprises, Joseph Burleigh," Anne told him.

"I have a few more I'm saving," he said with a smile. She laughed.

"Let's go back," Anne said, turning back in the direction of the boarding house.

Once in their room, Anne and Joseph stood, as they had on the first night of their marriage, facing each other. Each knew that this night would be different, but neither knew quite how to proceed.

Finally, Joseph stepped forward, put his arm around his wife and pulled her gently towards him. Leaning over, he put his lips on hers with increasing pressure until suddenly he felt her whole body respond. Her tongue came out and the resulting kiss was more passionate than he had expected.

"You have some surprises left as well, Anne Burleigh," he said, pulling her even closer. She could feel his manhood through her light skirt as he could feel vibrations running through her body.

They pulled apart, panting. Without a word, Anne reached over and began to unbutton Joseph's jacket, which she dropped to the floor. She slipped the waistcoat off his shoulders and left it to fall on top of the jacket. As she pulled out his shirt and reached for the buttons on his britches, Joseph stopped her hand.

He carefully unlaced her bodice which fell to the floor behind her, starting a new pile of clothing. Her skirt and pockets, untied, simply slid down. At that point, Joseph curled his arm around her waist again and pulled her back to him. Anne whimpered slightly as she returned his hard kiss.

The rest of their clothes hit the floor in moments. The newlyweds fell on the bed still clinging lip to lip, but with their hands roaming each other. Anne arched against Joseph who leaned over to kiss her breasts, biting them slightly. Anne's eyes opened wide and then closed for good. She groaned as Joseph's mouth moved down her body to caress between her legs, an area that was now moist and hot. Reaching for his already engorged penis, Anne stroked it with increasing vigor.

He took a breath, pulled back and thrust into her. She stifled a moan and he rocked back and forth slowly at first and then faster. It didn't take long for the pent-up passion they both felt to explode inside Anne's body. Joseph arched and cried out then collapsed onto her chest without pulling himself out.

They both panted, covered with sweat, letting the heat of the act and of the summer evening dissipate in their sweat. When Joseph could breathe evenly again, he lifted himself up to look at her. "You are the most beautiful woman I have ever seen," he said, leaning over to kiss her on her forehead. "With the most attractive freckles."

"I hate my freckles," she protested. He just smiled in response.

"You're damned good at this," she added.

He laughed again, which caused him to fall out of her. He rolled over with his back against the wall. "Well," he said, "there's at least one thing we won't ever fight about."

CHAPTER FOUR

26 June 1721 - Hampton, Virginia

Joseph drove the wagon from the stable to the boarding house as soon as they had finished an early breakfast. Anne waited on the front step with the trunks and valise. In a small canvas bag, she had packed some food and cider for the road. Joseph estimated it would take them a day to get to the plantation.

She wore a loose, shortened gown over her shift and petticoat without stays or corset. *Might as well be comfortable*, she told herself. *Women clothes be damned if I don't have to.*

After the porters helped Joseph lift the trunks onto the wagon, which had already been loaded with some chairs and boxes of household goods, Anne handed him the valise. He stored it behind their seat bench where they could get to it easily. He held out a hand which Anne ignored as she climbed up onto the wagon box on her own. The porter began to smirk but a sharp look from Joseph stopped him. "Good luck to you," he called out as they drove away.

The terrain was fairly flat even where there was only a trail and not a wagon track to follow. Anne sat silent, looking out at the rivers and streams. *Seems to be a lot of water hereabouts*, she mused. They drove past many fields of tobacco leaves. Here and there they passed a bit of forest.

"Most of the land's been cleared for farming," Joseph told her.

Occasionally they saw a path or road veer off beside a field. With her spyglass, bought in York Town, Anne could sometimes see a house in the distance. Most were one story with deep porches. The two-story houses had second floor porches which were always covered by roof and furnished with chairs.

"People here rich?" she asked.

"No, not really. Some small farms and some bigger ones. The biggest plantations are farther north near Williamsburg."

"How far is that?" Anne asked, looking at Joseph.

"Another twenty-five or so miles beyond our place." Joseph glanced at her cautiously, encouraged by her curiosity.

"And how far to that?" she asked, wrinkling her brow.

"About twenty miles from here." He turned back to the track ahead which had suffered from the early summer rains. The wagon jogged back and forth through the ruts.

"What's there?" she asked.

"Where?" he replied.

"Our place." She pronounced "our" as a two syllable word.

"A house. Two stories. Big porch. Parlor and kitchen downstairs. Two bedrooms upstairs. Not much furniture though. Table in the kitchen." He tossed his head back towards the wagon. "We're bringing chairs. And a rocker. Got a good deal from a family heading further south."

Something about the way he said it made Anne look at him sharply. "Good deal, eh?"

"Yes," he answered, looking sideways at her with a grin twitching around his mouth.

"Took advantage, did ye?" The timbre of her voice did not indicate disapproval.

"A good deal," he insisted, refusing to rise to the bait.

"Father said crops are planted." She was again looking out at a long, narrow field growing tobacco.

"Yes. We have almost 500 acres. And slaves to work them. Two house slaves, five yard slaves and sixteen for the fields. Came with the property."

Anne drew in a breath sharply. Joseph looked at her. "What's wrong?" he asked.

"I won't have slaves," she said coldly. Her auburn hair almost crackled with the force of her feelings and her freckles flared red.

"Oh." Joseph didn't know what to say. *You can't run a plantation without slaves,* he thought but he waited for Anne to speak.

"I won't have slaves," she repeated. Joseph didn't respond.

After some consideration of how best to proceed, Joseph took a deep breath and asked, "What about servants?"

Anne thought about it. *I won't have slaves. My father has slaves, including my mother in all but name. I've seen the slave trade. I've worked with escaped slaves. It's brutal and vile and I won't have it.*

Before she could respond, Joseph turned the horses to the side of the path. "I think it's time we talked about what we need and what we want," he said. He climbed off the seat and led the horses to some grass near a chestnut tree. Anne stared at him in surprise, then hopped off the wagon and joined him under the tree.

She looked him straight in the eye and, with a smile, said, "I was a pirate. I sailed with former slaves and saw the slave trade close up and at Father's plantation. I won't have slaves and changing what we call them won't make a difference."

Joseph looked back at her. "I know you were a pirate. That is why I wasn't surprised when you lifted the brooch in York Town." He swept a hand towards the ground under the tree to indicate that they should sit.

Anne sat cross-legged facing him. "My father wanted me to marry a plantation owner. A man who dealt in human beings as property. I refused. Then I met James Bonny, a sailor, and married him. Father didn't approve and so we ran away. I think part of him was relieved, though. I was difficult." *How stupid I was. But all sixteen-year-olds are, aren't they?*

"Women aren't usually allowed on pirate vessels, so I pretended to be a man. Men's clothing is far more comfortable than women's anyway. I was used to it since my ma dressed me as a boy from a child. Kept people from realizing who I really was – the bastard daughter of a married lawyer." Her voice trailed off. Joseph sat silent, listening.

"But I was a fast learner and by the time they realized I was a woman, they all liked me and knew I could pull my own weight. When the British offered amnesty, the bastard coward my husband turned informer. I left him, met Jack Rackham in a bar in Nassau. We sailed his ship *Revenge* for a while until she went aground. Then we took the *William* and kept on. That's when we met Mary."

"Mary Reade?" Joseph asked.

"Yes. She'd been an actual soldier, can you imagine? Her ma dressed her as a boy to fool her dead husband's mother. Their boy had died and Mary's father was long gone. It worked, too. Until the granny died. Mary was so much a boy by then that she joined the army. Went to France and fought. Fell in love with an officer." Anne chuckled. "That caused some dissent in the ranks, I can tell ye."

Joseph nodded.

"Well, when they found out it was worse than two men loving, which is what they'd thought, but actually a woman in their ranks, they threw her out. She made her way back to London then crewed a merchantman headed for Nassau. We met up with her there. She was a looker, too. Jack fell hard."

Joseph glanced over at his new wife. He didn't see any kind of jealousy or anger on Anne's face. *I might have felt different*, he thought.

"After *Revenge* wrecked, we took the *William*. She was a good, fast ten-tonner. A sloop. Had a decent crew or so we thought." Anne paused, remembering.

"In the end, they failed us. So did Jack. Barnet came after us – British captain sent by Governor Lawes who was the bastard who sentenced me." She glanced over at Joseph for the first time. He put a hand on her knee and squeezed it. She looked away again. "Jack was drunk. They were all drunk except me, Mary and one sailor. Sleeping it off. Mary and I saw the ship coming and raised the alarm but the damned men were too far gone to help. We did what we could but they got us."

She stopped, the memories overwhelming her, a single tear running down her cheek. "Couldn't hold them off. Barnet took us all. Jack was hanged, disemboweled I'm told. Put in a cage, gibbeted on Deadman's Cay. Body's still there. The rest were hanged and left swinging around the harbor as a warning." Anne's voice had taken on a hard tone.

"Mary and I pled bellies," she looked over at Joseph. "I never asked Mary but I suspect that Jack was father to both. She died of a fever in prison before her babe ever appeared. Mine lived. A boy. I got to hold him for a little while then they took him away." She sniffed and Joseph saw tears rolling down her cheeks and splattering on her shift.

She may be a pirate, but she's got a woman's heart.

"Yes," Joseph responded with a smile. "But you weren't ... hanged."

"Ye knew all this and yet, ye took me on?" She didn't look up, her mind still in the prison.

"Indeed, that's why I took you on, as you say."

Anne looked up in surprise. "Why?" she asked.

"Your father made me an offer. Take his beautiful, headstrong, dangerous, nay, murderous, auburn-haired daughter off his hands in exchange for money, a plantation and a new life." Joseph said. "Seemed like a good bargain."

Anne stared at him. She thought for a moment, then, tilting her head sideways, looked at him with narrowed eyes. "Why would that have been a good bargain, Joseph Burleigh?"

Joseph's blue eyes twinkled. "I wondered when you'd stop thinking about yourself and ask about the man who married you for money."

She stared at him. "And why was it then? A bargain?" she asked.

"I had some ... difficulties of my own to deal with. In short, I needed to get out of Carolina and I needed money to start over. You were the perfect solution to my problems."

"Solution?" Anne almost screamed. "What are ye, Joseph Burleigh, that I am yer solution?"

"'Was,' Anne, not 'am.' I was a forger, quite a good one, a highwayman, and a swindler." He said. "Captain Stoutley was recommended by a friend who is a smuggler and a pirate, in fact."

Anne's mouth dropped open. "And my father made a bargain with you?"

"Yes. He knew something of my profession. In fact, that's how we met. One day I waited in some trees not far from your father's plantation to intercept him. I had heard in the town that he was in the process of buying some land from a neighbor. A Mr. Gunn. Do you remember him?"

Anne shook her head. "I left young. I think I might know the name but that's all."

Joseph nodded. "Gunn was a Scotsman who had tried to grow tea. But the crop failed so he decided to move north to Boston and try his hand at something else. He needed money to move so he approached your father whose land adjoined his. They struck a bargain." He laughed. "Like too many Scots, our Mr. Gunn couldn't hold his liquor – or his tongue."

"So I lay in wait. And sure enough, along came your father, on horseback to buy the Gunn property. I waylaid him and demanded the coin I thought he carried. But he refused, stating that he wasn't carrying coin anyway but credit notes. 'I would not be so careless as to carry actual coin,' he told me.

"We faced each other for a few moments while I considered whether credit notes would be useful. I had determined by then that I wished to give up my life of crime. Being a highwayman is tiring, dirty, wearying work. And it was getting around that I was forging and swindling. All probably much less exciting than the open seas and piracy," he added.

"It has its moments, piracy," she admitted.

"Then your father winked at me. 'Perhaps we can help each other,' he said. 'I have a daughter in need of a new existence.' Needless to say, I was taken aback, but he was so genial that I thought I might as well listen to what he had to say. So we rode to a nearby bridge, dismounted, let the horses eat and drink while we talked. When we were done, I had agreed to take his wild pirate daughter off his hands and he had agreed to stake me to land and a new start." Joseph finished and looked at Anne.

She started to laugh and then couldn't stop. *My father found a land pirate to take his sea pirate daughter off his hands.* When she finally Maria regained control, she wiped the tears from her eyes with her kerchief. "Did ye have no qualms?" she asked.

Then Joseph laughed. "Of course, I did, my dear. But I had been living a hard, treacherous life among hard men -- and women -- and I thought I could handle you. Besides," he added, "once he showed me your miniature, I was in for life. And so, here we are," he concluded.

"We are a pair, then. A pirate and a forger. Perfect for each other." Her green eyes flashed with humor.

"Perfect, indeed," Joseph answered her. "Maybe. We need to talk about our new life and what we want it to look like."

"Agreed. I want children to start," Anne was staring off into the distance.

"As many as you're willing to bear," Joseph responded.

"And I won't be housekeeper." Joseph started to protest but Anne put up a hand. "I've no calling to it and no skill. If we have people in the house who can run it, they will."

"As the wife, it's your ultimate responsibility, Anne. Didn't you help run the pirate ship?"

"Sometimes. But I won't do it. I'll do other things but not that. No keys round my belly. Ever." She looked at his disturbed face.

"Well, we can see how that goes," he said.

Anne leaned back against the tree and said, "I have a proposal." Joseph sat up straight and nodded for her to go on. "We can have 'servants' – house and field – but they have to be paid and taught to read and other skills. They get decent houses and good food." She paused. Her expression darkened. "And families will never be separated or sold. Ever."

"Aren't you afraid they'll take it into their heads that they don't need us?" Joseph was aware of the plantation owners' fears that given leeway, slaves would rebel, run off, murder them or at least refuse to work. He also understood owners' firm belief that plantations could not be profitable without slave labor.

"No. Give them a decent life and they'll stay. Why wouldn't they?" Anne turned and grabbed Joseph's arm and leaned into him, looking him straight in the eye. "This is not negotiable," she said.

Joseph looked into the distance, thinking through what she'd said. "You were raised on a plantation. Your father owns slaves. What turned you against it?"

Anne pulled a blade of grass and started chewing on it. "The children," she replied.

Joseph looked at her quizzically. "What children?"

"All of them. My father sired several then sold them off. Plus in the West Indies, I saw slaves beaten, raped, killed. Sold. Mothers hysterical. Fathers held back by chains." She gulped and took a long, deep breath.

"My mother was a servant," Anne continued. "She had no rights and even when we came to Carolina, my father saw her as a servant. But she was lucky, she got to pretend she was more. Lady of the house. But she had no more choice about her life – or mine – than the slave mothers did."

Joseph reached out and touched her arm.

"I fought back. And then I ran. Far away as I could from him, from the slaves, from the children who couldn't run." She looked down again. "I never really escaped them, though. Men escaped from slavery – whether black Africans or red Indians – help crew most pirate ships. And the islands are also worked by slaves. Which is the other reason I am against it. I know those people. They were friends and colleagues."

"All right. We'll have servants, not slaves," he said. "But this arrangement cannot get out. It would draw attention to us. The neighbors would view us with suspicion, at a minimum. It's not safe."

Anne nodded. "Then we will tell the servants that if they wish to enjoy the benefits of life on our plantation, they must agree never to discuss how they live." She put a hand on Joseph's cheek. "Thank you," she said. Then she stood up. "Let us to our new life. And God help us both."

"And the servants," Joseph added.

Later, when the sun shone high overhead, they stopped by a stream to rest and water the horses and to eat their picnic dinner under a cluster of cypress trees. The needles that carpeted the ground made for comfortable seating.

"There are the two house sl…" Joseph caught himself. "Servants. One's a cook and one cleans and sews. All you have to do is tell them what to cook and clean or whatever needs doing."

"Don't they know?" she asked.

"Generally, yes. But they'll look to you for leadership."

"Well they aren't going to get it. But I'm sure they can manage. If there's a conflict, I'll hear it. Otherwise, I'm happy to let them go at it. And if there's anything ye want to eat or drink, tell whoever the housekeeper is." Anne downed a gulp of cider.

"My dear wife, if it helps, please remember that I don't know anything about running a plantation either," Joseph said, shooting a sideways glance at Anne. "But I have confidence."

"Possibly misplaced," Anne muttered. Joseph looked at her and stifled a laugh.

"Absolutely misplaced, Wife, but there nonetheless. I suggest you grab some for yourself." Joseph kissed her on the cheek, stood up and gathered the horses and wagon.

It was late afternoon when they came to a big stand of willow oak trees planted in an "L" shape on their right side. A lane lined with more of the tall trees led off from the right side of the wagon towards the northeast.

"The house is down there," Joseph said pointing at the wagon track. "Welcome home."

"Can't see anything but plants and trees," Anne said, leaning out of the wagon.

"House is a mile away. That's our tobacco there, on both sides." Anne heard the pride in Joseph's voice, which she could yet not share.

"Then let's get there. I'm hungry and jolted enough for one day, in fact for a lot of days," she grumbled.

Joseph cracked the reins and turned the horses into the roadway.

CHAPTER FIVE

26-27 June 1721 - Great River Plantation, Virginia

The track was smoother than the main road so the wagon jolted less although Anne wasn't paying attention. She strained to see a house but all around her were fields stretching away in the distance. Finally, they rounded a bend and there it was: a two-story, white-washed house with a widow's walk on top and a wraparound porch on the bottom. *A widow's walk? To see if those sailing' in the fields come home safe?* Anne wondered.

A woman with very black skin, wearing a yellow calico gown, looked up from sweeping the porch as Joseph called out, "Hello."

She turned towards the side yard and yelled, "they here." Another woman, with lighter chocolate skin, pushed open the front door and looked out. To the right, Anne saw six small wooden cabins without doors. Outside each was a log bench and on the bench outside the nearest one sat five African men. One stood up and strolled over to the wagon. He looked to be about forty or forty-five. The other four were younger but rose more slowly. By the time Joseph brought the wagon to a halt, all five men and the two women stood between them and the house. A small boy hid behind Maria's skirts.

Joseph jumped down. "I'm Joseph Burleigh," he said holding out a hand to the older man who came over, wringing a felted hat in his hands, and shook hands, looking wary all the while. He was short and stocky with a balding head wrapped at the bottom by salt and pepper hair. His shirt hung down almost covering his canvas trousers.

"I's Caesar," he said. He turned and waved a hand behind him. "I's the foreman. And them's Ben, John and Ebo. Rest of the fiel' han' working. Ladies is Maria and Letty. The boy's Maria's Samuel."

Each stepped forward as his or her name was spoken. Ben was tall and thin, in his late teens, with close-cropped black hair curled tightly against his scalp. He wore trousers but no shirt. John was covered by canvas slops. He stood almost as tall as Ben but had a broad chest and thick limbs. Anne guessed he was in his mid-twenties. Ebo, the youngest of the men, wore trousers and a loose shirt. His hair was long and stringy, wound into tight, almost fuzzy curls. *Sixteen or seventeen,* Anne thought. Samuel was much lighter than his mother which made Anne wonder if the former owner was his father.

Anne climbed off the wagon. "You must be Maria," she said to the darker woman with the broom. She held out her hand which Maria stared at. Anne finally grabbed her hand and shook it. Maria's eyes widened in surprise. "What do you do, Maria?" Anne asked.

"I cook, take care of the house, in charge of shopping. I's the housekeeper." Maria raised her shoulders in a gesture that looked like pride to Anne.

"Wonderful," Anne said, turning to the other woman.

She walked down the steps and stood next to Letty. "I's Letty. I's the do-all woman," she said. "I does the laundry, cleaning and stuff." She reached out and shook Anne's hand without prompting.

"How many are in the fields?" Joseph asked.

Caesar stepped forward. "Bout twenty-five of 'em."

"You don't know how many?" Joseph asked.

"Now 'n' agin one leaves for a while then come back." Caesar said without any indication of approval or disapproval in his voice. "Lotta weedin' and stuff to be done. This group," his hand encompassed the other men, "they work round the house fixin', tendin' to the hosses, what needs doin'. Not fiel' hands."

Joseph nodded. "Thank you, Caesar," he said. "Now, let's get these things unpacked." He walked around to the back of the wagon. "Maria, I do hope there's supper soon. We haven't eaten since midday."

Anne walked slowly up the steps into her new home. The inside was clean: the walls covered in faded flowered paper. The entry hallway opened on the left to a parlor with a table and empty shelving. The parlor walls were covered in wallpaper, also faded, with exotic animals.

Anne took it in quickly and then moved down the hall to the back of the house where she found the kitchen. There was another table -- for preparing food and eating –which, as Joseph had promised, was without chairs. The wall on the left was lined with shelves filled with vegetables and stacked jars of preserves.

"We got a nice garden out back. Herbs too. Good for medicine and cookin'," Maria said. Anne nodded. On the top shelf she found three plates, two tankards and two glasses.

"Good we brought plates," she said. A sink on the right wall contained a big pitcher. Below that were hung several pots and pans. A small fireplace covered the back wall.

"Where do you cook?" she asked.

Maria pointed out the door to the right of the fireplace. "Cookhouse out back. Jus' use this for heat mos'ly."

Anne nodded and turned to find the two women standing behind her waiting, she suspected, for instruction.

"Ye heard my husband, we're hungry. We got food here?" She knew she sounded angry although she wasn't. "I'm sorry. I'm tired and hungry is all. Can you feed us?"

"So sorry. I get you some food right away," Maria said. Just then

Joseph and Caesar brought in the first of the four chairs they had taken off the wagon. "And you gonna be able to sit too," she added.

By the time Maria had set the table with plates of cabbage slaw, thick slices of bread with butter and slabs of ham, the rest of the furniture had been brought in and Anne was upstairs inspecting the bedrooms. The bigger one contained a decent-sized, roped bedstead with two mattresses: one with cotton ticking filled with chaff and the other filled with "flock" of wood fibers. The bed sat against the back wall. She could see the kitchen's chimney outside the window on that wall. *Will be warm come winter,* she thought. A well-patched quilt made from worn out skirts, Anne guessed, covered the bed. On the left side of the room sat a modest wardrobe while a small table and chair occupied the other side. *Not much here but bigger than a ship's cabin,* Anne told herself. She opened a door on the right wall beside the table and discovered the widow's walk which overlooked the yard, cabins and the fields beyond. *That'll be nice,* she thought.

In the other room, Anne found a small bed with a single mattress ticking filled with chaff. The room had a small, carved wood chest and a wooden bench but no other furniture. *A child's room,* she thought with a slight pang. She shook off the feeling.

As she turned to leave, John and Ben showed up on the landing carrying the heavy trunk. Anne directed them to put it down near the wardrobe. When Ebo and Caesar appeared with the smaller one, she directed them into the other bedroom. *Joseph can have his own dressing* room, she thought. Finally, Joseph arrived with the valise. He put it on the table as he looked around.

Standing in the sparsely-furnished bedroom of their new home, Joseph pulled Anne to him and kissed her hard on the mouth. "A new day, Pirate," he whispered with a wink. "These slaves won't know what hit them."

Anne held his eyes. "Won't they be surprised, Forger? Now all we have to do it make this life work though neither of us knows what the hell we're doing."

"True," Joseph answered her. "But we've made good with less, my girl. At least I have. Let us go start anew." He let her go and bowed out of the room.

Downstairs, Anne and Joseph ate awkwardly with Maria and Letty looking on. About halfway through the meal, Anne looked up at the servants. "Have you eaten?" she asked.

"No, ma'am. We waits till you's done," Maria answered.

Anne looked at Joseph who was steadfastly chewing and avoiding her gaze. He peeked at her and saw her eyes narrow but he said nothing.

"Do ye get enough food? Do the men?" Anne asked.

Her concern surprised the women who glanced at each other with questioning eyes. "Yes 'm," Maria said.

"Same as us?" Anne asked. She had put down her fork and was looking at them.

"Well, we eats what's left, course," Maria answered. "'S enough."

"The men work hard. How much food do they get? Who prepares it?" Anne was determined to dig into the reality of the plantation's relationship to its workers. *Not slaves.*

"Da womenfolk does," Maria's voice now sounded wary. "Some the fiel' han's are women. They do the lighter work and they take care of the men."

She thinks I'm trying to catch her out, Anne realized suddenly.

"How many women are there?" she asked.

"They's seven women fiel' han's. Eighteen men. The women makes the food when they come in." Maria's manner had become defensive.

"Where do they get the food?" she asked.

"Leftovers from main house and some extra we grow, vegetables. Once a month, they gets a chicken." Maria watched Anne.

"The workers need enough food to keep going, Maria. And the women, too. Can ye help out? Do some extra cooking for them so when they get back, the women can rest a little?" Anne looked at her astonished face.

"Is that a problem?" she asked.

"No, Miz. I guess not. Never done before, is all. I'll need extra money for supplies." Maria's perplexed face tried a smile.

"Good. Just make whatever ye're making for us only a lot more. Can ye adjust what ye cook to feed more?" Anne waited. "If any of the women want to cook for their men, just be sure they have what they need."

Maria nodded. "Yes, Miz. I might need some help from Letty."

"Then we will tell Letty to help. And if there's anything I can do," she stopped as she heard Joseph choke on his bread. She glared at him but his face remained inches from his plate. "Let me know. If we plan ahead, should be all right. I have some experience in getting supplies to feed a lot of men," she said.

"Yes, Miz. We can do that." Maria looked over at Letty whose expression was as astonished as hers.

"Good. We'll start tomorrow by figuring out what supplies we'll need." Anne said. She went upstairs to unpack, leaving the two women staring at her retreating figure.

The next morning, Anne and Joseph gathered all of the slaves in the yard under a huge oak tree on the east side of the house. They brought over the benches from the cabins and the kitchen chairs and sat, waiting. Their confusion and curiosity were palpable.

Anne passed out glasses and tankards of cider. The slaves looked at each other bewildered. The last owner had whipped every one of them the day before he rode off over a week ago.

"We want to talk to you about how we're going to run this plantation," Joseph began. Anne sipped her cider slowly, listening.

"My wife and I," Joseph acknowledged Anne with a wave, "do not believe in slavery.'"

The slaves, as they had always been, stared in astonishment. Joseph had their full attention as the cool cider sat in glasses undrunk.

"We need workers. And you know how to do the work. So we need you. And you are not in a position to venture out on your own, so you need us." He stopped, looking around the gathered group. All of them nodded, several with mouths hanging slightly open. They looked like they were in shock.

"Here is what we propose. We will see that you have plenty of food," Joseph paused and lifted his tankard, "and drink, as well as sturdy clothing, warm things for winter. Your cabins will be given doors for privacy and there will be plenty of wood for heating them in the winter. We will teach you to read, if you want to learn."

He looked at the faces surrounding him. This was clearly nothing they had ever envisioned. "And we want you to learn skills. If you can do the blacksmithing and the leather repair and the mending and the sewing and the cobbling, we all benefit." He looked down at Anne who was again concentrating on her cider.

"And we will pay you," he added. An audible gasp escaped from every person surrounding them.

"You gon' pay us?" asked Maria, her eyes wide.

"Yes. It won't be a lot, but it will be pay for work. That's what laborers get. You aren't slaves any more. Maria, you are a cook; Letty's a housemaid. Caesar, you're the foreman. Ben, John and Ebo, you're the yard workers and the rest of you," he swept his hand to the others, "are field workers."

The slaves stared at him, not quite believing what they were hearing.

"There is one thing we have to insist on though," Joseph continued. Their lowered heads began to shake.

"We can't let the neighbors know," he said. At that, the heads popped up and all eyes went back to his face. "They think that if we treat you with humanity and kindness, you will kill us in our sleep. Mistress Burleigh and I don't think that's true. But we cannot let them know what we're doing here. It would put us all in danger." He looked each of them in the eye. "Which means that if any one of you takes a liking to a slave from another plantation, you cannot tell that person how we do things here. We'll try to get that person to work for us, but we can't guarantee it. And you will have to watch yourselves, especially if you've been drinking." Joseph looked around. "If you don't think you can do that, we'll try to find a humane plantation to send you to. Do you agree?" he asked.

"Can we have a moment, suh?" Caesar asked. Joseph nodded and sat next to Anne, who smiled at him as she handed over a glass of cider.

The gathered slaves of the Great River Plantation talked. They shouted. They cried. They argued. Joseph and Anne waited.

Finally, Caesar came to them, the others following behind him.

"We good with that," he said. "And we thanks you."

"Wonderful," said Joseph. He went and shook each servant's hand. Anne followed and did the same.

"Ebo," Joseph continued, "I want you to learn to tend the horses. They're important to the farm and to us. We will be getting a pair of riding horses soon. And some goats and cows. I want you to tend to all the animals."

Maria looked up. "Samuel love the hosses," she said.

"Wonderful. He can be the stable boy." Joseph smiled at Maria whose return smile was full of gratitude.

Anne stood with the women. "Maria, I will help ye organize the house but I'm no good at cooking." Maria nodded. "Or sewing." She looked to Letty who grinned. "I'm leaving the running of the house to you two. Come to me if there's a conflict but otherwise, you have my permission to do what you already do."

"I sew real good, Miz," Letty said.

"Wonderful." Anne then turned to the women who worked in the fields. "Maria's going to make some of the food for ye so ye don't have to do so much work when ye get in at night. We'll make lots of stew or bread or whatever, and ye can come get what you need for your cabin." The women stared and then, as one, nodded. "If you want to cook, just let us know what you'll need. Take as much as you can from the kitchen garden first."

"Thank you, Miz," said a short, stout woman named Julia. "No one ever treat us so good." She lived with her man Wilbur, another couple and, as Anne discovered, a year-old girl in one of the cabins. The other women agreed. Most lived with all men in their cabins.

"Any of you boys good with building?" Joseph asked, looking from one man to another.

Caesar raised his hand. "I built them cabins," he said with pride.

"Good. We'll take a look at them and see if they can be improved. When the crop comes in, I'd like to add to the main house. For today, I want all you men to walk with me through the cabins and the fields. Tell me everything you know about living here and growing tobacco."

Joseph returned to Anne. "That went pretty well," he said.

"Yes, but they will have to be convinced, Joseph. We'll have to earn their trust. It will take time ... and fulfilling our promises," Anne said. Joseph nodded and left with the men.

Anne turned to Maria and Letty. "Ladies, we will go through the house and the gardens. You can show me our new home and tell me what you do." She dusted off her skirt and headed towards the house. Maria and Letty followed her.

As Joseph and the field workers walked towards the cabins, Caesar came up to walk beside Joseph. "This for real, Massa?" he asked.

"Please, call me Mr. Joseph. Yes, it's for real. We want everyone here to have a good life. This isn't just about us. It's also about all of you. We work together, we all thrive."

The now-former slave nodded, "T'ank you, suh."

"Mr. Joseph is fine, Caesar. Show me the yard." Joseph patted Caesar on the shoulder.

A month later, Anne and Joseph gathered them together again under the big tree in the front yard. All had worked hard on the crops and on improving the cabins. Not one had asked about the promised pay.

"If you would queue up," he began. He pulled out a bag of coin. Their eyes widened and they looked at each other. Whispers passed through the group. "I have your pay," he said.

One at a time the workers on the Great River Plantation stuck out their hands into which their employer, not their Master, put a Spanish pistole. The first two, Caesar and Maria, took the money as if it might explode, but by the time Ebo reached Joseph, the others' faces showed smiles and tears. Something just short of freedom had come to Great River.

CHAPTER SIX

22 November 1722 - Great River Plantation

Joseph raced down the rows of tobacco, Caesar on his heels. *What the hell happened?* Ben had come running screaming about a fire. When he turned, he could see smoke billowing in the distance.

By the time he reached the end of the row, two hundred yards from the house, he could see that the wood and brick cook house was fully engulfed and that despite the best efforts of the servants, the fire had spread to house ten feet away across a tree limb. The walls of the kitchen were smoldering, and the wall was blackening up to the second floor – Anne and Joseph's bedroom.

The servants brought buckets and threw them one by one onto the flames. "Form a line," he screamed. He ran to the well and started hauling up the bucket. By the time it hit the top, Caesar was beside him with a pail. He filled it and Ebo stepped forward with another one. Looking around, he saw men and women behind him lined up, each carrying some kind of pail or bucket. Even eight-year-old Samuel stood in the line.

"Spread out between here and the fire. Pass the buckets. It'll go faster." The group formed the line. "Let the cook house go. Stop the house burning," Joseph yelled as he pulled up another bucket. The line shifted to concentrate on the house.

Suddenly, he realized who was missing. "Where's Mistress Anne?" he yelled.

Behind him, Maria called out, "She safe. Passed out on the front po'ch."

"Passed out?" *Shit,* Joseph thought. *I'd bet that she started this somehow. She's been so moody lately.* Then Joseph focused his attention fully on the pails of water leaving and refilling.

In twenty minutes, they had the fire out in the kitchen with one wall burned but holding. "The cook house," he yelled and the line shifted slightly. It took another half an hour to put that fire out. They dumped water on the glowing embers.

When Joseph called it done, and Caesar had poured the last bucket, the group collapsed, panting. Joseph leaned against the well, breathing hard. Once his heart stopped pounding, he inspected the damage. The cook house was a total loss. The back wall of the kitchen had burned and there were scorch marks above it to the second floor, but the walls were intact. Inside the kitchen, smoke covered the walls and water sat on the floor in puddles. The south wall had a big hole in it.

"Damnation and hellfire," Joseph snarled. *This will cost money we don't have.* He looked over the ruins. Standing out above the smoky, charred pile of wood were the hearth and the brick ovens. *It could have been worse.* Joseph sighed. *We don't have to rebuild the ovens and Caesar can reconstruct the building in brick which we can ill afford. At least the kitchen wall still stands.*

"We take care o' this, Missr Joseph. You tend to her." Maria took Joseph's arm and turned him towards the front porch.

He didn't move. "Caesar, start working on a new cook house. Let me know what you need. We'll do it in brick this time."

He nodded. "Yessir. Get on it soon's the coals cool."

Maria had gone inside to clean up the kitchen with Letty. Joseph followed them inside.

"Maria, what happened?" he asked.

She took a deep breath. "We seen it coming. She come down this mornin' an' I could see she upset. Angry. Don' know why though. I ask about the food and chores for the day, hopin' to take her out of that fit but it didn't work. She jus' yell at me to do my ..." Maria hesitated but Joseph nodded a *go ahead.*' "Damned work."

"She say anything else?"

"Well, I tol' her the cow done drop her calf. Thought that was good news but that really set her off." Maria still saw Anne's face melt into fury when she told her about the calf. "I don' know why but it sure did."

Joseph shook his head and sighed. "I don't know either, Maria. She been drinking lately? Seemed liked she was."

Maria nodded. "Mos' every day, Missr Joseph. I didn't say nothin' because it ain't my place." She stopped to be sure he wasn't angry with her. He shook off her concern. "Never thought it'd go this fur."

"How did the fire start?" Joseph asked.

"Not sure, Missr Joseph. She in the cookhouse. I went to get water. Turned around and saw the fire. Ran yellin' for her, but she didn' answer. Ran round the house and found her passed out on the po'ch with the jug beside her."

"So she started it somehow?" Joseph had known that in his heart but wanted confirmation.

"B'lieve so. They was a stool knocked down and on fire. Broken crock," Maria stopped, taking a breath. "Rum crock on the floor, flames comin' off the spilt drink. Walls already burnin'." Tears welled up in her eyes. "I so sorry, Missr. Joseph. I wasn't gone too long. Knew she'd been drinkin' but never expected," her voice quavered and she slumped to the ground sobbing.

Joseph knelt down and put an arm around her. Looking out the window, he noticed that the morning's puffy cirrus clouds had given way to dark thunderheads. *If she'd started the fire later,* he thought, *the storm might have put it out.*

"Not your fault, Maria. She was a disaster waiting to happen." He hugged her and gently lifted her up standing. "Take a drink of rum and compose yourself."

Maria dabbed her eyes with her apron and took a long, deep breath. "I will. You look to her."

Joseph inhaled a deep breath which was, unfortunately filled with smoke. Coughing, he thought, *God damn her.*

He walked around the side of the house to the porch where he found his wife -- dead drunk and passed out, her body leaning at a sharp angle, almost out of the rocker. He took in everything: the auburn hair snarled and tangled hanging down, the dirty shift with nothing over it, the snoring that came with the alcohol.

He leaned against the porch rail, his mind racing. *It's been coming,* he thought. *I could feel it. She's been slipping back, slipping away. Last week's shopping trip triggered her. Seeing the slaves whipped in the town square. The anger. And she can't let loose. Except at us. And the damned drought.*

Just the day before, he had overheard Anne screaming at Maria that they should be glad to have such good employers and stop asking for help in running the god damned house. Maria had tried to talk her down. "I jus' want to do things how you and Missr Joseph want them done," she had said.

"I don't care how they're done," Anne had screamed back before she left the kitchen and stomped down the road.

Maria had come out of the house to watch her and saw Joseph also watching from the edge of the field. She shrugged her shoulders. Joseph came over to her. "She's going through a tough time. Not sure why – maybe because the crop will be so small. I apologize for her and I know she will when she returns."

But she didn't.

She never wanted this, thought Joseph. *We thought she'd adjust, but she's struggled every day.* Joseph's mind ranged back to the times Anne's anger and fiery spirit had raged against the restrictions of her new life. She hated the town. She hated the other wives and daughters. She hated Society. She didn't want to run the house. She wanted to be left alone. She hated farming. *The only thing she likes is sex*, he thought. In the early days, he believed she would adjust easily. She was smart and had captained pirate ships. She took on the task of making the house her own with some enthusiasm, but that had waned over the last two months. *What happened?*, he wondered with a sigh.

Joseph couldn't come up with a specific incident but he knew her attitude had changed, beginning with the realization that the drought had decimated the crop which meant they would not have the assets they had hoped for. She spent most of her time in the stable. He had found two beautiful mounts for them to ride, and Anne had gone off almost daily into the far reaches of the property. Exploring, he thought, but she never said where she went or what she had done.

He found her one day coming out of the stable, her skirt covered with mud. "What have you been doing?" he asked.

"Teaching Samuel to clean the harnesses and saddles." She walked right past him.

He left her to herself, to find herself. He was there for her but didn't push. *That was a mistake,* he told himself now.

She stirred, pulling her head up and straightening herself. "God's blood, Jack, watch them cannons," she cried out, still mostly asleep.

Joseph cringed. Jack Rackham again. But was it really Rackham or just that life that colored her sleep? He didn't know how to ask.

He decided to let her sleep it off and headed back to the smoldering ruins of their cook house and kitchen.

"Not much to be done for now, Maria. She's out cold." He tried to keep the bitterness out of his voice. "But she's safe on the porch."

He joined the men by the ruins of the cook house. "Can any of this be saved?" he asked.

Caesar shook his head. "Not much, suh. The hearth maybe. We wait until after the storm then clear her out the rest t' way."

A rumble of thunder rolled around them. "Won't be too long," Joseph said. "Let's get some canvas over this hole in the house before it hits."

John and Ben ran to the barn and came out struggling with a canvas twenty feet long and forty feet wide. *Glad I picked that up on my last trip to Hampton*, he thought. It was a torn sail from a ship in harbor and he'd talked the ship owner into letting him have it for free just to get it off his hands.

The men dragged the canvas over to the house. Caesar stood on a ladder with a hammer and nails. He attached the canvas to the burned wall on one side then moved the ladder and nailed it in on the other side. Joseph took his big knife and ripped a seam so they could go in and out. *Shame but can't be helped. Another one on Anne.* He shoved down his feelings of resentment.

Although it was mid-day, the storm clouds had killed all of the morning's sunlight. "Let's take cover. No sense anyone getting hit by lightning," Joseph called over the din of the increasing wind. As if to confirm his point, a bolt shot through the sky just off to the west. The group scattered.

Joseph ran to the porch. Anne was still moaning in her sleep, her head again fallen to the side. "Damn you," Joseph cursed again. "Why do I love you so?" He put his arms under her and lifted her out of the rocker. "Letty, open the door," he yelled.

Letty appeared, wide-eyed and scared, as thunder cracked again, almost overhead. As he carried Anne inside, the first crash of hail hit the roof. The wind blew it onto the porch. *Saved you again, I did*, he said to his unconscious wife as he put her on the bed and covered her with a quilt.

CHAPTER SEVEN

22-25 November 1722 - Hampton, Virginia

That evening, after a tense, cold supper in the parlor, Joseph went back into the fields and Anne walked the grounds, working off the pain thumping in her head. She needed to think and to do that, she had to get past the drunk. Maria had given her a container of water laced with turmeric to help. *She was nicer about it than I would have been*, Anne thought.

The rainstorm had passed and the air smelled fresh and clean. Leaves colored the ground. The air held the crispness of fall. Anne saddled her mare, Rover, and rode for an hour before she let herself think. She collapsed under a slippery elm tree by a small stream, which she had named Mary's Run for her lost friend.

That was amazingly stupid, she chastised herself. *Getting drunk and then damned near burning down the house.* She sighed. *The old ways won't work here. Didn't work all that well then either, if I admit it.*

Facing the dual problems of a much-reduced crop and therefore less income combined with the pregnancy she now knew was two months gone, at least, Anne shook her head. She thought about the babies she'd given birth to but had been taken away from her, by death and by the government. She thought about the plans she and Joseph had to expand the house, improve the inside, and get new furniture – all to have been paid for with tobacco profits. *We'll be lucky to have enough to plant next year.* She tried to cry but had no tears left. Between the horror of the slaves in town and the terror of their disappearing assets and now a baby, she was spent. *Maybe I should get rid of it,* she thought.

Anne realized with a start that she wanted this child. This one alone of her three pregnancies was conceived in a partnership with someone she loved. James was already gone from her affections when she had the baby in Cuba, and Jack, well, Jack had gotten both Anne and Mary pregnant. She admitted to herself that she hadn't fought hard to keep the result.

There has to be a way, she decided. *There's always a way. Even if it doesn't always work out.* She grimaced at her memories of the final battle on the *William*. *But there was a way even to escape hanging, wasn't there? The baby. Saved my life, he did.*

But what options did they have? Most of the money from her father was gone – put into building more cabins for the workers and paying them. Buying more food. A twinge of guilt crossed her consciousness, but she dismissed it as quickly as it had arrived. *No, those were things that had to be done.*

Staring out at the stubble of a field slashed and burned after the tobacco that survived had been picked, she pictured the fields when they had arrived in May. *Tall and swaying. The not quite derelict house with that strange widow's walk. Like they have by the sea.* She caught her breath. *Like the sea. The sea that I know. The life I can do. Where I don't feel constantly out of place and fearful. But how?*

An hour and a half later, Anne ran into the yard and up the stairs to her bedroom. She rummaged in the truck that her father had given her, pulling away a false bottom on one side. She pulled out a bag – the last of the coin her father had given them until the crop came in.

"The crop's in, Father," she said to it. "Now we must find a way to plant another."

She had fallen asleep by the time Joseph came to bed, trying to remain angry but himself spent with the effort, as well as the work it had taken to save the house and to try to hate his wife. She looked so sweet lying in their bed, her hair spread out on the pillow. *Anne Burleigh, you are trial to be sure. But damn me, I love you.* He undressed and joined her, falling asleep almost immediately.

Anne woke and heard the clock chime three. She looked to Joseph, sound asleep, and got up. She put on a shift and a coat against the late fall coldness, and tiptoed downstairs carrying her sea boots. When she reached the ruined kitchen, she put them on, shivering at both the destruction and the chill coming through the canvas.

She walked outside and strode briskly under an almost full moon to the nearest tobacco field, now burned and no longer waving plants that looked like ocean waves. *It'll have to do,* she told herself as she stepped onto the ashy earth. She began to run down the row, slowly at first, getting her sea legs, then faster and faster. As she ran, she waved imaginary cutlasses at imaginary foes rising from the ashes. Slash left; slash right. She thundered down the long row and when she got to the end of it, she turned and ran back. When she got far enough away from the house so she couldn't be heard, Anne Bonny started shouting orders. "Man the guns. Furl the sails, ye scabby cur. I'll run ye through before ye can reload that blunderbuss, coward." She reenacted a battle. She set the ship on course and ordered the sails adjusted. She bucked wind and waves and naval ships belonging to the Crown. After almost an hour, she came to the end of a far field and knew she was ready. She fell to the ground panting until she had caught her breath, then picked herself up and went back to the house.

She left the sea boots downstairs as she went upstairs. She pulled the valise out of the trunk, and filled it with a few necessaries: a hairbrush, a toothbrush, stockings, an extra chemise and petticoat. Then she dressed in the simplest women's clothes she had – a full ensemble to look respectable but nothing that might make her stand out. She went to the bed, looking fondly at Joseph in the moonlight. She kissed him softly, went downstairs, put on her boots, and went to the barn. She saddled Rover and tied the valise to the saddle.

By mid-afternoon, Anne had reached the harbor at Hampton. She had heard Captain Stoutley tell Joseph that more and more ships were picking up and off-loading cargo there. The Hampton Roads, he had called it. A waterway at the entrance to Chesapeake Bay, Hampton also provided direct access to the Atlantic, making it a good spot for cargo between Virginia and the West Indian islands.

Anne found a stable for Rover near the harbor. Once the horse was taken care of, she picked up the valise and headed for the docks. Once there, she began inquiring for a merchantman looking for investors. *If I can find a good cargo, my father's coin will double or triple.* By the time evening came, she was frustrated and tired. Although she had uncovered several leads, none would take her on. Captains didn't trust red-haired women who claimed to have money but didn't look the part. *I should have worn my best garments,* she thought with regret.

She trudged up a street several blocks from the dock, knowing that any place too close would be unsavory. *I can handle myself but I don't want to,* she thought. The eight inch knife she'd brought was stashed in her boot.

A sign proclaiming "Bowditch House" caught her attention. She went inside and got a room. "Is there a respectable but not too expensive place to eat nearby?" she asked.

"King's Raven – just down the high street," the proprietor told her, pointing to the left.

Anne thanked him. She remembered the place from their arrival and found it easily about two blocks away. The inn had two big dining rooms, one with a bar. She went into the other one. *Ladies would never go into the bar side*, she thought, surprising herself. *I guess I have learned a bit in the last months.*

She took a table near a window – always preferring to see to the outside and protect her back, especially since the dining room was not well lit. She asked for food and cider and sat staring at the people walking by.

"May I sit with you, Mistress Burleigh?" asked a familiar voice.

Looking up in surprise, Anne saw Captain Bartholomew Stoutley standing over her.

"Captain Stoutley," she said. "What a pleasant surprise." She motioned to the seat across from her own.

"I saw you sitting here alone and I decided you needed a companion." He bowed to her and sat.

"Thank you. It is difficult for a woman traveling alone."

The waiter came by and Stoutley ordered food. He had brought a tankard with him.

"What brings you here alone, Mistress Burleigh?" he asked.

"I am so glad to see you. I am searching for a merchantman to invest in and have had no luck. None will speak to a woman." She tried to keep the anger out of her voice, with only partial success.

"Ah, yes, that is true." Stoutley's expression was all sympathy and understanding.

I do like this man, Anne thought. *Joseph's friend did us a good turn in finding him.*

"But I must ask, why do you need to invest? Was the crop not as good as you'd hoped?" Stoutley asked.

"No, I'm afraid not. We had not enough water and half of the crop failed." Anne took a deep drink of the cider. "We have a little left to invest and since I have some familiarity with shipping ..." She hesitated while she thought of a reason she would have familiarity with shipping. "...through my father's businesses." *That makes some sense.*

"Ah." Stoutley's food came as he drank from his tankard. He gave her a quick, furtive glance.

As they ate, Stoutley inquired after Joseph and how they had found the plantation, crop failure notwithstanding. Anne answered his questions, happy to have someone to talk to. Her account was mostly honest.

When the food was done and another round of drinks procured, Stoutley sat back in his chair and looked thoughtfully at Anne.

"I have an investment that might suit you," he said finally.

Anne perked up. "Oh Captain, that is good news. What might it be?"

"It's a smuggling ship. Current owner is now in jail, I'm afraid, and looking for a buyer." He held her now wide-eyed gaze of surprise.

"A smuggling ship? Why would you ..." Before she could finish, she realized that Stoutley knew who she was.

"Who told you?" she asked.

"Your husband. He's quite proud of you, actually."

Joseph is proud of me? How could that be? When we married, he didn't even know me.

Her confusion showed on her face. "Yes. Joseph and I have mutual friends. You were quite a find, he told me. A woman who wouldn't care about his past and who was strong enough to work with him. He was quite pleased," Stoutley said.

"And he told you who I was?" Anne continued to be astonished at her husband's feelings and indiscretion.

"Yes. He knew I would find you as fascinating as he did. I am pleased that your marriage is working out well, but not surprised. Joseph is a good man and tolerant." Stoutley took another drink. "The smuggling ship can be had quite cheaply and is fully staffed. There's a Sailing Master, two Mates, Helmsman, Bo'sun, Second Mate, Cook/Surgeon, and a Carpenter plus twenty-five able bodied seamen who are already familiar with the routes she takes."

Anne took a deep breath. This was utterly unexpected but an opportunity. *If we could get a run or two in before winter, and before the babe gets too big, we can make up the losses from the tobacco.*

"Tell me about the ship and the cargo she's been carrying," Anne said, leaning forward.

Stoutley described a sturdy Baltimore clipper: a two-masted topsail schooner. "She picks up rum, molasses and tea from the West Indies and delivers it to customers from New Jersey south to the Carolinas. The contacts would come with the purchase."

Anne sat back, thinking. "What do they want for her?" she asked.

Stoutley named the figure – a bit over the amount Anne had to spend. He saw her concern. "I will lend you the balance to be paid on return, with interest of two percent." He noted her surprise. "An opportunity to invest in a true pirate is one I cherish," he said, leaning closer.

Anne stared at him, thinking hard. Finally she said, "Then let us do it." She reached her hand across the table to shake on the deal.

He took it but held it as he leaned forward. "What about Joseph?" he asked.

Anne held his eyes. "He will be fine. He trusts me." *When I'm not drunk*, she added to herself. "When can I see the ship?"

"I will arrange for it tomorrow if possible. The owner, as I said, is unavailable so I'll have to find those who can make the sale. I assume you can remain in Hampton a day or two if necessary?" He watched her closely.

She hesitated. *Joseph will be worried. Frantic maybe. Angry surely. But this is our best chance and when I return with a plan, he will accept it.*

"He gave me leave to do what I could," she lied.

Stoutley snorted. "I'm sure he didn't, but he is your husband not mine. Where are you staying?"

Anne told him and he said he would send word as soon as those who could sell the ship were found. They rose and walked to the door together.

"Thank ye, Captain," she told him, tears coming to her eyes, which really surprised her. *It's the damned pregnancy – makes me too emotional*, she told herself as she pulled herself together. "Ye'll never know how much this means to us."

He hugged her. "I do have some idea, my dear. Now go rest up. I will contact you soon."

She nodded and left, walking up and down the streets, thinking, before she returned to the boarding house. Once there, she undressed and fell into bed and into a much-needed, deep sleep.

The next day passed slowly, waiting to hear from the Captain. She walked the docks and talked with some of the sailors, who assumed she was a whore, a belief she quickly corrected. She visited dry docks and marine suppliers and craftsmen. She might need sailmakers and carpenters and besides, she had time to kill.

By evening, she was once again exhausted as she headed for the boarding house. As she walked in, the proprietor called to her. "There is a message for you, Mistress Burleigh," he said.

She read the note.

> *Dear Mistress Burleigh,*
>
> *I have found the pertinent persons. Please meet me at the King's Raven at 1:00 tomorrow afternoon. They will join us there.*
>
> *I am yours affectionately,*
>
> *Bartholomew Stoutley, Captain*

Tomorrow, Anne thought. *A new beginning in an old life.*

The next morning dawned clear and very cold, a brisk onshore wind blowing. Anne rose and went down to the small breakfast room. Her coffee had just arrived when she saw Joseph standing in the doorway.

"May I join you?" he asked as he approached her table. She nodded.

He sat across from her. She tried to judge his face but it was impassive. *The liar's face,* she thought.

"Are you well?" he asked.

"I am, Joseph. Thank you," she answered, her mind full of questions.

The server arrived with her food. "My husband has just arrived. He would like a meal as well," she told the girl who nodded and left.

"How?" she began. He put up a hand.

"Stoutley is a friend, remember?" Joseph said and Anne felt a rush of relief roar through her body.

He is not angry. She was surprised at how delighted she was to see him and how happy that he was not angry with her, which he had every right to be.

"He sent word. I came as quickly as I could." He reached out for her hand which she put in his willingly.

"Did he tell you why I came?" she asked.

"Yes. If you are willing, I can take care of Great River while you're gone." He squeezed her hand.

His food came and they ate, a comfortable silence between them.

"Let's go for a walk," he said. "When is the meeting?"

"At one," she answered, heading for the door.

"Then we have time."

They walked down the street, quiet and lost in their own thoughts. "Have you seen the ship yet?" Joseph asked.

"Not yet. Stoutley says she is in good shape and has a full crew. Plus all the contacts I will need." Anne stole a glance at her husband. She could see him thinking through the project. *He'll be alone at the farm but not really. Letty and Maria would take care of the house and he'll be out in the fields finishing the burning and getting ready for winter. He'll be plenty busy.*

"It sounds like a solid plan, Anne. I will miss you horribly but we'll manage and the money will keep us going next year." Joseph took both of Anne's hands and held them right. "Just be sure to take care of yourself and come home."

"I promise," she said, squeezing his hands back.

They strolled down to the harbor. Anne pointed out a ship that might be hers – a Baltimore clipper – so that Joseph could see what it looked like. "They're sturdy and good for both ocean travel and sailing along the coast," she told him.

Eventually, they reached the end of the docks. There was a large grassy area, as yet unbuilt upon, just ahead. Joseph steered them that way.

"Let's sit here. We can watch the harbor and talk," he said.

Talk? Anne looked at him but couldn't read his expression.

They sat in silence for a few minutes. Then Joseph spoke. "How far along are you?" he asked.

Anne gasped. *How could he possibly?*

She gulped. "Not quite three months," she answered. Then looking at him, she added, "How did you know?"

He looked back, love in his expression. "I am not inexperienced, Anne. I knew your courses had not come. Maria confirmed it when I asked her."

Anne's mouth dropped open. "How did she know?"

Joseph laughed. "She's a woman. And she and Letty do the laundry. She knew your courses hadn't come too."

Anne hung her head. "I am so sorry, my dear. That day... the fire ..." Tears began to run down her cheeks.

Joseph pulled her to him, her head resting on his chest. "I know," he said. "Houses can be fixed. I'm just glad you are safe and have not run away from me."

She sat up. "Is that what you thought?" she asked.

"I feared it. I thought the baby might be too much and you might decide to ..." He left the thought unfinished.

"No, my dearest Joseph, no. This baby means the world to me. I got drunk out of fear and horror – fear that we could not take care of the babe and horror at the slave market."

He looked at her, then pulled her to him and kissed her tenderly. "This babe is ours and we will take care of it. We are doing what we can about the slaves. You must let go of what others do. We simply cannot save them all." He stroked her hair and held her as the tears continued to fall. She wiped her eyes with her sleeve.

When she quieted, he pulled the neck kerchief out and wiped off her face. She blew her nose noisily and then laughed. "I've made a mess of this piece of cloth. Let me take it. I can clean it in the basin in the room." She put the wet kerchief into one of her pockets.

"Let's go back to the room until the time comes for the meeting," he said, kissing her again.

"Yes, Joseph, let's," she answered.

The meeting went well. The ship was as described and the price, including all the contacts and the guarantee that most of the crew would stay aboard, was also as Stoutley had described it. By the end of the meeting, Anne owned a sailing ship in her own name, at Joseph's insistence, a crew, and the means to make money smuggling. She was to take possession the next week after she had returned home to collect her things.

And so began her new career as a smuggler – and as a mother.

CHAPTER EIGHT

2-5 May 1730 - Off the coast of Virginia

Howard Wilberforce, cook and surgeon, looked up from the hold ladder. He watched the captain, wet, red ponytail blowing from under a slouch hat, standing on the listing quarterdeck of the two-masted, square-rigged *Betsy D,* yelling up to the crew. "Strike the tops'ls, boys. They'll take us down." The gale almost blew away the words. Henry Boots, able-bodied seaman, quickly went to work then climbed down the ratlins and landed a foot from the Anne.

She saw Wilberforce. "Get that damned hatch battened down, you fool." Wilberforce grinned at the strength of the lady's voice. "Aye, aye, Captain MacCormack." He went below.

She turned to the Bos'un. "Mr. Mayfield, blow three longs and a short to bring the tops'ls down." He blew three long shrieks and one short on his whistle. Men scrambled up the ratlins to get the sheets down; they were catching too much wind. Anne Bonny Burleigh watched the rain tear at their slops as they climbed.

Rainwater poured off the captain's leather slouch hat as the seamen gathered in and tied off the sails. The ship righted itself. "Keep sou'souwest," she screamed to the helmsman, Richard Sylvanus, a former slave, who turned the resisting wheel with his muscular arms as water drenched his striped shirt. Even though he was only a few feet away, the storm shattered the words.

Anne went over the trip in her mind as she watched Sylvanus struggle with the wheel. *Damn the weather. Favored us to Curaçao for rum and molasses and Suriname for tea, then we lost our luck. It forced us to shelter on Cuba and then near St. Augustine. Royal Navy ship showing up didn't help. At least the drop off went well and the Betsy D wasn't damaged badly. So glad to be on our way home to Hampton, but then this god damned storm blew up without warning.*

Anne cursed the new Sailing Master, Phineas Thompson. *I should never 'a' taken that nap or trusted him.* When the storm hit at eight, the Second Mate found Thompson below decks -- drunk. After rousting him, the officer pushed the groggy Sailing Master up top.

"Damn yer hide, Mr. Thompson," she cursed at the bald head poking above the hatch. "Ye shoulda seen the signs of the storm. Get yer ass up here."

Thompson groaned as he held onto the safety line and slipped across the drenched planks toward his angry captain. "I need to find us place to lay up. Watch the deck, ye knave, if ye can." Anne slapped him upside the head for good measure. Using the safety rope, she slid down into the heaving bulk of the vessel.

Making way through cursing, staggering men – all of them soaked to the skin – Anne sat down at the cabin desk, pulling out the charts. Moving the magnifier down on the sea chart, she looked about where they were likely to be. *We should be near Rehoboth. We might make it. If we can get to Indian River, there's a spot we can wait her out.* Plotting their last known location and the direction and speed of the wind, she nodded. *That should work.*

Climbing back on deck, the Captain tied a rope to the mainmast and then around her sopping wet breeches. Waves washed over the deck as she struggled up to the wheel, playing out rope behind. One particularly bad wave knocked everyone on deck down and threw the

Captain to the railing. Luckily, the rope held. Struggling to stand, Anne finally reached the Helmsman. Shouting in his ear over the shriek of the winds, she told him to steer the ship to the west. The seas raised the ship and slammed her down repeatedly, but she righted every time. The black storm showed no signs of letting up. Hail fell along with rain and thunder cracked overhead. After a harrowing half-hour, Able Seaman Jimmy Jones, standing aloft, leaned down and shouted, "Land ho."

Sylvanus looked astonished. "Din't tink we'd make it," he yelled.

"No faith, Mr. Sylvanus," Anne replied, clapping him on the back. In another half an hour, the *Betsy D* had arrived dipping and rolling into Rehoboth Bay where she turned south into the river channel. Once the ship got as close to shore as possible without grounding, she dropped anchor. The drenched crew furled the sails, shinnied down the ratlins and fell into the hold, pulling the hatches closed behind them to wait out the fierce storm.

Anne went to her cabin without looking at the half or fully naked men, a skill she had learned over years of sailing. She peeled off her wet clothes and changed into a dry shirt and breeches, then ordered the Sailing Master's appearance. He knocked and she called out, "Come." Thompson opened the door and slunk into the cabin. Raising a knuckle to his forehead in the traditional salute of British sailors, he quaked in fear.

"Mr. Thompson." Anne stood looking out the picture window without bothering to turn. "What the hell were ye thinking?" Slowly turning to face him, Anne's eyes glowed a deep emerald green.

"I'm sorry, Ma'am." Thompson ducked as an eight-inch jack knife barely missed his ear, lodging in the door behind him. The flash of anger that crossed the features of the Captain at the mistake stopped his heart. "Um, Captain."

"Sorry ain't helping, Mr. Thompson."

Thompson gulped. "I took our readings and watched the sky. Red all dusk; no sign of a storm. The boys invited me for a taste of rum and well, I got carried away." He stopped and took a deep breath.

"Yer thirst damned near drowned us." Anne turned and slammed a fist hard onto the charts on the table. "Ye're confined to quarters. There'll be a trial when we reach home."

"In my defense, and I know it isn't enough, I'm rather new and these damned spring nights are hard to read."

Anne dropped down into the desk chair. "I agree, Mr. Thompson," she said. The Sailing Master breathed a sigh of relief that he quickly regretted. "But I trusted ye. I gave you the responsibility and ye failed me." Thompson was always surprised how well the Captain could sound like a man.

"I'm sorry, Captain. I won't ever let it happen again."

"No ye won't. And neither will I." Anne glared at him.

Thompson saluted and scurried out of the cabin.

The storm raged for another day. The officers took turns braving the winds and driving rain to be sure the ship hadn't sustained damage. They found one spar hanging, but otherwise the ship had held. When the weather cleared, the carpenters went up to fix the spar and within a half day, they were under sail to Hampton.

When the ship was safely moored in the harbor, Captain MacCormack called a consul of the crew: six officers, and twenty-five able bodied seamen.

Mayfield looked at the assembled crew and asked the seaman next to him, "What the hell is this all about?"

Jimmie Jones replied, "Captain does infractions this way. Says that since we all need each other to make the ship run, we should all agree on crimes and punishment."

"Really?" Mayfield asked. He had been added to the crew as Bo'sun when Anne could find no other. Lord Thomas Mayfield, fourth son of the Earl of Dunham, had been Bos'un on a Royal Navy vessel until he was thrown off for inciting to mutiny, but with a letter of recommendation by a baronet named Woolrich, new to Virginia. "Isn't that how pirates handled such things? I hear they treated everyone equally."

Jimmie detected a very haughty tone in the man's voice. "I wouldn't know," he said, and moved away from the Earl's son.

Anne stood in the Foc'sl with most of the officers and some crew. She looked up at those on the Quarterdeck. "Our sailing master took it upon himself," Anne began, "to get drunk instead of doing his job. Put us all in danger." She paused, then added, "partly my bad judgment, but it was his responsibility nonetheless. Mr. Thompson will make his own case. That's how we do things." *And that's one reason my crew is loyal.* "His fate is up to you. If ye want to keep 'im for our next trip, say so. If not, I'll look among ye or around the docks for a new Sailing Master who does his duty." She stepped back and extended an arm out to invite Thompson to step forward. He moved slowly, looking furtively at the crew, many of whom scowled at him.

"I made a mistake," he began, wringing his hands. "And we all very nearly paid the price. But we didn't because of the skill of our Captain." He turned and gestured towards Anne whose face remained impassive and almost hidden by the slouch hat.

"'Tis my first trip as full sailing master and I regret that I failed you. But I have learned and I won't do it again. My navigation's good and got us down to Curaçao and Suriname and back with a full cargo delivered safely and paid for. Give me a second chance, lads, and I promise as God's my witness ..." He took a deep breath then continued. "I will not drink the demon rum when my skills are needed on deck." Thompson looked pleadingly at the other officers and crew, avoiding a glance at the Captain. "Give me another shot, boys, and I will not let you down," he repeated. Then he bowed and backed away as Anne stepped forward.

"Flog the bastard." A voice rang out in the ensuing pause.

The Captain's eyes went straight to the man on the deck above.

"Shut up, Mr. Mayfield. Ye may be son of an earl, but on this ship we don't flog anyone - ever. This ain't the Royal Fucking Navy." Mayfield glared arrogantly down at the Captain from his puffy eyelids as his lank light brown hair blew in the wind. Anne spit. Mayfield was a hero to the youngest crew members simply because of his birthright, and disliked by most of the rest because of his haughty demeanor. Rumors abounded that he'd been telling the younger crew that Anne wasn't qualified to be captain. *Damn him. He's an arrogant, manipulative cur, that one. I knew he'd be trouble before I even hired him.*

Mayfield laughed with the able seaman standing beside him—not looking down to the captain. "Bo'sun!" Mayfield slowly turned, tipping his hat very slightly. Anne had to restrain Wilberforce from launching up the ladder to him. "Do ye have anything else ye'd like to add, Mr. Mayfield?"

"He should be punished. Peremptorily. A strong captain would see it done." Mayfield's upper lip curled in a sneer.

"Are ye challenging me, Bo'sun?" Mayfield didn't move. Anne continued, "We're all equal on this ship, from earls' whelps to blacks who were slaves, to red Indians, to red-haired Irish bastards like me." As the crew giggled, the Captain didn't move. Mayfield's acolytes were moving away to either side. He frowned then bowed slightly, giving Anne a condescending look.

"We'll take the vote then. Those in favor of keeping Mr. Thompson as sailing master, say 'huzzah'." Most of the crew shouted out. "Those opposed, say 'nay'." A few of the crew standing by Mayfield booed loudly along with the Bo'sun himself.

Anne turned to the Sailing Master. "Mr. Thompson, for now, ye'll retain your position. But mark my words, if ye endanger this crew again, it will not go so well for ye. Yer punishment is forfeiture of one-quarter of yer shares."

"And Mayfield." The Captain's hard green eyes looked up at him, "I will not tolerate insubordination on my ship. Ye will not be sailing with me again. But since we are at the end of our voyage, no punishment seems necessary." Mayfield smirked as he made an exaggerated bow.

Bastard.

Thompson put knuckle to his forehead and whispered, "Thank you, Captain," as the crowd dispersed.

Down below, Anne packed her sea bag. She wore her finest breeches, shirt and jacket. The slouch hat had been packed in favor of a tricorn with gold trim and feathers. The jolly boat waited beside the ship.

"I'm off, boys," she called out. A cheer went up. *Every one of them would be broke and ready for another trip in six months' time. If I make one.*

The jolly boat took Anne and her sea bag to the dock. The King's Raven was just up the road.

The next morning Anne Bonny Burleigh, wearing her finest bodice, skirt and petticoat, left the King's Raven and climbed into a carriage for home.

CHAPTER NINE

6 May 1730 - Great River Plantation, Virginia

As Anne's carriage pulled up to the three-story plantation house, she marveled at how far they and Great River Plantation had come since they had arrived only eight years before. She stepped down into three small children and Letty, the former seamstress now nanny, who had poured out over the wrap-around porch to greet her. As Anne encircled the three children: five-year-old Joe and four-year-old twins Maggie and Lizzie, she noted that Letty had once again been unable to keep her fuzzy hair contained under her mob cap.

"Letty, my darling girl, did you lose the hairpins I left ye?" Anne stood to hug the servant who was only a few years younger than she.

Letty giggled. "I didn' lose 'em, Miz Anne. But I was in a hurry t' see you." Anne laughed and hugged her again.

The children danced around their mother, shouting for her attention. She put her arms around them and sank down into a squat. "Joe, what is that? A new frog?" Her tow-headed son, with his father's blue eyes and his mother's freckles, held out a small, slimy, green amphibian. "Ye must put him back in the pond. He will be very unhappy if he has to live in your bag much longer." Joe nodded so hard his blonde curls bounced to his shoulders and back. He ran off, barefoot as usual.

The twins, as they always did, stuck together. "Did ye wash your teeth while I was gone?" Anne asked them.

"Yeth," Maggie said, pulling herself up proudly and showing them off. She was five minutes the older and tended to take the lead. Both girls had inherited their mother's deep auburn hair and green eyes, although Lizzie's right eye tended to wander. Anne hoped that when she learned to read, the eye might strengthen.

Lizzie tugged at her skirt.

"Lizzie?"

"I ate all my pottage," she said with a wide grin. "And look what I found, Mama." She reached into her pocket and pulled out a bird's egg.

"Oh my, Lizard," Anne exclaimed. "Where did ye find it? How beautiful. Did Maria say ye could keep it?" Lizzie nodded vigorously.

Maggie pushed her mother's shoulder. "She found it under the big tree out by the barn pond," she said. "I told her not to go by herself, but she wouldn't listen."

Anne looked sternly at Lizzie. "You girls aren't supposed to go there by yerselves," Anne reminded them. "You must take Letty with you. Ye must have gone too, Maggie, or you wouldn't have known where she got it." Anne guessed. The absolute silence that followed told her that she was right. "Ye must be more careful. Children have drowned in ponds. I will teach ye to swim next summer, but for now, ye must not go alone." The twins nodded sheepishly. Anne hugged them both and handed them over to Letty who had watched the confrontation with amusement.

"I tole them girls not to go by theyselves but they headstrong. Your chil'en all headstrong."

Anne looked at her, surprised, both at the girl's willingness to speak the truth about the twins and at the observation itself. *She's absolutely right though I never noticed it,* she thought. "They take after their mama, I'm afraid."

She stood up as Maria, the cook and head housekeeper came out. Letty took the twins' hands and walked with them back into the house.

Hugging Maria, her first real friend in Virginia, Anne asked, "How was the household? How is Joseph?" She hesitated for a moment, then added: "And where is Carrie?" Carrie was a force to be reckoned with at the age of seven. When Anne had left for the voyage, only Carrie had steadfastly refused to come down to say goodbye. It had hurt, but Anne recognized her own rebellious nature in her eldest child.

"She fine," Maria said. "She been mopey since you been gone. Missr Joseph in the fiel'. They out in the back section. Got some of them little grasshoppers in the t'bacca. I made garlic spray and sent some flour to dust the plants."

Anne looked concerned.

"Not to worry, Miz Anne. It not too bad," Maria said.

The third maid, Angeline, stood on the top step of the porch. Anne climbed up and hugged her. "I done finished them two dresses we remake from last year," she said. "Cut down that calico for Miz Burleigh, but the girl need a new fancy robe, mebbe two."

"Thank 'e, Angeline. I'm very excited to see the clothes. I'll pick up some fabric for Carrie next time I'm in town." Anne smiled and squeezed the maid's arm. Angeline had been with them for a year. When Ebo had fallen in love with her, the Burleighs had purchased her and initiated her into the world of Great River. The two had married as soon as she came to the plantation. Angeline beamed and followed her mistress and Maria into the house.

Anne pulled off her calfskin gloves as she climbed the stairs. She noted that the new, powder blue wallpaper with small butterflies had gone up. *Looks nice*, she thought. At the top of the stairs, she turned left to the new part of the building where the children's rooms had been added with last year's smuggling profits.

She found Carrie on her bed, reading. Her daughter had inherited

Joseph's dark brown hair. *And my temper*, Anne thought. Carrie looked up when the door squeaked.

"Hello, Mother," Carrie said, rising to a sitting position.

"Hello, my darling. What are ye reading?" Anne knew that like herself, her daughter must be approached carefully.

"It's a new book the vicar gave me at church last Sabbath. It's stories by Mother Goose."

Anne sat on the bed and picked up the book. "It's beautiful," she said. "Do ye like the stories?"

"Yes, Mama. I've already read it once." One way in which she and her daughter differed was in the love of reading which Carrie had developed at an early age. Anne had come to it much later when there was a lot of down time on ships.

"I am happy to be home," Anne sighed.

"When are you leaving again?" her daughter asked with a slight wobble in her voice.

"Oh my darling, not soon. I have missed you so." Carrie's stern façade broke as she fell into her mother's arms, hanging on as if for dear life. *This is getting harder and harder*, Anne realized with a deep sense of loss at having missed so much of her children's childhoods.

Anne stood up, lifted Carrie's face up with her forefinger and kissed her on the forehead. The girl finally smiled. *Joseph's deep blue eyes*, Anne noted not for the first time. *I cannot resist either one of them.*

After she had changed into a simple shift, petticoat and skirt with a fresh apron, she went downstairs. "I am starving, Maria," she said, sitting at the table. The cook had already prepared a plate of bread, cheese and sausages, which she set down in front of Anne along with a small tankard of beer.

As she ate, Anne's eye caught a smudge of black near the ceiling to the right of the door that led out to the cook house. *We missed that spot*, she realized, surprised that she hadn't noticed it before. The fire almost eight years earlier had destroyed the cookhouse and badly damaged the kitchen although they had managed to put it out before it engulfed the whole house. Anne choked on a bite of Maria's bread thinking back to that day, very little of which she remembered.

Just then the door slammed open and Joseph was upon her. "Welcome home, my beloved wife," he said. He kissed her hard.

"Joseph," she cried although she had enjoyed the kiss.

"Nothing they haven't already seen," he responded. "I even kissed you after the fire, not that you remember."

"I was just thinking of that day," Anne said, pointing to the black smudge.

"Oh dear. We'll get that painted over right away. I have missed your skills of observation, my dear. Although they sometimes present a problem."

"Oh you mean problems like when new things I haven't ordered show up in the house? Or when we go to town and Samuel has to pour you into the carriage? Those problems?" Anne looked him in the eye, then kissed him.

"Can I get a bit of food, Maria? Upstairs?" Joseph asked her with a wink.

"Surely, Missr Joseph. I'll put it outside the door." Maria watched the two head up the stairs, the last piece of bread in Anne's mouth.

Their clothes came off quite a lot faster than they'd been put on. The bed shook with their lovemaking for almost half an hour. When they were satiated, Joseph opened the door and pulled in the bread, sausage and cheese and a cool pitcher of hard cider with two tankards.

"Tell me about the voyage," he said as he poured the cider. Lying back on the bed with the food between them, he listened to her tale of bad weather, bad luck and her own bad judgment.

"I'm thinking maybe I've lost my touch, Joseph. Maybe 'tis time to let go." Anne took a deep draught of the cider.

"You've said that before, you know. More than once. The sea is in your blood and I'm not sure you can shake it."

"Possibly. But I missed ye and the children so this time. And I made mistakes. Death to a sailor." Anne sighed.

"'Tis your choice, my darling. We would love to have you home, especially Carrie. But I learned long ago that you must do what's right for you and we have to adjust."

"That sounds so selfish and unfair when you put it that way," Anne said.

"Maybe, but it's who you are. I fell in love with your miniature and I was warned by your father. I love every bit of you. Luckily for you, I'm not easily enraged."

Anne sat up and looked at him. "Have ye ever been enraged at me?" she asked.

"A few times – besides the fire, of course. But you need to be who you are and I'm a confidence trickster. I can adjust more easily. And it hasn't been that often anyway. I get mad at you but rarely enraged."

"Oh Joseph, ye are the kindest soul. And yes, ye're a chameleon, able to change as circumstances require. Father did well." She leaned over and put the plate on the ground with the two tankards.

"And there's one thing we know we'll never argue about," she said with a sly smile.

CHAPTER TEN

21 May 1730 - York Town, Virginia

Three weeks later, Anne and Joseph rode into York Town in the carriage for market day. Samuel, now sixteen, could handle the horses as well as any man. Anne admired his ability to be careful and cautious without being frightened of either the horses or the roads. Since Joseph sometimes had too good a time in town, having a driver made for a safer journey home.

Anne loved going shopping, although she couldn't get away every week. Not only was it a change from the routine of plantation life, but it was a chance to see the friends she had made since moving to Virginia and to show off a bit. She had never lost her love of expensive things, now bought rather than plundered. The twice-a-year voyages meant they were able to lavishly furnish the plantation while the tobacco profits supported the farm, allowing them to buy another fifty acres to plant in maize corn, fifty more in hemp, and to make the additions to the house.

Anne and Joseph got out at the Commons. Samuel drove the carriage behind the stable where he spent time socializing with other young black people, a couple of free men but mostly slaves. None knew how Great River was run.

Joseph kissed Anne, then strode off towards the livestock pens. He called back to her, "I need goats to control the weeds in the yard."

Anne's first stop was the milliner's. *Carrie's growing so fast,* she thought with a slight sadness at the milestones she had missed while at sea. *She needs a new polonaise for church and social wear.* Anne thought of the clothes stored away in a trunk in the basement. *When she's twelve, we can pull those out. Angeline can rework the blue taffeta with green and yellow flowers and add a new red underskirt and do another in reverse. Then we can add some new ribbons and lace so they will seem as if they are new gowns altogether.* Anne could picture them. *But for now, we need something sturdy that she can pass down to the twins.* A bolt of fine lawn with delicate orange flowers and bright green leaves that would go well with Carrie's complexion caught Anne's eye. She put it down and kept looking. She liked to see all the options before deciding, something she'd learned as a ship's captain. *What lovely cambric,* she thought, picking up a bolt of the French linen. *The vines and leaves are beautiful. Might as well get enough for a pair of dresses since the twins will soon grow into them,* she thought.

The younger children got hand-me-downs until they wore out; day dresses were turned and reworked as necessary. With four active children, someone always needed something. She noticed some fine red wool that would make a perfect riding jacket for Carrie. It would last through the others as well. *Some fine yellow linen for a lining. What a nice brown worsted for Joey. He gets all new clothes, lucky him.*

"Have ye some yellow linen, Mistress?" she called out to the proprietor, Emily Hemmings. Anne had learned the grammar and syntax of how the locals spoke but had never been able to fully eradicate her Irish accent.

"Indeed Mistress Burleigh. I just got some in. I'll bring it out." Emily disappeared into a back room.

Anne picked up a velvet shoe with a short heel decorated with Spitalfields silk and green embroidered flowers. *An extravagance but lovely with the lawn. The shoe would set off both of the new gowns.* She turned the shoe over, considering its quality. *Good workmanship, but we took better from that merchantman out of Carolina. Such beautiful china he had, too. Damn Jack for tossing all the plate overboard.* She sighed. *He was such an idiot, which is why he's hanging a gibbet and I am not.*

A tap on her shoulder jolted Anne out of her reverie. She turned to see the smarmy smile of Mistress Lydia Starke, the wife of the sheriff. Anne's senior by ten years, Lydia had long been a thorn in her side, criticizing her to others for not being quite proper enough, and nosing around asking about new things as Anne brought them in. Anne generally managed to change the subject.

"My dearest Anne, it's been too long," said the older woman as she air-kissed Anne near her cheek. Anne acknowledged the comment but remained wary. *Not long enough.* Mistress Starke was the worst gossip and busybody in James City County. Her indiscreet husband passed on all the county's failings to his wife.

"Good to see ye, Lydia," Anne lied.

Mistress Hemmings came out with the linen, acknowledged Mistress Starke and then showed the fabric to Anne. "That's lovely, Mistress Hemmings. I'll need thirty yards." She handed over the red wool and the brown worsted. "I will need ten yards of each, please. And a few other things. Can you measure it for me while I look around?" Anne asked.

"Of course, Mistress Burleigh. Take your time." Anne was always polite to Mistress Hemmings -- and all merchants -- and never asked for credit. As a result, she was a popular customer.

As she walked across the store to a table with boxes of buttons. Lydia Starke followed her.

"You have been away again, I heard," said Lydia, leaning over the table across from Anne. At Anne's questioning look, she added. "William ran into Joseph a bit ago and inquired after you." Her tone indicated a completely innocent conversation, but Anne knew that it was never innocent with the sheriff.

Anne took in a quick breath but covered it with a cough. Picking up a packet of blue buttons that would bring out Carrie's eyes, she said, "I was visiting my father in South Carolina. His wife has been ill." She dropped the buttons into her bag and turned to the ribbon display. She tried to concentrate. *I need at least three colors for the dresses to present at their best.* She rubbed several between her fingers, trying to hide her agitation.

Mistress Starke hovered, picking up ribbons and placing them down without ever looking at them. "Oh, I am so sorry, my dear. How is she?"

Anne turned to the other woman. "She is recovering, thank 'e," she replied holding Lydia's hard stare.

"Oh good," Lydia paused. "You know there's a new Baronet in Williamsburg. Name of Woolrich. Just came over from Jamaica. Quite good friends with my husband's cousin the Burgess. You remember him, don't you?"

"Isn't that nice," Anne replied as she turned back to the table, picked up ribbons of gold, blue and green and a bolt of lace and walked calmly back to the counter. "If ye would be so kind as to wrap this up for me, Mistress Hemmings. I will also need six yards of the pale blue alamode."

Mistress Hemmings nodded as she made notes on a paper receipt. "Anything else?"

Anne looked at her own notes. "Ten yards of the usual yellow calico. We seem to go through it so quickly. And packets of yellow, purple, orange, green and dark blue embroidery thread. That should do it. When can ye have this ready? I'll stop back to pay and pick them up."

The milliner nodded. "About an hour?" she asked, looking up.

"Perfect," Anne said with a smile. She shook Mistress Hemmings's hand and turned to go, running directly into Lydia who had followed her to the counter. "It must be nice to afford such lovely things, Anne," Mistress Starke said, attempting but failing to affect an innocent look.

"From one who is always elegantly attired, Lydia, I must consider that a compliment. Good day," Anne said as she walked firmly out the door and onto the street.

Once outside, Anne took a deep breath. She walked briskly away from the milliner towards the general merchandise store, muttering obscenities under her breath. There, she bought enough fine candles to last for a month. They had acquired a new servant named Rebecca, and had taught her to make ordinary fat candles. She was only fifteen, but learned quickly. *Samuel has his eye on her*, Anne thought, remembering that she had seen them walking behind the barn the day before. At the time, she hadn't given it much thought. *How delightful*.

Anne gave Mr. Windler a list of what they needed: flour, sugar, tea, and other necessities that they couldn't grow or make. The goods, he said, would be ready in an hour. Finally, she visited the bootmaker where she ordered new riding boots for Carrie and pair for Joseph as well.

"Will they be ready in three weeks when we return to town?" Anne asked.

"Shouldn't be a problem, Madame," he told her. Anne thanked him and left.

She looked around and was relieved not to see Mistress Starke. A group of women had gathered under the shade of a large oak tree in the commons. She knew them all, and most she considered friends.

Sally Madison waved to her from the edge of the square. She had been heading towards the group at the oak tree as well. "Anne, so good to see you again so soon," she said. Anne came up and hugged her. Sally's fine brown hair flew around her face outside her mob cap. Anne thought she looked like she was surrounded by spider webs.

"How are you and the children, Sally? I heard Josiah had a cough," Anne responded.

They chatted for several minutes until three other women joined them. All exchanged pleasantries and tales about their families as well as news from the plantations and from the town. The vicar's wife came by last.

"Mistress Burleigh, it's so nice to see you. You haven't been to services for too long," she scolded.

Anne took Louisa Fontaine's long, slender hand, squeezing it warmly. They had become close friends when Maggie almost died from a fever two years before. Louisa came to help care for her and stayed for almost three weeks until she was out of danger. They had been fast friends ever since.

"It's been so busy at the farm," Anne said. "We just haven't been able to do much since the last Assembly in Williamsburg."

Louisa nodded. There were many plantation owners in the congregation who came only occasionally. Since the Burleighs donated to the parish, Louisa was content with their attendance when they could be there.

She pulled Anne to the side as the other women continued to talk. "I heard something, my dear, that I wanted to mention to you."

Anne froze. *Oh shit.* "Yes?" She leaned in to listen.

"Sheriff Starke asked me about you. He said he wondered how you had come to be able to add on to the house and acquire so many new things. Seems he has taken it into his head that you might somehow be involved in something nefarious. Which neither Francis nor I believe for a moment." Louisa stopped, blushing.

"Nefarious?" She hesitated for effect. "Ah. No, Louisa. My father has done well and has gifted me with tobacco credits to help us out," she said. "Ye do know I've been down to visit him? His wife has been ill and he needed some assistance. He does know how to express his gratitude although," she leaned over conspiratorially, "he isn't as good at expressing his love." She straightened up. "I believe the funds were his way of thanking me."

Louisa's face lit up. "Oh Anne, I'm sure you're correct about that. Francis told him that we know you and Joseph well and that you are exemplary Christians. I am so embarrassed that I've even mentioned it."

"Please, dear friend, do not question yourself for a moment. I'm sure the sheriff believes it is his job to keep an eye on the county and something he saw as out of the ordinary would naturally peak his interest. If Francis gets a chance, tell him he has my permission to reveal the truth to Sheriff Starke. With my gratitude."

Louisa nodded happily. "I think Sheriff Starke's head is swelling because of that new Baronet just in town who is fast friends with his cousin. Between you and me," she lowered her voice to a whisper, "we don't need more Baronets, earl's sons, or lords around here."

Anne stopped breathing. "Earl's sons?"

"Yes, came with the Baronet ... what is his name? Baronet is named Woolrich. The other one was Royal Navy – third or fourth son no doubt. Name of May something. I don't remember. I think the sheriff is jealous that Joseph has become close to Lt. Governor Gooch through the Tobacco Act work he's done. It's very un-Christian but also very human."

Anne had a flashback to the prison in Jamaica: a man standing at the bars to her cell, telling her he was glad she was would be hanged since the fever the pirates brought to town had killed his wife and son. They called him Woolrich, and he'd spat at her as he left. *And he's a friend of Mayfield.* Her heart ran cold.

She buried the feeling and replied, "Oh my, I go to a sickbed for a while and so many things happen. Well, if the sheriff mentions me again, feel free to tell him I would be happy to talk with him directly, as would Joseph."

"If I get the opportunity, my dear, I will." Louisa hugged Anne. "Personally, I'm just glad you're back."

Anne and Louisa rejoined the other women and chatted under the oak tree until it was time to collect their husbands and return home.

Anne walked quickly to the animal pens in search of Joseph, praying she would not run into Lydia Starke again. She didn't. She found Joseph behind a barn surrounded by friends. She saw a jug being passed from man to man.

It's good we have Samuel to drive, she thought. *Men and drink.* She shook her head as she strode towards the group.

"Joseph, I have finished my purchases. We will need to stop by the milliner and the grocer to pick up some things." Joseph looked up with a slightly blurry look, which worried Anne. "Is Samuel nearby?" she asked.

He pulled himself up, swaying. "Of course, Mistress Burleigh. I shall fetch the boy."

Samuel appeared from behind the barn. In a moment, he appeared, driving the carriage. As he held the door for her, Anne noticed that there were no goats tethered to the back. She leaned out the window. "Joseph," she called. He was still talking with the other men. *I hope he is not too far gone,* she thought, her annoyance rising. *I have been through enough today.* Samuel went to stand next to his employer, quiet but watchful, until Joseph saw him. He shook hands with the other men, calling out, "Until next time."

He made his way, rather unsteadily, to the waiting carriage. Samuel stood behind him to be sure he didn't fall back as he got in, then closed the door.

Anne called out the window to Samuel, "Stop at the milliner and the grocer, Samuel." Samuel grunted the affirmative as he climbed up to the driver's seat.

Once they had picked up the packages and were on their way home, Anne turned to Joseph, who sat staring out the window. "I saw Lydia Starke," she said. "And Louisa Fontaine." She waited, but Joseph didn't respond. "The sheriff is making inquiries."

Joseph turned slowly to look at her. "I know. He asked about you the other day," he said. "Louisa? She is not one for stories."

Funny, thought Anne, *he doesn't sound the least bit drunk.* She cast a sidelong glance at her suddenly sober husband.

"No, but William Starke made some negative comments to Francis. Who, she says, defended us. Lydia, of course, was positively dripping with curiosity and innuendo."

Joseph snorted. "That is her natural state, Anne."

"True but there's more," Anne continued.

"Mayfield and the Baronet – yes, the men were talking about them. They're making quite a splash in Williamsburg," Joseph said as he turned again to look out the window.

"They'll be coming after me, Joseph," Anne said.

Joseph looked at her. "Why do you say that?"

"Well, Mayfield was the bos'un I took on stupidly. And I just had a memory of a man standing at my cell in Jamaica as I lay in the filth about to give birth, spitting on me and saying he'd be glad to watch me hang. The guards called him 'Woolrich'."

After a moment, Joseph sighed. "Something must be done about the sheriff. Starke is asking too many questions, which leads people to wonder where they would not otherwise. As for this Baronet and Mayfield, we'll hope nothing comes of them. Starke won't be able to prove anything," Joseph added. "And we have the advantage of our hard-earned good reputation."

"Joseph, if he keeps asking, people will start to question and they may find something that would be ..." she left the thought unfinished.

"I will take care of it, my dear." Joseph took her hands into his and squeezed them.

She looked into his eyes and saw something there she had seen only rarely, a hardness that spoke of anger and determination. He kissed her on the cheek and turned back to the window. It occurred to her that he had not gone to town for goats at all, but to find out what was being said. She slid over, wrapped her arms around his arm and nestled her head on his shoulder. Anne Bonny Burleigh had always liked adventure. Joseph was one she was still in the middle of.

CHAPTER ELEVEN

23 May 1730 - Great River Plantation, Virginia

Anne stood on the front porch watching the servants and field hands assemble. Some brought chairs; others stood or sat on the grass. At the front, facing the crowd, stood Ben and Caesar, the de facto leader of the workers, talking intensely. Anne went inside and found Maria in the kitchen.

"What's going on?" she asked.

Maria looked up from the vegetables she was peeling. "Gonna have a trial," she said.

"Why?" Anne asked, sitting across the table.

"Jason – that tall fella, works the hemp fields. 'Cep he ain't been workin'. Ben caught him smoking somethin' back behind the barn."

"Oh dear," Anne said. "So what will happen?

"Don' rightly know. I thinks Caesar is gonna be judge with Ben behind him. You white folks have a name for the fella who stands with the judge, don'cha?" Maria looked up from her potato.

"Bailiff," Anne said. "How bad an offense is this for a field worker?"

"Pret' bad, Miz Anne. Takes all the hands to get the crops in, grown and out. We ain't got any bodies to spare here so one worker not workin' is bad."

"What kind of punishment will he get?"

Maria chuckled. She looked straight at Anne. "If it was me, I free 'im."

Anne's eyes flew open. "You'd free him as punishment?"

"Yes 'm. He find out pretty fast how good he got it here. It's an ugly world out there and I doubt he'd get five mile before some hunter picks him up and tears up the papers."

Anne thought for a moment, remembering what Sarah had told her when she said she'd free the slave if she inherited the plantation. "I think that you're right Maria, as usual."

An hour later the trial broke up. Anne and Maria took the laundry out to the line. Samuel came running over. "He gonna have to make soap and they givin' him two more rows, Mama."

Maria nodded. "Seems fair to me son. Now you git – hosses need feedin'."

"Yes 'm," he said as he ran off.

"I don't think that boy knows how to walk. Ain't walked since he learned to run."

"Why soap?" Anne asked. *So much about running this place I don't know yet. But that was my choice.*

"Well, ain't a fun job. In fact, 'bout the worst they is." Maria picked up a sheet and giggled. "Hands in lye all da time. Ugh. He been hankerin' after Liza who does the soap making."

Anne laughed. "Caesar is a wise man," she said.

Maria handed the other end of the sheet to Anne. It took two of them to get the sheets on the drying rope without dropping any part into the dirt. Usually Letty helped, but she was busy with the children. Ben had been trying unsuccessfully for two years to get grass to grow under the laundry lines. Every time Anne suggested they simply move the lines, he got upset and assured her that soon – very soon – there would be grass and no need to move them. *Next year*, Anne thought, *we're moving the lines. Ben will just have to deal with it.*

She was standing behind a sheet, pinning it up, when she heard the sound of horses trotting up the drive. She quickly stuck a second pin onto it, glanced over at Maria who nodded, and then moved out from behind the laundry. She instinctively straightened her mob cap and wiped her hands on her long work apron.

Anne waited at the end of the drive for the four horsemen to arrive, wishing Joseph hadn't gone into York Town that day to pick up some new china they had bought. She knew all four men. Sheriff Starke rode in front on his tall roan. Behind him she saw Burgess John Holloway and Justice Archibald Blair, both from York Town. The fourth man was Jimmy Snaggle, their neighbor Zachariah Waterford's overseer – a cruel man with a reputation for harsh treatment of slaves and for being a drunk. Waterford's property adjoined Great River to the south. Anne had seen Snaggle at the slave market and on Waterford's property when she was in their adjoining fields.

"Sheriff," she acknowledged the lead rider. "To what do we owe the pleasure of this visit?"

"Where is Mr. Burleigh?" he asked. The implication that Anne was unable to talk to him herself irked her, but she had gotten used to the local attitudes towards women.

"He is in York Town. Ye might best have remained there to talk with him. But since ye've come all this way, how can I help ye?"

Anne heard the front door open and turned to see Maria coming out of the house carrying a tray with four glasses of water. *Poisoned, I hope*, Anne thought as she acknowledged Maria. The servant offered a glass to each of the horsemen. Once the Sheriff accepted his, the others did as well.

"This is a business matter, Mistress Burleigh."

"Indeed? I run this plantation so I am quite familiar with its business." She stood and waited as Maria collected the empty glasses and headed back into the house. Anne gave her a slight nod – their signal that the yard help would be quietly gathering in case Anne needed them.

Deliberately ignoring local protocol that said she should ask them into the house, Anne stood and waited. Whatever they wanted, it wouldn't be good.

"Mistress Burleigh, we have been informed that you are harboring a runaway slave."

"Ye have, have ye?" Anne responded. "By whom?"

"Mr. Snaggle informs us that his employer Zachariah Waterford is missing a house slave."

"Has he looked thoroughly?" Anne asked. "Young girls are easily misplaced."

"This is not humorous, Mistress Burleigh. The girl is worth a considerable sum of money. And has been trained at considerable effort."

She turned to Justice Blair. "Mr. Justice Blair, I'm sure you are aware that my husband just prevailed in a court case against Mr. Waterford who was grazing cattle on land that, in fact, belongs to Great River?"

Justice Blair coughed and hemmed as he turned pink. "Yes, Mistress. I heard that case."

"So my husband told me."

The overseer moved his horse closer. "That got not'in' to do wi' this, woman. A nigger girl run away and we know you gots her."

"Then you are better informed than I am," Anne said, holding Snaggle's gaze. She looked from man to man then turned and called out, "Angeline." The young woman appeared at an upper window. "Would you be so kind as to ask Samuel to fetch Rebecca from the tobacco barn?"

"Yes 'm'," Angeline said and disappeared.

"If you gentlemen will excuse me for just a moment, I have something in the house that might help clear up this confusion." Anne turned without waiting for an answer. She walked as slowly as she could into the house, and into the office they had added across from the parlor. She unlocked a cabinet and pulled out a file. Removing a piece of paper from the file, she then lifted out a ledger which she looked through for a moment before taking it outside.

The horsemen were, as she had expected, getting a bit antsy and angry at not having been asked to dismount. But Anne had learned all the rules – including the one that said it was polite to offer them the opportunity to dismount as well as the one that said they couldn't until the option was given. She saw no reason to offer.

Anne stood in front of them holding the ledger without saying a word. In a few minutes, Samuel came around the corner of the house with a young woman of sixteen at his side. When she saw Snaggle, she shrunk back. Anne turned. "Samuel, help Rebecca forward if you would."

Samuel took the girl's hand gently, whispered something in her ear, and then brought her forward.

Anne turned back to the men. "Is this the girl you claim went missing?"

The overseer jumped off his horse and started to stomp towards them, his hand on his holster. Before he got past the Sheriff, Starke jumped down and grabbed him by the arm. "That's the bitch," Snaggle screamed.

Rebecca started to cry. Samuel put his arm around her. Anne stepped in front to cover them.

"I have a ledger here. We keep meticulous records, Sheriff. We purchased this girl legally from Mr. Waterford, and I have the receipt with his signature to prove it. If you will put Mr. Snaggle back on his horse, I'd be happy to show this to you and," she looked at the Burgess and the Justice, "to you other gentlemen. But I do not want Mr. Snaggle anywhere near me or mine."

The Sheriff turned the struggling Snaggle around and managed to pull him back to his horse while talking to him in a low voice. The overseer, however, kept screaming: "Damn nigger lovers. You see the way she treat them likes they was white? She's a damned fucking nigger lover. Ain't got no right to tell us nothin'. Besides she's a goddamned woman. Her word don't mean shit."

By the time the two men reached Snaggle's horse, it was clear that the Sheriff had had enough. "You shut up, Snaggle before I haul you into jail for disturbin' the peace. First, you apologize to Mistress Burleigh for your language." He waited.

Snaggle groused under his breath but finally said, "I 'pologiz for saying that."

"Good," Sheriff Starke continued. "Now, I happen to know that Mistress Burleigh owns an equal share of this place along with her husband and I want to hear what she has to say. So get up on that nag o' yourn before I hog-tie you to him."

Snaggle glared from the Sheriff to Anne then mounted his horse, with his hand on his gun. The Sheriff sighed. "Gimme the gun, Jimmy. There'll be no violence here. If Mistress Burleigh's claim is true, we all go home. If not, we'll take the girl back. That's the deal."

"I ain't giving up my gun," Snaggle snarled.

"Well, it'll be a long afternoon then, Jimmy Snaggle. Because I'm not leaving this spot until you do." The Sheriff turned his back to Snaggle and leaned on the horse.

Anne and the others waited. She could hear Rebecca whimpering behind her. She put down the ledger and laid her hands on the girl's shoulders. "You live at Great River, Rebecca," she said softly. "You're ours."

The girl looked up, tears streaking down her face. She nodded slightly, biting her lip.

"Good girl. Be strong." Anne hugged her and glanced at Samuel who gripped the girl even tighter.

When she turned back around, she saw Snaggle handing the gun down to the sheriff who strode forward. "Mind if we all dismount to look at these?" he asked.

"Of course not, Sheriff Starke. Except Snaggle." Anne motioned to a bench under a tree next to where the men had stopped.

"Take Rebecca to the porch and sit there," she instructed Samuel. He put his arm around Rebecca's waist to lead her up the steps.

Anne sat on the bench and the men sat next to her. She opened the ledger and handed it to Starke. She pointed to the line that said "18 March 1730. Purchased from Zachariah Waterford one Negro slave girl aged fifteen. £15 to be paid in tobacco."

The next line read: "19 March 1730 – tobacco delivered to Waterford; girl brought home."

Anne handed the Sheriff a receipt which she had pulled from a separate file. It read:

RECEIPT
Paid in full: £15 in tobacco hands by Joseph Burleigh to Zachariah Waterford.
Dated: 19 March 1730
(signed)
Joseph Burleigh
Zacharias Waterford

Anne looked at the Sheriff. "In my experience, Sheriff Starke, most folks don't keep good records. But we do."

"May I show the Justice and the Burgess?" he asked.

"Of course." Starke passed the ledger and receipt to the others. "But I will not allow Overseer Snaggle to see. His own master should have a copy. And I don't trust him not to tear it up." Anne's eyes remained calm and steady as she addressed the sheriff.

"I understand," he said.

After the three men had examined the documents, they excused themselves and moved away to confer.

She rose and waited where she had greeted them.

Sheriff Starke returned the ledger and the receipt. "We are satisfied, Mistress although I wonder that Mr. Waterford believed the girl a runaway."

Anne looked at him with a raised eyebrow. "You more than anyone Sheriff know that Zachariah Waterford spends far too much time in the tavern to even remember to come home nights."

Starke chuckled. "You have a point, Mistress Burleigh. My apologies for the intrusion."

She expected him to turn and leave, but he didn't.

"I wanted to mention one other thing."

Anne took a deep breath. "Yes?"

"It has been noticed that you and your husband have been making considerable additions to your property which would seem to be of a cost beyond what the tobacco crops are bringing in."

"Noticed?" Anne asked.

"Yes. I wondered ..."

"I'm afraid this is not your business, Sheriff. But if you must know, my father has been generous because I have been returning to South Carolina to help him attend to his wife who has been quite ill."

The Sheriff bowed. "Sorry, Madame. I had no idea."

"There is no reason you should have had, Sheriff Starke." An edgy anger crept into Anne's voice. "If your business here is finished, I have much work to do."

"Indeed. Thank you for clearing up this misunderstanding."

Misunderstanding my ass, Anne thought.

"You're welcome."

She remained where she was until all of the horsemen had disappeared far down the entrance road. She noted that the sheriff kept the overseer's gun.

She sat down next to Rebecca and wrapped her arms around her. "Cry, my child. All you need to. No one should have had to go through the kind of terror you have. And while I am alive and here at Great River, you never will again."

She lifted Rebecca's chin and kissed her on the forehead. "Now, go into the kitchen and get a glass of cider from Maria and a biscuit and when you're ready, go back to work."

Rebecca nodded. "Thank you, Miz Anne. Thank you." She returned the hug and went into the house.

Anne sat on the swing a long time, remembering the day Samuel brought Rebecca home. She was covered with bruises, dirty and wet from hiding in Mary's Run and the maize fields, starving, and terrified. *Thank god for Joseph's forgery skills and Waterford's drinking.*

She rocked back and forth, thinking about how far they'd come since the day they'd arrived. *I've learned how to talk Society and I've learned the rules and how to use them to our advantage when needed. We've managed to keep servants who aren't slaves and to prosper. Even though it took more than the farm income to do it. But I will never be one of the so-called gentry. Never.*

CHAPTER TWELVE

25 May 1730 - Great River Plantation

"Joseph," Anne called out to her husband who was riding in from a maize field he'd been helping to plant.

He waved and rode up to where she stood beside the front porch. "Yes, Wife?"

"I would like to ride out with you," she said.

He bowed. "I do not require a formal invitation, Anne. Change and meet me in the barn."

When she had pulled on her dark brown riding coat over a teal satin waistcoat and linen shirt and donned the men's breeches she had made just for riding, she pulled on her short boots. She sighed with the joy of wearing men's clothing again.

As she walked briskly to the barn where Joseph had already asked Charlie, the stable boy, to bring out her mare Rover and saddle her, Anne picked up an apple from a barrel by the doorway and fed it to the mare, who happily took the offering. Samuel had graduated to driver. Charlie brought over the mounting step and helped her up. Unlike other local women, Anne never rode sidesaddle, preferring the control and comfort of riding astride.

Joseph led the way out of the barn, but Anne quickly passed him and galloped south through a fallow field. Joseph laughed, spurred his horse and tried to catch her. He knew he would fail, but they both loved the chase.

After riding for a mile, Anne slowed down so Joseph could catch her, which he quickly did. "Where are we heading, Anne?" he asked. He had seen her ride in this direction but since she usually came this way when agitated, he had never followed her.

She looked over at him. "I have decided to trust you with my special spot," she said. He doffed his hat to her and swept it forward. "Lead on."

It took them about half an hour to reach the small grove of Slippery Elm trees at the edge of Mary's Run. Anne slid off her horse and let Rover enjoy the abundant grass.

Joseph dismounted and followed her lead. He looked around. "'Tis lovely, Anne. I thank you for bringing me here."

She smiled and untied a blanket from her saddle. Laying it on the ground, she sat and patted the spot next to her. Joseph sat down beside her.

"I found this place the day I knew I was expecting our first child – after the fire. I confess I came here considering whether to dislodge the baby. I was distraught."

Joseph took her hand and kissed it. "I am not surprised, my dearest. I cannot imagine what that felt like, but I am glad you made the choice you did. It must be difficult to lose the freedom of a single woman."

Anne frowned at him. "'Twas more than that, Joseph. I had two babes before and lost them both. One disappeared in Cuba, and the other was taken from me in prison. I wasn't sure I wanted that pain again if I were to somehow lose another." She looked off into the distance. "But when I found this stream and the trees and the view..." she waved her hand in front of them. "This beauty and serenity, I thought I could bear the fear."

Joseph leaned back against the tree and waited. He knew well enough that she had brought him here for something momentous.

"I have given thought lately to selling the *Betsy D*," she said. When he didn't respond, she went on. "The Sailing Master failed in his duty partly because I did not take enough care in governing him." She paused again, gathering her thoughts. "And I took on a Bos'un who should have been hanged, not hired." She sighed, staring off into the distance. "I wonder, Joseph, if my time in smuggling has lost its necessity. I sorely miss the children." At his raised eyebrows, she added, "And you, of course. When that first crop almost failed, with Carrie on the way, I was frantic. That's why I ran away to Hampton. To invest in a merchantman – something I knew. When Captain Stoutley told me about the smuggling boat – all crewed and with contacts – it seemed like a godsend."

Joseph nodded. "It was. I understand your panic. When I found the last of your father's credits missing, I became frantic myself. I feared you had simply run away."

Anne caressed his cheek. "I know, Joseph, and I am sorry for the anxiety I caused." She blushed. "For that and for the fire."

He kissed her hand. "It doesn't matter now."

"But now." She turned towards him. "I am getting weary and careless, which is death to a seaman."

"Or woman," Joseph added.

She shot him a withering look. "I'm a seaman, Joseph. I dress as a captain should – as a man. It's an addiction, I guess, the life. Here things are so quiet and predictable." Joseph raised an eyebrow. "Mostly," she added. "But now I am wearying of the sea." Tears filled her eyes. "I missed the twins' birthday. I meant to get home but the agent was not on the shore when we got there and we had to wait. Then there was a squall and the sailing master damned near drowned us. And then there's Mayfield ..."

Joseph looked at her curiously. "The Earl's son? The man you shouldn't have taken on?" he asked.

She nodded absently, still staring out at the fallow field. "Yes. Bad judgment. He's a rotter, that one."

"For a pirate?" Joseph asked.

"He's no pirate," Anne responded. "He's worse ..." Her voice took on a deep sneer. "A gentleman. Never to be trusted." She shook her head. "He challenged me – in front of the whole crew. Bastard."

Joseph sat while she fumed.

Anne gulped and took a deep breath. "So I wondered. Can we afford to sell the *Betsy D*? If I am truly ready, and I'm not yet certain about that, would you want me home all the time?"

He stared at her incredulously. "My dearest wife, I want you with me always." He paused. "It is hard on us at home with you gone. The children miss you and ask why you are not here. I miss you." He grinned. "In our bed and other times." She rewarded him with a smile.

"Not even counting the increasing gossip," he added. "But are you sure you want to give up that life?" he asked.

"No, not yet. But there is another consideration," she began.

"Sheriff Starke," Joseph said.

"Yes. His inquiries persist. He is having some impact, Joseph. Some of the women are asking questions when we visit. You know how people are. A good story is better than a true one."

"Only in this case, the good story is, in fact, true," he pointed out.

Her head bowed. "Yes." She leaned forward and picked at the grass. "And now there's Mayfield and Woolrich who may recognize me. I am weary, but I am also afraid. The smuggling has sustained us, but we have money now, and the risk increases with each voyage. I do not want to lose all we have built."

Joseph nodded. "I have been considering asking you about leaving the sea as well. I am glad you brought it up." He tilted his head to look at her. "We need you here more than we need the extra funds," he said.

Anne fell backwards into his arms. He kissed the top of her head, running his fingers through her hair. "Mmmm," he murmured. "I do love you so, Anne Burleigh. And your lovely auburn hair." She snuggled more deeply into his embrace.

They sat together until the sun had crept low on the sky to the west. Anne looked up. "There will be a storm, Joseph. With winds I think."

He looked at the sky and saw dark clouds on the horizon. "A bad one?" he asked.

"Very bad. We should get home and batten down the hatches." She rolled to her knees and stood up, reaching down a hand to her husband.

He took it and when he was on his feet, he turned to his wife. "Quit, my darling. For Great River. For the children. For me. For you. For us."

Anne gently stroked his cheek with her hand. "I love you, Joseph Burleigh," she said. She reached for Rover's reins. With a leg up from Joseph, she settled into the saddle.

Joseph mounted and they turned the horses towards the house. "Oh, Anne, I almost forgot to tell you. A message came from the Lt. Governor. There's a hearing on the tobacco inspection bill on the eighth. And, I have been told, Gooch is having an Assembly at the Capitol. I know you dislike politics but …"

Before he could finish, Anne interrupted him. "If there is dancing, I will go," she said. "You knew I would want to, you scamp." She flicked her whip at Joseph who recoiled in mock horror. He urged his horse into a gallop home.

CHAPTER THIRTEEN

11 June 1730 - Williamsburg, Virginia

Anne stood on the balcony overlooking the Williamsburg Capitol's General Court which had been transformed for the evening into a lively assembly. As she looked down upon the dancers moving gracefully through their sets, she mentally appraised the value of the jewels glittering on their bosoms, hands, wrists and ears. Her practiced eye added the room up to almost £200. *Not a bad haul*, she said to herself, *if one could pull it off. About what we took off that Spanish frigate.* Her own neck showcased the emerald and diamond parure with matching earrings that was a birthday present from her husband on the day she turned thirty. She fingered the pinchback brooch pinned to her bodice. *If only they knew where that came from*, she mused.

Not naturally graceful, Anne had added the ability to seem so to her repertoire over the years. *I have also learned to seem civilized, domestic and feminine,* she thought as she descended the stairs into the entryway and made her way into the court. The room was paneled with dark wood and had high rectangular windows. The area used by plaintiffs and defendants, as well as lawyers, had been turned into an area for the orchestra. The judges' seats above sat empty.

She looked around at the crowd of guests as she came through the door, finally spotting Joseph up near the Governor's Chair chatting with Lt. Governor Sir William Gooch. They had become friends through a shared interest in the Tobacco Inspection Act which was being written for the House of Burgesses, although it would ultimately have to be approved by the Crown. The law would require Virginia tobacco to be inspected to assure that it met certain quality standards which would make it more profitable. Joseph served on the board that helped the General Assembly draft the language. He supported the effort so that prices for their own high-quality crop would continue to be strong.

Sally Madison was talking with Amity Loudoun near the back of the room. Anne slipped through the dancing couples to join them. She glanced out the tall windows at the darkening sky, the moon already blotted out. *Thank goodness the rain held off*, she thought as she approached her friends. *It'll be ugly later though.* She could hear the wind starting to pick up over the music.

Anne perked up as she approached her friends. She admired Sally, whose plantation lay just to the south of theirs, for her willingness to wear her hair piled up a foot high above her natural height of almost six feet tall. *I wonder how much of it is actually her hair and how much is wool*, Anne always wondered. Her own dark auburn curls were piled up but not to great heights and only lightly powdered. She was proud of her hair, its unusual color and even its betrayal of her Irish heritage.

"Anne Burleigh," exclaimed Sally. "It has been far too long. Where have you been keeping yourself?"

Anne laughed. "I might ask ye the same Mistress Madison. We have been planting, of course. Tobacco, maize and wheat. And we added a field of hemp. The ships always need rope so we thought we'd try it. Such a lot of work to keep everyone fed and productive during planting time. Were ye not doing the same?"

Before Sally could answer, a short, thin woman with a pox-scarred face joined them. Anne kissed Rebecca Gooch, the Lt. Governor's wife, on the cheek, being careful to dodge the three beauty marks glued to it. "That is a lovely bracelet, my dear," Anne commented, fingering the foil-backed topaz and chrysoberyl piece. "Eighteen carat?"

"You have such good taste in jewelry, Anne. Yes it is. A gift from my late mother." Rebecca waggled her hand so the gems flashed in the candlelight. "My husband and yours are deeply into tobacco talk. I don't know how you tolerate the country life," she said. She shook her head, sending the powder on the white curls of her wig flying and the feather on top waving briskly.

"Why Rebecca Gooch, ye can't possibly know its joys until ye've tried them," declared Anne. "Dust, horse messes, field slaves, tobacco stains on everything and children who run wild. It has much to offer a gentlewoman."

Rebecca laughed. She adored living in the Governor's palace and had furnished it lavishly during her time there. "At least in the palace, I needn't worry about horse messes. And the only stray tobacco ends up next to the spittoons."

Anne continued. "There are rewards too, you know. We have streams and trees to lie under when it's hot and plenty of help so we needn't work too hard. Plus the children are in good health from running in the fresh air."

"My dear Anne, everyone knows that fresh air is dangerous. Full of pestilence," declared Amity Loudoun with alarm. Amity had never been out of Williamsburg, the protected child of older parents. She was tiny, less than five feet tall, her petite figure made more so by the tightly-laced stays she wore. Amity never wore a wig; she decorated her brown hair with jeweled pins. *Easily £5 worth*, admired Anne. Amity's red brocaded skirt fit perfectly, showcasing her tiny figure. Anne sighed inwardly at the expansion of her formerly trim waist under the stress of childbearing. She refused to tightly lace her bodice.

"Amity, you must have the best seamstress in Williamsburg. The embroidery on your petticoat is exquisite." Amity blushed and curtseyed a thank you.

"I can't speak for the air in town," Anne said, "but it is not pestilential in the country. We have lots of good water and fresh food to harvest and slaughter. We want for little except society and niceties which we can find elsewhere so there is much to recommend it." Turning back to Sally, Anne added, "So far this season, the weather has been ideal. Don't you agree?"

Sally nodded that she did, setting her girandole earrings bobbing. Anne calculated that they had cost at least £10. *Easily the best in the room*, she mused. She laughed at herself. *Old habits die hard. I have enough fine jewelry of my own now. Why do I still mark what others wear?*

Across the room, Joseph continued to talk with the Lt. Governor. "Do you foresee the outcome of the Burgesses' vote this week?" Joseph asked.

"I believe it will pass but then we have to send it to Parliament for approval so it will be awhile before it's in effect," the Lt. Governor replied.

Gooch pointed out a man standing across the room speaking with Burgess Goodwin.

"Joseph, I want you to meet someone who has recently arrived in Virginia. Sir Jonathan Woolrich, a Baronet. He comes from Jamaica -- a friend of Burgess Goodwin." Gooch leaned over, putting his arm over Joseph's shoulder. "I'm told he's quite a skilled swordsman and has a penchant for duels, so be careful, my friend." Joseph could smell the brandy on his breath.

"I have heard of him. What brings him here, William?" Joseph asked.

"Rumor is he's fallen on hard times. He had some financial reversals over a lost shipment of slaves. He's been asking around trying to find an inexpensive vessel with the money he has left. Plans to use the profits to start a new farm. Plucky man to start over at his age – he must be forty-five or fifty."

Joseph nodded.

"Goodwin says he has not been the same man since his wife and one son died of fever about ten years ago. His daughter has married and removed to England. His remaining son married and there are three children, I believe. He gave them his plantation in Jamaica, to help them out, he said. He showed up about a week ago with a young man – a Lord Mayfield, son of some Earl or another. Apparently promised the parents he would look after the boy."

Joseph looked carefully at the Baronet -- a tall, portly man in his late-40s with puffy, piggish eyes, wearing a short, tightly-curled white wig, meticulously dressed in breeches and a coat of gold voided velvet in a lace pattern. *He looks a villain.*

"After the ship was lost, he says he gave his plantation to his son. He says it wouldn't support all of them so he came here to begin over. The Earl's son is a sailor, we're told, so I presume he will captain a vessel if Woolrich finds one."

Joseph looked curiously at the Baronet. "He does seem a convivial fellow," he remarked. *A totally false one. It takes a confidence man to see another.* Woolrich was laughing heartily at something Goodwin said.

"He is indeed. I ask a favor." Gooch looked at Joseph. "I have obligations and must leave shortly. So I am unable to act as his host."

"What about Goodwin?" Joseph asked.

"He also must to leave in only a few minutes. Another social obligation."

Joseph wondered what social obligation might outrank a party at the Governor's Palace. He suspected some kind of gambling. "I'd be delighted," he said.

"Good man," Gooch said.

Following the Lt. Governor, Joseph walked to where Goodwin and Woolrich stood, still laughing.

"Benjamin," Gooch said, getting the Burgess's attention. "I have brought Joseph Burleigh to host Sir Jonathan." He smiled.

Joseph bowed to Goodwin then turned to face Woolrich.

"Sir Jonathan Woolrich, let me introduce you to Mr. Joseph Burleigh, a prominent citizen of Virginia and responsible for much of our new tobacco inspection law."

Joseph then bowed to Woolrich, who merely nodded in response. *Arrogant bastard, as I thought.* "A pleasure, Sir."

"Mutual," Woolrich replied, his voice cold as a spring stream.

"I would be happy to introduce you around," Joseph added. He waited as the Burgess, the Lt. Governor and the Baronet exchanged good-byes.

Joseph took Woolrich around the room, introducing him to friends and acquaintances. Having been in Williamsburg so often, and regularly at both the Capitol and the Palace, he knew most of the guests.

"I understand you are staying with a young man, an Earl's son," Joseph said.

"Yes, Lord Thomas Mayfield, fourth son of my old friend the Earl of Dunham. He was in the Royal Navy, quite the exceptional sailor, I'm told. But he is now looking for something independent. I said he could stay with me and I would look after him until he is settled. The Earl invested heavily in my plantation, so I was happy to return the favor."

Investment isn't a favor, thought Joseph, but he didn't say anything.

After a while, he spotted Rebecca Gooch with some friends across the room and led the Baronet that way, not seeing Anne who was partially hidden by a post.

The ladies were chatting about children and husbands when they heard Joseph's voice. The other women backed up and dipped slightly. Anne stepped out, gasped then stepped back quickly.

"Mistress Gooch," she heard Joseph say. The man was well-dressed and wearing a diamond stick pin in his cravat. *It has to be Woolrich, the bastard who spat at me in prison. Why the hell did Joseph bring him over here? Then she realized she'd been hidden as he walked over.* She saw Rebecca curtsey slightly. As the Lt. Governor's wife, she had top status.

"Ladies, may I introduce Sir Jonathan Woolrich, Baronet, recently moved here from Jamaica." As he extended his hand towards each woman, he introduced them. "Mistress Gooch you have met. Mistress Madison. And Mistress Loudoun." At that moment, Joseph realized that Anne was behind the post. He gulped. "Anne," he said. "Come meet the Baronet." She knew she would have to and that Joseph did, too. She turned and curtseyed to Woolrich, keeping her head low. The Baronet bowed to each woman in turn without taking his eyes off of Anne.

Does he remember? Or am I just familiar?

"So nice to meet you, Sir Jonathan. Are you in Williamsburg long?" she asked, hoping that the pounding of her heart could not be heard over the music coming from the far end of the long, narrow room.

"As long as it takes to find a new plantation to invest in," he replied. He hesitated for a moment, then asked, "Have we met?"

Anne shook her curls without a moment's hesitation, pulling her lace fan in front of her face. "No, I don't believe so," she replied. "Were you at the Ball two nights ago? You might have seen us there." She fluttered the fan with unnatural vigor until she realized it and slowed down.

"No, I have only just arrived," he rejoined, still staring at her. She turned away.

Once Woolrich had uttered standard pleasantries to the other women, Anne shot another look full of daggers at Joseph. This time, he raised his eyebrows with a slight shrug that said, "I didn't see you." Then he turned to Woolrich. "You must meet our Mr. Guthrie. He is most familiar with local properties."

"Indeed," responded Woolrich. "A pleasure, ladies." He bowed, left leg extended, in perfect form. The women curtseyed in return. "Perhaps we can chat later," he said to Anne. She kept the fan over her face and did not respond. *Over my dead body,* she thought. That was, after all, what he and Jamaica represented to her.

Thank God, she thought as she watched them walk away. Anne shot her husband a grateful look when he glanced back.

Sally watched them go, concern on her face. "Why on earth did he think he knew you, Anne? There's something ... unsettling about his manner."

"Insincere to its core," Rebecca sneered. "I wouldn't trust him with a chicken."

The others laughed. "Well, my dearest Rebecca, your chickens, belonging as they do to the Lt. Governor, are more valuable than most," Anne said, her deep green eyes sparkling in the candlelight.

They resumed their conversation where it had been interrupted. Anne tried to pay attention, but kept thinking of how Woolrich had looked at her. They had shared all the latest gossip when Rebecca hefted a deep sigh and said, "I must mingle, ladies. Politics always."

"My father will be looking for me as well," Amity said, dropping a curtsey to her friends.

"Rebecca loves it, ye know. Politics," Anne whispered to Sally, who agreed.

They chatted about the crops and the children for a while longer until Sally pled the necessity to join her sister-in-law. "I see that she has been cornered by the Reverend Matthews." She almost groaned out the words. "I must go to her rescue. Will I see you before you leave?" she asked.

"No, my dear. We're going home tomorrow. We have danced these three nights running and must return to real life. The children can be difficult if we're gone too long. But I'm sure we will see each other in York Town soon." Anne kissed her friend on the cheek then patted her behind to send her on her way. Sally looked back waving as she glided into the dancing.

Anne needed to use the privy, so she headed out to the gardens that led to the brick outhouse. Outside, she saw Joseph and Woolrich talking at the north corner of the building. Grateful for the darkness of the black skies, she edged along the wall until she was close enough to overhear their words.

"Your wife," the Baronet said, "seems familiar somehow. Did she reside in Jamaica?"

"Oh no, she's from South Carolina," Joseph answered.

So he's probing, she grimaced. *Damn him.*

She walked quickly to the privy, relieved herself, and then returned inside. She sat near the orchestra, as far from Woolrich, who had gathered a following, as possible. As she fanned herself in the heat, she watched thunderclouds gather. After so many years at sea, Anne could feel barometer falling.

At midnight, Gooch returned to preside with his wife over a light meal of bread, chicken, fruits and nuts.

Anne had lost sight of Joseph. That wasn't unusual. He was far more gregarious than she. But he had neglected her need to dance, so she resolved to find him after the food was cleared away and the music resumed.

The orchestra struck up again and dancers filled the floor. She tracked Joseph down for the Contredance and then had several neighbors for partners for a minuet, a gavotte, and canarie before the clock stuck two. When it did, the orchestra began to pack up.

The thunderstorms held off, she thought, *but not for much longer. We'll be lucky to get back to the boarding house dry. I'd best find Joseph before the storm breaks. I expect he will be ready.* Even the chatty Joseph would be wearing out after three straight nights of conversation.

Anne watched clouds race across the dark sky. She looked around and realized that the room had emptied. Suddenly, a figure stepped out of the shadows from behind the courtroom's bar. She caught her breath as fear welled up her spine: Woolrich.

"Mistress Burleigh," he said in a frightening soft tone.

Stopping short, she showed her surprise. "Ah. Mr. Woodland, is it?" she asked.

"Sir Jonathan Woolrich, Madame. At your service." He bowed. She dipped slightly, hoping he couldn't see the evil eye she shot him.

"I must say, my dear Mistress Burleigh, that I was surprised to find you here." Woolrich's forehead undulated as he talked like he had caterpillars walking under his skin. His dark eyes all but disappeared under the bushiest eyebrows she had ever seen -- either gray or powdered to look so.

"I'm sorry? Sir Jonathan, is it? What do you mean?" Anne felt the terror creeping into her heart.

"Well, I thought you had been hanged, my dear woman." Woolrich's voice had gone flinty hard and his lips pursed into a thin, hard line, turning almost dead white. Then they lifted slightly into what might be a smile, albeit one filled with malice.

Anne caught her breath, her composure struggling against the fear that threatened to waylay it. She looked out at the courtroom. There was no one there. They had all gone into the entry way. Her breath caught in her throat.

"I have no idea what you mean, Sir. Why on earth would you think I had been hanged?" Her fear was giving way to anger. Her deep green eyes hardened to emeralds.

"Why, you are the pirate Anne Bonny. I was at your trial. I visited your cell. I heard you had been carried out dead, so I assumed you were hanged. I did wonder why you weren't gibbetted." His visage remained intense and unmoving.

Anne took a deep breath, determined to remain calm, or at least to seem so while she figured out a way to escape him. Her back felt the wall behind her. Woolrich had stepped between her and the exit door, cutting off that route. "You are much mistaken, Sir. I have no knowledge of such a woman and I am certainly not she." She found herself surprised at how calm and indignant she sounded despite the fear snaking through her heart. She turned and tried to push past him.

Woolrich lunged forward and with his right hand, pinned her arm against the wall, his whole body blocking her. He twisted her so she faced him. "Yes you are, you strumpet. I would know you anywhere. I took quite an interest in your trial – in all the pirate trials. Went to every single one. My wife and son died from fever brought to town by you pirate scum. And as I told you in prison, you and that bastard partner of yours, Rackham, took my ship as your last prize. So I went to every day of every trial and watched every hanging. Pleaded your belly, you whore."

Anne gasped at both the ugliness and truth of his statement. His grip on her arm tightened. She squirmed but couldn't break free. He pushed her back flat against the wall.

"Let me go, you swine. How dare you?" She drew a breath to call for help, but Woolrich clapped his other hand over her mouth. She screamed anyway, hoping that even a strangled sound might bring attention.

"Oh no, my dear woman. I have you now. But I am a kind man," he continued, raising an eyebrow as if he were taking a high road. Anne snorted despite herself at the word "kind." "I will let you go if, and only if, you do me a service."

Anne's eyes opened wide. She mumbled enough so that Woolrich took his hand off her mouth. "I am not that woman," she protested.

"Perhaps not," he continued. His cold confidence distressed her more than his physical restraint. "But it does seem rather coincidental that there is a red-haired smuggler sailing the coast."

Anne stared at him. *Mayfield.* "I have no idea what you're talking about. I have been to sea but thrice, once with my father who is a merchant out of Carolina, and twice to Carolina to nurse his wife," she asserted.

Woolrich laughed, a sound as oily to Anne's ears as a rendered pig.

"Our friend Lord Mayfield might argue different." He looked at her with an icy gaze.

Anne gulped. *Damn him – and herself for bringing him aboard.* She said nothing.

"His father was a friend of mine. Asked me to look after the lad. Seems he had some difficulty at home and in the Navy." He looked for a reaction but Anne gave him none. Her heart raced but her blood felt cold and hard.

"It seems he then fell in with a smuggling crew. Red-headed captain. Thought it was a man at first but then found out different. Runs the ship like a pirate vessel. Mayfield chafed, shall we say, at the captaincy of a woman." Anne continued to hold Woolrich's gaze without speaking.

"So when I saw you, I thought, 'oh yes, that explains it.' And it does, doesn't it?" He waited.

Anne took a deep breath. "What do you want?" she hissed.

"Your vessel. I have a cargo in need of transport and mine sank." He let go of her wrist, confident that she would not bolt.

"What kind of cargo?" she asked.

"I am glad to hear you will be reasonable. An accommodation that will help us both. You can retain your anonymity; I get my cargo."

"What kind of cargo?" Anne asked again, this time slowly and deliberately.

"Slaves, my dear. Just slaves."

Anne's heart sank. "Just?"

"Yes, one load should render me solvent." Woolrich looked down his nose at her.

"Slaves? Human beings?" She spat the words at him.

He was unfazed. "Cargo, my dear woman. Goods. You do live in

Virginia. You must be familiar with the concept." Sarcasm crept into his tone.

"Familiar I am," she said, thinking hard. "From where?"

"The cargo will be picked up in Jamaica and landed in Baltimore. My agent there will take charge of it." He watched her.

"And my compensation would be?" Anne held his gaze.

"Not being arrested and hanged for piracy and smuggling, which would also prevent the disgrace of your family. And would protect your crew. Lord Mayfield, of course, can identify all of them." Woolrich smirked. "And £50 in tobacco notes," he added.

Blood money, she thought. "I must think on it," she said after a moment. "My crew may not agree to sail and without a crew, I can't go out."

"I recommend you convince them or 'twill go hard on them as well as you," Woolrich's tone hardened even more. "But I will need to know no later than a fortnight hence. You can contact me at the King's Arms. We can make the arrangements by courier."

Anne took a deep breath to hold in the anger and fear that threatened to consume her. "I will inform you within the fortnight," she said.

She glared at Woolrich and stepped forward until he moved back to let her out. She walked deliberately to the doorway and out into the entry space between the two round halves of the Capitol. Gritting her teeth, she screamed as a huge crack of thunder rang over the building.

"Anne?" Joseph's voice came through the door. "Where have you been? I was getting worried." He appeared, holding her cloak.

"I was delayed by Sir Jonathan," she said through her clenched teeth.

"Oh dear. Tell me about it later. For now, the storm is upon us and you are safe with me. Let us get to the boarding house before the skies open," he said, placing the cloak around her shoulders.

Grateful for the cover of the incoming storm, Anne followed him to the carriage and climbed in without another word.

Joseph stopped to say goodbye to apothecary Robert Davidson, the former Mayor of Williamsburg. As the doctor looked up, Anne, with a great effort, waved gaily to him.

"Dr. Davidson, it's so nice to see you," she called out. "I want to let ye know that the medicines ye gave us for the fever have worked wonderfully well. Both Maggie and Eddie were afflicted this winter but both came through without harm."

Davidson laughed. "It's always a pleasure, Mistress Burleigh. Your appreciation exceeds all expectations." He bowed back to her.

"We must go, Robert. I will see you next time I am in town." Joseph shook Davidson's hand.

"Always a pleasure, Joseph."

By the time they got to the boarding house, the sky was dropping hail and rain so hard that Joseph had to carry Anne into the building. He didn't see her tears.

CHAPTER FOURTEEN

12-13 June 1730 - Great River Plantation

Anne sat deep in thought all the way home. Joseph mostly left her to herself. He knew she would open up when she was ready. And he knew she was brooding about whatever Woolrich had said to her. *It couldn't have been good. If only I'd seen her before I took him over.* Joseph sighed. *But the man would most likely have seen her eventually anyway.*

The road was sloppy from the heavy rains and hail of the night before, so the carriage rocked and bounced through the whole journey. Bursts of wind had left the road strewn with branches and limbs as well as two tree trunks. It had taken all three of them – Anne, Joseph and Samuel – to pull the trunks to the side so they could get the carriage through. By the time they reached home, they were muddy, tired, jostled and irritable. Their homecoming was full of children, chores and unpacking. They never had a chance to talk. By nine o'clock, Joseph was in bed, sound asleep.

Anne, however, remained wide awake. She went over and over the encounter with Woolrich, wondering if there was any way out of his proposal. At one in the morning, she pulled on her sea boots, took her matched cutlasses from their hiding place under the floorboards beneath the writing table, and walked outside towards the nearest rows of tobacco -- about two hundred yards from the house.

The fields were quiet in the night. The heat of the afternoon had dried out the mud. Anne liked the tobacco at night. No shouts or songs from the field hands. No orders barked by the field manager. No birds squawking. No children screaming. Just her boots moving up and down in the dirt, the breeze rustling through the big leaves like the wind off a Quarterdeck. Since that first time when she knew she was pregnant, the fields had calmed her and cleared her mind. She had taken to the fields with every pregnancy, knowing that each child would draw her inevitably further into domesticity and home -- and away from the sea.

She looked up at the sky. The darkness of the new moon allowed the stars to shine brightly. Anne knew them well. Venus and red Mars both glittered, as did the constellations of Hydra, Orion, and Ursa Major. She imagined her past twinkling up above: Mary Reade in the Seven Sisters of the Pleiades; Calico Jack in the looming figure of Orion with its glittering belt; and James Bonny -- Hydra, the snake. She laughed at her younger self who had thought of her marriage and piracy as romantic adventures when they were, in reality, violent, bloody, dangerous and ultimately futile and deadly. Yet she still felt the excitement of the smuggling voyages.

She reached the far end of the row. She turned and ran down the next row, the cutlasses in her hands slashing at the plants as she flew by them. Screaming rage and anger out of hearing of the house, Anne pounded between the rows, slashing left and right in a windmill like action. The emotions she had been holding in poured out of her throat and her hands as she envisioned her boots on Woolrich's neck with every step, the cutlasses cutting him to shreds.

Woolrich. Bastard. Watching all the trials like they'd bring back his wife and child. And mine for his ship. Mary and I were a spectacle – the female pirates. Mary, poor Mary. Rest of the stupid crew were left on gibbets around the harbor for years. Jack disemboweled. As much as Anne had resented her father ransoming her and arranging her marriage to Joseph Burleigh at the time, she was grateful now.

She remembered the handsome man who had stepped in front of her father to introduce himself as her husband to be. His deep blue eyes still spoke to her in ways she could not name. *I did not know such a partnership was possible. Nor did I miss the joy of the children when they were taken from me first in Cuba then in prison. Now* ... A tear slid out of her eye before she could stop it. *I do love them so. All of them.*

Did Woolrich have proof beyond his word? His remembering me wouldn't likely be enough if I denied it – or would it? He's a Baronet, damn him. And there's Mayfield. She slowed down, her arms dropping the cutlasses to her sides. She found herself at the far side of the field again, panting heavily. *A five row night, damn me.*

Mayfield's an Earl's son. The young crew idolized him. But they will learn the ways of the upper classes, probably the hard way. He'll be believed because he's aristocracy. It's all we pirates and smugglers fought against – that privilege, the power. And now I'm up against it. I wonder would our friends, gentlemen and lords, quickly forget our reputation and friendship and believe their "equals"? And what of the family? We are all in danger. As are the crew – Mayfield knows them all. "God damn it," she shouted.

And the Sheriff. Woolrich could bring him in as well. His cousin's a Burgess. Damn them all to hell. She lifted her right arm and slashed through an entire tobacco plant with single swing of the cutlass while uttering a wrenching scream. Then she fell to the ground sobbing.

After ten minutes, she wiped her face and blew her nose with her neck kerchief while gulping air and trying to tame the horror that rested in her gut. *I'm trapped,* she realized. *Just when I was ready to get out.* She sobbed again, her head bobbing uncontrollably. When she felt herself regaining control, Anne stood up, wiped her face and nose again, then, red-eyed, turned back towards the house and started walking home.

What can I do? I have no choice. But if I'm going to do this evil deed, it must be the final act. Woolrich has to get to Sheriff Starke through his bastard cousin to back off. I need to be free of this, free of smuggling, free of threat when this is done. Her abhorrence of slavery rose to her gullet but she stuffed it back down. *First I save myself, the family and the crew. Then I will see about Woolrich. When this is over, I will see him hanged or better. Somehow.*

A candle dimly illuminated the kitchen as she stepped through the door. She was surprised to find Joseph sitting at the table with a cup of tea, looking up at her. Without a word, she laid the cutlasses against the door jam, took the kettle off its hook and poured more hot water into the teapot he had left on the table. Taking a mug off the shelf, she sat down and stared blankly out the window. The clock struck four.

Joseph got up, took the lid off a plate and pulled out two corn cakes. He poured Anne's tea, put it down on the table in front of her, placed one of the cakes next to it then sat back down.

"Woolrich?" he asked, staring out the window at the gloom.

"Yes," she responded.

For a few minutes, they drank tea quietly. Anne found to her surprise that tears were again streaming down her cheeks. *I thought I'd gone dry.* She snuffled slightly and took the damp neck kerchief from her sleeve.

"What did he want?" Joseph asked, breaking the silence. He turned towards his wife.

"He's a true son of a viper, that one," Anne started. "He wants me to ship cargo on the *Betsy D* to get himself out of debt."

Joseph looked at her over his tea cup. Her face in the dim light looked haggard. "What kind of cargo?" he asked.

She put down the mug and turned to him. Leaning over the table, she whispered, "Slaves, Joseph. He wants me to bring in a cargo of slaves." Her voice cracked at the end.

"From your reaction and what I heard about him, I feared that was the case." He put down the cup.

Joseph knelt at Anne's feet, picked up her hands and gently kissed them. She looked into his eyes, grayish in the low light of dawn. She saw love and acceptance in them – and worry. She cried softly with relief. She fell into his arms and the two of them remained entangled until her crying stopped.

Joseph pulled her up, put his arm around Anne's waist, and said, "It will be light soon. Get some rest. We can talk later. Enough for now." Anne nodded, spent. She kissed her husband softly on the lips, grabbed her cutlasses and went upstairs. She fell on the bed still dressed in her shift. Within moments, she was asleep.

The next morning broke clear and hot, the air misty. Anne got up late, ate breakfast then went looking for Joseph. She found him in the barn saddling Charlemagne, the tall, grey stallion they had just bought for his riding mount. He looked up as she came through the opening into the cool shadows of the stalls.

"Good morning," he called to her. She smiled as she walked over towards him.

"Want company?" she asked, scratching Charlemagne's nose. The horse nickered a hello.

"Always, my dear," said Joseph. "I've been waiting for you, in fact." He leaned over and kissed her cheek. "Charlie, go get the mare, will you?" The stable boy nodded and headed to the other end of the barn to bring Rover out to be saddled.

"Did you get any sleep?" she asked as she reached into a bucket for a carrot to give Rover who shook her head as she bit the treat. Charlie pulled Anne's saddle off the wall peg and threw it over her back.

"Some. But the Devon cow calved this morning. A strong, healthy heifer, but a difficult delivery. Ben came for me. Should be another good milker."

Anne smiled. She always thought it amusing that the servants came for Joseph for all matters occurring outside the house – even birthings. *I'll look in on them after our ride,* she promised herself.

It took Charlie about ten minutes to saddle the mare after which he helped Anne mount up. Joseph waited for her then turned Charlemagne out the south door. Anne followed. She loved riding; it felt like freedom. Spurring her horse past Joseph, she headed out into a fallow fields ahead.

They galloped for a while until they were out of sight of the house and the working fields. Anne slowed Rover so Joseph could ride beside her. They traveled in a comfortable silence until they came to a to Mary's Run. The fields on the other side of the stream belonged to the Madisons and had also been left fallow.

She slid off Rover's back and let the horse loose to graze; Joseph did the same. Then she plopped down onto the grass under the biggest tree whose leaves shaded a large circle beside the clear water of the little stream. The brook would dry up in a month or so, she knew from experience.

He sat down and pulled a handful of strawberries out of a small bag, handing several to her. "What a treat," she exclaimed, "I didn't know they were ready. Thank you, Husband."

They chewed on the fruit for a few minutes, then Joseph turned to look at his wife, "Have you decided?" he asked.

She moved her hands to squeeze Joseph's. "I remain torn," she began. "'Were it any other cargo, I would be less so. But ye know how I feel about slavery. As does my crew, some former slaves themselves." She sighed. "I don't see I have a choice, really. If I don't go, he will press the issue and with Mayfield a witness. It will not go well, I fear."

Joseph leaned back against the tree. "I agree. The aristocracy rules by intimidation, not by quality. But rule they do and his word would go before yours. If it were Woolrich alone ..." his voice trailed off. He sighed. "But then he is a Baronet so he would get the benefit of his rank as well. As opposed to we mere ordinary folk. And he's likely to have contacts in Jamaica who would testify for him."

"What is being said of the good Baronet, Joseph?" she asked. She could always rely on him for gossip.

"William Gooch is suspicious. Says Woolrich told him he left Jamaica so his son would have his estate for his family," Joseph said. "A generous and kindly man, or so he wants to appear. But William also heard that he is low on funds because his last ship went down. All hands and all cargo – more than 200 slaves – lost at sea. Put him in a bad way financially which corroborates with what he told you."

Anne nodded. "I can probably convince the crew to take slaves this once if we treat them well. I will have to warn them that they too are at risk. But I hate the very idea." She groaned and put her head in her hands. "He offered to pay me. £50 in tobacco notes. A tiny plus, I suppose." She sighed.

Joseph cocked his head in thought. "There is also the sheriff," he noted.

"Yes, another scurvy bastard."

"Woolrich knows Burgess Goodwin, as do I. The Burgess, although not fond of his cousin, would support him against you. He's very protective of family." Joseph leaned forward, chin resting on his hand which was braced against his knee.

"I don't see a way out, truly," he began. "But add one more condition before you agree. Woolrich must get the Burgess to call the Sheriff off. He can tell Starke that you sailed on one of his ships to see your father in South Carolina, like you told the women." He watched for Anne's reaction.

"I have already thought of that. At least when this is over, I will be free from all of them." She looked up, trying to keep more tears from welling in her eyes. "Freedom. It's what piracy is about. And what slavery destroys."

She leaned over and put her head on his shoulder. He put his arm around her and hugged her tight. "I love you," he said. "You are a remarkable woman and I am proud to be your husband and that you are the mother of my children. Although you have never been easy," he added, "you have always been worth it. And when this is over, we will be free." *I hope*, he thought.

She tilted her face up to him, again caressing his cheek. "I have no regrets. Most of all for loving you." She reached up and kissed him hard and passionately. She joined with him under the tree. If a child happened, she might be able to put off the evil voyage.

When they were done, they lay in each other's arms looking up at the sky. "I will send a message this afternoon. Is Samuel free to take it to town?"

"I will take it. I have goats to buy." Anne shot him a look and he shrugged.

They headed home, both of them thinking that Woolrich might well not be satisfied, but neither one saying it out loud

CHAPTER FIFTEEN

15 June 1730 - Great River Plantation and York Town, Virginia

Anne went for an early morning ride, hoping the exercise would calm her mind. When she got back to the stable, she didn't feel any better, but she was determined that somehow they would prevail. *So much that could have destroyed us before, and yet we have managed to thrive. And now this.* "AND WE'LL DAMNED WELL SURVIVE THIS, TOO," she screamed to the barn. She handed Rover over to a startled Charlie and went looking for Joseph, but he had already headed for town.

Joseph bought two goats at the livestock yard and then went to find a courier. He knew several who routinely rode between local towns and the Capitol delivering messages. Joseph's work on the Tobacco Inspection Act had required him to utilize more than one. Today he was looking for his favorite: Nicholas Lawson. Lawson was reliable and discreet, especially for a price. And he lived near the plantation.

He had in his pocket the letter to Woolrich:

Jonathan Woolrich, Baronet
Dear Sir,
My wife, Anne Burleigh, accepts your offer with one addi-

122

tional condition. It is our understanding that you are acquainted with Burgess Goodwin whose cousin, William Starke, is the sheriff of York Town. Starke has been making inquiries about my wife's absences to visit her father and about our access to funding to improve our homestead. It would please her greatly if you would suggest to Burgess Goodwin that Mistress Burleigh's absences and finances are not of concern.

If that is accomplished, I believe we can begin preparations immediately. Please advise.

Joseph Burleigh

His first stop was the merchant's shop. "Mr. Windler, good morning." Joseph saw the merchant in a far corner of the darkened store. The lack of light kept the goods fresh and the heat at bay, if only a little.

"Mr. Burleigh. Always a pleasure. Mistress Burleigh is not with you?" He looked around the store.

"No, I'm afraid my wife had to help with cheese-making today. She did send a small list, however." He handed over a list he and Anne had put together that morning. "Add to that a dozen cigars if you would be so kind," Joseph added. "My wife is not fond of them so I smoke only out of sight." He chuckled and Windler joined in.

"You are not alone in that, Mr. Burleigh. Not at all alone." He took the list.

"Have you seen young Nicholas Lawson?"

"Two days ago he rode through. I'm not sure whether he's back yet. Have you a message for the Capitol?" Mr. Windler spoke while reading through the list.

"Indeed. Tobacco Act business as usual," Joseph answered.

"Check with old Wilson at The Golden Lamb. Nicholas is often found there." He looked up. "I can have this ready in an hour, maybe less."

"An hour is fine, Mr. Windler. I appreciate your diligence." Joseph reached to shake the merchant's hand.

"Mondays are slow, Mr. Burleigh. I am glad to have the custom," Windler said.

Joseph walked up the street to the tavern, grateful for its relatively cool interior after the humid heat of the Virginia summer. He waited until his eyes adjusted to the low light. He spotted his neighbor Ben Madison enjoying a pint of cider. *Ben loses more hair every day,* he thought. *I am grateful that it is not so with me.* He sidled up next to him at the bar and waved to the barkeep.

"What he's having," he said.

Ben turned quickly and jumped off his stool. "Joseph," he cried as he slapped his friend on the back. "Where've you been keeping yourself these last days? I hardly saw ye at the Assembly the other night." He laughed boisterously, causing the simple broadcloth vest that restrained his barrel chest to make a valiant effort to pop open.

"So an hour isn't much, Ben. I must remember to bend your ear for longer next time." He laughed. "'Tis always good to see you, my friend," Joseph added. "And to share a pint of Wilson's fine cider. Best in York Town." The bartender put the mug in front of Joseph, who raised it in a toast.

He took a deep drink. The men chatted about the goats Joseph had purchased. "Best I've seen in a long time," he noted. "Both good milkers, I'm told. I hope so for what I paid."

Ben put down his tankard. "I wanted to tell you, Joseph, that comments have been made."

Joseph looked hard at the bar, collecting his breath. "Sheriff Starke?"

"Yes, so you've heard." Ben sounded surprised. "I thought you should know if you didn't already."

"I have heard. The truth is that Anne's step-mother has been ill and she has gone south to assist. Her father is grateful," Joseph said.

Then, with just a trace of bitterness creeping into his voice, he added, "For which, the sheriff indicts her a criminal."

Ben nodded. "Yes, 'tis unfair and not the first time Starke has made unwarranted accusations."

"I hope you will defend my wife's honor if it is impugned, Ben." Joseph leaned back to look at his friend.

"Indeed I have. As has Sally. Goody Starke is not reluctant to pass on her husband's gossip, I'm afraid." He patted Joseph on the shoulder. "Rest assured, your reputation is solid with us and shall remain so. And we will defend you to anyone saying otherwise."

"Thanks, Ben. We would do the same." Joseph lifted the mug and downed the last of the drink.

"I am in need of a messenger. Have you seen Nicholas, by any chance?" he asked the bartender.

"He was here this morning. I can ask for him," Billy stopped wiping the bar in front of Joseph and picked up the empty mug.

"Would you please?" affirmed Joseph, tossing half a pistole onto the plank to pay for drink and services about to be rendered.

"Wait here." Billy left the bar and went into the parlor. In a few minutes, he came back.

"He's in the dining room finishing a late breakfast," he said.

Joseph nodded. "Thank you, Billy." He turned to Ben Madison, "Ben, always a pleasure. Say hello to Sally for me."

"I will indeed, Joseph and best to Anne." They shook hands.

Joseph walked into the dining room on the other side. There he found Nicholas, a young man of eighteen who routinely rode between Williamsburg and York Town with messages.

"May I join you?" he asked, pulling out a chair.

Nicholas looked up, his left eye twitching into a wink as it always did. Joseph noticed that Nicholas's thick, straw-colored hair had been pulled back into a ponytail at the nape of his neck and tied with a yellow, instead of the usual black, ribbon. He wondered briefly whether the color hinted at some sort of rebellion in the young man. He'd always liked the boy and this small gesture only improved his opinion. *Anne has certainly influenced how I look at people,* he realized. Nicholas's mouth was full, so what he mumbled Joseph didn't know, but it sounded affirmative, as it should be for a regular paying customer, so he sat down.

Nicholas gulped tea and swallowed hard. "What can I help you with, Mr. Burleigh?" he asked. Joseph knew Nicholas was courting the Brewster girl and that he was saving his money towards their marriage. He also knew Nicholas to be discreet and paid him extra for that.

"I have a message for Williamsburg," Joseph said. He pulled the folded packet out of his pocket, verifying that the seal was solidly intact. He handed it to Nicholas. "How soon can you get it there?"

Nicholas read the address. "Woolrich? He's that Baronet out of Jamaica, is he not?" He looked up in surprise.

"Yes. Anne's father asked us to forward a letter. He does business in Jamaica and apparently had some with Woolrich. We have been holding this letter but when we saw him the other evening, Anne asked me to have it sent on."

Nicholas nodded. "Of course, Sir. I can be there tonight if you will. 'Twill be a hard ride at this hour, though."

Joseph held out a full Spanish pistole, twice the usual fee. "Will this help?" he asked.

Nicholas brightened. "Very much, Sir. I will have it there by nightfall. Is there a reply expected?"

"Very likely," Joseph told him. "Can you wait to return until tomorrow if required?"

"Indeed. I can stay with my cousin Catherine. There will be a slight extra fee, though." Nicholas said.

"Another half pistole, perhaps?" Joseph held out one more.

Nicholas nodded vigorously. "Yes, indeed, Sir."

"And an additional coin, a full Spanish real I came by recently, to bring any reply to the house?"

Nicholas positively beamed. "I will do it. Thank you, Mr. Burleigh. As always, I appreciate your patronage."

Joseph stood up and put on his tricorn. "My best to Mistress Brewster when you see her. Anne and I are both quite fond of her. A lovely girl."

Nicholas's face went red. "She is. She is," he said.

Joseph went out through the parlor door into the hazy sunshine. "There's an evil job well done." He scowled, but caught himself when he saw Sheriff Starke across the street. He bowed in the man's direction then turned on his heel back to the barn to retrieve the horse and goats, and head for home.

CHAPTER SIXTEEN

17 June 1730 - Great River Plantation

Anne saw Ebo talking with the rider as she hung up the wash with Angeline. *Nicholas.* She recognized him as he came closer.

Nicholas dropped the horse to a walk, and stopped at the front of the house. "I don't want to dirty your laundry, Mistress Burleigh," he said as he dismounted.

Anne came over to him. "Ye're a thoughtful young man, Nicholas. Thank 'e." She noticed that today's ribbon was bright red. She had seen that the boy had a rebellious side before Joseph had.

He met her at the front porch. "I had to wait an extra day," he began as he rummaged through his leather pouch. "But Woolrich paid me extra so you owe me nothing."

There was something about the way he said the man's name that caught Anne's attention: "Woolrich" without a "Sir" or even a "Mr." *What has the son of a whore done to irritate Nicholas?*

"Ye found Sir Jonathan well?" Anne ventured, raising an eyebrow.

Nicholas looked up, a trace of fear running across his face. When he saw her look, he said, "He could charm the honey from the bees. Too bad I'm not a bee."

"At the moment," Anne replied, "he's a necessary evil."

"I can believe he's 'evil,' all right." Nicholas found the folded paper and passed it to Anne. "I hope you don't have to have more dealings with him." His eye twitched. "Or at least that I don't have to."

Anne took the packet. "What did he do, Nicholas?"

"I saw him with one of the kitchen slaves at the house where he's residing. She's a lass of only ten or twelve and he had his hands all over her." Nicholas's disgust was apparent. "I interrupted them, thank the Lord, and she ran off. But his intent was clear."

Anne nodded, filing away the information for future reference. "Are ye in favor of slavery, Nicholas?" she asked.

He looked at her warily for a long minute. "No I am not, Mistress Burleigh. I do not believe the Lord intended us to enslave other human beings." She saw his gaze go to Angeline, still hanging sheets on the line. "I have noted, however, that some people treat their workers better than others." He looked back at Anne. "Your people are well-fed and content. I commend you for that."

"Thank you, Nicholas. We need their labor but that does not mean they have to be abused. I will not allow anyone living at Great River to be mistreated," she said.

"I am happy but not at all surprised to hear it, Mistress Burleigh." He bowed. "I must be off. I have a message for Mr. Madison."

"Of course," Anne replied. She dug into her pocket and found the coin Joseph had given her in case Nicholas appeared. She handed it to the messenger. "For ye. My best to Amy Brewster."

Nicholas took the coin as he blushed again at the mention of his girl. "I will tell her, Mistress. But you needn't pay me extra as Woolrich did."

"We honor our commitments, Nicholas. And I'm sure you can use it." Anne responded.

"I can indeed. Thank you, Mistress Burleigh." He mounted his horse. Lifting his tricorn hat, he swung the horse around and trotted back down the drive.

"Angeline, can you finish here?" Anne called out, fingering the message anxiously.

"Of course, Miz Anne. Almos' done." Angeline's disembodied voice floated to Anne from behind one of Joseph's shirts.

Anne went inside and put on her boots. She had seen Joseph heading for the livestock pens after breakfast. He had been teaching Charlie to tend to the goats. She found him there, leaning on the split rail fence smoking a cigar.

"Caught you," she called.

He turned quickly, attempting to hide the cigar behind his back. Then he laughed at her triumphant expression. "You did, my dear. You did." He saw the packet in her hand.

"Nicholas?" he asked.

"Yes. And the boy saw Woolrich trying to take a young slave girl – ten or twelve he says. The boy was disgusted, for which I give him much approval."

"Yes. I am not surprised. I have heard rumors. Any information we can gather could be useful," he added.

"I leave that to ye, Joseph. I have my hands full." Anne's grim face reflected her mood.

"Shall I read it or will you?" he asked.

"You," she said. Her stomach was in knots. She knew what the answer would be and dreaded it.

Joseph unfolded the packet, smoothed it out and began to read.

> *My dear Mister Burleigh,*
>
> *Thank you for your letter of yesterday. I agree to your conditions and shall implement them immediately. Please advise when your ship can sail. I will send instructions and letters of introduction by courier as soon as I know the date.*
>
> *Yours &,*
>
> *Sir Jonathan Woolrich, Baronet*

Anne sighed. She moved closer to Joseph and leaned into him, breathing in the cigar smoke which didn't bother her as much as she pretended it did. He put his arms around her. "So it begins," she said with resignation.

"Sooner to end," he responded. "I will go to town in a few days and see whether the Sheriff is still making inquiries." Anne nodded vacantly.

She took a deep breath then let it out slowly. "I must contact the crew. This will not be an easy sell, but they are at risk, too," she said, wiping her hands on her apron as if to wipe the vile Sir Jonathan away.

"And I must see to the corn crop. The hail did some damage. Caesar's been out there all day." Joseph kissed Anne and carefully returned the unsmoked remains of the cigar into his leather case. Anne wrinkled her nose at him and left. As he watched her go, a shiver of fear ran up his spine. *When this mess is done …*

CHAPTER SEVENTEEN

4 August 1730 - York Town, Virginia

Charlemagne plodded slowly down Bacon Street. Joseph felt an ache when he looked out across the bluff to the ships anchored in the river. Anne would be leaving soon. He turned the horse up Main Street and down through the Great Valley to the Commons. He found several others tied to the railing and put Charlemagne on the end. "At least you'll have company, my Great Charles," he said as he slapped the horse on the rump.

His first stop was the cooper's shop. They needed ten new barrels for this year's cider crop. The cooper assured him the barrels would be ready within a month.

Joseph visited the tailor's shop. Angeline, in his opinion, made perfectly beautiful women's clothes – and children's – but he was not impressed with her breeches, waistcoats and jackets. The tailor, however, created exactly the look he wanted.

"Good morning, Matthew," he greeted the man who came out from the back room. "I see your hair hasn't yet changed color." Matthew Forcythe had hair even redder than Anne's – a bright hue where hers was a deep auburn. He had once confessed to Joseph that he'd give anything for plain, brown hair. It became a friendship joke between them.

"Joseph, good to see you. Another set of clothes?" Matthew's small blue eyes danced with the light from the window.

"Just a riding jacket," Joseph replied, fingering the ragged bottom of the one he wore. He had spent most of his clothing money on garments designed to impress the Lt. Governor. This jacket had been his since before he met Anne and it was showing its age. *Now that I have funds...*

He looked through the fabrics. Like Anne, he loved to finger the pieces to gauge their density, their smoothness, and how light the material would be to wear.

Matthew brought over a bolt of dark green broadcloth. "This just came in. No one has bought the color yet. It would go well with your skin tones," he said.

Joseph liked both the idea and the color immediately. He rubbed the material in his hands. *Good quality*, he thought. "This will do," he said.

"Buttons?" Matthew asked.

"Yes, I think the ones on this jacket can be reused, Matthew. No sense in spending extra money."

The tailor nodded. "I had heard that you have done well recently. The merchants say that you have almost totally refurbished your house and added on to it." He turned to take the bolt to the cutting table.

Joseph stared after him. *Damn. It's gone farther than we thought.* He followed Matthew to the table.

"We had a little windfall – from Anne's father. She helped his wife through an illness." Joseph watched as the tailor measured out the material.

"Ah. That explains it then," Matthew looked up. "Not that it is business of mine, Sir," he added.

Joseph shrugged. "Curiosity is universal, Matthew."

"Actually, Sheriff Starke had asked about your spending when he was in a couple of weeks ago," Matthew said as he cut.

Bastard. No wonder everyone in town knew.

"But he did not mention it when he was in yesterday, so I suppose his curiosity was quenched. I do not like gossip in my shop." He put down the measuring tape, made a note on a piece of paper and then turned to Joseph. "It is not my habit to gossip about anything I hear or learn, Mr. Burleigh. Rest assured that any information or even suggestions that come into this shop do not leave by my lips."

Joseph suppressed a laugh – Matthew had just passed along the gossip he claimed to avoid. Joseph patted the shorter man on the shoulder. "I never doubted that, Matthew. But others are not so discrete."

"No, sadly, they are not. I was glad the sheriff made no more mention of it." He leaned closer, although there was no one else in the store. "He is a gossip and no mistake. We would be served better by another, but that will not happen while his cousin is a Burgess."

"I fear it will not. Now to business," Joseph said as brightly as possible, ready to leave both the conversation and the tailor. "The cooper will have barrels ready for me in less than a month. Can you equal that?"

The tailor thought for a moment. "That would not be a problem." He grinned. "I will even talk with Henry so that the barrels and your jacket are ready at the same time."

Joseph smiled. "That would be most kind," he said. The men shook hands and Joseph left.

Outside, he looked around the square to see whether Sheriff Starke was in sight. Not seeing him, Joseph headed for the Wilkins Ordinary.

Inside, he ordered a beer and sat at a table along the back wall. The Ordinary was the best place to uncover local news. His last trip in town about a month ago had revealed that the Sheriff's rumors continued. He wanted to know whether Woolrich had kept the last part of their bargain.

The waiter brought the tankard. "Thank you," Joseph said.

Over two tankards and an hour and a half, Joseph was able to talk with six different friends, all of whom mentioned both that Sheriff Starke had made comments and that he seemed to be retracting them. They were all relieved and all told Joseph they were glad that he would no longer be the subject of such unwarranted scrutiny. Joseph thanked them one by one, repeating the story of Anne's father to each.

He rose to seek the relief of the privy when Nicholas Lawson appeared in the doorway. He looked around, spotted Joseph and came over to him immediately.

"I am glad to have run into you, Mr. Burleigh. 'Twill save me a trip." The boy sat across from Joseph.

"I have a letter for you," he said, digging into his leather case. He pulled out several before finding the one addressed to Joseph.

Joseph took it suspecting that it was the paperwork for the slaves.

"Thank you, Nicholas. I hope you were compensated for taking this all the way to the farm," Joseph said.

Nicholas nodded. "Oh yes, Mr. Burleigh. A bonus indeed to find you here." He turned to go, then swung back to face Joseph. "That Woolrich is a bad 'un, Mr. Burleigh. I told the Mistress that and I still think it. I hope you'll not have much doings with him in the future."

"We sincerely hope not, Nicholas. Thank you for doing this."

Nicholas doffed his hat, bowed and headed out the door.

Joseph watched the boy leave, then walked to the privy. When he was done, he paid the waiter and headed out into the bright sunshine. It took a minute for his eyes to adjust but when they did, he noticed Sheriff Starke chatting with Vicar Fontaine. He lingered behind a huge oak tree, watching. The Sheriff's countenance was amiable and the vicar smiled and nodded as the Sheriff spoke. *This is promising*, Joseph thought.

After a few minutes, Starke left, and the Vicar started back towards the church. Joseph intercepted him as he was about the turn onto Church Street.

"Francis," he yelled. The Vicar turned around and stopped to wait for Joseph to catch up.

"Joseph, I'm so glad to see you. I was just talking with Sheriff Starke about you and Mistress Burleigh."

"A positive conversation, I hope," Joseph said as he reached out to shake the Vicar's hand.

They walked down the street towards the church. "I have been much distressed by some of the questions he has been asking about Mistress Burleigh's activities, Joseph. I know you are aware of them. They have generated concern about your respectability, which, I firmly believe, is utterly unwarranted. I have told him so on several occasions, but until today, my protestations had no apparent effect." The clergyman walked with his hands folded behind his back, looking at the street for the most part, but occasionally glancing up at Joseph as he talked.

"And today?" Joseph asked.

"He tells me now that he has it on good authority that your good fortune is wholly respectable." The Vicar stopped as they reached the front of the Grace Episcopal Church. "It must have been a trial to your wife to have to travel so far. I have always thought her heart was pure, but her actions in assisting her father confirm that. Louisa and I are relieved as well that the Sheriff is no longer questioning the source of your prosperity."

"Thank you, Francis. That reminds me, I intend to make a contribution to the parish this Sabbath. Anne and I have missed too many services. We simply cannot get in every week, as you are aware, but we will be there this week."

"That is most generous, Joseph. You have been loyal supporters even though you are not able to attend always. We hold you in the highest regard."

Joseph bowed. "It is our pleasure. Your work among the parishioners is exemplary," he said. "As are your sermons ... which cannot be said of all pastors." He smiled.

"Thank you, my friend. It is always good to hear that," the Vicar said.

Joseph held out his hand. "I must be gone, Francis, but I will see you in a few days."

The Vicar shook it vigorously. "I look forward to it, Joseph. I believe my homily will be on the subject of gossip." He said as he strode up the steps into the church.

Joseph felt a weight had lifted off his shoulders as he made his way back to the town square where he consciously put on a pleasantly neutral look. *At least that bastard's kept one promise. Let's hope the rest of this horrible project goes as well.*

CHAPTER EIGHTEEN

11 August 1730 - Hampton, Virginia

It took Anne almost two months to get word to the crew that she was sailing again. She did not tell them where they were going or why. *I'd not get any of them to show if I tell them the real purpose.*

She sat at a table in the King's Raven dressed in her captain's clothes drinking beer while waiting to see who answered the summons. She had not sent a message to Mayfield. She wondered whether he would get word from either Woolrich or the seamen who surrounded him on their last voyage. She sincerely hoped she would not have to confront him, but she was prepared for the worst.

The door opened, letting in a ray of light. She recognized the silhouette immediately: Richard Sylvanus, her helmsman. A Muslim native of Mali in West Africa, he had been brought to Barbados as a slave, but, within a year, he had killed the master by strangling him with manacles. Taking his wife and daughter, Sylvanus escaped to the Moskito Coast of Honduras and joined the Moskitos Zambos, a colony of escaped slaves and native Carib Indians who lived there. Leaving his family with the Zambos, he had gone to sea on James Bonny's first vessel, which is where Anne met him. When she needed a Helmsman for her smuggling crew, she sought out Sylvanus first. He had sailed on every journey with her since.

She waved to him to take a seat. "Welcome Mr. Sylvanus," she said.

"Well, Captain, we together again." He shook hands with her as the waiter plunked down a tankard of small beer.

"A pitcher of this plus one of rum and several more tankards, John," Anne told the waiter. He nodded and left.

Richard never drank anything harder than small beer, but she expected more crewmen soon. "Surprised to hear from you so soon," he said, downing a huge gulp.

"I hadn't expected to go out yet," she said. "But a situation has come up."

Sylvanus raised his eyebrows. "Situation?"

If she could get him to crew a slave ship, the others would be go along.

"Yes. An unfortunate one," she said, holding his gaze.

"What cargo?" he asked.

She gritted her teeth. "Slaves." Her voice barely rose above a whisper as she watched his reaction. As she had expected, his face showed nothing.

"I have been identified by a man who was at my trial in Jamaica. He's connected somehow with Mayfield who told him about our smuggling voyages. He knows the names of my crew. His wife and child died of fever supposedly brought to Jamaica by pirates, and apparently the last ship we sank belonged to him, so he's out for blood. My life and the crew's freedom, and possibly their lives as well, are all now at risk." Anne watched Sylvanus.

He continued to drink without taking his eyes off Anne. Finally, he nodded and waited. "Who?" he asked, his tone suggesting that he could guess.

"A Baronet named Woolrich," she answered.

"Ah," he said. "With Mayfield. He a bad man." He lifted the empty tankard towards the waiter who nodded and disappeared behind the bar. "You believe we all at risk?" he asked.

"I would not be here otherwise, Mr. Sylvanus. I have no more love for slavery than you. But I do have love for my family, my life and my crew." She sat back, still watching for his reaction.

"Hmm," he murmured as the waiter reappeared with two pitchers and five tankards. "Where the cargo?" Sylvanus asked.

"Jamaica – going to Baltimore." Anne watched carefully. His carefully blank face was starting to melt a little.

"One trip?"

"Yes," she answered.

The waiter appeared again. "Food?" he asked.

"A trencher of meat, cheese and bread, if you will," she said smiling at the boy. He nodded again and left.

The door opened. The man standing in the light would have been completely missed by most people. He was of medium height, stout, his long, light brown hair tied in a ponytail with a black ribbon. Dressed all in brown, as usual, he was an expert at blending in.

Anne waved. "Mr. Wilberforce, welcome." She put a hand out to a chair.

Howard Wilberforce had only arrived in the colonies in 1725. Although his life in England was a mystery, his skills as both surgeon and cook made him immediately popular to any crew he sailed with. He had joined Anne on her last two voyages. He sat down and poured himself some rum.

"A sailing already?" he asked.

"Situation," Sylvanus answered.

Wilberforce's eyes flew open. "Do tell," he said.

Anne told him the same story she'd relayed to Sylvanus. His reaction was cautious.

"So, you are at risk. Your family is at risk. But I have no family," he said.

"Mayfield knows you. So you are at risk. All of the crew are. But more importantly, Mr. Wilberforce, I need your skills both as cook and surgeon to keep the cargo alive." Anne waited, hoping his ego would be appeased.

He bowed his head. "I am most flattered."

"Good but it is the truth nonetheless. I am being pressed to this service, unwillingly, but I do not intend that the *Betsy D* will be run as most slave ships are," she explained. "We will take care of the people we transport. They will be fed and cared for. They will not die on my ship from neglect and bad hygiene." The passion in her voice was matched only by its softness.

Sylvanus nodded again. Wilberforce looked at Anne for a long time.

"So you intend to keep them alive to be slaves," he said.

"Yes. As much as I hate being forced to make this trip, I am determined to at least treat them as humans and to do the best I can for them," she responded.

"So I'd be tending to how many?" Wilberforce asked.

She knew then that she had him. "Crew of seventeen. Cargo, I am told, of one hundred and fifty or thereabouts. We will build bunks and hammocks below decks, add lanterns for light, assure there is air, and provide latrines." She turned to Wilberforce. "We need a cook willing and able to feed a huge group of people. And one who is also a surgeon is of the utmost value."

She looked from Sylvanus to Wilberforce. "You two are the linchpins of this operation. Without you, we have no chance of a humane journey. The composition of the rest of the crew is less important."

"Anyone else signed on?" Wilberforce asked.

"I reached out to you two first. Without you, I don't know how I can make the trip safely."

"Bos'un?" Wilberforce asked, his expression darkening.

"Not Mayfield. I managed to find Mr. Potter," she replied. Clarence Potter had sailed on two previous journeys. Unfortunately, he was ill when they had set out the last time which is why she had brought Mayfield aboard, to her great regret.

"Good man," Sylvanus said. Anne breathed a quick sigh of relief.

"Anyone else?" Wilberforce drank deeply from his tankard.

"Expect to hear from Harkness today. Any objections to his return as Second Mate?" Anne looked from one to the other but both shrugged. Harkness was well liked, which was essential for that job. "Asked him to find me riggers and able-bodied seamen. I've invited the other officers in to talk this afternoon, but with you two on board, I'm confident they'll sign on."

The waiter brought two trenchers of food. "Saw the size of the mouths to feed, did ye?" she asked, looking at the huge mounds of food. The boy nodded with a grin.

"Master Gunner?" Sylvanus asked.

"Taking most of the cannon out. Need the room for the cargo." The word was a little cowardly but saying "slaves" was worse.

Wilberforce's eyebrows lifted in surprise. "No cannon?" he asked.

"We have four – two on each side just in case. But no Master Gunner. I'm going to have Potter train a couple of the seamen to use them. And why would we need gunners? This is a legal shipment," Anne said.

"Why indeed, Captain?" Wilberforce responded with a wink.

"You with me?" she asked.

Sylvanus looked away towards the small window on the west side of the room. "Yes," he said.

Wilberforce nodded. "Oh, why the hell not. Usual shares?"

"Yes, but I'll go without since the profit won't be great."

The men looked at her, surprised. "I'm in it for my life," she explained. "And my family and for you."

"Understood," Wilberforce said with a bow. Anne's skill, determination and sense of fairness had long since engendered a deep loyalty among her crew.

"We have a lot of work to do. The Carpenter, Stephen Kilrun, has men coming on board tomorrow to alter the hold. We sail in a week's time. Mr. Wilberforce, figure yer needs and give me a list. Mr. Sylvanus, can ye oversee the rigging crew? When I find them," she asked.

Both men muttered "yes," then rose to leave.

"It's not a voyage I want to be making," Anne told them. "But if I have to, I'm grateful ye're along, both of ye." She stood and shook their hands, then watched them head out the door.

"Let's hope we have a full crew in a week," she muttered to herself as she sat back down to wait for any other crewmen who received the summons.

CHAPTER NINETEEN

18 August 1730 - Hampton Roads, Virginia

The hot, humid afternoon air encased Anne as she walked to the dock. She had been on shore to hunt down the last three riggers who had signed up only the day before. They trudged behind her now, dragging their sea bags and sweating in the hazy sunshine.

"Come along, ye scurvy swine. Ye should have been aboard hours ago. If I didn't need bodies so badly ..." she let the threat hang in the air. Captain MacCormack had come to fetch them. The riggers were all young men in their early twenties who signed on for adventure. Anne knew, if they didn't, that they'd regret it but for now, she just needed everyone on board so they could cast off with the evening tide in about two hours' time.

At the dock, she hailed the *Betsy D*'s jolly boat. Henry Boots, one of Anne's long-term seamen, rowed the boat over to the wharf and she stepped in. The riggers followed. She didn't know their names; she didn't care.

With all aboard at last, Anne set about to check on her officers. She found Sailing Master Thompson on the Quarterdeck with maps and a sextant. "Just want to be sure everything's set properly," he said, turning back to his maps. She was relieved that he was sober.

The riggers had dropped their bags below decks and were learning how to shinny up to the tops'ls. The ones who had arrived yesterday had practiced before, but they would all have a great shock when they tried to climb a mast that was rocking wildly. Anne laughed as one of them – *Timothy was it?* -- slid back down, burning his hands.

"Ye'll be wanting gloves. Did I not tell ye?" she asked.

The seaman blushed. "I brought 'em. They're in me sea bag," he said.

"And much good they'll do ye there, lad. Go get 'em before ye go aloft again." Anne's mothering instincts had been getting stronger the last couple of voyages. It worried her.

She stopped at the helm where she found Sylvanus talking with Harkness. "Your riggers are mighty green, Mr. Harkness," she pointed out.

He grimaced. "They'll learn soon enough, Captain."

Anne slapped him on the back. "Good to have you back on board," she said turning to Sylvanus. "Eh, Helmsman?"

Sylvanus agreed. He and Harkness fought like cats and dogs, but when they weren't fighting, they were best friends. The Second Mate had brought a doctor to Sylvanus's wife when she came down with fever. The quinine he gave her had saved her life.

"The tide should be turning about five bells, just after two-thirty. Mr. Thompson is ready." The men nodded so Anne moved on.

She found Bos'un Potter in the crew quarters playing dice with the seamen and riggers who did not need training. They all rose when she appeared. "No need, gentlemen. We ain't at sea yet," she said. "But we will be afore too long so be on yer toes."

Potter bowed. "Yes, Captain," he said.

Potter turned to the other men. "Ye're sailing with the best captain in these waters, bar none." The men looked at the Captain wide-eyed.

Potter added, "Captain MacCormack can read the tides, the weather and the birds better than any I've sailed with. I ain't never seen Captain be wrong when predicting a storm coming on us."

Anne waved a hand dismissively. For now she was Andrew Mac-Cormack to the new crewmen. She knew they'd figure it out before the voyage was over. By then, she'd have shown them her stuff. Besides, there would be no way to get off the ship until they got to Jamaica. She didn't think she'd lose any. As she turned to leave, each man lifted a knuckle to his forehead.

"Carry on, boys. Leave the sailing' to me," Anne said. She nodded to Potter, who bowed as she left the room.

Anne went up to the focs'le and walked across to the cargo hatch leading to the hold where the slaves would be kept. Taking a deep breath, she climbed down into the belly of the ship. It was dark, but not as dark was usual for a slaver. Sugar and rum didn't need light, but people did, so she'd had several portlights, which, unlike portholes, could be open or closed, cut towards the top of the hold, as far above the water line as possible to give the slaves both light and air. She'd also had the carpenter rig sails on the upper decks to funnel air below. *I won't have people dying for lack of decent air to breathe.*

Lanterns had been placed around the huge room and barrels full of candles to light them lined one wall. The outside wall of the hold had been fitted with bunks – three high – all with simple straw mattresses and a single blanket. Hammocks had been hung three high around much of the rest of the room. *One hundred fifty people need fifty rows with three bunks or hammocks each,* she had calculated. The carpenters managed to squeeze them in and leave a space for a long table and benches for eating and socializing. Latrines had been created on each side. The slaves themselves would be responsible for emptying the buckets.

Although the conditions were far better than on an ordinary slaver, looking at the changes hit Anne hard. The reality of what she had agreed to undertake suddenly overwhelmed her. Tears rolled down her cheeks. She hid behind some barrels, sobbing at the horror of what this ship would be doing: taking human beings to slavery. It took her a full five minutes to get the sobs under control. She pulled out her neck kerchief and wiped her eyes.

I can't show weakness. None of the crew are happy about the purpose of this damned voyage, but we need it to get rid of the sorry bastard we serve.

She climbed back up to the deck. She ran into the Sailing Master holding his sextant to the afternoon sky. He turned when he saw her. "Tide's turning," he said, gesturing towards Bos'un Potter who was yelling for the seamen and sending the riggers aloft.

"Weigh anchor," he barked. Seamen standing in a line hauled the anchor chain up out of the harbor.

The ship moved. *Quickening, like a babe,* Anne thought. *Both are always exciting – signifying a new adventure.*

She stood at the stern of the schooner as Sylvanus turned her towards the harbor entrance. She watched Virginia slip away to port until land was no longer visible. She sighed as the *Betsy D* began its journey to transport slaves.

That night as the crew sat eating bread and cheese and downing small beer, Anne stood on the bottom of the steep stairs leading down into the crew quarters. She took off her worn slouch hat, and waited for them to quiet. She had brought Sylvanus down to stand with her, leaving the First Mate, Jenkins, at the helm.

"Men," she began when the room had fallen silent. "This is not our usual voyage. To start with, it's a legal cargo." A few men laughed. Anne had learned the art of starting any speech or conversation with something positive if possible. There was little positive about this voyage, but that small fact was one thing.

"Unfortunately, as most of ye know, the cargo are people. Slaves direct from Africa or from the West Indies." She waited to see if there was a reaction. A little murmuring ensued but quickly died down, all eyes on the captain.

"I'll tell you straight out. I don't take to slavery. For people of any color or country. Not for black Africans, mulatto West Indians, nor for the red Indians whose people massacred our own. I don't give a damn whether you approve or not. On my ship, slavery is vile.

"Because of that, this is a voyage I don't want to make – my officers don't want to make. The only one wants it is the man forcing it on us. He has us by the balls, men, and no mistake. So we will do his bidding -- this once. But only once. And when the opportunity arises, I can assure ye that we will see to it he pays the price."

She waited as her words sunk in. Then cheer rose up. She waited, realizing that this was a family she would miss if she stayed with the other one permanently.

"We can only make the best of it. These people are to be treated as people. They are not, while on this vessel, cargo. Ye've all no doubt been down to gawk at the hold." Heads nodded. "So ye know we've rigged their quarters as best we can -- given the numbers and the space we have. Once they're on board, Mr. Kilrun," she pointed to the ship's carpenter, "will be adding canvas walls to separate men from women. It's not much, but it's better than they had getting to Jamaica."

"We get this done, boys, get them delivered safely, and put this behind us. I'm counting on ye to take this chain off my neck – and off most of yers, the ones who've sailed with me before." She waited, but no one spoke. "The evil bastard we're doing this for knows most of ye through that scurvy dog Mayfield, so only the new boys are not at risk here. That said, I thank ye for coming. For my sake and for yer own. If ye need to talk with me about it, any of ye, my cabin's open. But if I hear of anyone deliberately harming one person in the hold, he'll answer to me." Her scowl reinforced the threat.

"Again, I thank ye all for coming. I'll thank ye more when we're home. Safe trip." She put her hat back on. The men rose as one, an honor to the captain that didn't happen often on a pirate or smuggling ship. She was touched. She swept her hat dramatically across her chest and bowed to the crew. Cries of "Huzzah!" rang through the space.

Anne climbed the ladder back up top and walked the length of the ship to her quarters. *Let's get this over with*, she thought.

CHAPTER TWENTY

26-29 August 1730 - Kingston, Jamaica

The trip from Virginia went without incident. Anne gathered the crew every evening to talk over how the boarding and housing of the slaves would go in Jamaica, trying to anticipate every eventuality. She knew they couldn't, but they'd get as close as possible. By the time the *Betsy D* anchored in the Kingston Harbor on the incoming tide the evening of the twenty-fifth of August, everyone on board knew his role.

"Mr. Jenkins," Anne called to the first mate at the sound of six bells at seven o'clock the next morning. "Have ye eaten?" She stood on the quarterdeck watching him climb out of the hatch. She and Jenkins were the only ones on board with private cabins. The helmsman and the second mate shared quarters as did the bos'un and the cook/surgeon.

Jenkins nodded, pulling down his best jacket as he came towards her. When he approached, she handed him the orders. "For the agent's eyes only," she reminded him.

"Aye, aye, Captain," he said.

Anne could not be sure who in Kingston might remember her. After all, a lot of pirates had taken the government's amnesty in 1718 when she and Calico Jack, among others, had not. Using a version of her birth name and having Jenkins act on her behalf kept her – and her red hair -- out of sight – just in case.

When she had carefully opened and re-sealed Woolrich's instructions, she discovered that he, too, was using a false name.

To Mr. Josiah Smith, Agent:

The bearer of this letter has been sent to retrieve cargo, viz 150 healthy African slaves consisting as follows:

72 adult males

62 adult females

10 children, various sex

To be transported by the bearer on the ship called the Betsy D per the arrangement made between myself and the seller, The Honorable Peter Manchester, for whom you are acting as agent.

Please assist the bearer in any way possible in loading the cargo onto the vessel safely.

I am, my dear Sir, your most humble servant,

Thaddeus Pennington

The crew had lowered the jolly boat with Boots on the oars into the water where it bobbed, waiting for its passengers. Anne watched Jenkins descend and looked for the second mate. She had a special mission for him. Harkness had spent time in Kingston in the last few years as a drunk and as crew on a number of voyages, carrying both legal cargo and cargo without manifest. He had friends there.

He came up to her, dressed as an ordinary seaman in slops. She looked him over with an approving eye. "Ye look the part," she said.

Harkness winked. "The part of a spy, you mean?" he asked.

Anne nodded. "Yes, Mr. Harkness. Yer history with these people means they'll trust ye. Especially if they think ye're drinking too much."

"There are great advantages to being underestimated," he responded.

"Something I am acutely aware of, Mr. Harkness. Ye've got yer mission, man. Come back when ye've got what we need."

Like Jenkins, Harkness saluted. "Aye, aye Cap'n." He climbed down into the jolly boat.

Potter and Wilberforce also stopped to check-in on their way into the port. "Have ye the lists?" Anne asked them.

"Yes, Cap'n we do. And we've already decided how to spread out to buy the victuals so they don't suspect the number we'll be feeding."

"Good." Anne told them. "And keep your ears to the ground. Anything you hear on Woolrich or Mayfield may be of use to us."

They both saluted and climbed down into the jolly boat. Boots pulled on the oars and Anne watched the little boat bob along to shore.

Wish I could go, she thought. *See some old friends.* She sighed. *No, most are gone. And I must be gone, too.*

She turned and almost ran into Sylvanus who had come quietly to stand behind her.

"Helmsman. You gave me a start."

He looked across the harbor at the beach and around at the few ships at anchor. "Bad time to sail," he said, his expression wrinkled with worry. "Sailing Master agree. Hurricane be comin'."

Anne nodded. "I know." She sighed. "I could see it in the water and feel it, but when you're being coerced, you can't always pick your moments."

"When this done ..." Sylvanus left the statement unsaid. Anne could feel his anger.

"Somehow, Mr. Sylvanus. We will find a way to bring him down. I promise. We already have compromising information and we're looking for more."

He nodded and looked at the harbor. "Ships be close. Best take that red hair below."

He was right. The sun shone brightly and there were two ships, both flying the Crown flag, within spyglass distance of the *Betsy D.* She pulled on her hat, thanked him and went below to wait for the news from shore.

She didn't see Harkness or Potter until two days later. When they returned, she knew from the smirks on their faces that they'd been successful. She called them into her cabin.

"Well, boys, you look like you not only found the canary but ripped it to shreds." Anne said. She was ready for some good news.

She pulled a decanter from the small cupboard and poured them each a glass of brandy. She watched while they drank as they sat back in the only two chairs in the room. She leaned against the table that served as her desk and waited.

"What'd ye find?" she asked.

They looked at each other until Wilberforce nodded to Potter who took a deep breath. 'Woolrich is quite the rotter," he began.

Anne sighed. "We already knew that, Mr. Potter. What else?" She held the decanter out.

He swallowed another mouthful of brandy and lifted the glass so she could refill it. "Seems he didn't leave Jamaica out of the kindness of his heart for his kin," Potter continued. "Seems as if he might have killed someone he shouldn't have killed."

"Do tell," she encouraged them.

"Seems the victim in the case was a special favorite of the Governor. Mulatto woman named Christy. And the thing is, he didn't just kill her ..." He drew out the word "kill" until it was almost three syllables long. "He raped her first. Hurt her pretty bad."

"Too bad for her; good for us," she said as she poured the men a third glass of brandy each.

"This woman – a mulatto? A whore?" She asked. They nodded. "Didn't know killing a whore counted for anything."

Wilberforce spoke up. "She was, as Mr. Potter noted, the favorite of the Governor. He managed to get an indictment issued for Woolrich's arrest."

"Really?" Anne was surprised. "And?"

"It worked – got him to leave Jamaica which is what they really wanted." Wilberforce put down the glass. "Charges would never stand but that's not why they were brought. Figured facing the prison, he'd flee and he did. They counted on his being a coward and it worked."

Wilberforce sat up. "The locals didn't take kindly to his getting away. The woman was quite popular with others besides the Governor. What took longer was tracking down the 'How.' How did he manage to get to Virginia?"

"Good question, gentlemen. And the answer?" Anne looked from one to the other.

"Seems he did have some friends after all," Wilberforce began.

Potter interrupted him. "More like the Governor's got enemies." Wilberforce nodded.

"There's a Lord Gentry who was up for Governor and lost the position. He smuggled Woolrich off the island."

Wilberforce continued. "Seems this Gentry ... odd name for a lord, don't ye think?" Anne nodded. "Anyway, seems this Gentry was in some sort of business trouble that our friend," he spat the words out, "helped him out with, so when the bastard got into trouble, Gentry found him a way out."

"Why Virginia?" Anne asked.

"Seems the Baronet had friends in high places – a Burgess. You knew that, didn't you?"

Anne affirmed the question. *I wonder if Burgess Goodwin knows who his friend really is.*

Wilberforce and Potter exchanged glances. Anne looked from one to the other. "What else?" she asked.

Potter spoke up. "We found a lad who'd traveled across with Sir Jonathan who told us his tastes don't just run to mulattos." He hesitated. "Or women."

Anne shrugged. "So? What about Mayfield? How is he connected to Woolrich?" Anne asked.

The two exchanged looks. "Now there's an interesting tale in itself, Captain," Potter began.

"The poor wee laddie got into trouble in Scotland. Seduced a Lady Campbell and stole almost £200 of jewelry from her." He looked at Wilberforce who shrugged. "And he left a bun in the oven as well," he added.

"That's when his daddy bought him a commission. By the time he got to Boston, he'd beaten up almost every able seaman, one to death. The Royal Navy decided they should cut him loose. So his father sent him on to Woolrich in Jamaica. For protection." Wilberforce shook his head. "Which Woolrich was happy to give him."

This story gets better and better, but could it be told to Burgesses if it came to that?

"How the hell did Mayfield come to us?" She asked, trying to remember the story he'd given her. *Something about being tossed from a Crown ship, which ain't a bad thing in my world, and needing money. I needed a Bos'un so I didn't ask enough questions,* she chastised herself. Then she shook it off. *We're smugglers, not babysitters. He knew the job and we needed a Bos'un.*

"Seems he got into a bar fight so Woolrich sent him to find gainful employment."

"Lucky us. Well, my friends, you did great work. If we must, can we prove this?" Anne looked from Potter to Wilberforce.

"Oh yes, Cap'n. There's at least a dozen sailors, seamen and officers, ready and willing to see the Woolrich hanged, despite his pedigree and Mayfield with him." Wilberforce held out the glass which Anne quickly filled again. "Not even counting some Royal Navy officers ... and his own father."

"And Lord and Lady Campbell," Potter added.

"Can we get these men to Williamsburg if we need to?" she asked.

"Some of them volunteered to come on their own to testify against Mayfield and Woolrich," Potter said.

"Woolrich has got few friends here. I think his son would testify against him if you asked." Wilberforce added.

"Well done." Anne picked up the decanter and returned it to the cupboard.

"Out with ye now. Sober up. We're loading cargo tomorrow and I need you both in a state to do yer jobs." She put a half doubloon in each of their hands as she shook them.

The men bowed and left the room, swaying and singing a bawdy song.

Well Mr. High and Mighty Sir Jonathan Woolrich and yer even worse friend the fourth whelp of an Earl, ye're not so much in control as ye believe, though ye don't know it. And ye won't until the time's right.

CHAPTER TWENTY-ONE

30 August 1730 - Kingston, Jamaica

Although the day had broken clear and sunny, Anne told the Sailing Master, "This weather won't hold." Thompson nodded agreement.

Mid-afternoon, they got the signal that the wharf was theirs. "Take her in, Mr. Thompson and let's get this over with."

The *Betsy D* sailed to the wharf in a light breeze. A long line of black and mulatto men, women -- a few cradling babies, and children were lined up and roped together. The crew put barrels of water and fresh meat on board first, letting the slaves rest in the shade across from the dock. When all the supplies were loaded, First Mate Jenkins signaled to the seaman guarding the slaves to bring them down. Before they got but a few steps, a tall, angry man came storming out of a warehouse next to the pier.

"I must see the Captain," he screamed in a voice so high-pitched that it sent all the crew into suppressed fits of giggles. He glared at them briefly then spoke again. "I am Josiah Smith, Mr. Pennington's agent and I demand to see the Captain before I let a single slave on board this vessel."

Jenkins looked up at the man's red face and unkempt wig and

smiled. "I represent the Captain, Mr. Smith. He is indisposed at the moment."

"I don't care if he's having kittens," Smith screamed. "I will not let this cargo move until I have seen and met with him."

Jenkins sighed. "Second Mate," he called. Harkness was standing not ten feet away and responded immediately. "Mr. Smith wishes to speak with the Captain. Would you be so kind as to let him know?"

Harkness nodded, wondering how Anne would handle this. The Second Mate went on board towards Anne's cabin but before he even got to the stairs, a figure appeared on the Quarterdeck wearing the Captain's uniform. It took Harkness a moment to realize he was face to face with Anne Burleigh, her auburn hair completely hidden under a powdered wig of the brightest white. His lips sucked inward as he stifled a grin.

"Captain," he saluted smartly. Anne looked at him, waiting. "The agent, a Mr. Smith, insists on talking with you before allowing our cargo on board." He emphasized the "our" for Smith's benefit. The cargo had been paid for the day before.

Anne looked up at the reedy, almost apoplectic, man stomping around the wharf. "All right, Mr. Harkness. If I must." She strode down the gangplank.

Once on the wharf, she bowed to Smith. "Is there a problem, Mr. Smith?" she asked.

Smith took a deep breath and managed to control himself. "No, Captain MacCormack, but I make a point of always dealing, at least in the final instance, with a ship's captain, not the Second Mate."

"Well, I am here, Mr. Smith. Again, is there a problem?" Anne looked him in the eye which meant she looked up from her five feet four inch height to his at least six feet.

She waited. Smith put out an arm to invite her into his office. She looked from him to the line of humans waiting to be taken on board. "The wharfage fees here in Kingston are stiff indeed, Mr. Smith. I must insist that you allow my crew to load our cargo while we ..." She hesitated, looking for the right word. "Consult."

Smith looked annoyed, but after a moment, he shrugged his shoulders and agreed. "So be it. The fees are indeed high."

Anne turned to Jenkins. "Proceed Mr. Jenkins. Let's get these people on board before we can no longer afford to." Jenkins saluted.

Anne walked calmly beside Smith into his office. He gestured her to sit in a chair across from his desk but she waved him off. "I prefer to stand," she said, keeping the timbre of her voice as low as possible.

"I just wanted to point out that I have done everything possible to provide for your needs. Is there anything else I can do for you?" He looked up at her.

He wants a bribe, Anne realized. *The balls on him.*

"Thank you, Mr. Smith. It's so kind of you and we do appreciate it. But I believe all our needs have been met." She smiled, waiting for his next move.

"Ah, well, there are quite a few ships in the harbor today and tomorrow. The Harbor Master is concerned about congestion. We wouldn't want any collisions, would we?"

I can't believe he thinks I'd fall for this, she thought. But on reconsideration, she decided that a small bribe might well be beneficial. She might need this man later and greased palms tended to loosen lips.

"Ah, Mr. Smith. I can see your point." Reaching into the pocket of her jacket, Anne pulled out a small pouch of coins. "Would the Harbor Master feel more comfortable in letting us go when we're ready if he were to have found, say two doubloons?"

Smith's face lit up but he managed to douse it quickly. "I believe he would be most flexible with just a little more incentive than that, Captain."

"And you know this, how, Mr. Smith?"

"He is my brother," the man told her.

"Ah well then, you would know his mind. Three doubloons then?"

Smith smiled affirmatively. Anne took three coins out of the pouch and put them on the desk.

"Thank you, Captain. Have you a departure in mind?" he asked.

"Yes, no later than tomorrow on the morning tide. It will take us the afternoon and evening to get the cargo settled in." Anne replied.

Smith stood up and held out a hand. Anne reached out and squeezed it so hard that Smith had to take in a gulp of air.

"Thank'ee, Mr. Smith," she said as she turned on her heel and left the room.

Down on the wharf, the line of slaves wound its way from the warehouses, across the wharf and up the gangway onto the ship. The sight sickened Anne and once again she swore, *I will break that bastard Woolrich no matter what it takes.*

She walked past the slowly moving line, seeing the sadness and fear on the faces of the people. A voice called out from behind her, "Hey, Cap'n – you been in Kingston before? You look familiar-like."

She turned slowly to see a lanky man wearing slops sitting on a barrel a few yards up the shore. Ned Hawkins, damn him. They had sailed together when she was with Bonny. Without the wig ... She shuddered a bit.

"No, I haven't had the pleasure," she called out. She turned back and walked deliberately onto the ship, heading straight for her cabin. When she got there, she ripped the wig off and tried to calm her pounding heart. *That was close*, she thought. *Let's get out of here as soon as we can.* She stayed in the cabin, listening to the noise of the people moving down into the cargo hold. Strange voices, hushed with fear, were audible on deck but muffled as they descended.

A pounding headache that felt like her head would explode from behind her eyes had gotten worse with the stress of the meeting with

Smith. *The crew can handle this,* she told herself as she laid down on the bunk, darkened the room, and fell asleep.

The sun was down when she woke from a nightmare, sweating. She'd been hanging on a scaffold with dozens of black faces below her jeering and crying out, "Coward." She had looked over and next to her saw the body of Calico Jack, his guts falling out through a large slash in his belly. Jack had smiled, "Don't let 'em get to you, Anne. We all do what we have to." His head flopped over and she realized he was dead. After that, she found herself falling into the sea and swimming. She was trapped under a dock and struggling to get to the surface ...

The loud knock that had woken her repeated itself. She struggled awake. "Come," she called out.

Jenkins appeared in the open doorway. "They're all in, Captain," he said.

Anne stifled a yawn. "How did it go?"

"As well as can be expected. They do seem to appreciate the better accommodations. About half of them speak English."

"Do ye have the manifest?" she asked. He handed her a paper with lines noting the names, if any, ages, and sex of the slaves. "Total here of one hundred forty-four persons," she read out loud. "'Seventy-two men, sixty-two women and ten children'." She looked up at Jenkins. "That seem about right, Mr. Jenkins?"

Jenkins thought for a moment. "Yes. Should be."

Anne nodded. "Well done, Sir. Extra ration of rum for you and the crew." She looked up as Jenkins quickly turned to leave. "But not 'til after yer shift is done."

Anne got up and changed into her usual breeches and a floppy white shirt, throwing an old blue jacket over it. Finding her way to the Galley, she looked in on the Cook. Wilberforce was in his element, pans swinging, pots banging. She had supplied him with two assistants since he was cooking for far more than the usual crew. "What's for supper?" she asked.

Wilberforce looked up. "Ah, Captain. You don't trust me, do you?" He laughed. "Got bread and pottage." He pointed to two huge pots full of a bubbling liquid that smelled, she had to admit, delicious. "Vege'bles is best. Some chicken in there too."

"Enough to fill a bowl each?" Anne asked. The bowls were stored in a cupboard in the hold.

"Aye. A full bowl and a chunk of bread. They probably ain't et that well for a piece. Need to start with something easy on the gut."

Anne nodded. "Well done, Cook. Carry on."

Back on deck, Anne slid into the line of people descending into the hold. Following a small woman who looked to be about her own age down the ladder, she was relieved that there was a little natural light left so they could find their way around the space. Seamen Boots and Jones were pointing men and women to the two sides of the room separated by a huge canvas wall. Another seaman, *Remington?*, was lighting the candles. The slaves looked around wide-eyed. She knew that the passage from Africa to Jamaica had been much worse than this.

Anne stood with the seamen and helped them direct the slaves until the hold was full. Then she stood up on the table. She motioned the people forward. The area by the table wasn't separated by the canvas.

"I am told that many of you speak English?" she asked.

Some of the slaves nodded. *Jenkins was right,* she thought. *About half.* The ones who didn't turned to others. As far as she could tell, most everyone either spoke the language or was near someone who did.

"We are taking you to Baltimore in the Maryland Colony. Although you are not free to make that choice, we will treat you as best we can." She waited while translations were murmured. Everyone stared at her.

"We will feed you twice a day at this table. Children and women first, then the men. You will have light. There is a place on each side," she waved to the men's side and then to the women's, "for a privy. You will assign one of your own, or more if you wish, to empty the pots twice a day, in the morning and again in the evening. Let Mr. Harkness, our Second Mate, know who is assigned that duty and he will assure they are able to get on the deck to do the job."

The crowd murmured and she felt the fear lighten just a little.

"You will be able to get on deck at least once a day -- in shifts because we can't fit all of you at once. If the weather turns bad, you will have to stay below for your own safety. If you need anything special, these seamen," she pointed to Henry Boots and Jimmy Jones who waved to indicate who they were, "will help you. Let them know. I am the Captain. I am responsible for your welfare. I will do everything in my power to get to you Maryland safely." *God help me*, she added to herself.

"Cook?" Anne looked around the Galley which appeared to be empty. Wilberforce and his two helpers appeared, lugging huge pots. "Women and children first. Then the men," she reiterated.

Nodding to the servers, she jumped off the table and headed for the hatch stairs.

Damn me, it's already an oven below. "Mr. Wilberforce." The Cook handed ladles to his assistants who were pulling bowls and spoons out of the storage cupboards and came over. He stood quietly. "They'll need water. As much and as often as possible," she said, her voice starting to crack with emotion. "And the sheets turned to bring air in. See to it." Wilberforce nodded as Anne turned and climbed up onto the deck.

Sucking in the fresh, warm air, she worked her way to her cabin where she promptly vomited into the chamber pot. Collapsing on her bunk, Captain Andrew MacCormack of the *Betsy D*, once again began to cry.

CHAPTER TWENTY-TWO

31 August 1730 - Caribbean Sea

The *Betsy D* sailed out of Kingston on the morning tide. The winds continued light, so she went with all sails furled. The tops'ils caught the winds aloft and moved her along at a reasonable, if not fast, clip.

Anne stood at the stern watching Jamaica fade into the distance with a great sense of relief. *May I never see yer damned shores again.*

"Mr. Thompson," she called out. Thompson came over from the Quarterdeck where he had been watching the sea ahead instead of the shore behind.

"Ye've set the course for Cuba?" she asked, knowing full well that he had.

"Yes, Captain. We'll go around her to the west then turn nor'east through the Strait of Florida and past the Bahama Islands, then north."

Anne nodded. It was the route they had planned from the beginning. "How long?"

"If all goes well ..." Thompson hesitated. Something about his tone caused Anne to look at him sharply.

"Yes?" she asked.

"Three days to round Cuba and another five or six home," he said.

"And if all does not go well?" she asked.

He looked at her and gulped. "Have you been watching the seas too?" he asked.

"Yes. All the signs of a hurricane." Anne said.

"I can feel it in my bones and I can see it in the water," he said. "There's a storm out there and a big one, make no mistake. Question is, how far?" He looked at the bright skies and slight chop ahead of them.

"And how long. Let's alert the crew though. I'd rather be prepared and not need it than found wanting." She nodded to Thompson, who bowed slightly and headed up to where Potter the Bos'un was standing talking to Sylvanus who held the wheel.

Anne descended into her cabin and pulled out her charts. *If the storm hits us ...* She stopped, realizing that she had thought "the storm" and not "a storm." *It's out there. I know it as sure as I live and breathe. Shit. Shit Shit.*

Spreading the chart out on the table, she took her magnifier and looked up and down the coast of Cuba. They needed a place to get out of the storm.

Storms come off Africa, she reasoned, *then go north or west. The winds howl right to left against sun-wise.* She looked closely at the charts. *Grand Cayman. Hardly anyone there. Good anchorages, deep water on the lee side.* She put the magnifier down on the paper and leaned over with her eye on it. *If the winds come, they'll blow us that way anyway. Where?* She moved the magnifier around the chart with her eye resting on it until she found what she was looking for. *Little Sound. Behind Booby Cay. That'd do it.* She sat up and heaved a sigh of relief. *At least we have a backup.*

She went up top and found Thompson. "I've had a look at the charts, Mr. Thompson."

He smiled. "And I as well," he said.

They spoke in unison: "Grand Cayman."

Anne added, "If we're right and we can't outrun her, she'll blow us that way. Be prepared to veer if need be."

Thompson nodded. "I've charted the course already."

"Well done. My head's been warning me since yesterday. Never fails. Headache behind my eyes and there's a bad storm heading for us." Anne rubbed her temples, which continued to throb. "Let the crew know, especially the riggers. They'll need to be ready to lower the tops'ls if it gets too bad."

"Aye, aye." Thompson bowed slightly and left.

Anne looked out at the swells running along the ship which was now moving at a good and steady clip as the wind has risen. *They're already getting' taller.* She staggered aft as the ship rocked. It was four o'clock, eight bells. Lifting the spyglass to her eye, she strained to see as far behind as she could. Puffy cumulus clouds floated over the ship, but in the distance, the sky was dark and getting darker by the minute. She could see the towers of some thunderclouds, but mostly the view was a deep, dark gray.

Getting closer, she thought. *But we have a bit of time yet.* Shaking her head, she went below decks to check on the slaves.

She found Henry Boots and Jimmy Jones at the table, playing dice with some of the men. "They ain't cheating' ye, I hope," she said to one of the black-skinned players. He laughed and pointed to the large pile of beans in front of him, the gambling currency of choice. The beans had been placed in bowls to keep them from rolling off the table.

"Ah well then, ye aren't cheating them are ye?" Everyone around the table laughed.

Henry and Jimmy stood up. "All's well, Cap'n," they said in unison.

"Good, glad to hear it. Everyone fed and watered?" Anne looked around. People were sitting on the bunks and on the floor. Others swung in the hammocks, many of them women with sleeping children on their chests. Her heart ached to hold her own four.

"Privies being emptied?" she asked. Henry pointed to a man and a woman carrying out buckets.

"Yes, Cap'n," Henry said but he stood up and motioned her to an empty area away from the table. "The ship's roll is starting to worry them."

"There's a storm coming, Henry. We're doing our best to outrun it, but we're also prepared to head towards the Caymans – sheltered cove there – if we can't." Anne told him. Henry bit his upper lip.

"Try to keep them calm. Tell them the ride's going to get a bit rough but to stay put and we'll get the boat into safe harbor."

"Aye, aye, Cap'n" Henry's face contorted with worry. This was only his second voyage.

"We'll do our damndest, Mr. Boots. But from you, all they should know is there's a storm. It'll be rough, but all will be well."

Henry nodded. "Do my best, Cap'n."

Anne patted him on the shoulder. "Good man," she said. "And Jones. Good job, both of ye. Extra ration of rum for each of ye after yer shift. Who's taking the next watch?"

"Kendall and Bennett," Henry told her. "At six bells. After supper."

"When you're done, lads, report to Mr. Thompson. He'll give you assignments for the storm."

The sailors nodded and put knuckles to their foreheads. Anne dipped her head to them and headed back up top.

She next visited the Galley. Wilberforce was busy boiling beef in a stew with okra and beans. She saw stacks of bread in a basket in a corner. "No weevils, I hope, Cook," she said, slapping him on the back.

"You gave me a start, Captain," Wilberforce chuckled. "No weevils. So far."

"All of us who eat your food appreciate that." Anne said, leaning against the table behind the cook stove. "But I have a serious matter to bring up."

Wilberforce wiped his hands on his apron and called out to his assistant, Billy James, who was chopping onions. "Billy, lad, come watch the stew for a bit."

Billy wiped his tearing eyes and nodded. "Glad to get away from these, Sir," he said, moving over in front of the stove.

Anne and Wilberforce moved out into the passageway. Crewmen squeezed past as they spoke.

"Sailing Master and I see a storm heading for us."

Wilberforce grimaced. "Thought so myself. Clouds to the south look a mite dark."

"Yes they are, Mr. Wilberforce. And we've seen signs in the water – long swells and bigger chop." Her eyebrows knit together as she grimaced.

He nodded. "We can feel the swells. Having trouble keeping the stew in the pot. We'll be sure the kitchen's shipshape and get something easy ready for breakfast in case we have to feed people in rough conditions."

"Good, Mr. Wilberforce. Thank you. After that, batten everything down," she said.

"Will do, Captain."

"One other thing. If it's bad – a hurricane ..." She paused.

"My surgical instruments and medical kit will be safely within reach," he finished.

"Excellent. The food smells good. When's supper?" She raised her nose and inhaled deeply.

"Not for the likes of you until the cargo's fed." His brown eyes twinkled at the rare opportunity to harass the captain.

She stuck her tongue out at him. "Well done, Cook. And well said." She slapped him on the back and turned to the stairs, climbing them quickly back onto the deck.

She climbed up to the Quarterdeck where Sylvanus stood with his large hands resting lightly on the wheel. "Ahoy, Mr. Sylvanus," Anne called out.

"What you need, Captain?" he asked without looking at her.

"Has Mr. Thompson been by?"

"'Bout five minutes," Sylvanus answered. His face remained expressionless, as usual.

"Good. I'm thinking tomorrow, perhaps midday. If we're right," she told him.

"He too," Sylvanus responded. He looked at Anne. "You sure?" he asked.

"As I can be," she said. He nodded and looked back to sea.

"Seen the swells. We be ready," he said.

Anne headed back for her cabin. She poured some water from the pitcher on her desk onto a cloth and rang it out. Then she laid back down onto her bunk and put it over her eyes. She prayed that her head would clear before all hell broke loose. And that she was wrong that it would.

CHAPTER TWENTY-THREE

1 September 1730 - Caribbean Sea Northwest of Jamaica

Anne awoke in the dark. Her temples pounded worse than before and nausea overwhelmed her. She had slept since supper and could sense that night was almost at an end. She could feel the seas rising, the boat rocking harder side to side, and hear the shouting of men on deck. The winds were whistling and shrieking even though the hatch above her cabin had been battened down.

She could barely stand with the ship rolling, but she managed to stagger across the room, pull on her slouch hat and go topside. Even in the low light of predawn she saw that the clouds above were darker and whipping by east to west. Sylvanus stood next to Jenkins, who had taken the wheel during the night. Anne had insisted that her Helmsman get rest. She knew he'd need it for the day to come. She held onto the windlass as a gust of wind threatened to blow her off her feet.

Anne found the safety rope the crew had tied across the deck, and was able to make it to the Quarterdeck, where she found Thompson watching the storm barreling down on them. "Can we outrun it?" Anne shouted.

"Doubt it. How long do you think before it's on us?" Thompson asked.

"Not long," she answered. "Can we make Grand Cayman?"

They watched as occasional patches of blue shone overhead, then vanished into the swirling clouds.

"I hope so," he said, fear permeating his voice.

"Stand by to strike sail," Anne screamed over the wind.

As the hurricane came closer and intensified, intermittent showers drenched the deck, blowing sideways with such force that Anne's face felt like it was being pummeled with needles. She heard the Bos'un yell, "Batten down the hatches." A belaying pin, the wooden pin used to secure the lines tied around it on the side of the ship, worked loose and flew out to sea just inches from her head. "Damn," she cursed.

The ship pitched over as the waves hit her starboard side. Sylvanus struggled to keep her going north, but he was forced west as the waves hit and shifted slightly. Harkness, the Second Mate, stood at his side yelling orders up to the men in the rigging.

"Best strike the tops'ls, Cap'n. The winds aloft are too strong. With the seas running so high, we're having to duck and weave to keep across the waves." Potter called to her without taking his eyes off the rigging and the men scrambling up it.

Anne looked up. The men aloft, holding on for dear life, waited for the order to strike sail. At that moment, a huge gust of wind heeled the ship over. Sylvanus was thrown back and barely kept one hand on the wheel.

"Mr. Potter, strike the tops'ls," Anne screamed over the howling wind.

The men hugged the ratlins as the masts swayed wildly in the wind and the increasingly heavy seas. Thompson screamed, "It's comin' in fast now." before he fell against the bulkhead behind Sylvanus, who had gone down to his knees and was struggling back to his feet. They were both tied to the wheel to keep from sliding away.

The next lurch of the ship knocked Anne off her feet. She grabbed the safety rope and held on as a huge wave crashed over the starboard side and swept across the deck. Anne tied the rope around the rail just before another huge wave hit them.

She crawled towards Sylvanus who had managed to stand and was turning the ship into the oncoming waves. The sailors struck the tops'ls. Sylvanus spun the wheel so the ship moved slightly to larboard, and with the sails coming down, the *Betsy D* straightened up several degrees. But before Sylvanus could get her square, another thirty-foot wave struck, sending one of the seamen screaming into the sea.

"Man overboard." Anne yelled, but she knew that in the clutches of the oncoming hurricane, he was lost. They couldn't stop, so even if he survived the fall, they'd never get to him in time.

"Shit," she screamed. One of the remaining men aloft had frozen. "Get those damned tops'ls furled." Mr. Potter blew three long whistles and a short. Whether from her voice or the Bos'un's whistle, the men seemed to have woken. He finished bringing the lower tops'l down.

The storm was fully upon them now. Sylvanus let it push the boat to the west, towards Cayman. "How far?" she yelled to Thompson.

"Forty miles, give or take," he called back.

"Mr. Sylvanus, how fast can we get there?"

"Don't know. If we keep speed and stay up, an hour, maybe hour and a half." He never took his eyes off the sea.

There was a shriek from the near the larboard gangway. Her heart stopped. *What the hell?*

Slaves were streaming up out of the main hatch onto the deck of the ship.

"NOOOOO." she howled, trying to be heard over the storm. Moving along the rope, Anne struggled forward.

She found Wilberforce, his two helpers, and the able-bodied seamen Boots and Jones trying to herd the slaves back into the Hold.

She hung onto the ladder and called to Wilberforce. "What the hell happened?" she asked.

"They opened the portlights – got too hot they said. Then a couple of the big waves came through and flooded the hold. Before we could calm them, they panicked and started running up the stairs."

Anne watched the disaster unfold as if in slow motion. First there were dozens of men, women and children on the deck screaming in panic. Then a wave, at least twenty or thirty feet high, swept over the deck and everyone vanished.

"Shit," Anne screamed again. She and Wilberforce made their way down the companionway. The ship righted itself again.

"Go back. Go back," she cried. She turned to Wilberforce. "Go around the other side; we'll have to force them." He nodded.

Thompson, who had arrived just as the wave swept the slaves overboard, joined Anne aft of the hatch. They waved their arms as they moved forward to try to get the panicked people back down into the Hold. On the larboard companionway, Boots and Jones were doing the same with Wilberforce kneeling by the hatch, helping people down.

As the crowd thinned and more slaves went below, Anne got close enough to ask Wilberforce, "How bad is it down there?"

"Bad. Flooded." he replied. "Four feet of water last I looked. We've got the pumps going." His sad, angry look touched Anne. "We got the portlights closed."

Only six slaves remained on deck when another huge gust of wind swung the ship sharply to larboard as yet another wave swamped the deck. Anne and Wilberforce grabbed two women who were swept off their feet. Two men disappeared. Gasping for breath, they pushed the women and the two other men down the hatch. The splashing at the bottom told them that none had put a foot on the ladder.

"Leave the wheel to Mr. Sylvanus, Captain. He can handle it." Wilberforce grabbed her hand to pull her down into the ship but she wrenched away.

"I'm the captain, Mr. Wilberforce." She turned to Thompson. "You both go below. Get the hold pumped best you can and get everyone settled. Put Boots on the hatch so they can't get back up."

She moved carefully back to the Quarterdeck - hand over hand on the safety rope. Once at the wheel, she lashed herself to it and stood next to Sylvanus, watching him manoeuver the ship. Consulting the ship's compass, Anne turned to the Helmsman. "Heading dead west," she yelled. He nodded.

"Speed?" she asked.

"Ten knots, give or take." He strained to see through the driving rain and dark clouds. The ship shook and rolled wildly.

Half an hour later, Seaman Jones, who was assigned to watch through the spyglass from the bow, shouted, "Land ho."

Anne held her breath, putting her own spyglass to her eye. After scanning the horizon twice, she saw it - a murky, dark shape off to the west. She pointed. Sylvanus turned the wheel a few degrees more to that direction, keeping the ship moving into the waves as best he could.

Within ten minutes, they could see a distinct point of land rising above the sea. "Water Sound," Anne called out. Sylvanus acknowledged with a nod. "Make for Water Sound, just below." Sylvanus nodded again.

The ship moved closer and closer, driven by the wind. Sylvanus maneuvered her around the point and past the Cay into the Sound. Anne pointed to a sheltered cove she'd used before when a Royal Navy ship had spotted them.

Thompson appeared out of the sheets of rain. "Water Sound?" he asked.

"Yes, Mr. Thompson. Stand by to drop anchor," she yelled.

"Aye, aye, Captain." Thompson, holding the safety rope, made his way forward. She saw him calling orders to the crew who dispersed to the anchor chains.

The *Betsy D* hove into a sheltered harbor at the back of Water Sound. The winds diminished – blocked by the rise of the island. Anne watched as the men struck all sail. She untied herself and went down to watch Bos'un's crew drop the anchor. When the ship was safely anchored, she thanked every crewman as she sent them down to the focs'le to dry out. "I'll be having the cook get ye some grub and grog," she told them.

Sylvanus remained at the wheel as she knew he would. When the rest of the crew had gone below, and she had instructed Thompson to tell Wilberforce to get food and rum to those who could stomach it, she made her way through the pounding rain to the wheel.

"Mr. Sylvanus," she began. Tears filled her eyes. She panted with relief and the sense that they'd been saved. She couldn't speak.

Sylvanus untied the rope that lashed him to the wheel. "I take break," he said. He threw his arm over her shoulder and they made their way down into the lower reaches of the ship.

They went straight to the Hold where they saw, with horror, the results of the portlight disaster. Everything was soaked. The lower bunks were still under water, although the bilge pump was pumping hard. Bos'un Potter, came over to her. "The slaves are taking turns at the pumps," he said. "We've dropped a foot so far."

Anne looked around. "How long to get it down to below the bunks?" she asked.

"Couple of hours, I'd guess," Potter said, scratching his head.

"Have ye done a count?" Anne asked, her voice trembling. *One sailor and god knows how many slaves.*

"Just a rough one. We took on one hundred forty-four slaves. So far, fifty adults unaccounted for." He waved a hand around the dark room; the only light coming from a lantern they'd managed to light. "But it's dark and there's too many don't know each other." He gulped then went on. "At least six babes drowned down here. Swept under the bunks, they were."

Anne's mouth opened then shut again. After a moment, she put an arm on Potter's back. "Carry on, Bos'un. Well done."

She left the Hold and found her way forward to the focs'le. The men were stripped down to their breeches. Everywhere, slops hung to dry. Some sat at the mess table, eating cheese and bread, or had brought the food to their hammocks. The ship continued to shudder and roll as gusts hit it, sending the hammocks swaying wildly. She noticed, gratefully, that the focs'le, at least, was only damp. *About an inch of water. They'll survive that without a thought*, Anne told herself.

She also noticed that they were quiet. Sitting down at the table, she looked around at the glum and, in some cases, angry faces. "Who was it?" she asked.

"Davy," said the man next to her without looking up. "Wilcox."

"Ah," said Anne remembering the young man of about twenty-five with lank dark brown hair and strange yellow eyes. He had a stutter, she recalled, and had sailed on her last three voyages.

"Damn," she said. She tried to remember if he had family.

"Has he a wife, Jeremiah?" she asked, realizing as she said it that the term should have been "had," not "has."

Jeremiah Roberts, who had also been on the three previous voyages, nodded. "Yeah. I think there's a child as well. And parents. In Boston."

"Damn," Anne repeated. "Can we find out? I want to help."

Jeremiah shrugged. "Yeah, probably. I think he has an uncle in Hampton."

"Would you check for me when we get in? And let me know?" She could feel all the eyes on the room in her.

"If we make it," Jeremiah said, finally looking at her.

Anne held his gaze. She was as unhappy about it as they, but she was the captain and had no time to mourn. He nodded slightly, acknowledging her concern. "Thank you," she said, stepping over the bench.

"Those draining the Hold will need help. It's flooded, as ye probably are aware, and the people are terrified." The men looked up. "Rightfully so," she added. No one spoke, so Anne continued. "Break into groups of three so ye can spell the men down there. The slaves are doing the pumping. Send Mr. Potter down if he doesn't have someone supervising. And to help if it goes badly."

Heads bobbed assent and the room filled with murmuring that Anne simply didn't have time for. "Another ration of grog when ye hear the eight bells – at four o'clock." She started to leave, then turned back. "You did the best you could out there. The ship's safe and at least a good number of the slaves."

CHAPTER TWENTY-FOUR

2 September 1730 - Little Sound, Grand Cayman Island

The wind and high seas buffeted the ship through the day and into the night. About three o'clock in the morning, Anne woke to relative quiet. She held her breath, listening. *The storm's passed. And so has my damned headache. Thank god.*

Pulling on clothes, she left the cabin and found her way up to the deck. The rain continued, but it wasn't slashing and it wasn't flying sideways any more. She trudged forward where she found Thompson peering into the darkness. Looking up, she could see a few stars. *A happy sight, that one.*

As they watched, the Carpenter appeared. Anne greeted him. "How bad is it?" she asked.

"Hold's a mess. Water pulled some of the bunks down. Found a fracture below the water line. We're fixin' it." He looked up at the masts. Two spars dangled, broken but trapped in lines as they fell. "Well, we won't have too much trouble gettin' those fixed, Cap'n," he said. "But the riggin'll take a while. We can get started soon as 'tis light."

Anne thanked him. "Mr. Thompson," she said, "as soon as ye can, plot us a course out of here."

Thompson responded with a huge yawn. "Since I know where we

are, or at least once I verify where we are, won't be too hard. What we don't want to do is run into the bloody hurricane farther north."

Anne agreed.

Thompson went on, "But since we have no way of knowing whether it will turn or no, I'll chart the straightest line."

"All right," Anne told him. "We'll get underway as soon as the rigging's fixed and the Hold's stabilized." She headed back to the hatch and slid down the stairs. There, she found two of the new crewmen, Timothy Kensington and Lackland Moreton, standing guard, both asleep on their feet. When she stomped a boot, they jumped in unison, eyes flying open. "All well?" she asked.

"Aye, aye Captain," Willie answered immediately.

Lackland looked at her a bit sheepishly. "At least we ain't heard to the contrary," he added.

"Good. Who's down working with them?" she asked.

"The Second Mate's been organizing the bilge crew," Willie said, rubbing his eyes.

"All right. I'll find you replacements soon as I can," Anne told them. The two boys thanked her with a knuckle to the forehead.

Anne pushed past them and into the Hold. Someone had placed candles in the lanterns and lit them. Although the scene was not as awful as the afternoon before, she could see the damage to the room. The water line had dropped to about a foot and the swaying of the ship had stabilized. People lay piled on hammocks and on the upper bunks. Several men sat at the table, their heads in their hands. Children whimpered, cried or screamed as mothers tried to soothe them. Everyone looked exhausted.

Anne walked over to the table and sat down. "Have ye had food?" she asked. Several heads slowly lifted. Grim faces nodded affirmatively. "Good." The man across from her had tears streaming down his face although he wasn't making a sound. She reached out to touch his hand but he pulled it back and his eyes went feral. "I am so sorry," she muttered, chastened by his look.

He held her gaze for another moment then lowered his head back into his hands.

"We did what we could," Anne said. Guilt and horror began to overwhelm her, so she stood up. Moving around the room, she spoke to as many people as she could and to the men pumping the bilge. "The worst is over," she assured them. They didn't look like it mattered to them at this point.

Making her way around the Hold, she climbed back up the stairs and headed for the Galley. "Mr. Wilberforce," she said, seeing the Cook/Surgeon standing over a table sewing up a gash in a black man's leg.

He looked up, nodded and then went back to work. Anne watched, impressed as always by his skill. The patient grimaced but didn't cry out. When Wilberforce was done stitching and had bandaged the wound, he handed the man a tankard. "Rum," he said. "'Twill help the pain a bit." The man downed the large mug in one long drink. One of the kitchen helpers propped the man up as he limped back towards the hold.

"Many injuries?" Anne asked.

"Enough," Wilberforce answered.

Anne sat down in a chair next to the table. She looked up. "Do we know how many dead yet?"

"Six babes, thirty men and twenty-three women." He turned and rested his buttocks on the table. "And one seaman." His voice broke as he added, "We couldn't stop them, Captain. They panicked and we couldn't stop them. The Hold flooded fast. It was dark. Screaming. Running. Climbing over people." He took a deep breath. "The babies got trapped under the bunks and we couldn't find them. No light. Just dark fear."

Anne pushed back her own tears, nodding as Wilberforce spoke.

"Well." She gulped. "That means, by my reckoning, we have eighty-five souls left to deliver safely."

"Safely. To be enslaved." Wilberforce responded bitterly and as if he were talking through a fog.

"Yes. But they already were. At least the ones left are alive. Maybe they'll find a way to escape in the end. They've survived this." Anne sat numbly, unable to move.

Wilberforce looked down at her. "You've too much heart for a pirate, Anne Bonny that was," he said.

"Do I?" she asked. "Or am I just a coward? I could have just told Woolrich no and tried to buy him off."

"Did you have the funds to do that?" Wilberforce asked with surprise.

Anne hesitated. Then she sighed. "No, we didn't. We've the farm. But nothing we could sell to pay him."

"I don't think he would have taken it, even if you'd offered." Wilberforce added, staring at his cook stove.

"Why do ye say that, Mr. Wilberforce?" Anne asked him looking up.

"I looked into the bastard after we talked. He's not just in this for the free ship. Son of a bitch is after you. He's talked you up all over Williamsburg – Anne Bonny, I mean." Wilberforce put his hand on her shoulder. "There's no way you could have gotten away from him besides this.

"Did you know his wife and son died from a fever he's sure was brought to Jamaica by pirates. And you're about the only pirate left for his revenge."

"I knew that He told me when I was in prison giving birth. But I wasn't even there." Anne protested.

"Doesn't matter. He's got his hand on your throat as he sees it, and he plans to squeeze the life out of you." Wilberforce put his arm around Anne. "I thought at this point ye should know. There'll be hell to pay with this lost cargo. God knows what he'll demand next but you'd best be ready."

Anne started to retch. Wilberforce found a bucket and let her fill it. Then he handed her a cloth to wipe her mouth and a glass of water to rise and spit.

"You need something to settle that stomach, Captain," Wilberforce announced. Anne sat, her head drooping over the putrid bucket. After a few moments, Wilberforce took it away and put down a bowl of broth and some hard tack.

Anne sniffed, wiped her nose and mouth and took a slurp. She waited. When nothing bad happened, she nibbled on the hard tack and took another spoonful of broth. Wilberforce dropped a mug next to her. The weak tea soothed her raw throat.

"Thanks to ye, Mr. Wilberforce. Ye'll save us all in the end." Anne told him. Wiping her face, she stood. "I'd best be going. Sun will be hitting the yardarm before too long. I hope." She gave Wilberforce a hug, a move that seemed to please him. "Be sure everyone's got something to eat who wants it. We'll sail as soon as we can."

"Aye, aye, Captain," Wilberforce said.

He watched her leave, shaking his head. Then he called his boys and started to pull potatoes and turnips out of bins.

CHAPTER TWENTY-FIVE

3 to 11 September 1730 - To Baltimore, Maryland

By dawn, the skies had cleared with only a few white clouds scuttling by. The winds had died almost completely. The Carpenter and the Riggers got the masts and lines straightened out so the *Betsy D* was able to sail out of Little Sound and away from Grand Cayman on the late afternoon tide. By then, no more standing water remained in the hold and the bedding on the bunks had been aired out and dried on deck. With fewer slaves, the survivors had more room, although none of them spoke of it. Most of the Galley's food had survived unspoiled and so the ship sailed north around Cuba and up the coast past St. Augustine and Charleston. Nine days later, three days past their scheduled arrival, they anchored off Baltimore.

Anne stepped off the jolly boat onto the dock wearing her captain's uniform and the powdered wig. A man dressed entirely in black but for a bright white shirt, stepped down to meet her. "You are Captain MacCormack of the *Betsy D*?" he asked.

"Yes, are you Mr. Johnson?" Anne responded.

"I am. Your paperwork?" As he reached for the papers Anne saw anger in his eyes. She held his glare. "Is there a problem, Mr. Johnson?" she asked.

"You are two days late, Captain," he answered.

"Three," she corrected him. "We survived a hurricane, Mr. Johnson. You're damned lucky we're here at all." She stood her ground without flinching.

His visage softened just slightly. "We heard there was a storm. But we thought you had left Jamaica in advance of it."

"We did. But not far enough."

He stared at her. She stared back, challenging him to say more. He coughed and stepped back. "Perhaps we could conduct our business at the tavern," he said.

"Perhaps we could. I could use a drink." She pushed past him up the dock. She'd dropped shipments in Baltimore before and knew exactly where the sailors hung out.

She walked to the Bos'un's Lament, then waited for Johnson to catch up. He was sputtering when he reached her.

"This is not a reputable tavern. I insist we go up to the King's Cavalry." He glared at Anne. She shook her head as she opened the door.

Inside it was dark, sweaty and loud – exactly what she wanted and needed to keep this transaction from the nosy ears of others. She went to a table at the back of the room next to the hearth.

Johnson followed her, muttering under his breath, which she ignored. "This is not a proper place," he hissed.

"Says you," she replied without looking at him. Her eyes ran around the room looking for anyone who might recognize her. Seeing none, she relaxed.

"Have a seat, Mr. Johnson. We can do our business here as well as anywhere."

Johnson gritted his teeth, sighed and sat down. He put his valise on the table. "I have all of the proper customs documents," he began.

"Do you? And do you have the proper payment?" Anne asked. She kept her own valise close by her side.

"Yes. Tobacco notes and notes of credit. As agreed to by Mr. ..." *He's trying to remember the alias.* "Pennington."

"Yes, Mr. Pennington it is, is it?" Anne echoed.

"Do you have the manifest?" Johnson asked again.

He's getting frustrated. Fine by me. He'll be a lot more than frustrated when he hears the news.

"The manifest?" he repeated through clenched teeth.

Anne dug into her valise and pulled out the paperwork which she slid across the table to him.

"This seems to be in order. 'One hundred and forty-four: seventy-two men, sixty-two women and ten children'." He folded the paper.

"There's a bit of a problem, though, Mr. Johnson," Anne began. "We ran into a hurricane."

Johnson's look froze. "Yes. You said that," he answered.

"We lost a rigger. Damned shame. He was a good man." Anne held Johnson's stare. Even in the darkness of the back corner, she could see him tense.

"And?" he asked again.

"Fifty-nine other human beings," she finished.

"Fifty-nine?" he blurted out too loudly. The room got quiet. He looked around wildly then ducked his head down until the room's conversations resumed.

"Yes, Mr. Johnson. Fifty-nine: thirty men, twenty-three women washed overboard. Six babies drowned in the Hold." She knew he could hear bitterness in her voice but she didn't care.

Johnson stared into the distance for a long time. *Figuring his losses. It's all coin to him. Bastard.*

"That changes things. I will have to recalculate payment." He looked at her warily, expecting an argument. He was disappointed.

"Yeah, I guess you would. Everyone'll stay on board while you do that, but we sail tomorrow so figure it out quick as possible. I'll meet you for supper at the King's Cavalry. Ye're paying. Six bells." She looked straight at him. "Seven o'clock to you."

186 - Carol Busby

Anne pushed the chair back and walked straight across the room and out the door.

On board, the crew switched off going ashore. Anne spent the day in her cabin, finishing up a report on the storm for the log. She told the crew to be ready to offload the cargo first thing in the morning. "They might as well have one more night with us. At least they're fed and not being beaten here."

At seven, she began to dress, putting on a fresh shirt, green silk breeches, a sleeveless, green silk embroidered waistcoat backed with worsted wool and a jacket with gold braiding. She adjusted the white wig on her head, making sure her hair was completely obscured or powdered. Out of her sea chest, she took a felted fur tricorn which she carefully perched on top. The small mirror on the wall reflected a well-dressed sea captain about to go out for the evening. *I do look good as a gentleman*, she thought.

On deck, the crew whistled and shouted as Anne strode to the larboard gangway. Before she stepped down into the jolly boat, she took off the hat and swept it across her body in an elaborate bow. Then she set the hat back on her wig and went down the ladder over the side.

At the King's Cavalry, she found Johnson sitting at a table in the middle of the room. She shook her head. *Doesn't want to face me in a corner, the coward.*

She approached and bowed. Johnson acknowledged with a returned bow, his face grim. Anne sat, placing her tricorn on an empty chair to her right.

"I had hoped to conclude our business before we ate. You are, again, late," he noted.

"Ship's business. Couldn't be helped," she replied.

Johnson pulled papers out of his valise. "The agreed to price was £100 for each adult man, £90 per woman, and £40 per child over the age of five." He looked up for Anne's approval.

Too bad none of your free babies survived, she thought.

"Those are the figures I was told," she responded.

"Do you have the current manifest?" he asked.

Anne hesitated, holding his gaze, then she reached into a pocket she had sewn inside the jacket and pulled out a paper with the current count of slaves on it. She handed it to him.

"Thank you," he said.

Johnson made some notes on a clean sheet of paper and then pushed it over to Anne.

She read the columns:

Men
42
£4200
Women
39
£3510
Children 5 to 15
3
£120
Babies
1
£0
Total
85
£7830

He's lost almost £5000, she realized.

"That seems correct, Mr. Johnson. When may I expect payment?" She belched and drank down a glass of water.

The look of disgust on his face pleased Anne.

"I will make the count at the unloading tomorrow and will present the tobacco and credit notes as soon as all are accounted for." He looked to her with a raised eyebrow.

"Satisfactory," she said. "We unload at nine o'clock, per the Harbormaster."

"Good," Johnson responded. He rose.

"You know this is blood money," Anne said, watching his face. "Money for the buying and selling of human beings. Blood money, pure and simple. I'm doing it because I was caught in a trap and I have chewed my leg off to get free of it." Johnson started to squirm and wouldn't look at her. "What's your excuse, Johnson?"

He collected his paperwork. He opened his mouth to say something but just as quickly closed it. Bowing to Captain MacCormack, Johnson left.

When she figured he was no longer nearby, Anne headed off to the Bos'un's Lament where she could find a dark corner and drink herself drunk without anyone bothering her.

CHAPTER TWENTY-SIX

12 - 16 September 1730 - Baltimore Harbor and Hampton, Virginia

It took two hours to unload the slaves, complete the paperwork and collect the payment from Johnson. By then the tide had begun to turn, so the crew hoisted anchor and sailed out of Baltimore Harbor. Once they had cleared the other ships, the rest of the sheets went up and the *Betsy D* sailed briskly south towards Virginia. Anne stood on the Quarterdeck, as she always did, watching Baltimore disappear. *A bad business concluded.* But she knew that it wasn't really concluded at all. There would still be hell to pay with Woolrich.

It was dark when the ship sailed into Hampton Harbor and anchored two days later. All hands were on deck to watch the town come into focus. When the anchor chain hit bottom, a huge cheer went up. Anne almost collapsed from relief at the end of this voyage, a feeling she had never had before. *It's always been a good thing getting home. But this time, it's damned good. If I was a praying woman, I'd be thanking the Lord.*

She sent the jolly boat ashore to request a time for the *Betsy D* to pull up to the dock to unload what remained onboard so that she could be fixed and fitted for her next trip, if any. She looked lovingly at the sleek lines of her ship. *Ye've been a good vessel, Betsy me girl. And I thank ye for that.*

The next evening, once the ship had been brought into dry dock and all arrangements made for her care, Anne, still dressed as Captain, gathered the crew at the King's Raven. Over a hearty supper and enough rum to render them all happy, she thanked them individually for sailing with her.

"Ye did what had to be done. And ye did it well and in as good spirits as could be expected. 'Twas an evil mission but we did the best we could with it." She raised her tankard. "To the *Betsy D* and to her crew, good and true." Glasses clinked all around.

Wilberforce stood and waved his hand for Anne to sit. "To the Captain. As brave a soul, and when possible, as kind a one, as I've ever had the privilege of sailing with." He raised his tankard then added, "And a damned fine sailor."

Tankards lifted, the sailors murmured agreement before downing their ale.

The crew ate and drank, and fondles the whores who came by, until they couldn't anymore. Some found places to sleep; others just curled up under the tables. The management of the King's Raven was used to that and Anne had made sure they were appropriately compensated. She took a room upstairs where she fell onto the bed and almost immediately into a fitful sleep filled with harsh dreams of black faces and roiling water.

The next morning, the crew lined up for pay. Anne thanked each one and passed along the share earned. She had cashed several of the tobacco notes in for Spanish reales to be sure they all got coin. Sylvanus approached her last.

She looked up, cocking her head to see all the way to his face. "Helmsman. The first in and the last off. As usual." She smiled at him fondly. "Have a seat."

He sat for a moment before speaking. "Cap'n," he said. "You did good. It be a bad situation. You should be proud."

His words touched her and Anne had to bite her lip to keep control of her emotions. "Thank 'e," she said. "Ye saved lives too, Mr. Sylvanus. We'd all be dead without ye." She put her hand over his on top of the table, a gesture that caused some attention from the other patrons but being mostly sailors themselves, they quickly looked away. The brotherhood kept secrets well.

"Here's your share and some more," she said, pushing a linen pouch across the table to him.

"Cap'n, I been talking w' Wilberforce. Your guy not gonna back off." He looked down at the pouch on the table.

Anne had been trying to forget her conversation with Wilberforce on that very topic. She took a deep breath then sighed, "No, probably not."

"'Specially when da cargo been lost," Sylvanus continued without looking up.

Anne peered at him curiously. "True. He'll be damned angry about that," she agreed.

"What you do when he say you got to be bring in second shipment?" Sylvanus finally looked her in the eyes.

Anne took in a deep breath. *What indeed?* She looked off towards the windows to the street. Men and women, well-dressed and poor, walked by, some holding their children's hands. Going about their ordinary business, their ordinary lives. She sighed.

"I won't do it," she replied.

Then Sylvanus smiled, his lips rising so slowly she almost didn't realize that's what he was doing.

"Ah, Cap'n, Wilberforce and me, we think you should go." He watched her surprised expression.

"You do?" she asked.

"Yes."

She stared at him trying to figure out what he was thinking. He and Wilberforce were as opposed to slavery as she was, and in similar danger. They were also as angry about losing both a crewman and almost half of the human beings they were transporting. She shook her head, at a loss.

"Why?" she asked.

"To crush devil. For good," Sylvanus declared.

Howard Wilberforce opened the tavern door and walked to their table. Sylvanus didn't react or take his eyes off Anne. *They planned this.*

Wilberforce sat down. "All square? Payments all made, Captain?"

"Yes, Mr. Wilberforce. All payments made. All square." She watched them exchange a conspiratorial glance.

"All right, ye two. What the hell are ye scheming?" Anne took a deep drink of rum and sat back to listen.

Two hours later, she looked from Wilberforce to Sylvanus and back again, shaking her head.

"Ye're either totally insane," she said, "or geniuses."

Wilberforce looked over his lifted tankard. "Both," he said.

"Both," Anne repeated. "Yeah, I think that's right."

She stared out the window at the sidewalk which had looked so inviting a few hours ago. But she didn't see the same scene now. Now she saw the privileged gentry – those who had good lives and never gave a moment's thought to those who didn't. And for whom black humans were property, not people.

"We'll need to tell the officers," she said, looking at the two men.

"We already sent that messenger of yours," Wilberforce said. "What's his name? Nathaniel?"

Anne nodded. She had noticed him sitting at the bar in the tavern earlier.

"He's collecting Mr. Thompson, Mr. Kilrun, Mr. Potter, Mr. Harkness and First Mate Jenkins. The rest of the crew only need to know that they'll be well paid. They should be here pretty soon." As if on cue, Phineas Thompson stepped through the door and made his way to the table. Within twenty minutes, the others had all gathered.

Anne, as Captain, explained the idea she had worked through with Wilberforce and Sylvanus. As had her own, their expressions moved from horror to astonishment to intrigue.

"Talk it over. I need the privy anyway. And if you prefer Mr. Wilberforce and Mr. Sylvanus to leave, they will seem to have the same need." She nodded at the two men and left.

After she'd been to the privy, she walked around town looking into lighted stores, a few of which were still open. When she figured enough time had passed, she went back to the King's Raven.

The men at the table were laughing and toasting and, as she walked in, broke into a sea shanty about a mermaid.

"Mr. Kilrun, ye've a great tenor. Ye should sing for us more often. Mr. Potter, however ..." She sat down.

The men quieted after a chuckle. Sailing Master Thompson spoke up. "If necessary, we're in."

"Good," Anne said. "Thank ye for yer compassion and bravery, and yer willingness to put this bullshit from Woolrich to an end. It will end. That much I will promise you."

Anne raised her tankard, and drained it. "I'm going to bed. I'm exhausted and we have a load of work to do. Ye all know how to get the ship together. Get as many of the same crew, but they must not know anything about this. They'll know soon enough when we have to tell them."

The men nodded.

"I'll head home tomorrow. Once I've contacted Woolrich, I'll send word. By Nathaniel. I trust him."

"He's a good lad," Wilberforce added.

"He is. Good night, friends," Anne said as she lifted the glass for the last gulp of brandy. "And if it happens, then to the success of our next voyage."

The others clanked glasses and stood with Anne. As she headed for the stairs to her chamber, she saw them all pour another round of brandy, laughing and joking.

When she had undressed and stowed the captain's clothes, she pulled out her women's traveling suit and organized her sea chest. She thought about being a captain. She may be able to run a ship as a man, but being a woman in the job could be lonely sometimes. She crawled into bed and as she fell asleep, her last thought was: *Tomorrow I'll be home.*

CHAPTER TWENTY-SEVEN

17 September 1730 - Great River Plantation

Joseph stepped forward to help Anne out. He took her hand as she stepped down then folded her into a crushing embrace.

"Thank god you're home and safe," he said, his voice husky. He pulled back, his arms still around her shoulders. "We heard about the hurricane."

"I am beyond happy to be home, my dearest husband. The voyage was harder than I could have imagined."

Joseph grimaced at her understatement. He was in Hampton when the news came in that a hurricane had hit Jamaica and a ship was lost. He waited another two days until word came in that it was the *Nuestra Señora de la Almudena* out of Panama that went down with the ex-Governor of the isthmus on board. When Stoutley told him about the storm, he collapsed into a chair, stunned.

Then he heard about the lost cargo, which he knew would have devastated Anne. He didn't mention it.

"Come inside and change into something more comfortable," Joseph said to Anne as the twins came tearing down the stairs to fling themselves on their mother.

"My angels," Anne said with joy. "How I have missed you."

"Maggie gots a cut, Mama," Lizzie informed her. Maggie held up her arm, pointing to a small scratch, smeared over with honey.

"She fell in da yard, Miz Anne. We take care of it." Anne gave Letty a big hug.

"Thank you, Letty," she said. Taking the girls by the hand, she walked up the porch steps into the house. She turned the girls over to Letty, saying to them, "I have to go change. Am I correct that your sister is upstairs?"

"Yeth, Mama. She's reading." Maggie rolled her eyes. "All the time."

"Don't sass, daughter," Anne told her, narrowing her eyes in warning. Maggie hung her head. Anne remembered her own stern mother. She picked the little girl up and hugged her. "Just be nice to your sister," she said. "It's harder on her when I leave." Maggie nodded. Anne kissed her forehead and put her back on the ground.

"Where's Joe?" she asked.

"He hoein', Miz Anne," Letty told her. "He's getting' to be a real good helper."

"Wonderful. We hope he'll take over the farm someday. Needs to learn how it works." Anne smiled.

"We'll get him, Mama," Maggie and Lizzie called out, jumping up and down until Anne, laughing, said, "All right. Bring him in. It's almost dinner time anyway." The two little girls ran off.

"Letty, tell Maria I'd like to have the whole family in for dinner today," she said.

Letty nodded and left for the kitchen.

Anne climbed the stairs to Carrie's room. *When will my child get over being angry with me?* She sighed. *And still one more damned trip.* She felt the weight of an almost unbearable sadness as she opened the door.

"Hello, my darling," she said far more cheerfully than she felt. Carrie could barely look at her. *What is she feeling?* Anne wondered. *Relief? Anger? Worry? All of them?*

She sat on the bed and put her arms around her daughter, folding the girl into her whole body and holding on tight. Carrie began to cry and sob. Anne held her until she was spent. Then Anne pulled off her neck kerchief and wiped her eldest child's face.

"You s-s-said you weren't going out again," Carrie stammered.

"I had not planned to, my dear. And I did so only because I had no choice."

"There's always a choice, Mama. You and Papa told me that." Carrie looked at her.

"No, my child. I wish that was true, but sometimes we must do things that we don't want to do because they are right or necessary. That's the choice – right or wrong, not whether to do something or not to do it."

Carrie thought for a moment. "You mean like having to wipe the dishes dry when they will dry by themselves?"

Anne kept a straight face. "Well, yes. But more like helping deliver a calf when the mother can't quite get it out."

Carrie nodded. "And making Ben marry Elzbah?"

Anne was taken aback. "What makes you think Ben didn't want to marry Elzbah?" she asked.

"He said he was giving up his freedom to marry her and make a good woman of her because it was the right thing to do." Carrie watched Anne with the intense seriousness of a seven-year-old.

"In a way, I guess. But Ben loves Elzbah and wants to have babies with her and the right way to do that is to get married." She looked at her daughter, amazed at the girl's perception. And the fact that she remembered the statement. *I shall have to be more careful of what I say in the future,* she thought.

"There are many bad things in the world, my darling. Few are worse than slavery. Our neighbors don't understand that and we can't convince them. They need to learn what is right. They would not let their workers marry. It's most important that we know the difference. And that we do the right thing. Letty, Maria, Angeline and the other men and women who work on the farm are not slaves. They're servants and field hands. But we have to be very quiet about that so that the neighbors don't misunderstand and get mad at us." She stroked Carrie's hair softly.

"I know that, Mama. That's why when Margaret Madison says Letty's a nigger slave, I just frown at her and walk away."

Anne's mouth dropped. It had never occurred to her that such conversations were going on. Margaret, Sally's second daughter, was only two years older than Carrie. She had not thought to hear such a thing out of her friend's daughter's mouth. She sighed. That was the world they lived in.

"Well done, Carrie. And if she says anything worse, come and let me know."

"I will, Mama." Carrie looked down at the quilt. "You're going away again, aren't you?" she asked without looking up.

"Yes, I'm afraid I may have to, my darling. Because I have a choice of good and evil and I have to choose good."

Carried nodded. "Is it slaves, Mama?" she asked, looking up.

Once more, Anne found herself astonished at the child's grasp of things. "Yes," she answered.

Carrie began to cry again. Anne held her face. "It will be for the good, my dearest girl. I can't tell you why right now but I will -- if we take the trip – upon my return. For now, you must trust me."

Carrie sat up, applying the neck kerchief to her face again. She gulped. "When?"

"I'm not sure. Probably within a month, maybe less." She knew that Carrie didn't really understand how long a month was, but that she would be aware that they would have some time.

"Good. I want to finish my sampler before you go. You can take it with you. For good luck." Carrie's wide blue eyes looked up at her mother.

"I'd be honored, my dear. Absolutely delighted." She kissed Carrie on the head, holding back tears. "Now, come help me change and we'll go down to dinner. I asked Letty to be sure everyone's together."

While Anne changed, she asked Carrie what had happened during her absence and how the other children had behaved. "They were not too bad," Carrie said diplomatically.

In the formal dining room that they had added with the funds from the last year's harvest, the Burleigh family sat down for dinner. Anne was always surprised at how much love she felt for those she had to leave too often and too soon. She found she had little appetite, preferring to watch them and listen to their easy banter. *I want this all the time*, she thought. *I don't want to be the returning guest any more.*

When Maria had cleared away the dishes, Letty came in to collect the children, leaving Joseph and Anne alone in the room. They sipped cider, simply enjoying being in the same place.

Finally, Anne spoke, softly. "It's not likely over," she said.

Joseph leaned back in his chair. "No," he replied. "He won't let go."

"No, not yet."

"Ever?" he asked.

"Maybe," she paused then sighed. "We can try to force the issue if necessary."

He watched Anne as she folded and refolded the napkin spread out in front of her. After a few minutes, he spoke. "You have a plan," he stated.

She looked up. "We do," she said.

"We?"

"Sylvanus and Wilberforce came to me. Last night. They know he won't back off too, especially after losing almost half the cargo." Anne folded the napkin one last time and set it aside.

"Let us walk," she suggested.

Joseph nodded. "Do let's," he agreed.

As they strolled around the grounds, Joseph showed her the stacks of harvested tobacco, corn and hemp, their newest crop. There was a foal in the pen, her mare Rover having given birth while she was gone. The chickens had been terrorized by a fox, so Caesar built a stronger fence around the coop. The farm prospered.

Anne told him the plan. "I won't lose you just for revenge," he told her. She could feel the worry in his voice.

"You won't," she said. "I have the best crew on the seas. And the most loyal. And they all have a stake in this. Woolrich could get all their names from Mayfield, probably already has, and they know it." She stooped to pick some Slender Gerardia which was blooming late this year. She loved the small, purple blossoms.

"It's the only way to best him, Joseph. At least that any of us could come up with."

"I can see that," he said, sighing. "He will, of course, press charges when you return."

"Yes, but we have a good chance to assure his failure. You have his story. We know Mayfield's story. And we know who he's likely to approach to identify me. There are only two or three men not hanged who would be able to. And they will take money from him and then deny me. Anyone else will have been bribed. We can cover that or let the fear of the courtroom oath do the work. Wilberforce and Potter spoke to those they could find. Several had already been approached."

She pulled him close and kissed him hard on the lips. "It's our only hope, so let's go at it as carefully as possible," she said.

Joseph nodded. "For now, let's go home and to bed."

Anne smiled. "My thoughts exactly."

CHAPTER TWENTY-EIGHT

15 September 1730 - Williamsburg, Virginia

The dining room at Marot's Ordinary was almost empty, which was not surprising since it was three in the afternoon. Anne and Joseph drank from a pitcher of beer as they waited for Woolrich to show up.

"Why am I not at all surprised that he's late?" Anne asked with sarcasm.

Joseph shrugged. "Did you expect different?" he asked.

"Absolutely not. Here's to his predictability," she lifted her tankard and clinked it on Joseph's. Their appointment had been set for two-thirty.

Finally, a bulky figure appeared in the doorway. The afternoon gloom hid his features, but they both knew it was Woolrich. He stalked into the room and sat in the chair they had left pulled out for him.

"Good afternoon, Mister and Mistress Burleigh," he said with a formality they both knew was utterly without respect.

Joseph looked up from his tankard. "Woolrich," he acknowledged.

"Have you the manifest?" Woolrich asked, oozing condescension.

Anne pushed the paper across the table. As he read it, his face went from condescension to fury.

"You lost half the cargo?" he roared. The two other drinkers in the room looked up sharply then, just as quickly, back down at their table.

"Well, strictly speaking, they aren't lost. I know where they are: at the bottom of the sea," Anne responded. "As is one of my riggers."

Woolrich glared at her. "And you think this a matter of jest?" he asked.

"Do you see me smiling? He was a valuable crewman," she said, holding his fierce gaze.

Joseph leaned over, waving his hand. "We are aware that not all of the ... cargo..." he put heavy emphasis on the word, "made it to Baltimore. But it was an act of nature. The Captain," he added, "managed to save the ship, the rest of the crew, and over half of the slaves."

"Over half," said Woolrich said. "And I am supposed to applaud this loss?"
"You should applaud that not all were lost," she responded.

Woolrich almost boiled over, but after taking a long, deep breath, he looked from Anne to Joseph and back again.

"You owe me another shipment," he stated flatly. Anne looked at Joseph with a raised eyebrow. This was precisely the response they had expected.

"We had an agreement – one shipment," she responded without emotion.

That seemed to surprise him, but Woolrich did not retreat. "Yes, one shipment of almost 150 slaves. Your delivery was fifty-nine parcels short."

Anne's eyes narrowed at the use of "parcels" but she maintained control.

"And?" she countered.

"You owe me either monetary compensation or another shipment," he said.

"Do I?" she asked coldly.

"Yes. And there will be consequences if I am not reimbursed," he snarled, sitting back in the chair.

Anne and Joseph considered his fury calmly, which infuriated Woolrich even more. His triumphant expression moved back to hostility.

Even though they found themselves exactly where they expected to be, they recognized it for what it was – a crossroads. One road led to a dangerous journey, another interaction with slavery, and a delay in any chance of Anne remaining at home for good, but had the potential of ruining Woolrich. The other guaranteed an indictment against Anne for which Woolrich held too many of the best cards. That might be unavoidable either way, but if their plan worked, it would at least give them more time to marshal their forces if some sort of indictment were forthcoming.

"May we have a moment, Sir Jonathan?" Anne asked.

The Baronet's expression indicated his belief that he had them. "Of course," he replied, gathering his bulk and moving to a distant table where he hailed a waiter to bring him a glass of wine.

Anne moved so that he could see neither of them. "This is our last chance to back out, Joseph. Are we sure we want to go through with it?"

Joseph covered Anne's hand with his. "It is indeed a risk. You could happen upon another hurricane. The season is still upon us." Anne nodded. "And there are always accidents at sea. Something dreadful could happen to you." Anne nodded again.

"On the other hand," Joseph continued, "if you don't, he will hound us. And even though we have evidence to discredit him and call his integrity into question, he remains a Baronet. And Mayfield is still the son of an Earl. We don't like it, but they have privileges and are given leeway that we ordinary folk are not."

"And," Anne added, "our witnesses are pirates and smugglers and may be looked upon with skepticism by a court."

"We also have the vicar," Joseph added.

"Yes, I'm sure the vicar will testify. But the plan will buy us time to strengthen our case against Woolrich. We haven't the money to compensate him and I wouldn't even if we did."

"True," Joseph agreed.

They stared at each other for a moment. Then Anne leaned over and kissed her husband tenderly on the cheek. "And with fingers crossed and trust that the gods are with us, we could prevail."

"We'll need all the help we can get," Joseph said as he stood up. "Sir Jonathan," he called out.

The Baronet glanced over with studied casualness. "Have you decided?" he asked, bringing the glass of wine to his lips.

"We have," Joseph answered.

Woolrich walked over to the table and sat down again. "And?" he asked.

"One more," Anne said. "But only one. And you agree never to bother us again."

Woolrich smiled benevolently. "Of course," he agreed. "Same terms, without the problem of Sheriff Starke?"

Anne sat back. "Not quite," she said. "I will need one-quarter of the sale price plus one hundred Spanish reales up front for repairs to the *Betsy D.*" She kept her gaze on Woolrich.

He considered, returning her stare. Finally, having done the calculations in his head, he nodded. "Agreed. But I will pay the money directly to the shipwright. In Hampton, I presume?"

"Agreed," she said, looking at Joseph. Woolrich would assume that he had the final say. He nodded.

"The repairs should be completed within a week. It may take another fortnight or so to gather the crew and supplies. How many in this shipment?" she asked, looking at Woolrich with undisguised disgust.

"I will send instructions," he responded. "By the same courier." He looked to Joseph who nodded again.

Woolrich stood and bowed very slightly. "Always a pleasure working with you," he said as he started to leave.

Joseph stood and put a hand up. "One more thing, Sir Jonathan," he said. "We want a contract. A written contract."

"I'll have my solicitor draw one up," Woolrich said.

"No need," Joseph responded, pulling a sheaf of papers out of the valise he was carrying. "All the terms are here. Standard shipping contract with the proviso of repairs to the *Betsy D.*" He put it down on the table. "Read it if you wish. Sign on the last page. We have already signed to save time."

Woolrich stopped and looked at the paper. "You drew this up, did you?" he asked.

"Oh yes," Joseph lied. In fact, he had the best marine solicitor in Hampton draw it up with the provisions stating that the cargo belonged to the buyer upon embarkation. But they were gambling that Woolrich wouldn't want to spend a minute more with them than necessary and that he believed that Joseph would not be capable of drawing up a binding contract that would run to the Baronet's detriment.

Woolrich stooped over the table, looked at the couple briefly, then grabbed the quill and scribbled his name. He tossed the quill back at Joseph.

He bowed as slightly as possible. On his way out, he looked back, a greasy smile emanating from his lips. "Our friend Mayfield sends his regards." Laughing, Woolrich left the tavern.

Anne and Joseph sat quietly for a few minutes, draining the rest of the beer. Finally, Anne put down her tankard. "That went as expected," she said. "Let's hope the voyage does too."

CHAPTER TWENTY-NINE

1 - 4 October 1730 - Hampton, Virginia

Anne spent a few days working with Wilberforce and Sylvanus to recruit new seamen. She had just filled her roster when a tall shadow crossed the table.

"Sorry, mate, we're full up. Maybe next trip." She didn't even look up from the paperwork. When the man didn't move and didn't respond, she raised her eyes.

"Mayfield," she said dread filling her body. "We have a full crew."

He leaned over. "Sir Jonathan suggested that it would be a good idea for me to come along," he said in the high-pitched voice that sent shivers through her.

"He did, did he? Well, too bad Sir Jonathan ain't the captain of this vessel, ain't it?" Anne held his eyes as she spoke.

Mayfield sat down. Anne looked back at her papers.

"He insists I go to sea with you, especially after what happened the last time," he said.

"No," she said. She began to gather the papers and stuff them into her valise.

Mayfield reached across and slapped his hand down on the last of the contracts before she could sweep them into the valise. She looked up straight into his eyes. The noise of the hand slamming on the table had silenced the room.

"Take yer damned hand off my papers, Mayfield," Anne said, holding his stare.

Mayfield's hand didn't move. "Jonathan wants me on that ship."

Anne thought hard. This was something they had hoped wouldn't come to pass. *God knows what the bastard will do if I send Mayfield back.*

Although his haughty look made her want to slap him, she took a deep breath and said, "We have a Bos'un. You can come aboard but as an Able Bodied Seaman."

Mayfield frowned, then nodded. "So be it, as long as I'm on board. And don't think for a moment that I won't be watching."

"I have no doubt of yer abilities in that direction, Mayfield. It's yer ability to be a Seaman I question." Anne put a Seaman's contract in front of the Earl's son which he signed with ridiculous flair. "I'll see you on board," she added. *And in hell.*

The day of departure dawned clear, a hint of fall crispness chilling the air. The *Betsy D* awaited the morning tide to sail once more to Jamaica. Anne gathered the crew on deck.

"Gentlemen," she began. "As you know, we have agreed to return to Kingston, pick up another load of slaves, and bring them to Baltimore to be sold."

The men watched warily. The extra pay Anne had offered had enticed many to go out again. Others feared for their fate if Woolrich was not appeased.

Mayfield stood among the crew as their murmuring quieted and all hands once again focused on their Captain. Anne continued, "we're taking on another load of slaves for the same bastard as before and for the same reason." She looked straight at Mayfield when she said it. "But I promise you this will be the last trip. The very last time any of us will transport slaves together."

"We've set up in the Hold like before only with a few improvements we learned from the last time. And we'll be sure the people down there know what to do if we hit a storm.

"Henry Boots and Jimmy Jones will be in charge of the Hold as before. If ye have any business down there, ye're to run it past them. And if they ain't sure, they'll come directly to me. Is that clear?"

She looked out over the group as every man, even Mayfield, nodded. "We sail on the tide so be sure we're ready." She looked around. "Dismissed," she said. The men scattered, talking amongst themselves, and she watched for any obvious fear or anger. *So far, it looks like we done good with this crew*, she thought as she headed downstairs to her cabin.

Anne sat at her table, staring at the door, sipping Madeira. The bells told her that an hour had passed and the tide would soon turn. There was a knock on the door. She called out, "come."

Wilberforce stepped over the threshold. "You did good, Captain," he said. "They're all working like clockwork and no awkward questions – so far."

"Mayfield?" she asked.

"Even him. He's been up on the rigging already. I guess the Royal Navy trained him well before they threw him out."

"Good," Anne responded. "Then let's get the hell out to sea, Mr. Wilberforce."

Anne went looking for Boots and Jones. They'd done well supervising the slaves on the first voyage, and both had become skilled at working the lines and rigging. She found them in the Hold sanding a table Carpenter Kilrun had just finished.

"Mr. Boots. Mr. Jones. A word," she called from the far side of the room, well away from the ears of the Carpenter and anyone else. The two came over, wiping their hands on the aprons they wore.

"Yes, Captain?" they said in unison.

"I need ye to do something for me," Anne began. "Most of the crew are the same as sailed the last time. They know who I am and how I run a ship. But we have three new seamen, not counting May- field ..." she paused to spit. The Seamen followed suit. "I need ye to fill them in on the rules on board the *Betsy D*. And be sure they know that Mayfield ain't a friend. He's our worst enemy on board."

"Why would Mayfield bother with them?" Jimmy asked.

"Because he's spying for Woolrich. Will try to shock the crew so they'll testify."

"Testify?" Henry asked.

"I suspect Woolrich won't let us go. Not after all is said and done. I'm afraid this ain't going to end our dealings with Woolrich, boys. But it's okay. We will get through whatever happens," she assured them. "I need you keep an ear out for what mischief Mayfield's going to try. I know he'll work on the crew somehow."

"We will, Cap'n," Boots said. He and Jones each spit on a hand, as did Anne, and they shook hands.

Good boys, those two, she thought as she went up the ladder to the Quarterdeck.

CHAPTER THIRTY

12 October 1730 - Kingston, Jamaica

Anne sat in Josiah Smith's office while he read the paperwork from Woolrich/Pennington. Mayfield sat next to her. She had decided to just do it herself this time, but the wig that disguised her auburn hair itched and she suspected it might be housing lice. *Last time I have to wear this horror. I almost feel sorry for judges and gentlemen. Almost.*

Mayfield insisted on coming. "Quite frankly, my benefactor doesn't trust you," he told her.

"Given that he's buying these slaves under a false name, that's a bit ironic, ain't it?" Mayfield grunted.

"One hundred and forty-five adults, ten children under fifteen and five babies under the age of one year." Smith read the manifest. He shuffled through the rest of the papers.

"These appear to be in order, Captain MacCormack," Smith noted. He had been a bit unsettled when Anne showed up at his office with Mayfield in tow.

"Good. We've asked the Harbor Master for use of the wharf in the morning." The *Betsy D* had arrived the day before and the crew had spent the day making final preparations in the Hold, while Wilberforce arranged for food and water.

Wilberforce, Potter, Jenkins, Harkness and Sylvanus had gone ashore to seek old friends and former crew in the taverns and brothels that dominated the harbor area. This time their mission was to convince the sailors that should someone might approach them regarding the pirate Anne Bonny. If so, they were to agree to identify or otherwise incriminate her. They would be very well paid indeed to agree, but to deny it should they be called before a tribunal. The officers also planted a story about her being brought out of the prison, dead and covered with a shroud which wasn't too far from the truth. They found several men who had already been approached by Woolrich's people and gave them coin not to testify for him.

"I shall speak with the Harbor Master and have the cargo ready to board when your vessel docks." Smith ventured a smile, albeit a wary one.

Anne stood and bowed, feeling the wig slip a little. *Damn.* She reached up and straightened it as she straightened up. "Very good. Thank ye, Mr. Smith. Until next time."

She knew Smith now expected a steady customer. "It has been a pleasure, Captain," he replied with a slight bow of his own. "Lord Mayfield." He acknowledged him with a slightly lower bow. *Typical.*

Anne left the office, running quickly down the stairs and out into the hot and humid afternoon. Mayfield followed slowly. She glanced down at the men gathered in the courtyard of a tavern, longing to join them. Instead, she walked a fast pace to the jolly boat. Boots put knuckle to his forehead as she and Mayfield came aboard. *The easy part is done at least.*

Back on board, Anne went straight to her cabin, threw off the wig and scratched her head, tossing her hair out. She changed into sea breeches and a shirt, brushed her hair out and tied it with a black ribbon. Then she put on the slouch hat.

She found Thompson sitting in a shady spot, looking over charts. "How goes it Sailing Master?"

Thompson looked up. "Well, I think. The charts for the route are good. How was the inestimable Mr. Smith?"

Anne laughed. "Pompous and greedy bastard as always. When I mentioned maybe seeing him again, he almost started drooling."

Thompson nodded. "I'm not surprised," he said. "They only care about coin. And His Lordship?"

"Behaved himself, thank God."

Below decks, it took a moment for her eyes to adjust to the dim light. The portlights were open, but the lanterns had not been lit. She looked around approvingly. The bunks had been made up with mattresses. The hammocks were hung, and the huge canvas room divider attached through grommets to a line at the top of the room. It was pulled back, but would be easily brought forward to separate the two sides. They had made other improvements based on the last voyage as well. The bottom bunks were planked off. Anne had no intention of losing a single baby to drowning if the Hold flooded. They had also installed an additional table so there was one for each side of the canvas, additional privacy and separation if the passengers so desired.

After walking around the entire ship, Anne felt confident. *Everything ship shape. It'll need to be.*

Returning to her cabin, she stretched out on her bunk and quickly fell asleep.

Three hours later, she heard a commotion on deck. Yawning, she stretched and stood up, grabbing the slouch hat to protect against the late afternoon sun.

When she arrived on the Quarterdeck, she saw her officer corps reeling around the Quarterdeck, slapping each other on the back and laughing uproariously. *Good sign*, she thought.

"Mr. Wilberforce. Mr. Sylvanus. In my cabin."

The two men staggered over and leaned against the capstan. She could smell the rum on their breaths, but something about their drunkenness didn't ring quite true. *Just like Joseph. We're all actors.*

She led the way down to the cabin and locked the door once the two men were inside.

Wilberforce spoke quietly. "We've got to all of them, we think."

Sylvanus nodded. "It gonna cost. Woolrich already been so we know how much."

Anne brightened. "Well, that is good news. Not surprised he got here first but first doesn't always win the day. Good work. They won't tell him, will they?"

"No love lost with any of them and that bastard." Wilberforce belched. "That woman he killed was pretty popular. Gave freebies to the boys now and again."

Anne nodded. "Although I am sorry for her, I'm glad for us."

"Yep. Dey all likes her. She run good house. Clean." Sylvanus said.

"More importantly, Captain," Wilberforce added, "she was honest and straight with them. That buys a lot of loyalty among thieves and criminals. Which we will benefit from."

"Good work, both of you." Anne slapped them each on the back. "I'd offer you an extra ration of rum but ..." She let the sentence hang in the air.

They both feigned shock then laughed.

"I do have a nice bottle of brandy, though. Come by after supper." Anne watched thoughtfully as the two men staggered off, hanging onto each other, and singing:

> *Come all ye young fellows that follows the sea*
> *To me, way hey, blow the man down*
> *Now please pay attention and listen to me*
> *Give me some time to blow the man down*

CHAPTER THIRTY-ONE

12 October 1730 - Williamsburg, Virginia

Joseph folded up the message from the Lt. Governor. He turned to Maria, who had sent Samuel to bring him in from the fields to receive it.

"He's called another meeting on the Inspection Act," he said. Looking up at the sky, he shook his head. "If I didn't believe keeping the quality of our tobacco high was good for business, I'd be too damned sick of these meetings." He sighed. "Too late to leave tonight. I'll ride first thing in the morning."

Maria nodded and went back into the house. With the mistress gone, she was in charge of packing the valise.

At dinner, Joseph told the children he had to go to Williamsburg and would be gone for a few days.

"When's Mama coming back?" Joe asked. Joe was always restless when Anne was at sea. The nightmares had been particularly bad this time.

"In a fortnight, I think, son. Letty will take care of you," his father told him. "You'll be the man of the house. I will expect you to help the womenfolk." Maria set down a trencher of potatoes, cabbage, and pork as he said it. He could tell from her bemused expression that the womenfolk didn't, in her opinion, need any taking care of. He also knew that the servants loved the children as much as their parents, and that he was leaving them in excellent hands.

"Mama will be back when she's back, Joe." Carrie had taken this separation better than most of the ones preceding it.

I wonder what Anne said to her. Whatever it was, it has calmed her fears.

"Can we go to the fields while you're gone, Papa?" the twins asked in unison.

"Yes but only with Joe or one of the field hands. Ben will take care of you. You are not," he paused for emphasis, "to go into those fields on your own. They're black with soot and open to all the creatures who usually hide in the tobacco."

"Like snakes and moles," Joe sneered at them.

The twins looked solemn. "We won't go alone, Papa, we promise," Maggie said. Lizzie nodded.

"Good. Carrie," he turned to his oldest child, solemn as usual. "I will need you to keep an eye on the others. Help Letty with them. And help Maria in the kitchen."

"Angeline is showing me how to embroider a new kerchief for Mama," Carrie said. "I will work on that as well."

"Your mama will be pleased," said her father. "I know she keeps your sampler near her heart."

We will all be relieved when Anne is home for good. Pray that happens soon. He sighed.

After supper, he went out to the cabins to let the workers know he'd be gone. He found Caesar chopping wood near the outdoor kitchen. It had been rebuilt in brick and expanded after the fire. There was now a two-oven brick fireplace as well as a second hearth for boiling and stewing. The small Dutch oven they had used in the early days now resided in the cabin Maria shared with her husband John and Samuel. The couple had "married" in the eyes of the Great River Plantation, even though the union had no legal status. Maria was now pregnant with their first child and everyone on the plantation awaited the birth. Samuel was especially pleased at the idea of a brother or sister.

When Ben had married Elzbah, Caesar built them their own cabin. He lived in a third one with Ebo. And Charlie the stable boy lived in a room they had built in the barn. The previous year, they had planted more corn, both to feed everyone living there and for a cash crop, and hemp. To work those fields, they'd bought three new slaves: Tuesday, Pompey and James, all strong young men in their twenties. The new hands had been astonished to find they were not slaves and had remained happily in the Burleighs' employ. Lately Joseph had noticed Pompey walking with Angeline. *A good match*, he thought.

Caesar straightened up when he saw Joseph. As the oldest and most experienced, Caesar was the foreman; he knew what to do in every eventuality. Not only had Joseph come to rely on his experience and wisdom, so had all of the field hands. Even Maria listened to him.

"I saw da messenger Missr Joseph. You goin' Williamsburg?" Caesar rubbed the small of his back. His hair had turned fully gray over the years, but he still retained most of his strength.

"Yes. Gooch wants another meeting on the Tobacco Act." Joseph looked at the pile of firewood. "You could get one of the boys to do that, Caesar. Lot of work for a man your ..." He stopped when the black man gave him a questioning glare. "I just mean, my friend, that the younger men could do the work. Your duties as foreman take precedence."

"I likes choppin' wood, suh," Caesar responded, sitting on the stump he used to split the wood.

"All right," Joseph said. He knew that the time would come when he too would resent the implication that his powers were receding. "I'll be gone a few days. Not sure how long. Miz Anne is likely gone for another fortnight."

Caesar looked at Joseph for a moment. Then he nodded. "She be stayin' when she back?" he asked.

Joseph nodded. "I hope so," he replied. "And so does she."

"That good. Those youngsters need they mama."

"They do. We all do." He spent the next twenty minutes discussing what needed to be done on the plantation while he was gone. Fences needed mending. Two of the fields hadn't been burned yet. Maria needed help with preserves and laundry. Rebecca had candles to make.

Joseph shook hands with the foreman and then moved from cabin to cabin checking in with the servants. He was greeted warmly in each cabin after he knocked, which he did even when the door was open. He and Anne had agreed that mutual respect was the only way their experiment in having slaves who weren't slaves would work.

As he prepared to ride off, the children gathered around. He hugged each one and whispered into each ear that the child should be good and watch out for the others. He also slipped each one a hard candy he had been saving for such an occasion. They followed him out to the barn, a sight that warmed his heart and broke it simultaneously. *Oh I hate to leave them.*

Charlie had Charlemagne saddled by the time the trooping Burleigh family got to the barn. Joseph thanked the boy and turned to the children.

"You take care of each other. And of everyone who lives with us." He smiled at them. "And mind the servants." He got a lift from Charlie and settled onto the horse's back.

The children walked beside the horse, except Carrie, who hated watching her parents leave. He blew each one a kiss and trotted down the lane to the Williamsburg road.

When he checked into Marot's, a letter waited for him. *From Gooch*, he thought, recognizing the handwriting.

> **My dear Burleigh,**
> **Our meeting is set for tomorrow evening at 6**

pm. But some concerns have come to my attention. Can you meet me at the Palace for supper this evening at 6:30? I will expect you unless I hear otherwise.

 I am, dear Sir, &c
 William Gooch,
 Lt. Gov., Virginia Colony

Joseph's heart beat faster. He could guess the reason for concern. He had hoped it would lay low until after Anne was safely home.

He sat at a table and told the waiter to bring him the day's supper and a pitcher of cider. As he waited for the food, another member of the commission, James Bradley, the lawyer who had drafted the initial language of the Act, approached the table. "May I join you, Joseph?" he asked.

"Of course, James." Joseph waved his hand to the empty chair across the table.

They chatted about the weather, which had been fine this fall, their growing families, and the local gossip. Dinner came – a large meat pie which they shared as they chatted.

Finally, Bradley leaned back in his chair, belched loudly and took a deep breath. "There's talk, Joseph," he began.

Joseph forced himself to look innocent. "Talk?" he asked.

"About your wife, Anne." Bradley waited.

"My wife? What on earth do people have to talk about Anne?" Joseph asked, eyes wide.

"Well, there's a rumor…" Joseph's eyebrows raised. The men had just discussed the evil of gossip. "I know, Joseph, but it's serious enough that I think you should be aware." Bradley again waited. Joseph waved a hand, indicating he should continue.

"There's a gentleman," he paused.

Joseph's expression didn't change. "No gentleman indulges in idle gossip," Joseph said.

"This man states that he saw Anne in Jamaica in 1720 and that she was a, how shall I say it, a woman of disrepute."

Joseph laughed out loud. "Anne? The daughter of a planter and lawyer? Who was never out of South Carolina but once on a trip with her father, a fully respectable man, to Jamaica on business?"

"He says otherwise. And claims he witnessed a trial. He refuses to say more."

"There is no more," Joseph answered. "She was once in Jamaica with her father. I believe she was fifteen or sixteen at the time. So that would be ..." He stopped to count. "About 1716."

"Do you have any explanation for his allegations?" Bradley asked.

"Her hair." Joseph looked directly at him. "My wife's auburn hair makes her stand out. She had been mistaken, more than once, for another woman with similarly colored hair. 'Tis the only logical source of the confusion."

Bradley thought for a moment. "Yes, you may have something there. Red-haired women are rare enough to be noticeable and common enough to be mistaken." He nodded to himself. "I wanted to warn you that these vile stories have made their way to the Lt. Governor," he continued. "He thinks very highly of you and your wife. I'm sure he will want to warn you, as I have, that the rumors are being spread."

"Are they being believed? That is the real question." Joseph leaned over the table towards Bradley.

"Some. The man spreading them has some friends. But those who know you well are merely perplexed as to why he makes these claims." Bradley looked again to Joseph as if for further explanation.

He thought for a moment. Then he cocked his head as if an idea had just come to him. "Is it that Woolrich? The man here from Jamaica?"

Bradley smiled. "Yes. I thought you might guess that. 'Tis he indeed. And his friend, young Mayfield. That boy's trouble. I've heard from friends in the Royal Navy. They tossed him out for insubordination and sodomy. His father doesn't want him back so here he remains. Although he has not been in town for a bit. Woolrich is a friend of the father, or so I'm told."

"What has Mayfield to say? I don't think we've ever met him." Joseph feigned interest.

"He claims Anne is a sea captain and a smuggler." Bradley laughed as Joseph stared at him incredulously. "Absurd, I know," Bradley continued. "I don't think anyone believes him."

"Perhaps he says these things to curry favor with his benefactor, Woolrich?" Joseph suggested.

"Perhaps. Either way, be wary of them when you meet. For some reason, they seek to discredit your family." Bradley flipped open his pocket watch. "It's almost four. Time has flown pleasantly, my good friend. I must be off."

They shook, patted each other on the back, and Bradley left. The waiter came by. "More cider, Sir?" he asked.

"Small beer, please, Harry. A pitcher." Joseph needed to think before his meeting with the Lt. Governor and this was a good place as any to do it. But by the time the pitcher was gone, he had not formed any sort of plan, although he had done his best to analyze all the angles to the problem.

Joseph wandered up Duke of Gloucester Street towards the Capitol. Strolling the grounds, he admired not for the first time its unique H-shaped building. He could see the Governor's Palace off to the north and the College of William and Mary straight ahead. Men, women and children bustled between the shops and the taverns, entering and leaving their homes.

Home, thought Joseph. *I do love it. And Anne. And the children. And the servants. Whatever I tell Gooch has to be designed to save it. All of it.*

Promptly at six-thirty, Joseph approached the door to the Governor's Palace. The butler let him in and left to tell the Lt. Governor that his guest had arrived. The entry always impressed Joseph, as it was meant to, with its geometrically-arranged weapons – swords, knives, guns – that covered the walls. He tried to picture what it would take to remove them in the case they were needed. *You'd think they'd want these things easy to hand in the case of attack by Indians or, perhaps, by the Spanish or French.*

The butler reappeared and escorted Joseph into the Palace's parlor where he found Lt. Governor Gooch sitting comfortably before a fire sipping sherry. Gooch put down his glass and greeted Joseph warmly.

"Joseph, come in, come in. Always a pleasure. Thank you for coming this evening. Wife is out visiting friends. Leaped upon the opportunity to dine with you."

Joseph bowed. "Sir, it's an honor as always to be invited to your home."

"You've done good work on this bill. Insight from the fields, as it were. Much appreciated." The Lt. Governor smiled and waved Joseph to a chair.

"How goes the plantation?" he asked. "I am convinced, Sir, that the prices will continue high and likely go higher still with the protections afforded by this law."

Joseph nodded. The Tobacco Act of 1730 required that all tobacco shipments be inspected for quality before being shipped. "Yes. With the quality guaranteed to be high, all of the tobacco farmers will get top prices for their crops."

"Agreed, my friend."

A slave came in to announce dinner. Joseph was always impressed by the livery the house slaves wore in the Palace. The long frock coats and waistcoats were periwinkle blue, the collars and sleeves contrasted in a dark rust brown. The breeches matched the brown. Gold buttons finished off the presentation. Striking, but not ostentatious.

They moved into the dining room through the entry. Joseph told the Governor how impressive the collection of weapons was. "For a reason, friend. To intimidate. They will not get us without a fight."

Joseph laughed. "But who are 'they,' Sir?"

"Anyone who underestimates the power of the Crown."

Slaves brought in the soup course and poured a heavy red wine. Joseph recognized the latter.

"Thank you, Kinya," Gooch said to the wine pourer. He turned to Joseph. "Kinya has been with us since we came here. His daughter Eliza works in the kitchen. It is so valuable to have loyal, hard-working help."

Especially if they have no choice and don't get paid, Joseph mused. He thanked Kinya as well.

While the slaves were serving the soup, Gooch asked, "How is your Anne?"

Joseph's hesitated for a second. "She's well, thank you, Sir. And Rebecca?"

"Well also. Visiting Mistress Wells. On a church committee of some sort." He dipped his spoon again. Without looking up, he said, "Have heard Anne might not be, shall we say, what she seems."

Joseph looked up with surprise. "What on earth do you mean, Sir?"

In between spoonfuls of soup, he continued. "Been said that she lived in Jamaica. Might have been less than respectable." He looked up then. "Not that we believe it, dear Joseph."

"You shouldn't," Joseph responded. "My wife comes from a fine planter family in South Carolina. She has never lived in Jamaica." *That's true enough. She lived on board ships.*

"Ah, Thought I remembered a connection to our south. Her father?"

"Is a planter and a lawyer. He remains in South Carolina and has remarried since Anne's mother died." He leaned back in the chair, watching Gooch. "Her step-mother has been ill the last few years. Anne has gone several times to help them out."

"Interesting. Good woman to help her father and step-mother."

"If I may inquire, Sir, who provided this ... information?" He chose the word carefully. They weren't yet accusations.

Gooch looked up. He waved a hand. "Not important. Someone claims to have known her in Jamaica." Joseph could feel Gooch watching his expression.

"Good god." Joseph stroked his chin as if in deep thought. Finally, he said, "Woolrich? He is just here from the island, is he not? We met him at the ball in June. Why would he impugn my wife's reputation?" Joseph asked, sounding both confused and angry.

"No idea, Joseph. No truth to it, of course."

An awkward silence fell over the table as they ate until Joseph decided to break it.

"You know, Sir," he began, "Anne's unusual hair color has been known to confuse people."

The Lt. Governor looked up hopefully. "Indeed?"

"Yes, there are so few auburn-haired women that people tend to mistake them for one another. It has happened to Anne several times. I suppose they are drawn to the beauty of the color and so do not spend time on the face or other features." He smiled.

"Thank you, Joseph. Might be right about the hair. 'Tis the first thing I noticed when I met your Anne." He smiled at Joseph, who returned it.

The remainder of the evening passed with nothing more said about Anne or Woolrich. Joseph left the Palace with a sense that the danger was out in the open but, for the moment, at bay.

CHAPTER THIRTY-TWO

15 October 1730 - Caribbean Sea near Honduras

The voyage began well, with only a few squalls. They caught the westerlies away from Kingston, blowing them towards the coast of Honduras, owned by the Spanish, but coveted by the British government. But their luck ran out when they found themselves in the doldrums – hot, humid weather without a breath of wind.

The crew suffered in the shade by doing as little as possible, which was easy since they couldn't sail. The slaves went up on deck in shifts. Anne was standing on the Quarterdeck in a small spot of shade when Mayfield came at her.

"Captain, I was wondering," he began. Anne looked up.

"Yeah?" she asked.

"Why are we over here? Why did we go so far west instead of north? We can't be far from the Moskito Coast. That's not the best way to get the cargo to Baltimore."

"Learned navigation in the Navy before ye tried mutiny instead, did ye?" she asked, looking off to the unmoving horizon.

"Some. But it doesn't take much experience as a navigator to watch the sun rise and the stars come out. We are too far west and I want to know why," he growled.

Damn the winds. Where are ye?

"Ye may be right, Mr. Mayfield," she said deliberately not using "Lord." "We'll look into it straight away when there's something we can do about it." She looked up at him from under the wide brim of her hat, her face impassive.

He stared at her for a moment, then commanded, "Do that," and walked away. Anne spit at his retreating body.

Another two days passed. The water supply was getting low despite rationing. Small fights began to break out. On the afternoon of the third day, a group consisting of almost all the seamen, led by Mayfield, came up to the Quarterdeck where Anne, Wilberforce, Sylvanus and Potter were talking about the changes they hoped they were seeing in the skies.

"Captain," Mayfield said, "we want to know what the hell's going on. Why are we here instead of on the regular trade route to Baltimore?"

Anne looked at the other seamen who were grumbling and had sour faces. She called a crew meeting.

"Gentlemen," Anne began. "We're here because we have no wind to move, but the officers and I are in agreement that it's coming. We should be on our way as soon as tonight. The seas are rippling and the skies are favorable." She saw the hope in their faces. "I'm yer captain for a reason," she added. "And these men," she waved an arm to include the others, "are officers for a reason. We know the seas." By his face, Anne could tell that Mayfield was not done. "Ye're also wondering why we're so far west." The seamen looked at each other and nodded. *Mayfield has done his job well.*

"We were told about a shortcut. By reliable sources. Who seem not to be so reliable after all." The seamen shook their heads.

"Unfortunately, we now need to restock water and some food, so since we are this close to the Moskito Coast, that's where we'll head when the winds come up. We'll stay long enough to replenish what

Mr. Wilberforce," she gestured to the Cook, "needs then we'll proceed along a more established route."

"A shortcut?" Mayfield asked, his voice rumbling with sarcasm.

"I am still the Captain, Mr. Mayfield. And besides the fact that ye did not address me properly, I make the decisions. This ship is my responsibility as are the people – all the people – on board." She waited. Mayfield pursed his lips until they went white, but he didn't say anything. The rest of the crew shuffled in the unrelenting sun. "Cook will bring water to ye all and to the people in the Hold. Everyone gets an extra ration while we wait for the wind. Then I recommend ye find a shady place and stay there until we start moving."

The crew, all but Mayfield, saluted her with their knuckles and spread out to where there was shade.

"Have ye an additional question, Mr. Mayfield?" Anne asked him.

He paused for a long moment. He tossed his damp, lanky hair, and without a word or a salute, he stomped up to the bow of the ship and sat in the shadow of a pile of rigging that was being repaired.

CHAPTER THIRTY-THREE

16 October 1730 - Cape Camarón, Honduras

The next morning, the wind picked up and the *Betsy D* was making way. It took another day to reach the coast of Honduras – known as the Mosquito or Moskito Coast.

They anchored off shore in the evening. Anne invited all of the officers to supper in her cabin. They all fit, barely.

"Mr. Sylvanus," Anne said, "Please tell the officers about the Moskitos Zambos." She turned to the other officers. "Mr. Sylvanus has lived with them and his family are currently in their care."

"Moskitos Zambos be descendants of escaped slaves who married wi' da native people. Dey have big camp near dis cape. Dey king called Jeremy. He a friend. Took in me and family when we escape from Barbados. I sent word ahead dat we be coming wi' a group of slaves who need help."

"Tomorrow, Mr. Sylvanus, take two or three of the boys with you and go ashore. Will the Zambos be nearby or will we have to wait for them?" Like all those who sailed the Caribbean, Anne was very aware of the Zambos' fierce reputation. They were aggressive and distrustful. They were known to undertake raids against neighboring local tribes and take captives as slaves or for sale as slaves to the British. The irony of this was not lost on Anne – or on Sylvanus. Without the

228 - Carol Busby

Helmsman, she would never have considered purposely sailing into their territory.

"Dey be near. Always watching," he said. Anne could feel his happiness at being close to a reunion with his family. It had been a year or more since he had seen them.

"Good. They won't attack if ye have other seamen with ye, will they?" she asked.

"No. Dey know me. But to be safe, best look like I captured da boys. That way dey not get the wrong idea." He said. "Dey don' trust white folk."

The officers hesitated, not wanting to offend the huge man, but when he grinned, they relaxed and laughed. "I would imagine not," said Anne.

"I want ye all with me when I talk to the slaves," she said. "Mr. Sylvanus, ye especially. With ye there, they are more likely to believe me. But before that, we need to inform the crew, with one major exception," she looked from face to face and they all nodded. Mr. Thompson would you please gather them on the Quarterdeck for me." Thompson nodded and left the room.

"Boots and Jones tell me the slaves are wary already. Happy with the conditions below but suspicious. Can't say as I blame 'em," Anne said.

"Mr. Wilberforce, have they been fed?"

"As we speak, Captain. A nice meal if I do say so myself," he smiled. "Same as ours."

"Hear, hear," called Potter.

"How long 'til the food's cleared out?" Anne asked.

"I'd guess another half hour. Give or take." Wilberforce popped a chunk of mango into his mouth.

"Second Mate, everything ship shape?"

"All tied down, anchored and secure, Captain," replied Harkness. "Mr. Potter's on duty."

"Good. Then let's finish the ale and go talk to the crew. After that, everyone to bed. We have a big day tomorrow. She raised her tankard. "To the *Betsy D* and her brave crew."

"Huzzah," called out the men as they clinked their tankards.

By the time Anne reached the Quarterdeck, accompanied by Potter and Harkness, Thompson was waiting with all the able bodied seamen. Except one.

"How did you lose him?" she whispered to the First Mate.

"Told him we were going to be passing out work duties for tomorrow," he whispered back.

Anne smiled. "Yes, that'd do it. Good work, Mr. Thompson."

She looked around at the assembled crew. Some, she knew, had figured out what they were doing. Most were simply curious. She took a deep breath and laid out the plan in full. She even told them that Mayfield must never find out what they were about and that she and the officers would take care of him. "Just be as natural as possible if you run into him," she added.

One of the crewman, a new man named Dabney, raised his hand. "This plan is devious at best and criminal at worst. I do like it, I admit, but what are your plans for Mayfield?"

Anne recognized him as having been recruited by the Earl's son as a spy, but that didn't bother her. She had asked around before she'd signed him up so she knew his heart was against slavery and that the plan would be something he'd approve of.

"We'll deal with him, Mr. Dabney. I know he has asked ye to spy on us." The rest of the crew looked at Dabney in surprise. He blushed bright red. "But if we are going to accomplish our goal, ye cannot say a word to Mayfield about any of this. Do you understand?"

Dabney looked around at the faces throwing daggers at him and gulped. "Yes, of course, Captain. You're in charge."

"Good. Then we'll have no problems with ye," Anne said. "Everyone go get some sleep except if ye're on duty in the Hold. A lot of work tomorrow." She looked around to see if anyone had any other questions, but no hands raised. "Dismissed."

The crew got up and moved as one down into the ship. They didn't talk or chat and their silence unnerved Anne a bit. *They're just shocked and trying to take it all in,* she told herself. *As long as they do what they're told tomorrow, all will go as planned.*

Early the next morning, the crew organized into parties to collect water, fruit and any meat they could find. The crew exempted Mayfield from this duty because, as they told him, they didn't think he'd do well at it.

"I grew up hunting," he protested, although without much vehemence.

"I'm sure if we had hounds to flush the iguanas from the bush, you'd be our man. However, this is a dirty, uncomfortable project and I cannot fathom that you really want to go over there," Wilberforce responded without even looking up at Mayfield.

Mayfield left without a word and went down to the seamen's quarters.

Anne came by and gave Wilberforce a questioning look. The Cook cocked his head towards the ladder down.

The crew gathered on the Quarterdeck. "First, ye should all eat. Cook has set food out near on the focs'le. When ye're done, ye have yer assignments whether to take supplies ashore or to seek out sources of food and water over there. Any questions?" Anne paused. No one responded. "There'll be rations of rum when we are all safely ashore and the ship is safely below the waterline. Dismissed."

The crew turned and headed up to the foc'sl while Anne and the officers remained behind.

Wilberforce stepped forward. "Mayfield," he said in a flat voice. It wasn't a question.

"We'll see to him when the rest of the crew are on their way ashore." Anne looked from man to man and saw no questions or confusion on any of their faces. "Quarterdeck as soon as whatever group you're supervising is away. For now, we need to eat too." She led the way to the table.

When all of the crew were ashore or on their way, the officers gathered on the Quarterdeck. "Anyone heard a peep from Mayfield?" Anne asked. They all shook their heads. "Good. So here's the plan." She set forth her plan to prevent Mayfield from leaving the ship and after some discussion, the group agreed on what was to be done.

Anne went to the wall next to her bed. She pulled up a loose plank in the floor and pulled out a velvet trimmed leather scabbard, gold pommel and the grip inlaid with precious gems. Mayfield had hidden it, but not well enough. Anne had seen him tuck it behind some barrels of corn. She had promptly taken it and hidden it under the floorboards. *Why he brought this, I'll never know.* Anne thought. *"Mutiny? Murder? He becomes captain?* It did look like a commander's sword.

Opening her door about a foot, she peered outside. Seeing the Bos'un outside the door, she softly called his name. Mr. Potter came over and she motioned him in. "Stay here and make sure no one else sees this," she said. The Bos'un's eyes widened at the elaborate scabbard, but he merely nodded, hid it under his coat and disappeared.

The crew had finished unloading supplies. They then joined Kilrun who was supervising the building of basic shelters for the slaves and sailors.

At three bells, one-thirty, the officers and crew gathered at the hatch to the hold. One by one, they descended into the ship. "Did you spice Mayfield's supper?" Anne asked the Cook. He nodded. No one would notice that the man was missing, since he refused to go near the Hold anyway.

Seamen Boots and Jones were already with the slaves, having gone ahead to light all of the lanterns. Anne stood on the table on the men's side of the Hold – the men to her left and the women to her right. The canvas divider had been pulled back. Babies cried and the ten young

232 - *Carol Busby*

children on board ran around, chased by their mothers. Despite these relatively homey surroundings, Anne could feel the tension.

"I want to tell ye first that ye have nothing to fear. The ship is in no danger. In fact, ye have probably realized that we are at anchor. The bay is calm and the weather fair. We don't expect a change at least for the next couple of days."

She had their full attention. "We are off the coast of Honduras. 'Tis a Spanish colony but this part of the coast is controlled by the Moskitos Zambos." She looked around. Only a few of the slaves seemed to recognize the name. She could tell which ones by the look of fear that crossed their faces. She waited while the English speakers translated.

"Our Helmsman, Mr. Sylvanus ..." She gestured towards him. "Has family in this area and knows the King. He has arranged for all of ye to go ashore and join with them. They were once slaves themselves, but escaped. They made families with the local tribes and now control the coast from here south for a long way." She had started to say to Nicaragua but realized that none of these slaves would likely know where that was.

She let that sink in, watching as the translators' took in the meaning of what she was saying. They turned then to translate to the rest of the group. Excited chat broke out.

Anne put up a hand and slowly the room went quiet again. "We will be joining ye on shore – the whole crew. The ship will go down so ye will be thought drowned. The Zambos should be here for ye soon. The Helmsman and the Zambos will take you inland to freedom." She waited for the translators.

"You will be free," she repeated. The translators gulped in unison then they translated. The entire room began to yell words that Anne could not understand. She looked at Sylvanus who was grinning.

He moved to the table. "Dey yes,' only in dey language."

"Oh good," Anne responded. She waited until the din had settled down and the translators were quiet again.

"We need yer help, though. Ye canna tell anyone who finds ye that we let ye go. Our safety and yers depend on it. Ye have to tell them the ship was attacked by the Spanish and then broke up in a storm but you survived. Will ye pledge to that?"

After the translators explained what was needed, the entire group rose as one. Sylvanus stepped forward, his hand over his heart. Every person in the group, including the small children, did the same. "On my honor," Sylvanus called out. The English speakers echoed him then called out words in the language the other slaves understood. The entire group repeated the oath.

"Good. And thank you. We hope this journey has been bearable, and we trust it will be the last undertaken without yer permission."

Boots and Jones shouted "huzzah" and the slaves joined in until the hold rang and echoed with happy voices.

"Have ye any questions?" she asked over the increasing din. When none spoke, she turned and looked to the officers who joined in the cheers. Then she raised her own fist and cried out, "Huzzah" herself, feeling at least as happy as they did. *We're all seeking freedom,* she thought. *And we all have a shot at it now.*

CHAPTER THIRTY-FOUR

17 October 1730 - Cape Camarón, Honduras

Anne watched the jolly boat and the dinghy being rowed back and forth between the shore and the ship. It was just dark and the last of their one hundred sixty passengers, no longer slaves, were on their way to shore. Sylvanus had spent the afternoon talking to each of them, getting names, places of origin. He had discovered several family units which were reunited and taken ashore together.

On the beach, the crew was busy as well. They chopped palm fronds to make shelters. The ones who had the skill, including several of the former slaves, showed the others how to weave roofs. One group spent the day chopping trees and erecting the trunks as poles to hold the roofs. They set the huts up as far from the water line as possible, but no less than ten feet from the edge of the forest. "Dey's critters in da bush you don't want be wandering in at night. Dat far out, not so many," Sylvanus had warned them.

The Cook commandeered the second jolly boat to bring the last of the provisions across. The officers would spend one more night aboard the *Betsy D* before she was scuttled the next day. The seamen would remain on shore with the slaves, watching over them and, if necessary, resolving disputes. Anne decided not to allow rum on shore until the entire ship was empty. *No sense encouraging trouble.*

Through her spyglass, Anne saw hammocks being hung under the huts and platforms being built from the bunks torn out of the hold. A lucky few would have mattresses. She had left it to the passengers to decide who slept where and on what. The seamen were happy with their hammocks which they were used to. Their sea bags and chests would go on the next trip once the freed slaves were all on shore.

What a scene, she thought, laughing at the children, let loose from the confines of the ship, running wildly up and down the beach. Mothers settled in, babes bound to their chests or nursing. She had to fight back tears – happy ones this time.

Potter came up to the Quarterdeck to join her. "How are things below?" she asked.

"Almost empty. Rather eerie, really." Potter watched the people on shore getting ready for a new life. "It's damned inspiring," he said.

"'Tis indeed, Bos'un." Anne handed him the spyglass which he looked through for a while.

"Where's Mr. Wilberforce?" she asked.

"Coming back." He handed her the glass which she put to her eye. She saw the bulky Cook in the inbound jolly boat just as it passed by the last group of men. The women and children had gone ashore first. Kilrun was with him.

"Good. As soon as possible, signal the officers ashore to return."

"Aye, aye, Captain," he replied, taking the spyglass which Anne offered him.

She went down to see the Hold for herself. *Never thought I'd be happy with an empty hold*, she thought. All the bunks and hammocks were gone, as were the lanterns. The tables had been dismantled and would also be taken ashore. The huge canvas had gone earlier to be transformed into a large tent for her use. There should be some benefits to being Captain, after all.

"Good job, boys," she told the seamen working on the table. It would be handy to have ashore. They might have to spend several days until the *Waverly* came by. It would give the men a place to eat, play cards, and pass the time. Her own work table was also being dismantled and would be taken to the tent.

In the Galley, she found the assistant cook preparing the evening meal: a fish stew. Harrison looked up from his chopping block full of onions and potatoes. "We caught a mess of snapper this morning. And we had some limes went a bit bad, but we're tossing the juice in," he said, knife in hand.

"Smells great, carry on," Anne encouraged him. She had put aside two bottles of good port knowing that would not be enough to render the officers incapacitated in the morning.

"Is someone cooking ashore?" she asked.

"Yeah, Cook is there and he's organized the women. Showed them the provisions and gave them some knives and spoons, and plates and bowls. They seemed to be pretty content."

"I can imagine," Anne commented.

Harrison put down the knife and wiped his hands on his apron. "You done a good thing, Captain. Might not get a chance to say it again so I'll say it now." He reached out a hand, a breach of discipline which Anne knew was heartfelt and spontaneous. She shook it.

"Ye as well. The whole crew in fact. I couldn't have done it without ye." Anne said.

She went back up top. The last passengers were unloading on the beach, greeted by Sylvanus who pointed them towards their assigned huts. Potter had disappeared, but then she spotted him near the bow signaling the officers ashore. *Damn I wish I hadn't given him my spyglass*, she thought, straining to see who was responding. Distant figures waved. She picked out Harkness and Thompson heading towards the water. Sylvanus was walking away with the last men, but he waved towards the ship to indicate he'd seen the flags. First Mate Jenkins was helping construct the canvas tent along with Kilrun. They hadn't seen the signal yet, but Boots had and was sprinting over to point it out to them.

Good, they'll be on board before dark. It was already four-thirty, the bell had rung while she was in the Galley.

She looked out to the beach again. Fires burned. Women carried aprons full of food back to huts. Several barrels of water had been positioned among the huts. *Not much more we can do tonight. I'll get reports. But it looks good,* she told herself.

The jolly boat carrying Wilberforce pulled up alongside. The Cook climbed up the larboard side to the deck. Anne went down to meet him.

"Report, Cook," she demanded.

"Food's ashore, Captain," he responded with a sweeping bow. "The ladies have pots, plates, cups, spoons and knives."

"Well done. Mr. Harrison's making a damned fine smelling stew, but I suspect he needs some kind of supervision, Mr. Wilberforce." Anne bowed to the Cook who returned the gesture and went below.

"Carpenter," she greeted Kilrun as he hopped onto the deck. "How goes construction?"

"Huts is up, many as we could manage. They'll have shade and some shelter if it rains. We expectin' any storms?" the carpenter asked.

"This time of year? Always, but nothing any time soon as far as we can tell." Anne pointed up to the cumulous clouds floating above them. Then she pointed to the sky above the island, facing west. "Red sky at night. Should be good weather."

"Since it may be awhile before rescue, I'd like to try to get better shelters built for the crew," he said.

"Excellent. Captain Stoutley is due in a few days, but we have no idea when the Zambos will come for the passengers." Anne said.

"Aye, aye. Got to check on the big tables. We'll get them taken apart and transported as soon as we can. They'll take a jolly boat each." Kilrun put a knuckle to his forehead and left.

Wilberforce reappeared. "Supper will be ready once everyone's back on board. Should I send Mr. Harrison to shore?"

Anne thought for a moment. "No, let him join us." Then she winked. "We'll need him to clean up."

Wilberforce laughed. "I'll make it seem an honor, Captain."

It took two trips in the dinghy to retrieve the officers. Potter and Jenkins came on the last one which they tied to the ship. The other boat had been secured on the other side. As each man disembarked, she told him to attend to supper in the officer's mess at six bells, seven o'clock.

"Mr. Sylvanus, would you come with me for a few minutes, please?" Anne asked. Sylvanus followed his captain towards the ship's bow. The eerie quiet was broken by the sound of snoring.

"Sounds like the Cook's dinner did its job." Anne commented. Sylvanus nodded.

They found Mayfield in the small "quarters" he had created for himself among extra spars, canvas, a mast and other replacement items necessary for any sailing ship.

Anne looked at Sylvanus. "You sure ye're fine by this, Mr. Sylvanus. You needn't be involved."

"I been lookin' for'ard to dis, Captain. Don't take it from me now." They watched Mayfield for a few minutes.

Anne rummaged among the canvas and pulled out a pillow and the elaborate sword which Potter had returned to her. She would leave the sword in the spare ropes curled around on the floor. She picked up the pillow, positioned it over Mayfield's face and brought it down, pressing as hard as she could. Sylvanus watched until Mayfield started to squirm. He held the body while the pillow did its work. Finally, when there was no more movement, Anne removed the pillow, put it carefully under his head, and checked his pulse. Sylvanus let go of his legs. For good measure, Anne clubbed him as hard as she could with a belaying pin. Blood began running down his face.

She nodded. Sylvanus picked up the rope with the sword tangled in it and put it over the body.

"If they find the ship," she began. Sylvanus nodded.

They headed upstairs to dress for the final farewell supper for the *Betsy D.*

CHAPTER THIRTY-FIVE

17 October 1730 - Moskito Coast, Honduras

Anne dressed in her embroidered waistcoat, jacket and silk breeches. She had tossed the wig into the water after they left Jamaica with no regrets. She brushed her hair until it shone and tied it back with a pink ribbon. Tonight she could be a female captain. *'Tis an occasion*, she told herself pulling down the jacket so it lay smoothly as it could on her woman's body. At the sound of the sixth bell, she left her quarters for the mess.

Even though they were smugglers by trade, the officers each had a "dress" uniform – some version of an outfit much like Anne's. Thompson's was dark blue with elaborate gold embroidery. Wilberforce's bulk was covered in pale yellow. His waistcoat and breeches were a matching green floral and lozenge silk with silver buttons. Potter opted for a dark, forest green with little embellishment. "I was brought up a Quaker," he had told Anne once when he caught her casting a curious eye over his suiting. Kilrun donned a black, voided silk velvet coat and twill breeches, also in black. Sylvanus's suit was the simplest of all – a plain white linen shirt covered by waistcoat, jacket and breeches of dark brown linen. Harkness's taste, however, outshone them all. His bright salmon voided silk velvet jacket was covered in gold buttons and braiding; his breeches were gold silk with birds embroidered on them.

Anne walked into this array of finery and stopped short. "Oh my," she sputtered. "I haven't seen this much elegance since the last Governor's Ball." She walked around the table taking in each man's outfit. It was the first time they had ever dressed up for her. She looked from one to the other with a bemused twinkle in her eyes. "You expected this, didn't you?" she finally asked.

The men nodded then bowed in unison.

"To quote the greatest of English queens, 'tis marvelous in our eyes,'" she said as she returned their bows.

Harrison appeared in the doorway carrying a bowl of the aromatic fish stew. Even the assistant cook had dressed in his best suit of clothing: all the pieces were deep gray and of worsted twill in perfect condition. "There is another bowl of stew and some fruits, so do not worry we might run out," he said. The officers broke into spontaneous applause. Harrison bowed and left.

Anne dished out the stew. The ravenous officers wasted no time or formality in digging in. Harrison came back shortly with another bowl and then again with a trencher piled with fruit and another with biscuits. On his last return, he brought in a huge blancmange which he set in the middle of the table. That stopped the meal as everyone "ooh'd" in appreciation.

"Well done, Mr. Wilberforce and Mr. Harrison. A last meal on board the *Betsy D* worthy of this venture of ours." Anne said.

Once they had finished dinner, Anne put out cigars and brought out the first bottle of port.

"Gentleman, tomorrow we begin a new and different adventure. One that will, with luck, provide us with true freedom from Woolrich and sufficient compensation to allow us to move on to whatever we want. As ye know, although the cargo belongs to Woolrich, the ship itself is insured, so when we return without her, we will be amply rewarded." She watched the men light the cigars. "Not by our shipper, of course." They all laughed.

"While we can and should enjoy this evening, as we will be well and truly stranded for an unknown amount of time, we must complete the plans to scuttle this lovely ship." Anne felt a twinge of sadness. The *Betsy D* had saved the plantation and provided her, and the men who sailed with her, a nice income for the last eight years. She was ready to move on, although she hadn't asked what the others would do. Because the ship had served them all well, scuttling her would be a bit like dispatching a member of the family. Nonetheless, it had to be done.

"Mr. Thompson, would you please review the plans?" The Second Mate outlined the plan to sink the ship with charges on board and cannon shooting each side.

"Does anyone have any comments on this? Or questions?" Anne waited.

"Will the jolly boats support the cannon?" Thompson asked finally.

"We brought them out in the jolly boats, Mr. Potter, so, yes, they will." Thompson smiled. "The cannon are not that large or heavy."

"Will the dozen balls suffice?" Jenkins asked.

"We believe so. We'd like her to go down as straight as possible so we'll shoot both sides simultaneously. I reviewed the procedure with a boatwright before we left, and his opinion was that it would suffice." He stopped at the look of alarm on the faces around him. "In confidence and under the guise of trying to understand what force might sink us?"

"Are we blaming this on a storm, Captain?" Harkness asked.

"Well, I had hoped to, but we been cursed with perfect weather," Anne said. "So, I think perhaps we ran into a Spanish buccaneer who wounded us before we got away. The ship went aground, then we were hit with lightning when a storm did come upon us." She looked around. The men nodded. "As for the slaves, well, some of them drowned when the ship went down. The rest ran into the jungle. We weren't able to catch any."

"Do you think he'll question why none of the crew were lost?" Harkness looked worried.

"We will have lost our Helmsman and Mayfield. Mr. Sylvanus will stay behind with his family. And Mr. Mayfield will not be joining us. As for the rest of us, we're experienced sailors and the slaves aren't."

The men remained thoughtful. Finally Wilberforce spoke up. "Helmsman, we shall miss you. You've done a most excellent job," he paused as a smile formed on his lips, "notwithstanding that the ship sank." Laughter filled the room.

"Well, the port is almost gone and we have a long day tomorrow," Anne said, standing and raising her glass. "To the *Betsy D,*" she toasted. The others stood and raised their glasses.

"To the *Betsy D,*" they repeated.

Anne downed her remaining port and slammed the glass onto the table. "And to bed," she said, bowing, adding to herself, *for the last time aboard my own ship.*

In her cabin, she took off her clothes and fell onto the bunk. *We have gone too far to change course now. God I hope it works.* She fell fast asleep.

CHAPTER THIRTY-SIX

The next morning, Boots and Jones each took a jolly boat and rowed to either side of the *Betsy D*. Anne had personally set the charges below with an extra-long fuse which she set on fire just before she jumped into the water and joined Boots in the jolly boat on the port side.

As soon as she heard the first explosion below decks, she yelled, "Fire when ready." Boots and Jones hit the ship with the cannon fire from both sides. As the *Betsy D* began to list to starboard. Jones rowed madly away behind her stern towards shore. The ship began to sink. Anne and Boots made it to shore where the Captain picked up her spyglass and watched her beloved ship go down. The crew had been given some rum and were celebrating around a bonfire with a few of the freed slaves joining in. Boots and Jones joined them.

Anne remained to watch. Seeing movement on deck, she adjusted the spyglass. To her horror, what she saw was Mayfield, panting, bloody and crawling among the fires and falling spars, lines and masts on the Quarterdeck. She gasped, adjusted the spyglass and looked again. Her heart skipped several beats. As she watched, Mayfield waved the sword and attempted to climb over the side just as the mainmast fell, crushing his legs. Although she couldn't hear over the noise of the ship blowing up, she saw that he was screaming. The ship continued almost straight down until only the tip of the mainmast showed above water. Then it too sank beneath the waves, and both the *Betsy D* and Mayfield were gone. *Typical, he tried to save the sword,* she thought. *For putting a useless symbol of wealth ahead of his own life, he deserved to die.* She lowered the spyglass and went to her tent.

The weather held dry and warm but not too hot. The open huts were comfortable. There was plenty to eat and drink. The crew gambled and chatted with each other and with the former slaves. Children ran wild on the beach. Wilberforce even managed to catch some crabs to throw into the stew.

Another day went by without incident, although Anne could feel tension rising. "Where are the Zambos?" she asked Sylvanus.

"Dey be here. Might be on raid or hunting. Not long," he assured her. "Dey know all goes on – fast."

He was correct. The Moskito Zambos showed up the next day, a mass of black and brown men carrying guns, swords, sticks, and knives. Sylvanus was in the woods with Wilberforce looking for edibles when Anne heard screams from down the beach. Before she could react, Thompson threw open the flap to her tent. "The Zambos are here and they're threatening the crew."

Damn, she thought, *I was afraid of that.*

"Where's Mr. Sylvanus?"

"In the woods somewhere. Looking for food." Thompson's eyes were wild with fear.

"Calm down, Mr. Thompson. Go see if you can find him. At any rate, he shouldn't be long."

"We could be dead before he comes back, Captain."

"Go, Mr. Thompson – NOW," Anne responded.

Putting on her slouch hat, Anne followed Thompson through the flap of the tent. Chaos greeted her. The Zambos were rounding up anyone white and holding them in a small area while trying to communicate with the slaves. Those who spoke English were trying to convince the warriors that the black people were not in danger and were, in fact, being freed by the white men. The Zambos held back, but continued to wave their guns and swords.

Anne walked far more calmly than she felt to the men interrogating the slaves. "I am the Captain here, gentlemen," she began, but before she could say more, two large men grabbed her by the arms and dragged her to where the rest of the crew was being held.

"We are freeing these people," Anne called out. She took deep breaths to calm herself. *Richard will be here soon.*

Once she was in the circle, she turned to the Bos'un. "Mr. Potter," she hissed. "Blow the Hail."

Potter froze, looking around at the men holding them penned. "They'll kill me," he stuttered

"Fine," Anne said, "then give the whistle to me." He moved closer to her and slipped it into her hand. She put it to her lips and blew six short, sharp, high-pitched notes. Dropping the whistle into the sand and stepping on it until it was fully buried, she looked around as if to find the source of the sound.

The Zambos also tried to find where the sound had come from. The groups on the beach quieted as the Zambos continued to argue with the slaves and threaten the crew.

After what seemed an eternity but was, in fact, only about ten minutes, Sylvanus emerged from the brush. Wilberforce and Thompson followed. The Helmsman called out a word Anne didn't recognize. The Zambos stopped in their tracks.

The ones guarding the crew looked suspiciously at the tall, black sailor. He glared at them as he waited for the rest to come over. Finally, one of them recognized him and they hugged.

As Anne and the crew watched, a conversation went on among the Zambos and Sylvanus. Wilberforce and Thompson joined the crew.

After fifteen minutes, Sylvanus came to the crew. "All well, Captain. Dey let you go now."

Sure enough, the Zambos guards backed away, heading over to where the slaves waited to begin their freedom. Ululations went up from the Africans. "Those good sounds. Happy," Sylvanus explained.

The Zambos worked with Sylvanus to organize the people into groups. The Helmsman remained until last to direct traffic as the groups moved off. As each passed the crew, they ran over and hugged and kissed their liberators, especially Anne, before disappearing into the bush. As the last group of ten people went past, Sylvanus came over and gave Anne a crushing hug. He held her hands in his. "You done good t'ing, Cap'n. Brave t'ing."

Anne thanked him, tears in her eyes. "We all deserve freedom," she told the big man.

"But we not all have chance to give it," he responded.

"Can ye get to Hampton some time round the end of the year?" she asked.

"I can."

"Good. I'll send word when we have pay," she said. *If I have to come back to Honduras, Sylvanus will get his share.*

Sylvanus held her hand for another moment, bowed, and turned to follow the last group away.

CHAPTER THIRTY-SEVEN

16 November 1730 - Cape Camarón, Honduras

Two weeks passed and the rescue ship had not arrived.

"Where the hell's Stoutley?" Jenkins asked Anne.

"I don't know, Mr. Jenkins. How could I?" Anne glared at him. "We gave him the time frame. Maybe he hit a storm." Anne had started to worry that Stoutley would not make it. They had agreed that he would "happen by" to rescue them around the third day but he was now almost two weeks overdue.

Potter, who stood next to Jenkins, spoke with more calm. "We are low on food, Captain. If we hadn't found the stream, we'd be out of water. And there's a storm coming."

Anne was aware of all of that. She had sent Wilberforce and Harrison out foraging several times with two seamen who claimed to know how to hunt. They brought back coconuts, mangoes and papayas, but no game, except a large iguana which they had barbecued, a meal no one wanted to repeat. Boots turned out to be quite a good fisherman, so they had eaten some snapper as well as horny lobsters and crab. *At least we have enough to survive – for a while*, she thought. The rum had long since run out. The morning sky had glowed a deep red. Now, in the middle of the afternoon, dark, towering clouds filled the skies.

To make matters worse, the mosquitos for which the Moskito

Coast was aptly named swarmed every evening. The men, and Anne, were covered with welts. Two of the seamen had come down with fever: one survived after several days of worry; the other was buried in the jungle.

"We're all fearful, gentlemen, but what can we do but wait?" Anne felt both helpless and responsible. "He assured us he would come," she insisted. "And Captain Stoutley is good for his word."

A huge thunderclap shook the air and the ground. The clouds piled up dark gray to black and the wind picked up. "Never even saw the lightning," Wilberforce said with a gulp.

"I suggest ye make sure everyone is inside a hut – with some food and water. If this goes on for a while, ye'll not want to come back out until it's over." Anne turned without waiting for affirmation and headed for her own tent. She had brought in a bucket of water as well as some coconuts and papaya that morning.

Inside, she sat at the table and thought through the consequences if Stoutley and the *Waverly* didn't show up. *We can survive for another week at least. If we eat the iguanas, longer. But the men are already restless and afraid, and another week will surely tip them over the edge.* She, like all those who put to sea, had witnessed the madness that came upon stranded, starving men. Murder and mayhem.

The wind doubled and the skies opened up. Lightning lit up the tent and the thunder that followed each strike came closer and closer until the light and sound occurred simultaneously. Rain fell in torrents. *Damned glad I put the bunk up off the sand. The hammocks will take care of the crew.* Rain poured down the sheets of canvas.

Over the din, she heard a shout. Opening the tent flap, she saw Harkness at water's edge jumping up and down and screaming, the rain gushing off his tricorn. "Ahoy. Ahoy," he shouted into the wind to a ship they could barely make out through the driving rain. No one on the ship could possibly have heard him.

The entire crew of the *Betsy D* joined him, including Anne, all jumping up and down, waving and screaming. *Damn the storm*, Anne thought. The ship going by didn't stop. It was rigged at full sail and sped past them almost before they had all gathered. When it disappeared, the crew went silent. The sound of rain beating on the sand continued. They turned, dripping, to Anne, disappointment, fear and anger in their eyes.

"My tent as soon as this damned storm is finished with us," she called out. She ran straight back to her quarters. *Oh, thank god, the Waverly. We are saved as long as they survive the storm*, she thought.

The storm raged over them for another two hours. She left watery footprints when she walked on the sand floor of the tent. She sat at the table, reading a book she had found at a store in Hampton called *Colonel Jack* by Daniel Defoe. Teaching Carrie to read had led to Anne's discovering that she loved books, too. She could identify with this story about an illegitimate child who turns to crime, marries multiple times and then resettles in Virginia. In fact, it was eerily familiar.

Late in the evening, Anne guessed around ten o'clock, the rain diminished. By midnight it had stopped. She waited, knowing the men would not be sleeping. There was a knock on the pole by the tent flap. "Come," she called out.

Wilberforce arrived first. "They'll be asking about a back-up plan," he said, seating himself on the bunk. *Where on earth did he find dry clothes?* "I heard some of the boys talking about it."

"Yes," she replied as she lit a second lantern.

The crew arrived in dribs and drabs. Anne offered them a seat, but, other than Wilberforce, they preferred to stand.

"Is everyone accounted for?" she asked, looking around.

Harkness counted the men and thinking for a moment to be certain, announced, "Aye, aye, Captain. All accounted for and present."

"Good. I suspect you are wondering whether I have a backup plan." Every eye remained on the Captain. "If absolutely necessary, we'll have to go find the Zambos, or let them find us."

The murmuring around the room indicated that the crew was not enamored of the plan.

"They'll kill us," Potter said.

"Maybe, but I think we can convince them not to until we find Mr. Sylvanus."

"But what good will they do us?" Boots asked. Others nodded agreement.

"They trade with British merchants. And they've been known to sell slaves in Jamaica. They can get us out of here to somewhere we can work our way home." The crew growled among themselves.

"Anyone got a better suggestion?" she challenged.

She let the men talk, although she noticed that Wilberforce, on the bunk behind her, was not taking part. She turned her chair to him. "You look like you are keeping a secret, Mr. Wilberforce."

"I believe you are keeping the same one, Captain," he replied.

He recognized the Waverly too, she realized.

Harkness spoke up. "It's a terrible plan, Captain, but we ain't got a better one." The crew mumbled agreement.

"I agree," Anne told them. "But, as it happens, I do have a better one."

The men stared at her, confused by this sudden change in direction.

"And that would be?" Harkness ventured.

"The *Waverly*," she said.

Although she had their full attention, Anne recognized that she would be unwise to string out the suspense for too long.

"You've never seen her, but I have. As has Mr. Wilberforce." She paused. The men were silent, watching her closely. "And that ship that went by us, gentlemen, was indeed the *Waverly*."

The men gasped and stared at her. Then smiles began to appear on faces, but were just as quickly lost. "But she went past," Jones said, a tremble in his voice.

"Aye, she did. I would have too," Anne responded. "The storm would likely have broken her up if she'd tried to get in." She turned to Thompson. "Surely Sailing Master, you agree?"

Thompson blushed. "I must confess I was not thinking that clearly. The hope of rescue overcame me."

Anne laughed. "As it did us all, myself included. But the fact is, that was the *Waverly* and god willing, she'll be back. I've no doubt she was watching for us and took note of where we are."

The men visibly relaxed.

"Then why did you tell us the alternate plan?" Potter whined.

"Just in case," Anne responded. "And because you wanted one."

"For now, gents, I suggest ye get some rest. I'd expect the ship here tomorrow or the day after at the latest – depends how far they were blown." She went around the room shaking hands with every member of the crew.

After they left, she picked up *Colonel Jack* again, this time reading with pleasure.

CHAPTER THIRTY-EIGHT

19 - 28 November 1730 - Moskito Coast to Hampton, Virginia

The crew of the *Betsy D* began to get restless again when the *Waverly* didn't show up the next day or the day after that.

I know Stoutley. If he can, he'll come, but I'll be feeling a sight better when his sails appear. Anne sent the crew back to their quarters.

Most of the men spent the days waiting at the water line, concerns about food supplies and back-up plans forgotten. Finally at dusk on the third day, Jenkins, with the spyglass, spotted sails.

"She's coming," he shouted. Those on the beach wrestled for the glass and everyone else, including Anne, came running. By the time they were fully assembled, the ship was easily visible.

Anne breathed a sigh of relief.

The ship dropped anchor not far from the remains of the *Betsy D*, which was visible from the top of the *Waverly's* mainmast. Cheers arose from the *Betsy D's* crew as the rescue ship came to a halt, dropped anchor and launched a jolly boat.

Captain Stoutley stepped off the boat first, a happy and relieved look covering his features. "We are here," he announced. A loud cheer went up from the crew.

Anne stepped forward. "Ye're a sight for sore eyes, Captain," she said as he enveloped her in a tight hug.

The crew of the jolly boat stepped on shore carrying bundles. Stoutley waved a hand at them. "We've brought you some dried meat," he said. "Unless you've developed a taste for iguana." He raised an eyebrow.

"We have not, thank ye. Had it once and that was enough," Anne rejoined.

For the next hour, Stoutley and Anne remained in her tent discussing the trip. He was astonished that Mayfield had come aboard. "Obviously ye had no choice, but the story changes now, doesn't it?" he said. "Mayfield went for the sword and was trapped?"

Anne nodded. "So sorry we're late. We got hung up in Providence. Rogers is in charge again and he's a suspicious bastard," Stoutley continued. "Wondered why we were departin' with such a small load of sugar. I had to convince him that we planned another stop or two to pick up some rum and slaves."

"Well, Captain, ye got here barely in time but barely is good enough. The men were starting to get a bit out of hand. I'm ... we're beyond grateful to have ye, even if late."

Stoutley smiled. "'Better late than never' as they say." He leaned over and squeezed Anne's hand on the table. "Ye know I'm fond o' ye, girl. Have been since we first met."

She squeezed back. "The feeling is mutual, Captain. Ye've been a good friend to us and we appreciate it more than we can ever repay."

Stoutley responded. "But ye'll try, will ye not?"

"Indeed we will. The insurance on the *Betsy D* will cover a lot of thanks."

"Ye got insurance on t' ship after the last sail?" Stoutley's mouth fell open slightly.

"Yes, Mayfield has enemies too, and one happens to be a Lloyd's partner." Anne winked. "The man's aunt was seduced and robbed by his Lordship – and left with a babe. He was happy to risk his reputation on this claim. Said he could find another job if need be.

The insurance is only on the ship, Stoutley, not on the cargo." Anne waited for the captain's reaction. "Woolrich signed our contract without reading it. So he doesn't know the cargo became his when we left Jamaica and is not our responsibility. He will have no right to compensation from me."

After a moment Stoutley started laughing so hard that he choked, and Anne had to get him a glass of the last of her Madeira to get him straight again.

"You are a wonder, my dear. An absolute wonder," he said, wiping his eyes.

"Not just me. Joseph found the man. I'm not me anymore without him."

Stoutly hugged her. "'Tis only true. Now let's go see what mischief's gone down while we've been gone."

The crew stacked everything they were taking with them into piles at the shoreline. The rest was being burned or buried in the jungle on the off chance someone came looking for the wreck site.

The *Waverly* had sent another jolly boat and a dinghy. The piles were quickly disappearing from the beach. Several shelters were aflame.

Anne and Stoutley made their way to the jolly boat where Wilberforce and Assistant Cook Harrison waited. "Who's left ashore?" Anne asked.

"Harkness, Boots and Jones," he responded

"Is there enough room to take all of us?" she asked.

"Close," Stoutley said, looking at Wilberforce's bulk and considering the addition of the other three men and the sea chest.

"'Tis all right," Anne said. "Come back for me. Captain should be the last rescued anyway." She turned back to where the tent had stood. It had been dismantled, tucked into the jungle and left for Sylvanus. Canvas was valuable.

When she grabbed her valise, she saw her book on the sand. She picked it up and brushed it off. *Well, Mr. Defoe, maybe ye'll make another book out of this adventure.* She put it in the valise.

Leaving the area for the last time, Anne walked out to the water line. Looking back, she watched the sun set. *Red sky at night. A good omen to get us home.*

The trip back to Hampton took a full week. The crew practiced their individual tales of hardship and harrowing experiences in losing the *Betsy D* until they all knew the stories and could answer any question put to them. They also memorized the story of Mayfield's misguided return to the ship to get his sword and his ultimate demise. "It's critical that everyone's in agreement," Anne told them. She helped the other officers drill the seamen. By the time they reached Hampton, she was confident that their stories would be believed.

She and Stoutley had spent every evening of the trip in his cabin talking over the next step in Anne's journey. Stoutley told her that when he was told about the rumors that Woolrich had uncovered something unsavory in Mistress Burleigh's past, he had scoffed to the gossips in her defense. "I brought the lass here from Carolina. Met her father. He's a respectable gentleman. And I know for a fact, she's been to the West Indies only once – with him on a business voyage."

As they pulled into the Hampton Roads on the morning tide of November twenty-sixth, a cheer went up from both crews. The day was fair and the seas calm. A light breeze assisted the tide in getting them into the harbor.

We can get ashore today, Anne thought. *There's a lot left to this journey, and I surely wouldn't mind getting it over with.*

The jolly boats started ferrying the crew to shore by four bells, two o'clock. Anne remained on board until all the men and their sea chests and bags were lined up on the dock where they were excitedly relating the tale of being chased and battered by a rogue Spanish ship, then grounding off Honduras where a storm had crashed into the ship which was hit repeatedly by lightning, until she caught fire and sank.

"We went ashore at the first strike," Thompson told a friend. "Managed to get our sea bags off but not much else."

Boots regaled other sailors with his stories of the horror of near starvation. "We had to eat them big lizards," he exclaimed. When the crowd made disgusted sounds, he added, proudly, "It weren't too bad, truth told."

Farther down the wharf, Potter described the slaves falling overboard in haste to escape the flames, and the arrival of the fierce Zambos, who took the rest of them away at gunpoint.

Word spread quickly around the port city that a shipwrecked crew had arrived and that the Helmsman and a seaman had died, the cargo lost. Then word flew around that young Lord Mayfield was not among the survivors. People flooded down to talk to the new celebrities. The crew reveled in the attention.

Anne, meanwhile, waited and watched from the focs'le until all of the crew and all of their bags and chests were ashore before she went to find Stoutley who was on the Quarterdeck. "Captain," she began. Stoutley gathered her in his arms in another tight hug.

"Captain," Anne exclaimed, looking around, aghast that they might have been observed.

Stoutley reassured her. "None o' my men are watching." They had been careful to treat Anne as a man throughout the trip. No one had been the wiser.

"Well, then," she began as she returned the hug. Then she reached out a hand. "Thank you," she said.

Stoutley squeezed her hand and then shook it. "It's been a real pleasure spending time with you, Captain," he told her.

They walked together to the ladder. A jolly boat waited in the water. Anne's eyes teared up. "Thank you, Bart," she said. "Until I see you again, Godspeed."

"And to you, Anne." She slipped over the side and sat in the boat watching Stoutley waving until they reached the dock.

Once there, she was mobbed by the frenzied crowd who shouted questions at her with rapid fire.

"Were you worried?" "Did you think you'd make it back?" "Did the Zambos frighten you?" "Did you really eat the big lizards?" "What happened to Lord Mayfield?"

Anne's heart raced. She wasn't used to the attention and the crowd began to frighten her. She also needed to get out of there before someone took a good look and realized she was a woman. *Wouldn't it be horrid if I made it this far only to be thrown off the dock by these idiots? Or discovered to be a woman?*

At that moment, the constable made an appearance, shooing away the crowds. He took Anne by the shoulder and eased her through the throng until it turned back to the more forthcoming crew members for information. Anne breathed a sigh of relief as they approached the King's Raven. She thanked him and sent him back to protect the crew.

"Captain MacCormack, welcome back." The owner, Mr. Rodgers, greeted Anne.

"Thank you, Mr. Rodgers. It's a relief to be back," she told him

Anne went to the bar where she found a messenger named Adam Darvin. Nicholas was not to be found so she engaged Darvin to take a message to the plantation that she had arrived safely in Hampton and awaited Samuel with the carriage.

When Anne finally climbed the stairs to the room, she found her chest had indeed been deposited therein. She sat on the bed, took a deep breath. As she thought, *"Step One is done,"* the strength, fear, hope and equanimity she had maintained throughout the trip abandoned her, and she found herself sobbing uncontrollably. After she regained control, she washed her face and let the waiter in with food and cider.

The next evening, Samuel arrived with the carriage. He found lodging among freed slaves so they didn't have to head out in the dark.

When morning broke, Samuel drove the carriage to the King's

Raven and waited for Anne at the door. She took bread and cheese from the innkeeper. Not daring to change into her women's clothes, she climbed in wearing her breeches and jacket.

At the plantation, she jumped out of the carriage and ran to Joseph. She hung onto him, panting to control herself and hold back the tears of joy and relief that threatened to escape.

Letty opened the door and the children, all four this time, came running. "Mama," they cried in unison. "You're home."

"Why are you dressed like that, Mama?" Carrie asked after the initial hugging had stopped.

Anne grinned at her daughter. "My clothing was stolen, Carrie. Can you imagine? I had to borrow these."

The twins hung onto her leg and Joe pulled on her arm. "Mama, I fell out the tree," he said, displaying a split lip. Anne looked at it and up at Joseph who shrugged.

"The doctor says it will heal fine," he told her.

"I am so very glad to be home," Anne told them all. "Let's go inside so I can change into my regular clothes."

After supper and with the children in bed, Anne and Joseph strolled around the yard, arm in arm.

"I was so afraid when you and Stoutley didn't come back on time," Joseph told her. "We had no news at all. No big storms and no word of anything that might have delayed your return."

"There was a storm – Stoutley got caught in it. The mosquitoes were fierce, and we had to eat an iguana. But we were lucky. Of the two men who came down with fever, only one died. And Mayfield, of course."

Joseph stopped and looked down at his wife in astonishment. "Mayfield?"

"He forced his way on. Woolrich's spy of course. I didn't have a choice. But the crew were warned, and the only time he questioned the route was when we hit the doldrums not too far off Honduras.

Then he asked why the hell we were so far west. I told him I'd been told about a shortcut that obviously wasn't a good one. He insisted we head north right away, but I told him truthfully that we needed supplies due to being unable to move for several days."

She paused. Joseph stood in front of her, worry on his features. "And then?" he asked.

"And then after the Spanish wounded the ship, she was struck repeatedly by lightning. The crew all made it ashore, but he insisted on going back on board to collect some fancy gold-handled heirloom sword that he'd hidden on board."

She saw the edges of Joseph's mouth begin to turn upward. "And despite our assuring him he would never make it off before the *Betsy D* sank, he went."

"And?" Joseph asked again.

"We thought we'd tucked him into bed below decks, but as she sank, I happened to see him crawling on the deck holding the damned sword until the mainmast fell on his legs. Moments later, he and the boat disappeared for good."

Joseph thought for a few minutes. "Stupid man," he said. He took her in his arms. "This is not over, but we've made it this far. We'll finish the deal safely. I feel it in my bones."

"It's my last trip for sure. No more *Betsy D*." Anne said.

She could see tears in his eyes. "Thank God it's the last, Anne. I couldn't take another trip."

Anne stroked his cheek. "Neither could I, my love. Neither could I."

They resumed the walk in silence. Finally, Anne asked, "When shall we face Woolrich?"

"Gooch sent a note that I need to return for yet another meeting in two days' time. We'll go together and get it over with." Joseph looked at Anne. "Are you up to it?"

Anne nodded. "Yes. In fact, I want it over with – the sooner the better."

"Good. Yes, the sooner we face what comes next, the sooner we can be free of it."

"He won't be happy," Anne said.

Joseph laughed. "That's an understatement, my dear. He wouldn't have been happy to have lost the cargo. To lose Mayfield as well is an even higher level of unhappy. But he hasn't all the cards any more, has he?" Joseph said.

Anne agreed. "Not all, but some. Nonetheless, it's our game now, not his. So we will deal the cards and see what happens. We have prepared all we can."

"We have indeed." Joseph directed their steps towards the house. "But for tonight, no thoughts whatsoever of Sir Jonathan Woolrich. Only of Anne and Joseph Burleigh, so happy and relieved that you are home."

CHAPTER THIRTY-NINE

3 December 1730 - Williamsburg, Virginia

The carriage pulled up to Thomas Cavanaugh's Boarding House in the middle of the afternoon. Although the skies were bright blue, there was a distinctive late fall crispness to the air that Anne loved. She took a deep breath as she and Joseph made their way into the house. Samuel and Angeline drove off to store the vehicle. They would stay in the slave quarters.

"Mr. and Mistress Burleigh, always a pleasure," the owner greeted them. He bowed very slightly.

"And our pleasure to return, Mr. Cavanaugh." Joseph returned the bow.

"I have a letter for you," Cavanaugh said, looking under the check-in table. "It's right here somewhere." He shuffled papers until he found the right one. "Ah, here 'tis. From the Baronet."

They looked at each other. *How did he know they would be staying at this boarding house?*

Joseph took the letter. "I wonder," he asked, "when this was delivered."

Cavanaugh didn't hesitate. "This morning. The messenger told me it was the Baronet's understanding that you would be in today which I confirmed." He bowed, believing that he had served his guests well.

"Ah. Very good. Thank you, Mr. Cavanaugh." Joseph kept a neutral face.

Cavanaugh called over a slave and had him take the bags upstairs to the room. When the door had closed behind him, Anne turned to her husband. "What the hell?" she asked. "How did he know?"

Joseph shook his head. "He probably sent some poor messenger all over town until he got a confirmation. Or maybe he just guessed. We have stayed here before."

"Maybe," returned Anne, her voice full of doubt. "Maybe we have a spy amongst us."

"Oh Anne, let's not jump to that conclusion yet." He unfolded the letter and read it.

> *Dear Mr. and Mistress Burleigh,*
>
> *I am eager to meet with you regarding the fate of our venture. I have been waiting quite a while for word. I do hope all went well. Please contact me as soon as you receive this so we may meet.*
>
> *Yours &,*
>
> **Sir Jonathan Woolrich, Baronet**

Anne and Joseph looked at each other in surprise. "If he has spies, they are not very well informed if he truly does not know what happened to the *Betsy D*," Joseph said. "And Mayfield," he added.

"Indeed. Or perhaps he's merely dissembling." Anne shook her head. "He is a liar of the first order."

"True but still, he is predictable. We know how he will react."

"Badly," Anne replied.

Anne told Joseph what her officers had found during their stay in Jamaica. "I don't think it would be much of an understatement to say they hate him there."

"Who doesn't?" Joseph shrugged.

"Ye make light?" Anne asked him, her voice tinged in anger.

"No, but one must find ways to alleviate the distress." Joseph responded.

"'Twas always yer way, my darling. One of the reasons I love ye so." She kissed him, which led to an embrace, which led to clothing flying around the room and the bed shaking with their love-making. Anne and Joseph's enthusiastic sexual encounters had always served to break tension.

They sent Nicholas back to Woolrich, suggesting a meeting at Marot's Ordinary in the morning. "Get him when he's fresh and feisty," Joseph suggested. "If we delay until later in the day, his anxiety level will rise and he will be more on guard."

"And more likely drunk which will only complicate things," Anne agreed.

At eight o'clock the next morning, the Burleighs entered the dining room at Marot's and found Woolrich already there. They exchanged stiff greetings. *He is anxious*, Anne thought.

"Sir Jonathan," Joseph greeted the Baronet, whose visage was grim and unfriendly.

Not even a pretense of civility, Anne thought. *I do wonder what he's heard.*

"Mr. Burleigh. Mistress Burleigh." He motioned them to chairs on either side of him. They ignored the gesture and sat next to each other facing their enemy.

"Let us get down to business," Woolrich said bluntly. "My agent informs me that no slaves have been delivered to him."

"I'm afraid we were unable to complete the voyage," Anne told him. She could feel Woolrich's anger radiating from his impassive face. "We were attacked by a Spanish warship. We barely managed to get away to a harbor where we could evacuate onto a beach. Then a storm hit and lightning set the *Betsy* D on fire. She went down. The Moskitos Zambos came and took all the slaves who hadn't drowned. The

Zambos sell slaves themselves even though they were once in bondage. We lost the Helmsman as well as a sailor to fever before we were rescued." She paused.

Woolrich looked from one to the other, the big question almost exploding him. "Mayfield?" he asked through gritted teeth.

Obviously, he does know what happened, Anne thought. "As I said, we managed to make it to a bay and got most of the supplies and sea bags on shore along with the crew, but then she sank in a thunderstorm after being hit by lightning." Anne kept his gaze.

"So you said. And Mayfield?" he asked again, his face almost apoplectic.

"I'm afraid Lord Mayfield didn't make it. Despite our pleas that he not do so, he insisted on going back for a family heirloom – a gold-handled sword, he said – that he had hidden on the ship. He made it back up on deck but the mainmast fell and pinned him just before the ship disappeared totally under the water." Anne looked down at the table. "We were, of course, horrified and knew that you would be as well." Looking at Woolrich, she thought, *I wonder if people really can explode.*

"We tried to save the remaining slaves but, as you may have heard, the Zambos there are fierce and not friendly to British sailors. We were not in a position to pursue them. Mostly, we were grateful they didn't take us, which was due to the intervention of the Helmsman who they did take."

Woolrich's equanimity, what little was left, totally vanished. "Why not?" he thundered. The six other patrons in the room looked up in surprise. He took a deep breath and asked again, more quietly, "Why not, Mistress Burleigh?"

"Because they would have killed us if the jungle didn't. We had little food, no weapons and absolutely no way to defend ourselves." She knew her calm would annoy him. *Says a lot about a man that he cares as much for his cargo as for his friend.*

"Damn you, woman. They say you're such a great sea captain and yet you've lost half the cargo on one voyage and the whole damned ship on another. Your contract states that you will deliver one hundred and sixty slaves, yet, you are able to deliver none." He looked from Joseph to Anne, his eyes enraged.

"The contract anticipates that we have slaves to deliver. Unfortunately, we do not. We barely survived ourselves." Anne's green eyes took on a steely glint. "Had we not been rescued when we were," she added, "we might have starved on that beach."

"That, my dear Mistress Burleigh, is not my concern. I am concerned with the losses you have inflicted on me, including the demise of a good, close friend and companion, the son of a benefactor of mine." Woolrich's voice could have frozen an erupting volcano.

"Inflicted on you?" Anne's asked loudly as she let her own anger show. "We damned near died, Woolrich. On a voyage we took under duress. I don't give a damn for your losses. I lost three good men and my ship for your voyages. All of them worth twice what the 'cargo,'" she emphasized the word, "was worth." She paused. "The slaves, by our contract, belonged to you as soon as they embarked, so we are not liable for them."

"What? I would never have signed a contract that said that. No reputable attorney would have written that way." Woolrich's face turned bright red.

"Did ye read it?" Anne asked.

Woolrich thought for a moment. "You bastards. No, I trusted you. That was stupid of me."

Indeed it was. Anne said nothing.

"Besides, the slaves, while not important to you, perhaps, were everything to me," Woolrich continued. He sat back looking from one to the other. Anne and Joseph returned his glare. "I'm afraid this means our agreement is breached."

It was the response they had expected and prepared for.

"What, exactly, are you saying, Woolrich?" Joseph asked him.

"That I have no choice but to bring your wife's true identity to the attention of the authorities." Woolrich's eyebrow raised. "And now there may be charges of murder besides."

"Murder? Because of a shipwreck?" Anne asked.

"I don't believe for a moment, Lord Mayfield would have be stupid enough to go back for a sword, heirloom or not?"

Anne looked at him. "Then you didn't know him as well as you thought. Because no one who wasn't stupid would have brought such a valuable item on board to begin with."

"You'll never prove it, any of it," Joseph responded.

"Oh, I believe I will. I have witnesses," Woolrich asserted.

Joseph stood and Anne joined him. "You'll never prove it," Joseph said as he took his wife's arm and walked out.

Lt. Governor and Mistress Gooch held a banquet that night for those attending the Tobacco Act meeting the next morning. Wives were invited. Anne and Joseph mingled with the other members of the Commission, most of them Burgesses or other high ranking ladies and gentlemen. They were relieved to find that not only was Woolrich not in attendance, his name was not mentioned.

As they proceeded into dinner, two by two, Anne leaned over to Joseph. "How the hell did we get included with this group?" It continued to astonish her how their status had risen so quickly, most of it attributable to Joseph's work on the Act.

"Persistence," he whispered back. He squeezed her arm. "And luck. If I hadn't come up to work for the Act, we wouldn't be here."

The banquet was spread out in the Supper Room at the back of the house. Tables for six had been set up around the periphery of the room. The guests filled their plates.

Anne and Joseph found places at a table occupied by Betsy Loudoun, the mother of young Amity. Although Betsy was almost twenty years older than Anne, the two had always gotten along well.

Joseph and her husband Charles were also good friends. Anne hugged her friend, asking after Amity. "She is quite well," Betsy positively beamed. Anne looked at her with a raised eyebrow. Betsy blushed. "She is being courted," she added.

"How wonderful," exclaimed Anne. "She is such a lovely girl. Any man would be blessed to win her favor. Who is the lucky gentleman?"

"His name is Isaac Phelps. He is a trained lawyer," she told Anne.

"Well done," Anne said. "How wonderful for Amity."

"Yes. We are pleased." She looked at her husband as he sat down. "I was just telling Mistress Burleigh about Amity's good fortune."

"Oh yes indeed, Mistress Burleigh. We are most pleased." Charles Loudoun was tall and stocky with perpetually red cheeks and endless good humor.

They were drinking their soup when another couple came by to take the fifth and sixth chairs. Anne looked up with a greeting smile that froze on her face.

Joseph and Charles immediately stood. "Burgess Goodwin, Mistress Goodwin, so nice to see you."

Anne recovered quickly, "Yes, please join us." Betsy smiled as well. Anne knew from prior conversations that the Loudouns were also not fond of the Goodwins, although with no reason other than their haughty attitude.

"Good evening, Mistress Burleigh. We haven't seen you for quite a while." Benjamin Goodwin put down his plate as he held the chair for his wife, Emily. "Have you been away again?"

Anne seethed, but kept control. "No, but the rearing of children and the running of a plantation keep me at home a good deal."

"Indeed?" Goodwin eyed her but said no more.

They managed to keep the conversation on innocuous topics – children, farms, tobacco and Assemblies that were coming up. *At least we have some things in common*, Anne thought with relief.

When the meal was over, the Lt. Governor and Mistress Gooch

rose and went to the entry hall to indicate that the evening had concluded.

As they were leaving, Gooch pulled Joseph to the side.

"Accusations have been made on a more formal basis, I'm afraid," he said. "Your wife must be prepared to defend herself."

Joseph looked at the Governor with alarm. "Surely you don't believe what the Baronet is claiming, Sir?"

"I do not," he said. "And between us, I do not like the Baronet. Nor do I trust him. But he has friends ..." He gestured towards Burgess Goodwin. "He's insisting on some kind of a trial or hearing. He swears he can prove that she is wanted in Jamaica and under a sentence of hanging. And he claims that she captained a ship on which Lord Mayfield sailed and that it went down and drowned him. He claims murder. I can scarce believe he would even suggest such a thing but he has and I'm afraid I can no longer let it go."

"I see," Joseph said with angry formality. "And when will this ... hearing take place?"

"I do not know exactly. He is still mustering his forces. I would suspect within a fortnight."

"I will tell Anne. She is as astonished by these accusations as I am. And as dismayed." He stood up very straight. "Thank you for letting me know, Sir. You are a good friend."

"And I will preside at this farce. Do what you must to prepare, but be assured, you will have allies there." Gooch shook Joseph's hand warmly.

Joseph bowed to the Lt. Governor and returned to Anne who waited in the foyer. "It's done," he said. "A hearing."

Anne nodded with resignation. "So be it," she said.

CHAPTER FORTY

5 - 14 December 1730 - Great River Plantation, Virginia

The day after returning home, Joseph rode to Hampton to alert Captain Stoutley. He carried letters from Anne to the crew who might have to testify that it was Captain Andrew MacCormack who sailed the *Betsy D.* The good Captain had succumbed to a fever shortly after returning from the voyage. She asked them to stand-by for word of the timing of the hearing. She assumed that Woolrich had already summoned the witnesses he planned to use against her.

With luck and our bribes, their testimony will do him no good in the end, Joseph thought.

While in town, he went around and visited the many friends he and Anne had made over the years. The vicar told him that Mr. Edwards, the magistrate of Spanish Town, was staying at the King's Raven.

Joseph found him in the bar, reading a newspaper and drinking ale.

"Mr. Edwards," Joseph said, "so nice to see you. It's been awhile."

Robert Edwards looked up. "Mr. Burleigh. Yes it has been at least a year. I don't come over that often. Please, join me." He gestured towards an empty chair. "I have heard that your wife is under some kind of suspicion."

"Yes, I'm afraid so. Baronet Jonathan Woolrich, from your island, came to us a few months ago and decided my Anne was Anne Bonny the pirate. Ridiculous but now he's asked for a hearing."

"I have met Anne. Lovely woman. That is indeed ridiculous. Anne Bonny is dead. But I'm not surprised at Woolrich. Know the man well. He killed a woman in Jamaica and I issued an indictment against him. She was a mulatto prostitute, well-liked by everyone, including the Governor." He looked at Joseph. "We feared that the sailors would kill him and we'd have to indict them. I never thought we'd convict but the indictment served its purpose. He left Jamaica. I am sorry to hear he landed on you."

"As am I. Would you be willing to testify at the hearing?"

"I'd prefer not to. But I can give you a sworn statement that the indictment exists. When is the hearing?"

"We don't know yet. At least ten days, likely more. Why?" Joseph asked.

"We sail tomorrow. I will come to the hearing with the indictment but would prefer not to be called as a witness. Woolrich has friends in the colony who are already angry with me."

"I will send word as soon as we get it," Joseph said. "Thank you so much."

When he returned, Joseph told Anne about Edwards.

Woolrich has his title and his self-conviction. The rest of his witnesses cannot be credible. And he no longer has the Earl's son to testify. Do we know who he might call?" Anne worried.

"Stoutley tells me he has met with Captains Kruetzer and Fairley who have already been noticed by Woolrich to testify. We do not know who else, but it's unlikely he'll find any who can definitively identify you." He saw the fear on Anne's face and pulled her to him. "We have come this far, Anne. We will not lose it now."

She looked into his eyes. "Thank you for marrying me, Joseph Burleigh," she told him.

"And to you, Mistress Burleigh."

Three days later, a week after their visit to Williamsburg, a rider came with a Summons.

To: Mistress Anne Burleigh

You are hereby summoned to appear before a tribunal of the Honorable Lt. Governor Sir William Gooch and five members of the House of Burgesses of the Virginia Colony to answer to the charge of being a convicted pirate by the name of Anne Bonny and the charge of having murdered one Lord Thomas Hewett Edward Mayfield.

Said hearing shall be held on Monday, 14 December 1730 in the chamber of the House of Burgesses in the Capitol of the Colony of Virginia beginning at 10:00 in the morning.

The accused shall be allowed witnesses of her choosing as well as legal counsel.

(signed)

David Underhill, Clerk

"Well," said Joseph when he had finished reading the Summons. "Looks like Lt. Governor Gooch bought us a little extra time to get witnesses here." He turned to Anne. "He is on our side, you know."

"That may be, Joseph, but he is not going to run counter to the Burgesses if they decide I am guilty of the charge of being Anne Bonny, or a murderess." Anne shuddered involuntarily as both fear and hope ran through her, leaving her a little light-headed. She staggered slightly.

Joseph caught her. "You must go lie down, Anne. This is becoming too much for you. You have done your part – scuttling the ship and collecting favorable testimony. Let me proceed from here."

"Thank you, my darling. For once, I will not resist." She leaned into Joseph's arms, kissed him fondly and went upstairs to collapse on the bed. She let the tears come, and when they had finished, she fell fast asleep.

Joseph went into York Town the next day to send a letter to Amity Loudoun's probable future husband Isaac Phelps, the lawyer. He had sought an introduction to the lawyer the day after the dinner party at the Governor's Palace. They had agreed that should a hearing be called, Phelps would represent Anne. He also sent a letter to Stoutley by a different courier informing him of the date of the hearing.

After that, Joseph sought out the vicar. He found Francis Fontaine in the vicarage writing his sermon for the coming Sabbath. The Vicar looked up slightly myopically as his glasses fell down his nose. "Joseph, a pleasure and a surprise to see you." He removed the glasses and came across the room to shake Joseph's hand firmly. "To what do I owe this honor?"

"I can use your assistance, Francis. Anne has formally been accused of being someone she is not, to wit, a pirate named Anne Bonny." Joseph watched the Vicar's face contort into anger. "If she is found to be this person, she will be sent to Jamaica to be hanged – the sentence the true Anne Bonny escaped somehow, apparently."

"Oh my. Please sit, my friend." Francis motioned to a leather wing-back chair in front of his desk. He returned to the other side and sat down.

"How may I be of assistance?" he asked.

"Testify to Anne's character. You know her, Francis. She is a kind and thoughtful woman and an asset to all in the area." Joseph leaned towards the clergyman as he spoke.

"Of course, Joseph. I would be delighted to extoll your wife's virtues for I know them well. And I know of no real faults that she has."

Joseph laughed. "She has red hair, Francis, and a temper to match at times. But she is a good woman and a wonderful wife and mother. More significantly, she is not this Anne Bonny."

"No, of course not. When do you need us in Williamsburg? I will bring Louisa. Anne will need the support of another woman."

"Thank you, Francis. The hearing is set for fourteen December, a Monday. Can you get to Williamsburg after the morning services?" Joseph asked.

"I can do better than that. We have a visiting missionary coming to preach that Sunday, so I will be able to travel to Williamsburg on Saturday. I always enjoy a chance to visit with Pastor Blair at Bruton Parish anyway," he said.

Joseph stood up. "You and Louisa have been good friends these years. If there is ever anything Anne and I can do for you, you know you need only ask."

"There is the matter of the church's bell ..." Francis began.

"Done," declared Joseph. "We had planned a donation for it in any case."

"Well, thank you both. Now go back to your wife and comfort her. We will pray for her and I have faith that she will not suffer harm beyond the trial itself."

Joseph shook the vicar's hand. "Thank you. Again and again," he said as he bowed and left.

Back at Great River, Anne sat rocking on the front porch. She had been feeling increasingly uneasy since the Summons arrived. Joseph watched her carefully, but despite her resting more than normal, he saw no decrease in her overall strength. It was now the ninth of December.

"Stoutley has sent back word," he said, settling into the other rocker. "He has gathered Potter, Harkness, Wilberforce, and Thompson. All will testify to your innocence, if you wish, and swear they have sailed under a captain named Andrew MacCormack who happens to have reddish hair. Boots and Jones are also standing by."

"Good," Anne replied. "Too many witnesses may cause problems. It might look like we're trying too hard. What does Lawyer Phelps think?"

"I sent him a query with that question. He wrote back that he tends to agree. He suggests only one or two of the officers and one of the crew. I think we should ask Wilberforce and Thompson plus Henry Boots. If Woolrich's witnesses fall apart, he'll still have his status behind him, so I doubt we can completely discredit them. We will put Francis Fontaine on to describe your impeccable character," Joseph added.

Anne looked at her husband's worried face. "Do not fear, Joseph, I am fine. I am merely reserving my strength for what will come. I want to be rested and ready."

Joseph looked at her with concern. "Are you sure, Wife?

"Oh yes," she answered. "I am still your Anne as I ever was." She fluffed her hair. "The auburn hair retains its power whatever its appearance to the contrary."

Joseph laughed. "Good. The board is set, Anne. The game will begin on Monday."

"Woolrich thinks he is the king and I, a pawn. He will discover otherwise to his detriment," she said.

Joseph rose and pulled Anne to her feet. "Anyone who underestimates you, does so at their peril indeed." He held her close for several minutes. He kissed her passionately and left before she saw the tears that welled into his eyes.

That night, at two in the morning, Anne Bonny Burleigh, dressed in her woolen captain's jacket and breeches and wearing her best boots, ran through the tobacco fields, now stubble, slashing left and right with cutlasses at enemies she saw in her head. When she was spent, she collapsed onto the front steps of the house, panting. *They will not know until it's over*, she swore to herself. Then she stood up and went to bed.

CHAPTER FORTY-ONE

16 December 1730 - Williamsburg, Virginia

The morning dawned clear and cold. Anne and Joseph crunched through the rust-colored, yellow and red leaves strewn on the sidewalks during their walk after breakfast with Francis and Louisa Fontaine. Anne had decided to wear her favorite outfit – a powder blue jacket and matching petticoat embroidered by Angeline with green and yellow vines and tiny flowers. She asked Angeline to also sew a small skull and crossbones on her bloomers at the waist where no one would see it. She'd dressed while Joseph was out so even he didn't know it was there. Then Angeline had piled up her hair and pinned on a straw hat.

The friends talked about anything but the hearing: children, Pastor Blair's sermon the day before, the weather itself. But the tension persisted until they heard the church bells ring out nine o'clock.

"We are meeting Lawyer Phelps at Marot's at nine-thirty so we must go back," Joseph told their companions.

Louisa hugged Anne. "I will be there for every minute," she told her friend. "If you need reassurance, look to me." She pressed a small gold cross into Anne's hand. "For strength," she said. The women kissed.

"We had a pleasant meeting with Mr. Phelps. You are in good hands," Francis said. Joseph nodded as they shook hands.

Anne and Joseph turned back to the Marot's Ordinary. Phelps waited for them in the semi-darkness of the wood-paneled dining room. He rose as they entered, pulling out a chair for Anne. Joseph sat next to her.

"How are you feeling, Mistress Burleigh?" Phelps asked.

Anne told him she was fine. "Confident in my innocence. But aware that this will be unpleasant."

"Yes, I'm afraid it will be. But I am here to help you and we have three excellent witnesses who will testify to your identity and integrity. I have done some research on Woolrich's witnesses and will do my best to call their testimony and integrity into question. Frankly, that won't be difficult." He turned to Joseph. "Mr. Burleigh, I must advise you not to react to what is being said. You may express outrage with your face but do not interrupt or call out. That will look ill to the Burgesses."

"I am aware of that, Mr. Phelps. I promise to contain my anger," he replied. Looking at Anne, he added, "But my wife is not always so circumspect." He squeezed Anne's hand as she scowled at him.

"I will restrain myself. I am fully aware that lies will be put forward. And that they will be refuted. I will prevail in the end. The process will be annoying but that is all it is. A process. Not a result." Anne said.

"I see I have worthy clients," he said. He pushed a piece of paper across to Joseph. "This is a list of those we will call to testify. Is there anyone missing?"

Joseph and Anne looked over the list:

> ***Howard Wilberforce***
> ***Henry Boots***
> ***Francis Fontaine***

"Will they be enough?" Joseph asked.

"Wilberforce and Boots will testify that they sailed with a red-haired captain by the name of MacCormack. I have a sworn statement from the gentleman you suggested I write in Jamaica attesting to the fact that he did the paperwork for two shipments of slaves for Mac-Cormack recently. And having a vicar on your side is never a bad thing," he added. "With the information I have on the Baronet's witnesses, they should be sufficient. If we bring on too many, it may seem we're trying too hard."

Anne nodded. "Do you have the list of Woolrich's witnesses?" she asked, knowing that most of those witnesses would fold under any kind of questioning.

"Indeed. Here it is." Phelps passed a sheet of paper across the table.

Captain Hogarth Fairley
Captain Jean-Baptiste Kruetzer
Robert Callaway

"Do you recognize any of these names?" Phelps asked.

Anne looked over the list carefully. She had known Fairley during her pirate days. Wilberforce had bought his favorable or at least uncertain testimony just before their last arrival in Jamaica for two bottles of Madeira.

Kruetzer had approached Wilberforce when he heard that Fairley got the wine. As a result, Kruetzer had been compensated with Madeira which, unlike Fairley who drank it all, he sold for ten pistoles.

Anne didn't know Callaway but Nicholas Lawson had told them that he was an Able Bodied Seaman who had arrived the day before and supped with Woolrich and his lawyer at the King's Arms. Nicholas said he looked quite too young to have known Anne Bonny during her pirate days. He was also too shaky to make a good witness, so they hadn't bothered to bribe him.

"I do not know any of these people," she told the lawyer.

"If they assert that you are Anne Bonny, they are lying. We have the right to question them after their initial testimony. That truth will come out." Phelps sounded quite confident.

I hope he can handle them, Anne thought. *And that the truth comes nowhere near this room.*

"We have prepared the best we can. Let us go to the Capitol and get this done," Phelps said, rising from his chair. He picked up his briefcase and led the way out of the inn.

The Burgesses' Chamber of the Capitol looked quite different from what Anne and Joseph were used to. Instead of an orchestra and an open area for dancing, two tables had been set up in front of the bar with benches for spectators lined up behind them like pews in a church. *I hope the spectators are few and friendly,* Anne told herself.

The high windows on each side of the room let in hazy sunlight but Anne knew a storm was on the way. The weak sunlight reflected on the dark paneling in an almost ominous glow.

Anne and Joseph followed Phelps to a table on the left, outside the rails that separated the Burgesses' area from where those being judged sat. They waited with Mr. Phelps. About five minutes later, the prosecutor, Erasmus Wilson, led Sir Jonathan Woolrich to the table on the right. Wilson, a prominent local attorney with an immaculate wig and piercing dark brown eyes that seemed to have no lashes, brows or emotion, represented Woolrich. Anne was relieved that they would be sitting parallel so she would not have to look at either of them.

Wilson and Phelps shook hands and conferred quietly for a few moments, nodding in agreement about something. She and Joseph both looked up questioningly when the lawyer rejoined them. "We have agreed to keep all of the witnesses outside in the entryway until they testify. That way their stories cannot be corrupted."

Anne was relieved to hear that. She had not relished the idea of being stared at from behind by them. As they waited for the Lt. Governor and the Burgesses to enter the chamber, she heard the shuffling of people entering the room and filling the benches behind her. Turning in her seat, Anne smiled at the Loudouns, including Amity, and the Madisons. Just behind them sat Sheriff Starke, his wife Lydia and Burgess Goodwin's wife. Anne ignored them. Louisa Fontaine sat on the far end of the first row next to the Loudouns. Francis, as a witness, waited outside.

A murmur arose as Rebecca Gooch entered. The Lt. Governor's wife stood in front of Mistress Goodwin and the Starkes until they finally took the hint and moved to end of the row. Before sitting, Rebecca came to Ann leaned over to take her hand. "We are with you, my dear," she whispered.

Anne's eyes began to well with tears, but she forced them back. "Thank you, Rebecca. It means everything to me," she said as the Lt. Governor's wife sat.

The door at the back of the room flung open, admitting John Fleming, the Bailiff, who closed it and then stomped with the force of his role to the front of the chamber.

"All rise," he cried. Everyone in the room stood.

"The Honorable Sir William Gooch, Lt. Governor of the Colony of Virginia and Burgesses Sir John Fuller, Lord Kendrick Simon, Sir Milton Avery and Sir Charles Goodwin." Anne's heart froze at the announcement of the last name. She looked at Phelps.

He leaned over, "We could not prevent him from sitting, I'm afraid. But he will not be able to do more than the others."

"Perhaps, but that's a vote against me before anyone has spoken," Anne groaned.

Joseph took her hand and squeezed it. "It will be all right," he whispered. *I hope.*

Gooch and the four Burgesses, all wearing the most formal of wigs which fell down below their shoulders, moved along the side of the room up to the seats at the far end on the north side. Gooch sat in the middle with two burgesses on each side.

"Be seated," the Bailiff called out. He turned and walked to the back of the room where he stood at attention by the door.

"Sir Jonathan," Gooch said. The Baronet immediately stood up. "Do you intend to proceed with these accusations?"

"Indeed, Your Lordship. I believe we all deserve the truth of this woman's true identity." Woolrich whirled and pointed a finger at Anne, anger coloring his face a deep blotchy red.

"My Lord, you will refrain from making such inflammatory remarks. This tribunal will be conducted in a civilized manner. You may be seated." Gooch glared down at Woolrich from the height of the Burgesses' seats. Woolrich bowed slightly and sat.

"Mr. Wilson, you will advise your client that we will not tolerate any more such statements. Or outbursts. Am I clear?"

Wilson stood and bowed. "My client will let the evidence speak for itself," he said.

"You will address all questions to the Bench. The witnesses will stand to the side and answer so that both we and your clients can view their faces. Understood?" Gooch leaned forward.

"Yes, Your Honor," replied Phelps and Wilson in unison.

"Good. Mistress Burleigh," Gooch looked at Anne who immediately stood. "I apologize for your having to go through this. Sir Jonathan has insisted and the Burgesses feel they need to know the truth of the matter." Anne nodded. "You are accused of being Anne Bonny, a notorious, convicted pirate who was sentenced to hang in Spanish Town, Jamaica on 30 November 1720, who somehow escaped her fate and became the respected wife of a prominent citizen of the Colony of Virginia. Do you understand the accusation?"

"I do, Your Honor," she replied.

"He has also accused you of being the captain of a ship called the *Betsy D* which went down off the coast of Honduras and that with it sank Lord Thomas Mayfield."

Anne gasped. She had hoped the murder charge wouldn't be

called. "I had not known of that accusation, Your Lordship. But it too is untrue."

Gooch nodded. "Well then, let's get this over with. You may sit. I will not require Mistress Burleigh to stand within the bar. She is not accused of a crime. Should Sir Jonathan prove to the satisfaction of this panel that Mistress Burleigh is, in fact, this Anne Bonny, criminal proceedings may ensue, but we are not looking at that today." Gooch surveyed the room.

Woolrich consulted feverishly with his counsel after which he sat back, pouting like a five-year-old from whom a candy had been taken.

"Call your first witness, Mr. Wilson," Gooch said.

Wilson stood again. "We call Robert Callaway, Your Honor."

The Bailiff went back down the aisle and through the doors, returning with a short, blonde man with a barrel chest dressed in a suit of brown worsted wool. The Bailiff swore him in.

"Now, what is your occupation, Mr. Callaway?" Wilson looked down at his notes.

"I'm an Able Bodied Seaman. A rigger in particular. I puts the sails up and down." The young man's voice shook and his body followed.

"And where do you ply this trade, Mr. Callaway?"

"Around the colonies and in the West Indies mostly. I work a lot out of Jamaica and Providence." His voice steadied and the shaking quieted.

"Jamaica and Providence," Wilson repeated. "Are you aware of a pirate by the name of Anne Bonny?"

"Oh yes, Sir. Of course. She's famous, she is." Callaway's body stopped shaking and his voice lost its quiver.

He's been well coached, Anne thought.

"Are you acquainted with her?" asked Wilson.

"Not personal like, but I seen her in taverns and whatnot," Callaway answered.

"And what did the woman look like?" Wilson asked next.

Callaway looked around, seeking his prey. "Oh, there she is," he exclaimed, pointing to Anne. She put a hand to her chest.

"And are you sure, Mr. Callaway?" Wilson walked out from behind the table and stood by the bar, only about two feet from the sailor.

"Yeah. Red hair and all," he replied.

"Thank you, Mr. Callaway. You have been most helpful." Wilson returned to the table and sat down.

Callaway started to leave.

Phelps immediately popped up. "Mr. Callaway, I have a couple of questions for you." Callaway froze. It was apparent that he didn't realize that Anne's lawyer could question him.

Anne slipped a note to Phelps who read it, looked at her with a raised eyebrow then turned towards the bench.

"Mr. Callaway, how old are you?" he asked.

"I'm twenty, Sir. Last Tuesday in fact," he answered.

Phelps looked down at Anne and nodded.

"Are you aware that Anne Bonny was sentenced to be hanged as a pirate?" Phelps asked.

"Oh yeah, but she wa'n't, was she? 'Cos here she is." His confidence had returned.

"So you say. Do you know when Anne Bonny was sentenced to be hanged?" Phelps continued.

"No. A couple years ago, I think." Callaway's voice had again gone soft.

At the table to the right, Anne could see Wilson's head droop. "Ah well, when did you first go to sea then?"

"'Twas ..." he hesitated grasping for the right answer. Without assistance from Wilson who was steadfastly staring at the table, or Woolrich, who was making gestures that made no sense, Callaway finished. "'Twas about four years ago."

"More or less?"

"Well, yeah. I'm not sure the exact date."

"So you went to sea four years ago when you were sixteen, is that correct, Mr. Callaway?"

Callaway brightened. "Yes, Sir. That's it."

Phelps pulled out another document. Addressing the judges, he held up the paper. "This is the transcript from the trial of Anne Bonny and her fellow pirates. The hearing was held 30 November 1720. By his testimony, Mr. Callaway would have been ten years old at the time."

Callaway looked wildly to Wilson, who was still staring at the table.

"Also by his testimony, he only went to sea four years ago. Therefore, his statements that he saw Anne Bonny cannot possibly be true." Phelps gave the document to the Bailiff, who took it up to the judges, who each looked at it cursorily and passed it on.

Callaway watched, shifting his weight from one foot to the other and back again. He finally raised his hand slowly in the air.

"May I speak?" he asked.

"Oh please do, Mr. Callaway," Gooch said.

"I might have been a bit off on the years," Callaway said.

"In what sense?" Gooch responded.

"Well, I might have gone to sea a bit earlier?" Callaway's response was a question.

"When you were ten, perhaps?" Gooch led him.

"Possibly."

The Lt. Governor broke into the conversation. "Mr. Callaway before you tread any further towards being charged with lying to this tribunal, I suggest you say no more and excuse yourself."

Callaway looked to Wilson who nodded back.

"Uh, all right, Your Honor. Thank you." He turned as the Bailiff opened the gate.

"No, Mr. Callaway, thank you," Gooch replied. Callaway fled.

When Callaway had gone, Gooch addressed Wilson. "I do hope you have better witnesses, Mr. Wilson."

Wilson gulped. "Yes, Your Honor. We call Captain Hogarth Fairley."

The Bailiff led in a man of middle age and medium height. His white, heavily powdered wig stood out against his darkly tanned complexion. The powder spilled onto onlookers as he stalked down the aisle despite the tricorn perched precariously on top. The Captain's glory was a bright green jacket with gilded brocade trim.

"Captain Fairley, would you please explain your background?" Wilson leaned forward, watching his witness closely.

"I have for forty years worked on merchantmen traveling between the African coast and the West Indies. I began as a boy and worked my way up. I now hire out to those who need a reliable captain." Fairley stood solid and proud.

"Very good. Now would you please tell this tribunal about your relationship with Anne Bonny?"

"I had none, Sir. But I knew of her. We all did."

"We?" Wilson asked.

"Yes, anyone who was in the West Indies when the pirates were in control. Until the amnesty in 1718, they were a force in both Providence and Jamaica." The Captain looked directly at the panel of judges, giving his answer with confidence.

He's got them, Anne thought.

"Did you see Anne Bonny often enough to be familiar with her person?"

"Not in a lewd sense, Mr. Wilson," Fairley's tone suggested that he was offended by the question.

"I meant only, Captain Fairley, would you recognize her?" Wilson reddened and bowed slightly to the Captain as an apology.

"Ah. Yes, I would. I saw her many times, including at her trial," Fairley said.

"And would you please look at the woman sitting at the table behind you – in the blue jacket?" Fairley nodded and turned slightly towards Anne. She kept her face impassive.

"Yes?" Fairley asked.

"Is that Anne Bonny?" Wilson asked with no emotion in his voice. Woolrich leaned over from behind him to watch Anne.

Fairley looked at her for a few moments. "It cannot be Anne Bonny," he said finally.

Anne suppressed a grin. *Good man.*

Wilson and Woolrich looked at their witness, aghast. "Why on earth not?" Wilson asked.

"Because I saw Anne Bonny's body carried out of the prison in Spanish Town in the spring of 1721." Fairley remained calm, impervious to the horrified expressions of the prosecutor and his client.

"You told Mr. Woolrich that Anne Bonny was not hanged."

"She wasn't. It's the truth. She died of a fever after the birth of a child in prison. I was there when they carried the body out." Fairley glanced from the judges to Wilson.

The lawyer took a deep breath and tried again. "Did you see the face of Anne Bonny when this body was taken out of the prison?"

"No, it was covered with a shroud." Fairley hesitated and Wilson was about to jump in when he added, "But I could see her red hair falling out behind the head. I am certain that it was Anne Bonny."

Wilson looked like he had been punched. Woolrich simply shook his head in disgust as he slammed his fist down on the table. Gooch glared at him. Woolrich muttered "Sorry, Your Honor," and Gooch let it go.

"Any questions, Mr. Phelps?" Gooch asked, not waiting to see whether Wilson wanted to ask more.

"No, Your Honor, thank you." Phelps answered.

"Captain Fairley, thank you for your testimony. You are excused." Fairley strode quickly out of the court.

Wilson and Woolrich consulted, both agitated, as the rest of the room waited. Finally, Gooch broke in.

"Mr. Wilson, have you another witness?" he asked.

"I beg your indulgence, Your Honor. I would like a word with my next witness before I call him."

"Mr. Wilson has had time to consult with his witnesses," Phelps objected. "This is a request to coach them. He either wants to call them or he does not."

"Mr. Wilson, I tend to agree. Just call the witness." Gooch cocked his head to the side, looking directly at Wilson.

"Captain Jean-Baptiste Kruetzer." Wilson said after a moment's hesitation.

The Bailiff retrieved the Captain whose appearance was far less splendid than that of Captain Fairley. His jacket and matching breeches were a dove gray -- simple and without embellishment. The only splash of color in his attire lay in his waistcoat of raspberry embroidered with small green palm trees. His hair was pulled back with a black ribbon. He wore no wig, only a tricorn which he removed before taking the Bible.

"Captain Kruetzer, what is your history at sea?" Wilson asked.

"I went to sea as a child of eight on a merchantman. When I was fifteen, I became an ensign in the British navy. These last years I have been captain of a ship transporting slaves from the African coast to the West Indies and Brazil." He spoke with a slight French accent.

"And are you acquainted with Anne Bonny."

"I was, Sir," Kruetzer replied.

"In what capacity?"

"She was in evidence in the ports of Providence and Kingston. And Port Royal, or what is left of it after the earthquake." Kruetzer addressed his responses to Wilson.

"Sir," Gooch called out. "Please direct your answers to this tribunal."

288 - *Carol Busby*

"Of course, Your Honor. My apologies." He bowed deeply.

"Captain, how well did you know Anne Bonny?"

"I knew her to talk to and greet. She was a pirate but occasionally provided useful information to me," Kruetzer responded.

"What kind of information, Captain Kruetzer?" Wilson asked.

"Where to find ..." He hesitated, considering his answer. "The best delights of the ports."

Anne heard sniggering from the audience. Gooch rolled his eyes.

"Captain, do you know Anne Bonny's fate?" Wilson asked.

"Oh yes, she was convicted of piracy and sentenced to hang," he replied.

"And did she hang, Captain?" Wilson moved forward, closer to the witness.

"No she did not." Kruetzer looked from Wilson to the judges.

"What happened to her?" Wilson asked.

"She was with child and therefore given a temporary reprieve," Kruetzer answered.

"So she was never hanged?"

"Not that I am aware of, Sir."

"And did you ever hear what happened to her after she was not hanged?" Wilson closed in.

"Only that she gave birth to a baby. And that the sentence was not carried out."

"Is she still in the prison in Spanish Town?" Wilson asked.

"I do not believe so. I visited a crewman of mine there just last month. There were no women being held," Kruetzer answered.

"Would you please look at the woman behind you in the blue jacket?" Wilson instructed.

Kruetzer turned toward Anne. She kept her face calm. "Yes?" he said.

"Is that woman Anne Bonny?" Wilson asked.

Kruetzer took his time. *Should be on the stage that one,* Anne thought.

Finally, he looked back at Gooch. "I cannot say for sure, but I don't believe so."

Wilson's mouth dropped open and Woolrich's face went bright red once again.

"Why not?" Wilson asked through gritted teeth.

"She has red hair, it is true, but it is not the red of Anne Bonny. Hers was lighter."

"Could that be a change that happened over the years?" Wilson asked, helpfully.

"I am not an expert in women's hair, Sir. She doesn't look quite like Anne Bonny," Kruetzer said, shrugging his shoulders.

Wilson shook his head. "But is it possible that she could be Anne Bonny?" he asked.

"Anyone with red hair could be," Kruetzer said. "But I do not believe this woman is."

Gooch stepped in then. "Mr. Phelps?"

The lawyer stood and shook his head. "Nothing, Your Honor," he said, sitting down.

"Thank you, Captain Kruetzer. That will be all," Gooch told him. The captain bowed to the judges.

"Mr. Wilson, Sir Jonathan." Gooch looked at the men. "Do you have any other witnesses?"

Wilson looked at Woolrich, who nodded. "Only one who is currently present, Your Honor. I call Sir Jonathan Woolrich."

Phelps immediately stood. "What does the Honorable Mr. Wilson mean by 'currently present'?"

"We have another witness who, we are told, is on his way and close by but not yet here. We ask the court to allow us to call him if he arrives before this proceeding has concluded."

Gooch looked at Phelps. "Mr. Phelps, given the relative informality of this proceeding, I suggest we not worry about an additional witness who may never materialize."

Phelps said. "Very well, Your Honor, but I must reserve a possible objection." He bowed.

"So noted," Gooch responded.

Woolrich stepped behind the Bar.

"Sir Jonathan, where did you reside before moving to Virginia?" Wilson asked.

"Jamaica, Sir. For many years."

"What did you there?"

"I was a planter, Sir. I grew sugar. And I owned several vessels for shipping." Woolrich looked directly at the judges, all of whom were watching closely.

"Why are you no longer in Jamaica?"

"My wife." Woolrich stopped and took a deep, dramatic, breath. "I'm sorry, Your Honors," he said. "My wife and son died and both of my ships were lost at sea, the last one to pirates led by Jack Rackham, Anne Bonny's lover. So I determined to leave the plantation to my only surviving son to support his family and come to Virginia to start over."

"I am so sorry for your losses, My Lord," Wilson said. Woolrich nodded acknowledgement.

"Would you say that you have made some progress in starting over?" Wilson asked.

Phelps stood up. "I don't understand the relevance of this question," he objected.

The Burgesses conferred quickly. "Where is this going, Mr. Wilson?" Gooch asked.

"Just to Sir Jonathan's character and strength, Your Honor." Wilson replied.

"He's a Baronet," proclaimed Burgess Goodwin. "There is no need."

"Thank you, Your Honor." He looked to the Burgesses and since they all looked bored and unconcerned, he continued his questioning.

"You resided in Jamaica during the peak of the pirate trials, did you not?" Wilson asked.

"Yes, I did. You see my wife died of a fever brought to Jamaica by those ..." He hesitated, choosing his words. "Filthy lawbreakers. After that I went to all their trials. One especially was a sensation and seats were limited, so I arrived early to be in the front."

"What trial would that have been, Sir Jonathan?"

"That of the pirates captained by Jack Rackham, Sir. They took my last ship remaining."

"Were those pirates found guilty?"

"Yes, and sentenced to hang, but two of them escaped the noose." Woolrich looked over to Anne and Joseph, his face bright red, his eyes glittering with hate.

"Which two would that have been?"

"The women: Mary Reade and Anne Bonny. Both pleaded their bellies."

"For those unfamiliar with that term, would you please explain, Sir Jonathan." Wilson looked up at the judges, none of whom seemed to be unfamiliar with the term.

"Yes, it means they were with child. They were spared until the babes could be delivered." Woolrich continued to look at Anne as he responded.

"My Lord, as with the other witnesses, I request that you address your responses to the bench," Gooch said.

Woolrich bowed. "I am sorry, Your Honor. I will henceforth."

"What happened to those two women?" Wilson asked.

"Mary Reade died of a fever before her babe arrived. Anne Bonny's was delivered." He paused. "And then she vanished."

"Vanished?" Wilson asked.

"Yes. There is no record nor verifiable story of her fate." Woolrich stated. "Which is why I was surprised, yet not surprised, to find her residing in Virginia." He looked once again at Anne, this time with an intensity that chilled her.

"Is that woman in this room?" Wilson also looked at Anne.

"Yes, right there. She goes by Anne Burleigh now." Woolrich pointed at Anne, who held his gaze without flinching while shaking her head slightly back and forth.

"You have also alleged that this woman, known as Anne Burleigh, captained a ship which was lost off the coast of Honduras, killing all of the cargo, all of your cargo, on board. Is that right, Sir?"

"Yes. And she killed Lord Thomas Mayfield, known to many here in Williamsburg," Sir Jonathan sneered.

"Thank you, Sir. Jonathan. I have no other questions, Your Honor." Wilson sat.

"Mr. Phelps?" Gooch asked.

Phelps stood. "Do you know the circumstances of Lord Mayfield's death or even for certain that he is dead?"

"He's dead all right. He'd be here if he weren't. She sank the ship and he went down with it. Told me a story about his going back for a family sword. Nonsense."

"Are you testifying then that you have spoken to Mistress Burleigh about these matters, Sir Jonathan?"

"Of course I have. She captained the *Betsy D* which carried two loads of slaves for me. The first voyage was caught by a hurricane and half the cargo lost. The other sank, or so she said, off the coast of Honduras, and the slaves were taken by the Moskitos Zambos. What nonsense."

"Since we are here because of Sir Jonathan's accusations, I don't believe I need to inquire further as to his opinion. But I do have one question, Your Honor," said Phelps.

"Ask it," Gooch replied with a wave of his hand.

"Sir Jonathan, why have you chosen to accuse this woman of being someone she is not?" Phelps asked.

"To serve the truth," he shouted, shaking his fist.

"Ah, the same truth as your other witnesses then?" Phelps followed up.

Woolrich turned to him. "You are being misled, Lawyer. And you have no right to bring my honesty into question. It is the truth. That is why we are here. This woman is a pirate, convicted and sentenced. She must be returned to Jamaica and hanged."

"That remains to be determined, Sir. Jonathan," Phelps answered calmly. "No other questions, Your Honor."

"You may step down, Sir Jonathan." Gooch said, his tone dismissive. "Has your elusive witness arrived, Mr. Wilson?" he asked. Woolrich stomped back to his seat.

"Gooch is getting fed up," Joseph whispered to Anne.

Wilson stood. "No, Your Honor. Not as of yet. Therefore, for now, I rest my case, but reserve the right to call the other witness should he arrive."

"Granted," said Gooch.

CHAPTER FORTY-TWO

16 December 1730 - Williamsburg, Virginia

"Mr. Phelps, I see you also have witnesses," Gooch continued.

Phelps stood. "Yes, Your Honor. I would like to call Howard Wilberforce."

Wilberforce wore the same splendid clothing as on the last night on the *Betsy D*, looking elegant and sophisticated.

"Mr. Wilberforce, what is your occupation?" Phelps asked.

"I am a cook and surgeon, Sir," he answered.

"And where do you ply these trades?"

"On merchantmen."

"Are you acquainted with Anne Bonny?"

"I have met her a few times. She sailed out of the West Indies, I believe. I sail mostly along the coast from Boston to St. Augustine. I have only been to the Indies once, when I was much younger."

"What was your most recent cruise, Mr. Wilberforce?" Phelps asked.

"It was from Charleston, South Carolina up to Baltimore," he responded.

"And what was the cargo?"

"Slaves," Wilberforce said.

"Who was the captain on the voyage, sir?"

"Captain MacCormack. Andrew MacCormack. A Scotsman." He watched the judges.

"And is there anything distinctive about this Captain MacCormack?"

"Aside from his being an exceptional captain both technically and as a leader?" Phelps nodded. "Ah, he has flaming red hair like so many of his countrymen." Wilberforce replied. "And a temper to match, I must say." He grimaced.

Phelps went on, "Where is this Captain MacCormack now? We would like to hear from him."

"That won't be possible, sir."

"Why not, sir?" Phelps asked, leaning forward.

"Because our ship was attacked by the Spanish and then struck by lightning. When she sank, the Captain went down with her." Wilberforce looked straight at the Burgesses as he answered. "I'm lucky to be here. So is Mr. Boots who waits outside to testify."

"I was unaware that you were on a ship that went down."

"Do you follow the shipping news, sir? Not the printed news but the news from the docks? Our ship may not have been officially reported." He looked at the Burgesses. "We were rescued, but only after barely surviving on a beach for several weeks."

"Well, good fortune for you and unfortunate indeed for Captain MacCormack, Mr. Wilberforce."

"Indeed, sir."

"For whom was the Captain sailing? Who was the sponsor of the voyage?"

"I do not know anything but his name. Pennington. I overheard the Captain mention the name once. Crew and officers aren't generally privileged to know that sort of information."

"Would you recognize Anne Bonny if you saw her?" Phelps asked.

"No, as I said, I believe she operated out of the West Indies and I work the coast. I've heard of her, though. Heard she was sentenced to hang but got a reprieve due to her ..." He paused. "Delicate condition."

"Do you know anything of her after that?"

"No, I'm afraid not. Rumors. Lots of rumors. But nothing concrete."

"Thank you, Mr. Wilberforce. I suspect Mr. Wilson has some questions for you," Phelps bowed briefly and sat down.

Wilson stood up and took a deep breath. "Is it not true, Mr. Wilberforce, that you were once a pirate yourself?"

Wilberforce looked back at the lawyer calmly then turned to the judges. "I might have associated with some pirates. But most of those I knew accepted the amnesty."

"Most?" Wilson followed up.

"Well, those that didn't are all dead now, aren't they?" Wilberforce replied.

"But Anne Bonny was not hanged, was she?"

"So I heard. I also heard she died in prison. And that she returned to England. And that she lives in Bolivia. When there is no finality, stories arise," he replied.

Wilson turned to Woolrich, who shrugged.

"No further questions, Your Honor," he said, sitting back down.

Wilberforce bowed very slightly as he strolled past Anne and Joseph without acknowledging them.

"I would like to call Henry Boots to the stand, Your Honors," Phelps said.

Boots's youth and innocent look were assets that Anne and Joseph counted on to help their case.

"Mr. Boots, what is your occupation?"

"Able Bodied Seaman, sir. On merchantmen." Boots looked at the Burgesses as he answered; he had taken instruction well.

"What was your most recent voyage?" Phelps asked.

"Up the coast with Captain MacCormack. He usually brings tea and sugar and things people can't get easily. This trip was slaves."

"Is he a smuggler, then?" Phelps asked.

"Don't know, sir. I work the riggin' and the sails. I don't ask about the cargo. Not my business."

"Very well. Have you sailed with Captain MacCormack before?"

"Yes, sir. Once before."

"Where is Captain MacCormack now, Mr. Boots?"

Boots shivered. "At the bottom of a bay off the Moskito Coast. We was hit by Spanish and then she was struck by lightning. The ship went down. Cap'n got everyone else on shore, he did, but didn't make it off in time."

"He was a brave man, then was he, Mr. Boots?" Phelps asked.

"The best Cap'n I ever served with, but I don't have much experience," he replied.

"Have you ever heard of or met Anne Bonny?" Phelps asked, looking down at his notes.

"Heard o' her. Everyone's heard o' her. But never met her – before my time." If Anne had not known Boots so well, she wouldn't have noticed the small drips of sweat on his brow.

"Thank you, Mr. Boots. Mr. Wilson may have some questions for you."

Wilson stood, eyeing Boots warily. "Were you on warm terms with your captain?" he asked.

"Warm as with any cap'n, sir. I didn't have a personal relationship with him if that's what you mean."

"Do you know for certain that your captain was a man?"

Boots stared at him. "I don't know what you mean," he said, blinking.

More sweat. Please be done quickly, Wilson, you bastard.

"Did you ever see him in any state of undress, for example, where you might have noticed his body type?"

Boots looked positively horrified. "No, sir. I would never." He looked up with wide eyes at the Burgesses as if they could explain this strange line of questioning.

Wilson waved a hand. "You may go," he said. Boots almost ran out of the room. Anne breathed a deep sigh of relief.

Phelps called Vicar Francis Fontaine to the bar. The Vicar extolled Anne's virtues as a wife, mother and citizen of James City County. He explained that the Burleighs were a happy couple who had contributed generously to the parish over the time they had spent near York Town.

Wilson had no follow-up questions. The Vicar joined his wife in the pew behind Anne and Joseph.

"If you wish to call no one else, Mr. Phelps, we will move to the summaries." Gooch said, looking left and right. The Burgesses nodded.

At that moment, the door at the back of the room slammed open and one of Wilson's clerks burst through. He made his way quickly, almost at a run, to the table to confer with the lawyer.

Anne and Joseph looked at each other and at Phelps who shrugged.

Wilson stood. "My last witness has arrived," he announced.

"Well, just in time, it seems," Gooch replied.

"Your Honor, even though this is an informal tribunal, I believe we have the right to know who this mysterious witness is. He or she was not on the list." Phelps sounded vexed.

Gooch nodded. "I agree. Mr. Wilson who is your witness?"

"He is the most material witness possible, Your Honor, and one whose testimony will be dispositive." Wilson replied, sending his clerk back to the door. The Bailiff followed.

"Yes, yes, who is he?" Gooch repeated.

"We wish to call … James Bonny, Your Honor." A loud gasp rose from the room.

Joseph cast a quick look at Anne whose face had gone white. He reached under the table and grabbed her hand and held on to it. He could see her jaw clenching and unclenching as she struggled to maintain her composure. He saw her lips move and leaned over. She repeated, in a voice so soft he could barely hear her, "I am done for." He squeezed her hands again.

"Not yet, my darling. Not yet," he whispered back.

Then he, like everyone else, turned to look at the man who emerged from the shadowy doorway and strode into the room. He was about five and a half feet tall, wearing a formal white wig. He walked carrying a mahogany cane with a silver knob. His body was lean but well-fed and strong.

As he approached the table, Anne turned slightly to look at him, hoping against hope that it was not, in fact, James Bonny. But she was disappointed in that and she struggled once again to maintain her composure. He was older, a little more filled out and better dressed, but he was indubitably her husband. She groaned almost inaudibly. Joseph squeezed her hand again and she squeezed it back, hard.

He leaned over to Phelps. "Must he be allowed to testify?" he asked.

"Yes, I'm afraid it would do us ill to object. But unless he lies, Anne is safe from him. And what he says will determine her fate."

Joseph took a deep breath as he felt Anne shiver.

They exchanged glances then looked towards the Burgesses and Lt. Governor. "Mr. Bonny, where do you now reside?" Wilson asked.

"In Cuba, sir, for the last six years." Bonny told the Burgesses.

"And before that?"

"Various places. Mostly Port Royal and Providence."

"What did you do there?"

"I was a pirate." Although most people in the room knew the answer, a gasp went up behind Anne.

"When did you cease being a pirate, Mr. Bonny?" Wilson's whole body exuded confidence as he stood straight, tall and calm. But Anne could see he was wound up like a top, ready to spin.

"In 1718 when the amnesty was announced," he replied. "I decided to take advantage so that I could live a more normal life. And because pirates who were caught would be hanged if they did not come in."

"Were you married at that time, Mr. Bonny?"

"Yes. But my wife Anne declined the amnesty. She never liked to accept the authority of others. So she left me and took up with another unrepentant pirate, Jack Rackham. Their ship was captured in 1720. The crew were hanged except Anne and another woman who was on board. The other woman died; no one knows what happened to Anne." Bonny spoke matter of factly.

"Do you know why we are here, Mr. Bonny?" Wilson asked.

"I was told that my wife might be here. As I have not seen her for more than a decade, I thought it prudent to find out." He looked at the judges as he answered.

"Yes, we thought so, too. What did you do after you accepted the amnesty?" Wilson asked.

"I worked for the government," he began.

As a damned informant, Anne thought.

"Then I was hired to run a sugar plantation in Cuba. I have done well over that time and now own my own plantation. Taking the amnesty was the best thing I ever did. That and remarry. My wife Jane and I have three lovely children."

Anne had to forcibly keep her mouth from dropping. *He's a bigamist*, she thought. *But then so am I.*

"Mr. Wilson, get to the point, please. We have been here too long already and are in need of sustenance." Gooch's tone was both stern and tired.

"Very well, Your Honor. Mr. Bonny, would you please look at the woman behind you wearing the blue jacket?" Bonny, who had been standing facing the judges, turned and looked directly at Anne.

"Is this woman your wife?" Wilson asked.

Bonny gazed for several minutes, holding Anne's eyes. Then he smiled softly and answered. "She is beautiful. I wish she was, but alas I do not know this woman. She and my missing wife share only the color of their hair."

Pandemonium broke loose behind Anne. The Burgesses' eyes flew open in shock. They leaned toward Gooch to confer. Woolrich immediately sprang up and yelled, "Liar! Traitor!" Wilson dragged him back into his seat.

Anne let out a deep breath that she didn't know she had been holding. Tears began to stream down her cheeks as she released her emotion and terror. Joseph let out his breath as well as he put his arm around his wife, pulling her to him, feeling her body shaking. "Thank god, thank god," he whispered over and over.

Bonny remained calm, waiting for the chaos he had created to subside. Gooch looked up finally. "We thank you for your time, Sir."

Bonny stopped at Anne's table, leaned over Phelps, and said, "I wish you a good life, Madame." Without looking back, James Bonny walked away from his wife for the last time.

CHAPTER FORTY-THREE

16 December 1730 - Williamsburg, Virginia

Anne looked straight ahead, unseeing, as the world around her exploded with noise and movement. She vaguely understood that the judges had declared her not to be Anne Bonny. She heard the sound of Woolrich screaming outrage. She felt Joseph put his arm around her and heard Louisa whisper, "It's all right, dear Anne. It's over." She tried hard to focus on what had happened and on what was happening now, but her mind was overwhelmed.

Joseph gave her a glass of water and told her to drink it. She looked at him uncomprehending. "Oh, my darling," he said, pulling her to him. She didn't respond.

Hearing her name, she looked up to see Phelps with a flask. "Anne," he said. "Drink this. You've had a difficult experience. This will help."

Joseph took the flask and put it to her lips. The fire of the brandy brought the world a little more into focus.

"It's over?" she asked.

"It's over. We can go." Joseph smiled. "As soon as you're up to it."

Anne took a deep breath and noticed the concerned look on Louisa's face. The tears had not stopped, but Louisa was dabbing them away with a pocket kerchief. "Thank you, dear friend," Anne said, sniffing.

Louisa stroked her cheek. "No need."

Anne looked to Joseph. "Let us go now," she said, having regained her composure.

"That's my Anne," he said.

They stood up and made their way through people congratulating them and shaking their hands. Anne was still dazed, but she responded as best she could. When they went through the big double doors at the back of the Burgesses' chamber, she blinked at the light streaming in the foyer. Her legs started to give way. She held onto Joseph who helped her stand until she nodded and they moved on, out of the building and into the courtyard. Samuel waited for them with the carriage. As Anne climbed in, she thought, *thank goodness Joseph had the presence of mind to have him be here even though it was in case we had to flee.*

She looked out the window at her husband. He was thanking the Vicar. As he moved towards the carriage, he also thanked Wilberforce and the two sea captains. Bonny had vanished.

By the time Joseph got into the carriage, the brandy was warming Anne's body and soul. She felt like she'd just woken from a horrible dream into a bright day. She started to laugh.

"Anne?" Joseph looked at her.

"We did it. We did it. It's over," she said.

Joseph squeezed her hand. "Almost." He spoke softly. Anne looked confused. "We must still get rid of Woolrich."

Anne nodded. "Yes. But how?"

"I will speak to him," Joseph told her. "And give him reasons to leave."

Anne thought for a moment, but her mind was still too overwhelmed to figure out the rest of Joseph's plan. "And then?" she asked. *At least he has some kind of plan.*

"Leave that to me, my darling. You've been through enough," Joseph told her, caressing her cheek. "Remember Mr. Edwards? The man from Jamaica who has an arrest warrant for Woolrich? Because Woolrich still has friends in Jamaica, I told Edwards I'd try to persuade Woolrich to leave without bringing him into it. The Baronet's a coward. With luck, he will fold when he knows we can expose him."

Anne thought about it. "As long as one way or another he leaves us alone. Forever," she said.

Joseph squeezed her hand. "I will look for him tonight. But for now, you need to rest. You are exhausted and not fully yourself. We'll get some dinner then I will thank our friends more fully while you take a long nap," he said. "I might even join you when you wake."

Anne sighed. "I would be delighted, my darling," she said, kissing Joseph hard.

They ordered food sent up, and Joseph took Anne to their room where Angeline helped her undress. When they had finished, he left the boarding house and headed for Marot's Ordinary. There, as expected, he found Wilberforce, Boots and Thompson with a pitcher of beer.

Joseph went to their table. "My good friends. Your assistance was most appreciated today." He sat and motioned for a tankard. "Even you, Mr. Thompson. We might have needed you to testify and your willingness will never be forgotten."

Wilberforce patted Joseph on the back. "You did well today as well, Joseph. And Anne. Is she all right? She looked quite pale."

Joseph took the tankard from the waiter and poured himself a beer. When the waiter was gone and the noise level had risen, he said, "Bonny was a shock to be sure."

"It was truly he?" Thompson asked.

"Indeed," Wilberforce answered. "I knew him some -- back in the pirate days. And he looked right at Anne. I know he recognized her."

"Why did he deny her then?" Thompson asked.

Joseph shook his head. "Don't know for certain. But I suspect that he wants to move on and forget that time in his life. After all, he's a success now -- his clothes and manner indicate that. And remarried. He's respectable and Anne being alive makes him a bigamist."

"I think you are correct, Joseph. I would bet that he was not happy to be called by Woolrich. If he hadn't come, Anne might have come back up to him again and again. This way, he is free," Wilberforce said.

"And so is Anne," said Joseph. He lifted his tankard. "To James Bonny," he toasted in a soft voice

"To James Bonny," the other three repeated.

The door opened and Mr. Edwards entered. Joseph waved to him then stood as he approached. He called to the waiter for another glass.

"Mr. Edwards, so glad you could come," Joseph said.

Edwards bowed slightly. "I am so pleased it came out the way it did. Imagine Woolrich finding Bonny."

"Yes, unexpected and it backfired." They all laughed.

"Mr. Edwards, may I introduce Howard Wilberforce, Henry Boots and Phineas Thompson. They came to testify on Anne's behalf." Edwards had been waiting in the foyer in case he was required to speak.

"A pleasure, gentlemen," he said.

Wilberforce stood and the other two followed his lead. "The pleasure is ours. But we must return to Hampton. The sea calls," Wilberforce said.

Joseph rose and shook hands vigorously with both men. "We will be down there soon," he said. "We hope to see you then."

"Excellent. We look forward to it," Wilberforce said.

"Indeed," Thompson added. The two men bowed and left.

Joseph sat back down. "I wanted to speak with you now that this is over. When do you expect to return to Jamaica?" he asked Edwards.

"In a few days. There's a ship that leaves from Hampton on the twentieth."

306 - Carol Busby

"Good. Can you remain in Williamsburg for another day?" Joseph asked.

Edwards thought for a moment. "I don't see why not," he said. "For what reason, may I ask?"

"I am resolved to get Woolrich to remove himself from Virginia. I want to persuade him, but if I cannot, would you be willing to tell your story to the Lt. Governor? He will surely ban the man should he refuse to leave voluntarily."

"Yes, of course. I would hope that this could be done without revealing my part in it," he said. "Woolrich's friends would not appreciate my interference."

"Of course. Sir William is a reasonable man. He'll be happy to have an excuse to throw the bastard out." Joseph said.

Edwards laughed. "Many of us in Jamaica were happy to have an excuse as well, although the specific incident was unfortunate."

As Edwards rose to leave, Joseph said, "I will let you know tomorrow how it goes."

"Please do – however it goes," Edwards replied.

After he had left, Joseph sat at the table thinking. The Lt. Governor had invited them to dine that evening, but Joseph had pled out because of Anne's exhaustion. When Gooch repeated the invitation for the next night, Joseph accepted. For tonight, he needed to find Woolrich where they could talk without being heard. *Shields Tavern*, Joseph remembered someone saying. *That's his favorite.* By the time he returned to the boarding house, Joseph had put together a plan.

Anne was awake when he came back to the room. She wore a shift and sat up in bed. Angeline knelt behind her, brushing out her hair. Anne greeted Joseph as he came through the door: "I am glad ye're home, Husband."

"You look much better," he said.

"I do feel much better, thank you." As Joseph leaned over to kiss her, she sniffed then kissed him hard on the mouth. "You smell like a brewery," she said, laughing.

"I had good conversations with friends," he answered.

"Angeline," said Anne. "Thank ye for now."

Angeline looked from Joseph to Anne, and took a deep breath. "You aks me to listen for talk 'bout dat man, Woolrich," she began. Anne and Joseph nodded. "Dere be talk." She stopped, blushing.

Anne recovered from the surprise first. "Yes, Angeline? Of what?"

"He attack one da servants at da Palace," she continued. "He ..." Angeline blushed deeply. Anne turned her so they faced each other.

"Yes?" she encouraged the girl.

"One da kitchen slaves. Girl about twelve is all. Waited for her outside t' house and den put hands on her." Angeline hesitated, blushed deeply, and added, "and mo'."

Anne looked quickly at Joseph whose eyes opened wider.

"What happened?" she asked.

"Her father saw dem. Pushed him off her. And she ran off." Angeline looked at her shoes.

"Does the Lt. Governor know?" Anne asked.

"No. It be slave word agin a gentleman's. But her father's Gov'nr's butler so Gov'nr will be mad even if he cain't do nuthin'," Angeline said. She looked up at Anne then over at Joseph. "He shouldn't oughta done dat," she said, tears streaming down her face.

"Ye're right, my dear. Thank ye for telling us. We will try to see that something is done about it." Anne hugged her.

Angeline nodded. She curtseyed and left.

Anne and Joseph exchanged glances. "Well, that's another piece of ammunition," Joseph said.

"Ammunition?" Anne asked.

"To convince Woolrich to leave. I will tell him not only that we know why he left Jamaica and can prove it, but that we will tell Gooch about the butler's daughter if he doesn't agree to our terms."

Anne thought for a moment. "What did ye ask of Edwards?" she asked.

"I wanted to be certain that he would be here to testify to Gooch if Woolrich doesn't take the bait. He doesn't return to Jamaica until Thursday. He did ask that we not tell Woolrich who gave us the information. I assured him we would not."

"No, hardly," said Anne. "I hope it works, my dear. Woolrich is unmoved by any sympathy that others might feel."

"I know. But he is has been caught out here and may decide to seek out other, more hospitable, places for refuge. He does seem to have friends."

"Indeed. When will you talk with him?"

"He frequents Shields. I will go over after supper."

"Be careful. I don't want to go home with only Samuel." Anne turned to her husband then and kissed him.

Anne returned to the boarding house after supper while Joseph headed for Shields Tavern hoping to find Woolrich.

He walked in and spotted his prey across the room by the huge, brick fireplace. Woolrich was talking to Burgess Holloway. Joseph could hear the anger and disgust in Woolrich's voice which was loud and slurred. Joseph moved to a corner where he would not be observed by them and ordered a cider.

From his dark table, Joseph watched as the men drank and laughed. When Holloway stumbled away to the privy, he pounced.

"Sir Jonathan," he greeted the Baronet.

Woolrich looked up, hatred in his eyes. "You bastard," he said. "What the fuck are you doin' here? I want nothing to do with you."

"I have a proposition for you." *Perhaps being rather drunk will make him more receptive*, Joseph hoped. "Something that would work to our mutual benefit. We have some funds to compensate your financial losses." He let the implication do its work.

Woolrich stared at him for a moment, then a wary smile crept up his face. "Indeed?"

"Yes," Joseph said.

"Well, perhaps we should talk." Woolrich looked up. "I see Burgess Goodwin coming this way," he said.

Joseph turned his head. Goodwin was halfway across the room coming towards them, blood in his eyes. "Tomorrow morning. Seven-thirty. Gordon Creek – I'll send you a map."

Goodwin arrived. "What the hell are you doing here, Burleigh? I didn't think they let the riff-raff in this establishment."

"Neither did I, Your Honor." Joseph bowed and left.

CHAPTER FORTY-FOUR

17 December 1730 - Williamsburg, Virginia

The sun, although it had not yet risen, was beginning to light the sky as Joseph went out the bedroom door, closing it silently behind him. He didn't see Anne's eyes pop open as he stepped out. Dark clouds blocked out any stars. He could sense that a big storm was coming and fairly soon.

As he moved down the street to the Palace, slaves were beginning to stir to life. He avoided them. Joseph saddled his horse and rode off.

The meeting spot at Gordon Creek near the mouth of the Chickahominy River was about an hour away. There was a clearing in the cypress forest which Joseph had found on a previous ride to the river to fish. The ground was covered with cypress needles and cones. As the sun lightened the overcast sky, Joseph walked around looking for escape routes, places Woolrich might be trapped against thick trees, and exactly where the creek ran. Once he had surveyed his battleground, he pulled out a whetstone, removed his sword from its scabbard and began sharpening. He had just finished wiping the weapon with a soft cloth and was returning it to its sheath when he heard a horse approaching.

Woolrich emerged from the trees and dismounted. He patted his own scabbard as he glared at Joseph. The former highwayman stood his ground until Woolrich stepped forward.

"I don't know how you got to Bonny, but when I figure it out, I shall have him brought back to tell the truth. This does not end with the hearing, Burleigh," Woolrich growled.

"We didn't get to Bonny. We've neither of us have ever seen him before. So I am not at as much of a loss as you as to why he testified as he did. Perhaps it was the truth after all." Joseph stood firm.

"What is your offer?" Woolrich asked.

"That I will not ruin you and have you returned to Jamaica in chains to face an indictment of murder," Joseph answered.

Woolrich's eyes flew open. "What? This is outrageous. And lies. You promised money, Burleigh?"

"I did? No, I think you're mistaken, Woolrich. You were a little in your cups when we spoke." Joseph's voice was hard.

"There is no indictment against me in Jamaica or anywhere else," Woolrich growled. "And I will not agree to capitulate."

Joseph pulled a paper out of his jacket pocket. "Here is a copy of the document, Sir Jonathan." He waved the paper. "If you go back, a lot of the victim's admirers are prepared to ignore the indictment and go straight to their knives, which you must have realized since you left in such a hurry." Joseph offered it to the Baronet. "I will show it to Gooch who will banish you from the colony. Or worse."

Woolrich grabbed it and read it. Then he tore it up. 'Now you have no paper," he said.

Joseph shrugged. "I did say it was a copy, did I not? The Lt. Governor will also be made aware of your rape of his kitchen slave."

Woolrich's stony demeanor cracked slightly. *Ah, he didn't know that I knew about that,* Joseph thought.

But Woolrich pulled himself together, and his face went again to its usual mask. *He's tempted but not quite convinced,* Joseph realized.

"She is the daughter of his butler – did you know that?" he continued. "No, why should you? And why would you care? She is a slave girl and helpless, therefore fair game."

"It's her word against mine. I am a Baronet."

"Yes, you are. God help the aristocracy. But the Lt. Governor will believe her father."

"You bastard," Woolrich howled, drawing his sword from its scabbard.

Joseph pulled out his own sword.

"I am a bit rusty," he said, slashing the weapon back and forth. "But not unskilled."

Woolrich growled as he approached, the sword extended, his arm bent for thrust. "I'll kill you right here and now."

Joseph countered the first parry, but the second one caught him on the arm, tearing his jacket. He backed up then ran forward, overwhelming Woolrich, whose own jacket split across the front. Neither had drawn blood. *He must have also put on extra layers of clothes,* Joseph thought.

Woolrich lunged and the two swords clanged against each other several times until both men backed up. Joseph could feel the slipperiness of the cypress needles and determined to move with care. He also vowed not to be the aggressor. He waited as Woolrich walked around him, swinging his sword. Woolrich plunged again, and Joseph parried the thrust, then moved back two feet. The clashing of swords went on for quite a while, back and forth, around the clearing, until finally, with a scream of rage, Woolrich went directly at Joseph, slashing until he caught Joseph's leg. A gash opened up and blood began to pour out. Joseph stumbled backward, but recovered to parry the next thrust. He even managed to score a cut across Woolrich's cheek.

Woolrich came back at full force. Joseph backed to set himself. But as he did, he put his foot down onto a dead limb which rolled, throwing him backward onto the ground. His sword flew out of his hand as he went down. Struggling to reach it, Joseph looked up at Woolrich's red face, grinning like a death's head, coming towards him.

"Great swordsman you are," Woolrich sneered. "Didn't account for the needles." He raised his blade for the kill.

Joseph threw a knife pulled from his boot. It hit Woolrich's shoulder, digging in deeply and sending the Baronet staggering backward. Joseph scrambled for his sword as the enraged Woolrich ran at him.

Suddenly, the world exploded in ear-shattering noise, blood and guts. Woolrich's body fell towards him but now with two gaping holes in his chest. Joseph closed his eyes as the heavy man landed on Joseph, knocking the wind out of him.

Opening his eyes, Joseph gasped for air. Anne was standing over him, two smoking pistols in her hands. She threw them down and turned to call something over her shoulder. Samuel appeared. He and Anne kicked Woolrich over and off Joseph who looked up at his wife bewildered.

"Ye didn't think I'd let ye go alone, now did ye?" she asked.

Joseph panted. "I did, but I should have known better," he said.

"Yes, ye should have. Ye're a brave man with a lot of skills, Joseph Burleigh. But killin' ain't one of them."

Samuel brought a wagon full of hay covered with pumpkins. Joseph looked questioningly to his wife. "We have to get rid of the body," she explained. "And the horse." She pulled him up to a sitting position. Anne cleaned the wound with a flask of water. She took another flask, this one filled with brandy, and poured it over the leg, giving the rest to Joseph to drink. She took a roll of linen out of her pocket and bound up his leg wound. "Wait here," she ordered.

She and Samuel dragged the body to the wagon, got it onto the bed, and slid it between mounds of hay. They covered it with the rest of the hay, put a tarp over it and the pumpkins on top. Anne hopped off, helped Samuel unhitch their horse and tie Woolrich's to the wagon. She gave Samuel instructions and watched him drive off.

When she got back to Joseph, he was shivering and a bit glassy-eyed. "Ye're in shock, my darling. But we must get ye on yer horse and back to town. Yer wound needs better tending."

"How? Where?" Joseph muttered, overwhelmed.

"First we go to the boarding house. Cavanaugh will help get ye upstairs and help ye change into clean clothes while I go get Apothecary Davidson to treat yer wounds properly." Anne gently rubbed his cheek.

"After that, I will send for Mr. Edwards and Lt. Governor Gooch so we can tell him the truth about Woolrich who, when ye confronted him with the facts, attacked ye and then rode off, wounded." Anne smiled. "It was a good plan, Joseph, just not complete."

I know this woman and yet I always underestimate her, Joseph told himself.

"Yes, he ran off, the coward," he replied.

Anne walked around kicking at the cypress needles until the blood was covered. She brought Joseph's horse over. She found a stump and helped Joseph up and onto his mount "I think I should take the reins, Joseph," she said. Her husband nodded in agreement.

As she mounted her horse, the rain began to fall -- obliterating their tracks.

Once she and Cavanaugh had settled Joseph into bed, Anne went for the Apothecary. "You did a good job with the wound, Mistress," he said as he unwrapped the bandages. "'Tis a deep one, I'm afraid." Dr. Davidson gave Joseph some laudanum for the pain and then cleaned, stitched up and re-wrapped the wound.

By nightfall, Joseph was shaking with fever. Dr. Davidson gave him some herbs to help, but could do little else. "He's strong, Mistress Burleigh. Give him time and the fever will pass."

I hate illness, Anne thought. She felt ashamed at her own impatience and vowed Joseph would never see it.

The fever lasted two days and on the third, Joseph woke Anne by shouting, "I'm starving, woman. I want food."

Anne rubbed her eyes and yawned. She kissed Joseph on the cheek. "Which ye shall have forthwith." Angeline, who had been sitting by the door throughout the two days, ran to get something.

As soon as Joseph finished eating, Anne sent for the Lt. Governor who had already been inquiring after her husband and Mr. Edwards. They arrived at the same time with Dr. Davidson.

"Come in, gentlemen. Thanks to ye for your concern and, Dr. Davidson, yer tender care of my husband. The fever has finally broken."

Lt. Governor Gooch came over to the bed and took Joseph's hand. "I am glad to hear it, my friend. I am almost perished of curiosity. What on earth happened to you? And did you know that Sir Jonathan vanished about the same time you were injured? I don't believe in coincidences."

"You shouldn't," Joseph said as Anne put pillows behind his back so he could sit up and face his guests. "Woolrich tried to kill me."

Gooch nodded. "I suspected as much. Details, man."

"I ran into him in the evening, drinking at Shields. He told me he'd like to resolve our dispute and would I meet him to discuss some accommodation. Although I didn't trust him, I agreed. He gave me a map to a place on Gordon Creek."

Anne handed Joseph a glass of beer which he drank deeply before continuing.

"He showed up and said that if we would pay him off with either his lost profits or a number of slaves equal to what he lost, he would agree not to pursue his claims. As you may imagine, I declined. Then in exchange, I informed him of two pieces of intelligence I had discovered that would ruin him." Joseph stopped.

Gooch's eyebrows rose. "And what would those be, my friend?" he asked.

Mr. Edwards stepped forward. "An indictment has been issued for his arrest in Jamaica over the killing of a woman." He handed Gooch the indictment which the Lt. Governor read.

"This woman," he asked, "was she ..." He stopped and looked at Edwards.

Edwards looked to Anne who nodded. "I am not so delicate."

"Yes, she was," replied Edwards. "A favorite of the governor as well as a lot of unsavory characters – sailors and whatnot. If he goes back, the indictment would probably fail because the woman was a mulatto. But the other aggrieved parties would not let him survive long."

"I think he realized that – judging from his face," Joseph said. "At that point, he drew a sword and I drew mine," Joseph added. "We fought until he got my leg. I slipped and fell to the ground. I was trying to retrieve my sword when I realized he was coming in for the kill so I pulled a knife out of my boot and threw it at him. It caught him in the shoulder and he staggered. I fell back from the pain." Joseph stopped, sweat dripping from his face. Anne held up a hand then wiped Joseph dry with her kerchief. He lay back with his eyes closed for a moment.

"The next thing I saw was Anne standing over me. Woolrich was gone. Some men don't like their women to outwit them, but I was extremely glad that she followed me."

The men turned to Anne. "I appreciate my honor being defended, but Joseph and I are partners and I felt it imperative to follow him at a distance. I saw Woolrich ride into the clump of trees. Sometime later, he came galloping out and rode away. That's when I went into the clearing and found Joseph on the ground, wounded. I got him on his horse with some difficulty and we rode back here."

The Lt. Governor stood thinking for a moment. "Well, if that bastard," he blushed. "Sorry Mistress Burleigh." Anne merely nodded. "If he shows his ugly face around my colony again, I shall be sure to deport him back to Jamaica."

Dr. Davidson stepped forward. "Do you continue to need my services, Joseph?"

Joseph looked at Anne. She shook her head. "Not at the moment, Doctor but my thanks for all ye have done."

Dr. Davidson bowed and left.

Gooch squeezed Joseph's hand, bowed and said, "Thank goodness for your wife. Mistress, if anyone should ever bring such an accusation against you again, I can assure you they will be removed from the colony immediately."

Anne stood and curtseyed to the Lt. Governor. "Thank you, Governor. We are most grateful for all you have done."

Lt. Governor Gooch bowed and left.

Anne sat back and looked at Joseph who was leaning back on the pillows and breathing heavily. "When can we go home?" he asked.

* * *

Late that afternoon, Samuel arrived in Hampton driving a wagon full of hay and pumpkins followed by Woolrich's horse. He made his way down to the docks where he sought out Howard Wilberforce who, when found, was chatting with a ship's captain. After a brief, private conversation, Wilberforce nodded, took a small burlap bag of coins from Samuel, climbed onto the wagon and drove off.

The Burleighs' driver found some friends among the slaves along the dock and managed to get a ride back to Williamsburg, arriving by noon the next day.

CHAPTER FORTY-FIVE

30 January 1731 - Hampton, Virginia

Anne and Joseph walked into the back room they had rented at the King's Raven to a round of applause. The insurance funds had arrived later than promised, but that had allowed time to get word to almost all of the crew, including, to Anne's delight, Richard Sylvanus. Everyone crowded around the couple hugging and shaking hands. Anne had dressed for the occasion in her favorite light blue silk damask robe with matching skirt -- the same she had worn to the hearing, but with a new petticoat of dark blue, quilted and heavily embroidered with swans and, hidden on each side, schooners.

The Burleighs had arranged a sumptuous feast of six courses, twenty different dishes including veal, fish and beef with puddings, roasted root vegetables and both fruit and pastries for dessert. They sat at three long, planked tables with Anne at one, Joseph at another and the officers at the third with the seamen spread among them. The waiters had been instructed to keep the rum punch coming in pitchers. When the last of the desserts had been eaten, Anne stood.

"My friends, and ye are all my friends, we come to a parting of the ways." The crew waved hands and booed to which Anne smiled. "Thank you for that, but this does not mean we shall never meet again. Just that it will be different. I will no longer be yer Captain."

The seamen watched her. "For now, let me say that ye were a splendid crew and we could not have accomplished any of what we did without all of us working together."

Wilberforce called out, "Or without you, Captain."

The others shouted agreement.

Anne smiled. "Thank you, Mr. Wilberforce." She nodded to Joseph who stood up and took a large linen bag out of his valise which he held up. "We have your shares, gentlemen. The insurance proceeds covered that and more so I have added a bit extra to each one."

Another cheer went up. The sailors raised their glasses. "To the Burleighs who keep their word," Boots cried. They all clinked glasses and drank deep.

"Joseph has a paper with the figures on it," Anne continued. "And the funds," she added. "He will meet with each of ye at that table in the corner." She pointed to a square table with a chair behind it placed in a far corner of the room, for privacy. "Please queue up and ye will be compensated one at a time. We have done a truly good and moral thing together – ye should all be proud." She sat to great applause and more shouting.

Joseph moved over to the table and sat down, spreading the paper in front of him. The men stood and Anne stopped them with a raised hand. They looked over at her and sat back down.

"I have one other thing to tell you before the money is distributed and ye start to go yer own ways," she said. "Our next child will be named Richard for our helmsman." She let that sink in. "Or Rickie, if it happens to be a girl."

The crew looked slightly confused. Finally Sylvanus asked, "When dat chil' comin', Cap'n?"

"In about five months," she answered.

At that the crew slapped each other on the back, as if they had produced this child instead of Anne and Joseph.

At that, the crewmen rushed over to Joseph at the table shaking his hand and congratulating him. "Thanks to you all," he said finally. "But you must queue up. Once you are paid, you are free to go wherever you want."

"Freedom," said Wilberforce. "We're all blessed in knowing you."

"And we in knowing you," Anne replied.

He came to her and took her hands. "I am so pleased for you," he said. "But the next one after must be named Howard, don't you think?" They both laughed.

"This will be five, Howard. There may not be another, but if there is, Howard he will be," she said. He kissed her hand before moving to join the queue.

Sylvanus was the last to be paid. After he had received his coin and tobacco credits, he came back to the table where Anne remained seated.

"I owe you, Mistress. My life, my chil'en's lives. Dose slaves' lives you done freed. You may never need me, but see you send for me if you do." Tears filled his eyes. "Da debt to you never be repaid."

"The joy of knowing that you and the Africans are free is enough repayment for me," Anne said, standing on tip toes to daub the big man's face with her kerchief. Then she smiled. "But if I do need ye, I will not hesitate to let ye know."

"Good," he said and, with a bow, he left.

Anne looked around the room. *I'll miss the crew,* she thought, *"and the sea life. It won't be easy but I always have the tobacco fields at night and the joy of family. I am content with my choice.*

Anne took Joseph's hand and squeezed it. "Let's go home."

GLOSSARY OF TERMS

Aft – The back of the ship.

Belaying Pin – A wooden rod around which ropes on shipboard are tied to make them fast; basically, a dowel with a handle. It also makes a good weapon.

Capstan - A revolving cylinder with a vertical axis used for winding a rope or cable, powered by levers that are pushed around.

Foc'sl – Slang for "forecastle" - The living quarters inside the hull of the ship.

Forward – The front of the ship.

Galley – Kitchen.

Hold – The space for holding cargo below the deck.

Jolly Boat – A ship's boat of medium size used for general work. Ships usually also had dinghies which were smaller but also did general work.

Larboard – The left side of the ship. Now called "port."

Lines – A line is a length of rope installed for a specific purpose. Sheets and forestays are examples of lines. Most often refers to running rigging (sheets, halyards, etc.).

Mains'l – Slang for "Mainsail" - The lowest square sail on the Mainmast.

Mainmast – The tallest mast on the ship. On a schooner, that is the mast furthest aft.

Pistole* – A quarter ounce gold coin.

Quarterdeck – The stern area of the ship's upper deck. The wheel that directs the ship is on the Quarterdeck.

Ratlins – Short for "ratlines": a series of small ropes fastened across a sailing ship's shrouds like the rungs of a ladder, used for climbing the rigging.

Real* – A one ounce silver coin from Spain was worth eight reales. Pronounced "re-al."

Rigging – There are two types: standing rigging - ropes/cables that keep the masts in place (stays, shrouds, etc.) which generally do not move, and "running rigging" – lines that move booms and yards to control the sails.

Schooner – A sailing ship with at least two masts (foremast and mainmast) with the mainmast being the taller of the two. The term derives from "schoon/scon" which means to move smoothly and quickly. They were very popular coastal ships in the 18th century and are still built today.

Sou'southwest – Directional term for a heading of south by southwest.

Spar – A pole or a beam.

Square Rig - Square rig is a generic type of sail and rigging arrangement in which the primary driving sails are carried on horizontal spars which are perpendicular, or square, to the keel of the vessel and to the masts. These spars are called yards and their tips, beyond the last stay, are called the yardarms. A ship mainly so rigged is called a square-rigger.

Starboard – The right side of the ship.

Tobacco Inspection Act of 1730 - The Tobacco Inspection Act of 1730 (popularly known as the Tobacco Inspection Act) was a 1730 English law designed to improve the quality of tobacco exported from Colonial Virginia. Proposed by Virginia Lt. Governor Sir William Gooch, the law was far-reaching in impact in part because it gave warehouses the power to destroy substandard crops and issue bills of exchange that served as currency. The law centralized the inspection of tobacco at forty locations. The colony drafted the law which then had to be passed by Parliament.

Tops'l – Slang for "topsail" – the sails (or sheets) at the top of a ship. *Betsy D* has 2 tops'ls.

Yard - A yard is a spar of timber on a mast from which sails are set. Although some types of fore and aft rigs have yards, the term is usually used to describe the horizontal spars used on square rigged sails.

*Since no coinage was allowed to be minted in the Colonies and the British did not want their coins circulating as a way of controlling commerce, most buying and selling was done with reales and pistoles or with tobacco notes – fiduciary instruments based on the value of tobacco.

OFFICERS AND CREW OF THE BETSY D

AND THEIR DUTIES

Captain – Andrew MacCormack/Anne Bonny Burleigh: Oversees the other officers; responsible for the welfare of the ship, the cargo and the crew.

Sailing Master – Phineas Thompson: In charge of navigation and the sailing of the ship. Directs the course and looks after the maps and navigational instruments.

Bo'sun (Boatswain) – Storm voyage: Thomas Mayfield; Other voyages: Clarence Potter: Responsible for the maintenance of the vessel and its supplies. Inspects the ship, sails and rigging daily and reports to the captain.

First Mate - Horace Jenkins and **Second Mate** - James Harkness: Apprentices to the Ship's Master, Bos'un, and Carpenter and on the *Betsy D*, the captain. Also took charge of hoisting the anchor and, during the voyage, checking the tackle daily.

Helmsman – Richard Sylvanus: In charge of steering the ship per the orders of the captain and Sailing Master

Cook/Surgeon – Howard Wilberforce: This is not a usual

combination of duties. On most pirate ships, the surgeon was often also the carpenter. Since Wilberforce is an expert with knives and a good cook, and since they are not likely to get into a battle, he acts in both capacities.

Ship's Carpenter – Stephen Kilrun: Responsible for maintenance and repair of the hull, masts and yards (sails). Works under the direction of the ship's Master and Bos'un.

Able Bodied Seamen – Henry Boots, Jimmy Johnson and others: Common sailors, needed to know the rigging and sails. On the *Betsy D*, they were also the riggers who climbed aloft to work the rigging and the furl/release the sails.

CPSIA information can be obtained
at www.ICGtesting.com
Printed in the USA
FSHW020735070521
81117FS